The Sorcerer's Codex

Hector L. Bones

I0609005

The Bones Family

Library of Congress Control Number:
Book Cover by Hector L. Bones
Illustrations by Hector L. Bones
1st edition 2025

Introduction

In every story lies a seed—a spark of curiosity, a yearning to explore the unknown. That is the essence of The Sorcerer's Codex. It is a tale born from the threads of imagination, woven with the mysteries of magic and the relentless pursuit of truth. This book is not merely a story; it is a journey into a world where ley lines hum with ancient power, where fragile alliances test the bounds of trust, and where courage is both a gift and a burden.

As the author, my aim was to create a world that feels alive, a world that beckons you to walk its paths, touch its magic, and unravel its secrets alongside the characters. Alaric Deymorne, the protagonist, represents the seeker in all of us—searching for answers, facing insurmountable odds, and growing with every challenge.

The Sorcerer's Codex is a tale of resilience and discovery, and it serves as a reminder that even in our darkest moments, there exists a spark of light waiting to be kindled. Whether you are a longtime fan of fantasy or stepping into this genre for the first time, I hope this story ignites your imagination and inspires you to seek the extraordinary in the ordinary.

With anticipation for the journey ahead,
Hector L. Bones

Dedication

I dedicate this book to my beautiful wife **Debbie N. Bones**, who has been a great support and source of inspiration. She is the most brilliant person I know to which I can count to bounce off ideas and help me through, but also helps me keep on track and complete our projects in life.

Without you **Debbie** my love I would have never got the courage to get this book out.

I also dedicate this book to my children who inspired me to put my ideas in paper and bring them to life. Thanks **Aerith Nyomi, Alisher Krystal and Aiden Kalel**, for being great kids and an infinite source of inspiration.

Synopsis

In the quiet village of Caerlyn, Alaric Deymorne dreams of a world beyond the fields and cobblestone streets. His longing for adventure leads him to a mysterious grimoire gifted by a passing mage—a book that pulses with ancient knowledge and beckons him toward the ley lines, the veins of magic that bind his world.

As Alaric follows the grimoire's clues, he is drawn into the halls of the Grand Arcanum, a prestigious academy where aspiring mages learn to harness magic's raw power. Here, he faces skepticism from peers, trials that test his courage, and the relentless guidance of Master Eldaryn. Despite his struggles, Alaric uncovers the ley lines' secrets, discovering their fragile balance and the ominous Spiral Nexus, an anomaly that threatens to unravel reality itself.

Joined by unexpected allies, including the sharp-witted Lira, Alaric embarks on a journey to understand the Nexus and the Codex's connection to it. Along the way, he encounters powerful artifacts, elemental forces, and creatures born of magic's volatile energies. As the stakes grow higher, Alaric must confront his own fears, balance ambition with restraint, and face the question: Can he wield the power to restore balance without becoming the very force that destroys it?

Blending epic fantasy with intricate world-building, The Sorcerer's Codex is a tale of resilience, discovery, and the unbreakable threads that bind destiny to courage.

Prologue: The Fractured Veil

The wind tore through the ancient forest of Alderran like a mournful wail, carrying with it the scent of damp earth and the electric hum of distant storms. Towering oaks stood sentinel around a clearing, their gnarled roots clawing at the soil as though resisting the chaos pressing in from all sides. The clearing was dominated by an ancient stone obelisk, fractured and worn, its surface etched with runes that pulsed faintly in erratic rhythms—a mirror to the instability of the world itself.

Kneeling at the obelisk's base was a man clad in dark leather, his trembling hands tracing the jagged grooves of a forgotten symbol. His breath formed fleeting clouds in the frigid air, and his voice barely rose above the whisper of the wind. "It's here... the nexus lies beneath us."

From the shadows, a taller figure emerged, their face obscured beneath the deep hood of a tattered cloak. They moved with an air of authority, their crystalline staff glimmering faintly, the veins of energy within it sparking with barely contained power. Each step resonated with purpose, the rhythm unbroken by the swirling energy that made the clearing feel alive with tension.

"Are you certain?" the figure asked, their voice smooth yet edged with steel. It cut through the air like a blade, commanding but calm.

The kneeling man glanced upward, his wide eyes reflecting both fear and desperation. "I can feel it. The ley lines converge here. The veil is thinnest in this place, but..." He hesitated, his fingers stilling against the stone. "It's unstable. To tamper with it—"

The cloaked figure raised a gloved hand, silencing him. "The fractures are spreading unchecked. If we wait, the damage will be irreparable. Begin the invocation."

The man hesitated, his eyes darting between the obelisk and the storm-like energy rippling through the air. Reluctantly, he retrieved a weathered tome from his satchel. Its leather cover bore the same ancient runes as the obelisk, glowing faintly in resonance.

"The nexus... it's too fragile. If we force it—"

"Do as I command," the cloaked figure snapped, their staff striking the earth with a sharp crack. A ripple of energy spread from its base, illuminating the clearing with a ghostly light. "Entire realms are at stake. We cannot afford hesitation."

With visible reluctance, the man opened the tome to a page of intricate diagrams and ancient incantations. His voice quavered as he began to chant, the melodic tones rising and falling like a haunting song. The runes on the obelisk flared to life, casting long, shifting shadows across the clearing. The ground beneath them responded with a deep, resonant hum, its vibrations palpable in the air.

For a moment, it seemed to work. The fractures in the obelisk appeared to knit together, the pulsing light stabilizing into a steady glow. But then the hum grew louder—angrier. The ground trembled violently, and tendrils of raw energy erupted from the soil, twisting and writhing like serpents.

"No!" the man cried, his chanting faltering. "It's too much! The nexus can't take this!"

The cloaked figure tightened their grip on the staff, their voice commanding. "Push through. The Codex's guidance is clear—we must mend the ley lines before the Spiral Nexus collapses."

But the energy spiraled out of control. The tendrils lashed violently, scorching the earth and tearing through the air with unrelenting fury. The obelisk shuddered, its fractures widening as bursts of light and shadow seared the night sky. The man dropped the tome, shielding his face as the air around him ignited with chaotic magic.

"It's unraveling!" he screamed, his voice breaking. "We've failed!"

The cloaked figure stepped forward, their movements steady despite the storm of energy. They raised their staff high, its crystalline tip glowing with a desperate intensity. "No," they said, their tone unyielding. "This is not the end."

With a swift motion, they plunged the staff into the nexus. A blinding wave of energy erupted outward, scattering the tendrils and momentarily sealing the breach. The clearing fell silent, the ley lines' hum reduced to a faint, mournful whisper.

The cloaked figure stood motionless, their staff now a dim relic of its former power. The man lay slumped beside the obelisk, unconscious but alive. The runes on the stone flickered weakly, their light fading into the night.

A Warning for the Future

The figure turned their gaze toward the horizon, where the faint glow of other nexuses pulsed like dying stars. They knelt beside the unconscious man, placing a hand on his forehead. "A new guardian will rise," they whispered, their voice heavy with resignation. "The Codex must find its heir."

They stood and looked back at the fractured obelisk, a shadow of its former self. The air still thrummed with instability, the ley lines beneath the forest struggling to heal. The figure tightened their cloak around them, their sharp green eyes reflecting the weight of their responsibility. "Balance must be restored. But the cost will be great."

With a final glance at the unconscious man, the figure disappeared into the forest, their silhouette swallowed by the shifting shadows. Behind them, the obelisk stood as a silent testament to the fragility of their world.

The Ley Lines Remember

The forest of Alderran had always been alive with whispers. The trees' gnarled branches carried the echoes of magic—memories of ancient rituals, the rise and fall of civilizations, and the countless secrets buried beneath the soil. Tonight, those whispers grew louder, resonating with the pain of the ley lines. They were alive, sentient in ways few understood, and they remembered every touch, every scar.

As the cloaked figure disappeared into the night, the faint glow of the ley lines beneath the forest pulsed weakly, as though lamenting their own fragility. Somewhere in the distance, the Spiral Nexus—the heart of all ley lines—shuddered, its fractures spreading like cracks in a mirror.

The world teetered on the brink, the threads of magic that held it together fraying with every passing moment. But even in the face of such uncertainty, the ley lines whispered of hope. The Codex—the ancient artifact that had guided countless generations—was still intact. And it would choose again.

Far from the clearing, in a secluded grove hidden deep within the forest, the cloaked figure paused. They leaned against a weathered tree, their breathing heavy. For the first time that night, they allowed themselves a moment of vulnerability. Their gloved hand brushed against the crystalline surface of their staff, now cracked and lifeless.

"How many more sacrifices will it take?" they murmured, their voice barely audible above the rustling leaves. The question lingered in the air, unanswered.

They looked up at the sky, where the stars flickered weakly, their light dimmed by the invisible fractures spreading across the realms. Somewhere out there, the Codex awaited its next heir—someone worthy of the burden, someone who could restore the balance that had been lost.

With renewed determination, the figure straightened. They could not afford doubt. The world's survival depended on their resolve. Adjusting their cloak, they stepped back into the shadows, the faint hum of the ley lines guiding their path.

Chapter 1: The Humble Spark

The Quiet Rhythm of Caerlyn

The village of Caerlyn was the kind of place where time seemed to drift like the Ashenbrook River that wove through its heart—steadily, unhurried, and always the same. Nestled in a valley of lush meadows and bordered by the dense, shadowy Alderran Forest, the village seemed untouched by the outside world. Cottages with thatched roofs huddled together along cobblestone paths, their whitewashed walls adorned with ivy and wildflowers. In the square, the market bustled with quiet energy as villagers traded freshly baked bread, woven baskets, and jars of honey.

It was a place of routine, of simplicity. The blacksmith hammered horseshoes in the same rhythmic cadence that had marked the days for decades. Shepherds led their flocks to the pastures at dawn and returned by dusk. Children played games in the fields, their laughter rising above the hum of bees flitting between blooms.

To the people of Caerlyn, this life was enough. But not for Alaric.

He stood at the edge of the forest, his gaze fixed on the distant hills that rolled endlessly into the horizon. A breeze rustled the leaves above him, carrying with it the faint, earthy scent of moss and pine. Somewhere beyond those hills lay answers—answers to questions that had burned in his mind for as long as he could remember.

"Alaric!" his father's voice called from the field, pulling him back to reality. "Get moving! The plow won't fix itself."

Sighing, Alaric turned and trudged toward the barn, where the old plow sat waiting. But as he worked, his thoughts wandered. He imagined towering cities of stone and glass, vast deserts of golden sand, and oceans that stretched so far they swallowed the sky. He imagined ancient ruins hidden deep in the forest, their secrets waiting to be uncovered. He imagined magic—not the simple charms and blessings whispered by the village healer, but true magic, the kind that could shape worlds.

A Life Too Small

That evening, as the sun dipped below the horizon and bathed the fields in golden light, Alaric joined his family for supper. The small, wooden table was laden with a humble meal of stew and bread. His father, Walter, a broad-shouldered man with weathered hands, ate in silence. His mother, Elise, a kind woman with soft eyes, offered Alaric a warm smile as she passed him a bowl.

"You've been quiet today," Elise said, breaking the silence. "Even for you."

Alaric hesitated, unsure how to put his feelings into words. "Just thinking," he said finally.

Walter grunted. "Thinking doesn't fix fences or fill the larder."

"Walter," Elise chided gently, but Alaric shook his head.

"It's fine, Mother," he said. "I'll do more tomorrow."

His father studied him for a moment, his expression softening. "It's not about doing more, boy. It's about doing what needs to be done. The world beyond this village... it's not what you think it is."

"How do you know?" Alaric asked, his tone sharper than he intended. "Have you ever been beyond it?"

Walter's jaw tightened, but he didn't reply. Elise placed a hand on Alaric's arm. "Your father just wants what's best for you," she said softly. "We both do."

Alaric nodded, though his frustration simmered beneath the surface. He loved his parents, but he couldn't ignore the pull he felt toward something greater. Caerlyn was his home, but it was also a cage.

The Arrival of the Traveling Mage

The next morning, as Alaric carried a bucket of water from the well, the sound of hooves echoed through the square. A hush fell over the market as a rider emerged from the forest path—a man cloaked in deep blue, his hood drawn low over his face. His black steed moved with an almost otherworldly grace, its hooves making no sound against the cobblestones.

The villagers froze, their gazes fixed on the stranger. Travelers were rare in Caerlyn, and those who came were rarely like this.

The man dismounted, his movements smooth and deliberate. He led his horse to the trough near the well, where Alaric stood rooted in place, the bucket still in his hands.

"Water for the beast," the man said, his voice rich and smooth.

Alaric nodded quickly, filling the trough. As the horse drank, the man turned his attention to the boy. His face was partially shadowed beneath his hood, but his sharp green eyes seemed to pierce through Alaric.

"You have the look of a seeker," the man said, his tone thoughtful.

Alaric blinked. "A seeker of what?"

The man smiled faintly. "Answers. Truths. The world is full of them, but they do not reveal themselves to the idle."

"I... I want to know what's out there," Alaric admitted, the words tumbling out before he could stop them.

The man studied him for a long moment, then reached into his satchel and withdrew a small, leather-bound book. The cover was embossed with swirling patterns that seemed to shift in the sunlight.

"Take this," the man said, holding it out to Alaric. "It may guide you."

"What is it?" Alaric asked, his fingers trembling as he took the book.

"A grimoire," the man replied. "But be warned—its secrets are not for the faint of heart."

Before Alaric could ask more, the man mounted his horse and rode off, leaving the villagers staring after him in silence.

The Grimoire's Mysteries

That night, with the village quiet and his family asleep, Alaric sat by the flickering light of a candle and opened the grimoire. The leather creaked softly as he turned the cover, and the scent of old parchment filled the air.

The first page bore a single symbol—a rune etched in shimmering ink. Its lines seemed to pulse faintly, as if alive. Beneath it, in elegant script, were words written in a language Alaric didn't recognize.

As he turned the pages, his heart quickened. The grimoire was filled with diagrams of strange symbols, notes on magical phenomena, and illustrations of creatures both beautiful and terrifying. Then he found the map.

It was folded neatly in the center of the book, its edges worn but intact. When Alaric unfolded it, he gasped.

Lines crisscrossed the parchment, connecting points scattered across the map. Each line pulsed faintly, glowing with hues of blue, gold, and green. Some of the points were marked with symbols—circles, stars, and other shapes he couldn't decipher.

"Ley lines," Alaric murmured, the term surfacing in his mind like a memory long forgotten.

He traced the lines with his finger, his thoughts racing. Some of the points matched locations he recognized—Caerlyn, the Ashenbrook River, the Alderran Forest—but others were far beyond anything he had ever seen.

As he stared at the map, a single thought consumed him: This was the key to something greater. To a world he had only dreamed of.

*****

Over the next few days, Alaric became consumed by the grimoire. He pored over its pages late into the night, sketching the symbols and making notes. But his obsession did not go unnoticed.

"You've been distracted lately," Elise said one evening as they tended the garden. "Is something bothering you?"

"No," Alaric replied quickly, though the truth was written on his face.

"You've always had a curious mind," she said, her tone gentle. "Just don't let it carry you too far."

Alaric nodded, but he couldn't ignore the pull he felt. The grimoire had awakened something in him—a spark of possibility that refused to be extinguished.

That night, he made his decision. He would leave Caerlyn. He didn't know where the map would lead him, but he knew he had to follow it.

"I'll come back," he whispered to the silent room as he packed his satchel. "But I can't stay."

A Narrator's Perspective: A World of Cycles

The world of Alaric Deymorne was one bound by cycles. The sun rose, fields were plowed, harvests came and went, and the people of Caerlyn lived within the small, familiar loop of seasons and customs. It was a pattern as old as the hills that encircled the village, their gentle curves cradling its inhabitants in a cocoon of safety and routine. But even in the most predictable cycles, there are moments when something extraordinary slips through—a spark that threatens to unravel the familiar fabric.

For Caerlyn, that spark was a boy who looked too often at the horizon.

Alaric's restlessness wasn't born of discontent alone. It came from something deeper, a gnawing sense that the world was larger than it seemed and that he was meant to understand it. He had heard the stories—fanciful tales of sorcerers who bent reality to their will, of ancient ruins filled with treasures and traps, of portals leading to worlds untouched by mortal feet. To the villagers, they were distractions. To Alaric, they were a challenge.

Flashback: A Childhood Glimpse of Magic

The first time Alaric glimpsed true magic, he was no more than seven years old. It had been a summer evening, the air thick with the scent of wildflowers and the hum of cicadas. A traveling healer had arrived in the village, her robes patched and frayed but her voice steady and kind.

Alaric had watched from the corner of the square as she knelt beside a farmer with a gnarled hand, her fingers tracing strange symbols in the air. For a brief moment, light danced along her fingertips, forming patterns too complex for Alaric to comprehend. When she finished, the farmer flexed his hand in astonishment, the pain gone.

"What was that?" Alaric had asked, wide-eyed, as the healer passed him by.

"Magic," she said simply. "But not the kind you'll find here."

"Why not?"

The healer had smiled faintly, her gaze drifting toward the distant hills. "Because magic seeks those who seek it. And most here do not."

Those words had stayed with him, planted like a seed that grew with every passing year.

Village Dynamics: Diverging Paths

Years later, Alaric still felt the weight of that seed, even as the villagers around him seemed content to let their lives remain rooted in the soil. He had tried to fit in, to embrace the life his father had laid out for him—a life of honest work and quiet satisfaction. But no matter how hard he tried, the questions remained.

At the market, the villagers often spoke of Alaric in hushed tones, their words carrying both admiration and skepticism.

"That boy's got a sharp mind," said Merrick the blacksmith one afternoon, his hammer resting against the anvil. "But his head's in the clouds. Never seen a lad so distracted by things that don't concern him."

"Maybe he's meant for more," said Hilda, the baker, as she arranged loaves on her counter. "Not everyone's roots run deep."

"Deep enough to keep him here, I hope," Merrick replied, his tone gruff. "The world's no place for dreamers."

Alaric often overheard these conversations, though he never responded. He knew they meant well, but their words only strengthened his resolve.

The Grimoire: Layers of Mystery

Late one night, as the moon hung high and silver light spilled through the shutters of his small room, Alaric sat with the grimoire open before him. Its pages seemed to shift under his touch, the ink shimmering faintly as if alive. He had tried to decipher its contents for days, but the language eluded him. The only thing he recognized was the map.

The ley lines fascinated him. Each glowing thread seemed to hum with its own rhythm, as though they carried the lifeblood of the world. He traced their paths with his finger, stopping at a point marked near the Alderran Forest. The symbol there—a jagged spiral surrounded by smaller runes—was unlike anything else on the map.

"What are you?" Alaric murmured, his voice barely audible.

As if in response, the runes seemed to glow brighter for a moment before dimming again. A shiver ran down his spine, but it wasn't fear. It was anticipation.

Narrator's Insight: The Call of the Unknown

The grimoire wasn't just a book—it was an invitation. Alaric felt it in every line of text he couldn't read, in every symbol he couldn't decipher. It whispered to him in ways he didn't yet understand, pulling him toward something greater. For all its mysteries, the grimoire also carried a weight—a silent warning that knowledge came at a cost. But for a boy who longed to see beyond the edges of his small world, the promise of answers was worth any risk.

Days after the mage's departure, Alaric found himself replaying their brief conversation over and over in his mind. The man's words had been cryptic, his demeanor both intimidating and intriguing. But one detail stood out: the grimoire was not a random gift. The mage had chosen him for a reason.

As Alaric sat by the riverbank, the grimoire balanced on his lap, he remembered the last thing the mage had said: "Its secrets are not for the faint of heart."

Had the mage seen something in him that no one else did? Or was it simply a test, a way of seeing whether Alaric would rise to the challenge?

Flashback: The First Question

When Alaric was ten, he had asked his father a question that seemed innocent at the time but carried far greater weight in retrospect.

"Why don't we ever leave Caerlyn?"

Walter had paused mid-step, his hands gripping the plow. For a moment, he seemed to wrestle with the answer before finally speaking.

"Because there's nothing out there for us," he said simply. "Everything we need is here."

"But what if there's more?" Alaric had pressed. "What if we're missing something?"

Walter had turned to him then, his expression a mixture of frustration and concern. "The world beyond those hills is bigger than you can imagine, boy. And not all of it is kind. Be content with what you have."

Alaric hadn't asked again, but the question had never left him. And now, with the grimoire in his possession, he felt closer than ever to finding the answer.

*****

The night Alaric made his decision, the village was quiet, the only sound the soft rustle of leaves in the breeze. He sat on the edge of his bed, staring at the packed satchel on the floor. Inside were a few essentials: bread, a flask of water, a small knife, and the grimoire. It wasn't much, but it was all he needed.

He glanced around the room, his gaze lingering on the familiar details—the wooden beams above, the worn desk where he had spent countless hours sketching maps and symbols, the quilt his mother had sewn for him when he was a child.

For a moment, doubt crept in. Was he doing the right thing? Was he being selfish, leaving his family behind for a dream that might lead to nothing?

But then he thought of the ley lines, of the spiral symbol near the forest, and of the healer's words all those years ago: Magic seeks those who seek it.

"I'll come back," he whispered, though he wasn't sure if he believed it. "I promise."

With that, he slung the satchel over his shoulder, opened the door, and stepped into the night.

The night was quiet as Alaric made his way through Caerlyn, his satchel heavy on his shoulder and his steps light with anticipation. The village, bathed in moonlight, seemed both familiar and distant, as though it was already slipping into memory. He paused at the edge of the square, taking in the sight of the well and the market stalls, now covered with tarps for the night.

His fingers brushed the rough wood of Merrick's forge as he passed. The anvil sat cold, its usual glow absent without the forge fire. Alaric had spent countless hours watching Merrick work, the blacksmith's hammer ringing like a heartbeat in the center of the village. He had always admired Merrick's skill, but the thought of a life spent shaping horseshoes and tools had filled him with a quiet dread.

"Goodbye, Merrick," he murmured, though he knew the blacksmith would probably scoff at the sentiment.

As he approached the stone circle at the edge of the village, a breeze stirred the trees, carrying the scent of damp earth and pine. The stones stood silent and imposing, their surfaces etched with faint carvings that seemed to glow faintly in the moonlight. Alaric knelt beside the largest stone, his fingers tracing the grooves of a rune that matched one in the grimoire.

"I don't know what you mean yet," he said softly, his voice almost swallowed by the night. "But I'll find out."

The circle had always felt alive to him, as though it was watching, waiting. Tonight was no different. The air seemed to hum faintly, a reminder that magic was more than stories—it was real, and it was calling to him.

A Vision from the Grimoire

As Alaric settled beneath the shelter of an old oak near the village's border, he opened the grimoire once more. The pages seemed to shimmer faintly in the moonlight, their shifting ink creating patterns that defied logic.

Exhaustion tugged at his eyelids, but as he stared at the map, the symbols began to glow more brightly, their lines pulsing in rhythm with his heartbeat. His vision blurred, and the world around him seemed to fade.

When he opened his eyes, he was no longer beneath the oak. He stood in a vast expanse of shifting light and shadow, the ground beneath him smooth and glassy like polished obsidian. In the distance, towering spires of crystal pierced a sky filled with swirling colors. The air buzzed with energy, and Alaric felt it thrumming in his veins.

Before him stood a figure cloaked in shimmering light, its form indistinct yet undeniably human. The figure raised a hand, and a voice filled the air—not spoken, but felt, as though it resonated in the core of Alaric's being.

"The lines are the lifeblood of the world," the voice said. "They connect, they sustain, they create. But they are fragile. And you... are the spark."

The figure gestured toward the horizon, where one of the spires began to fracture, its crystalline surface splintering into shards that scattered like stars. Alaric's heart raced as the vision faded, the grimoire snapping shut in his hands.

*****

As dawn approached, Alaric made his way to the edge of the village, the pack on his back weighing heavier than the belongings it carried. He thought he had slipped away unnoticed, but a voice stopped him just as he reached the old gate.

"You're really leaving, aren't you?"

Alaric turned to see Lysa, a childhood friend who had always seemed to understand him better than anyone else in the village. She stood with her arms crossed, her dark hair falling in loose waves over her shoulders. Her expression was a mix of sadness and understanding.

"You knew I would, eventually," Alaric said, his voice softer than he intended.

"I hoped you wouldn't," she admitted. "Or at least, not yet."

There was a long pause as they stood under the pale light of the fading stars. Finally, Lysa stepped forward and placed something in

Alaric's hand—a small, woven charm made of threads in green and gold.

"For protection," she said. "Or luck. Whatever you need most."

Alaric's throat tightened. "Thank you."

Lysa hesitated, then smiled faintly. "I'll miss you, you know. Even if you do have your head in the clouds."

"I'll miss you too," he said, and he meant it.

As he turned to leave, her voice stopped him once more. "Find whatever it is you're looking for, Alaric. And don't forget where you came from."

"I won't," he promised. "I'll come back. Someday."

The Narrator's Reflection: Crossing the Threshold

As Alaric stepped beyond the boundaries of Caerlyn, the world seemed to shift around him. The air was crisper, the colors sharper, as though he had stepped into a realm just slightly out of sync with the one he had always known. He didn't look back. The ties that bound him to his home had been cut—not with a knife, but with a quiet understanding that the path forward would not allow for hesitation.

For most, the horizon is a distant boundary, a place never reached and rarely imagined. But for Alaric, it was the first step on a journey that would take him far beyond what he could comprehend. He did not yet know what lay ahead—the dangers, the discoveries, the sacrifices—but he carried with him the spark of something rare: the courage to seek the unknown.

*****

The sun crested the hills slowly, bathing Caerlyn in golden light as the village awoke to another day. The scent of baking bread drifted from Hilda's oven, mingling with the earthy aroma of dew-soaked fields. Alaric walked one last time along the cobblestone paths, his boots scuffing against the worn stones. He avoided the square, knowing the familiar chatter of the villagers might sway his resolve.

Instead, he headed toward the small grove behind his family's farm, a place where he had often retreated as a child when the world felt too small. The grove was quiet, its trees casting long shadows over the soft grass. He knelt by a stream that trickled gently through the clearing, cupping the cool water in his hands and letting it slip through his fingers.

In this moment of solitude, he allowed himself to feel the weight of what he was leaving behind—the steady rhythm of life in Caerlyn, the warmth of his mother's smile, the steady guidance of his father, and the companionship of friends like Lysa. These were the roots that had anchored him, but now they felt more like tethers.

A faint rustling broke the stillness, and Alaric turned to see his mother standing at the edge of the grove. She carried a small bundle wrapped in cloth, her expression unreadable.

"I thought I might find you here," she said, stepping closer. "You always came here when you had something on your mind."

Alaric stood, brushing grass from his knees. "I didn't want to leave without saying goodbye."

Elise nodded, her hands tightening around the bundle. "I knew this day would come," she said softly. "You've always been restless, always looking beyond the horizon. I see it in your eyes, the same way I saw it in your father's before the world hardened him."

Alaric frowned. "What do you mean?"

She smiled faintly and placed the bundle in his hands. "He wasn't always like this, you know. Once, he dreamed of seeing the world, of finding something greater than what Caerlyn could offer. But life doesn't always give us the choices we want."

Alaric unwrapped the bundle to find a cloak lined with soft fur and a small, leather-bound journal. He ran his fingers over the journal's cover, his throat tightening.

"I stitched the cloak myself," Elise said. "The journal was your father's, from when he was younger. Maybe it will help you find your way."

"Thank you," Alaric whispered, his voice breaking. "I'll miss you."

She reached up, cupping his face with gentle hands. "I'll miss you too, my love. But you've got a fire in you that can't be contained. Follow it, and don't let fear stop you."

As Alaric returned to the house to gather his satchel, the villagers began their morning routines, each taking note of his absence in their own way.

Merrick, standing in the forge, looked toward the path leading out of the village and grunted. "So the boy finally did it," he muttered. "Well, I suppose every blade has to find its own edge."

Hilda, arranging loaves of bread on her stall, shook her head with a wistful smile. "I hope he finds what he's looking for. The world needs dreamers like him."

Even the shepherds in the fields paused to glance toward the horizon, as though sensing the shift in the village's rhythm. Caerlyn was small, but its people knew when one of their own had outgrown its boundaries.

*****

Alaric's father stood by the gate as he prepared to leave, his expression guarded. For a long moment, neither spoke.

Finally, Walter cleared his throat. "Your mother told me you were leaving."

Alaric nodded. "I need to find my own path."

Walter's jaw tightened, but he nodded. "I won't pretend to understand, but... I was young once too. Just promise me you'll be careful. The world isn't as kind as the stories make it seem."

"I will," Alaric said. "And I'll come back. Someday."

Walter hesitated, then placed a hand on Alaric's shoulder. "You've got my journal. That means you've got a piece of me with you. Use it well."

The words were simple, but they carried the weight of a father's love and a lifetime of unspoken regrets. Alaric nodded, unable to find the words to respond.

*****

As Alaric crossed the boundary of Caerlyn, the morning light painted the world in hues of gold and green. Each step felt both liberating and daunting, the path ahead unknown but filled with possibility. He carried the grimoire close to his chest, the journal tucked safely in his satchel, and Lysa's charm tied securely around his wrist.

The road wound through the Alderran Forest, its trees ancient and towering. Shafts of sunlight pierced the canopy, creating patterns of light and shadow on the forest floor. Alaric's thoughts drifted to the ley line map in the grimoire, its glowing lines leading him to places he couldn't yet imagine.

He paused at a clearing, turning back to catch one last glimpse of the village through the trees. The sight stirred a pang of homesickness, but he pushed it aside.

"Goodbye, Caerlyn," he murmured. "I'll make this worth it."

As he turned and continued down the path, the weight of the grimoire seemed to lighten, as though it, too, recognized the journey had truly begun.

The Narrator's Perspective: A Spark Ignited

For most, leaving home is a slow, steady process—years of preparation, careful goodbyes, and plans laid out with precision. But for Alaric, it was an inevitability, a single step that marked the start of something far greater than himself. The grimoire was no mere gift, and the ley lines were no ordinary map. They were threads in a tapestry that stretched across worlds, and Alaric was destined to follow them.

In time, the boy from Caerlyn would become more than a seeker of truths. He would become a spark that ignited change, a light that pierced the veil of the unknown. But for now, he was just a boy with a satchel, a map, and a fire in his heart.

The Quiet Rhythm of Caerlyn's evening faded into the sharp chill of night, and as the stars began their steady march across the darkened sky, Alaric lingered by the hearth. The grimoire gifted by the mage lay unopened on his lap, its weight pressing on him like a question left unanswered. Beside him, his mother moved about the modest home, tidying up before retiring for the night.

"Mother," he began hesitantly, "Do you remember the healer who came to Caerlyn when I was little? The one with the magic?"

Elise paused, her hands stilling over the edge of a woven blanket she was folding. Her gaze softened as she looked at her son. "I remember," she said, her voice gentle. "You couldn't stop talking about her for weeks. You even tried to draw the symbols she made in the air."

Alaric smiled faintly, the memory vivid despite the years that had passed.

Flashback: A Childhood Glimpse of Magic

It had been a warm summer evening, the air alive with the hum of cicadas and the faint scent of wildflowers drifting from the meadows. Seven-year-old Alaric had crouched behind the well in the village square, his small hands gripping the rough stone as he watched the healer at work.

She had been unlike anyone he had ever seen. Her robes, though patched and worn, shimmered faintly in the fading sunlight, as if they held remnants of the magic she wielded. Her movements were precise and deliberate, her fingers tracing intricate patterns in the air that left glowing trails behind them. The farmer she was tending to winced as she pressed her hands against his gnarled, swollen knee, but her calm voice soothed him.

"Just breathe," she said.

Alaric had watched, wide-eyed, as light began to pulse from her fingertips. The glow intensified, spreading in a gentle wave over the farmer's leg. For a brief moment, it was as if the world had paused—the cicadas quiet, the villagers hushed, and even the wind stilled. Then the light faded, and the farmer flexed his knee, astonishment replacing the pain in his eyes.

"What was that?" young Alaric had blurted, unable to contain himself any longer.

The healer turned, her expression soft but tinged with weariness. "That, young one, is magic," she said simply.

"Can anyone learn it?" he asked, stepping closer.

She chuckled lightly, her gaze drifting toward the distant hills. "Magic seeks those who seek it. But it's not for the faint of heart, boy. The world beyond these hills isn't kind to dreamers."

Her words had lingered with him, planted like a seed that grew quietly, persistently, in the corners of his mind. In the years that followed, Alaric had tried to replicate the healer's glowing patterns with sticks and chalk, only to fail repeatedly. Yet the memory of her magic never faded, and the belief that there was something more to the world beyond Caerlyn became an unshakable part of him.

Back in the present, Elise sat beside him, her hands folded in her lap. "You've always been curious," she said softly. "Even as a child, you wanted to understand things most people in this village never question."

Alaric hesitated, then spoke. "Do you think it's wrong for me to want more than this?"

Her expression grew thoughtful. "No, Alaric. But wanting more comes with its own burdens. Your father once wanted more, too."

Walter's Journal: A Father's Abandoned Dreams

The next morning, as Alaric prepared the plow for the fields, Elise approached him with a small, leather-bound book. The edges were worn, the leather cracked and faded from years of handling.

"This was your father's," she said, placing the journal in his hands. "He doesn't talk about it much, but maybe it's time you saw it for yourself."

Alaric opened the journal carefully, the faint smell of aged parchment wafting up. The first few pages were filled with neat, precise handwriting—a stark contrast to the rough, calloused man Alaric knew his father to be.

Entry: Year 982

The hills beyond Caerlyn are endless, their ridges beckoning like the waves of the sea. I wonder what lies beyond them. They say there are ruins in the forest to the north, remnants of a time when magic was as common as sunlight. One day, I will see them for myself. One day, I will leave this place.

Alaric frowned, flipping further into the journal. The entries became sporadic, the handwriting more hurried, almost angry.

Entry: Year 984

The fields need tending. The roof leaks again. Aerith's sick. I've no time for ruins or magic. Maybe it's best I let these dreams die.

The final entry was short, almost scrawled.

Entry: Year 986

The world beyond the hills isn't for men like me. Let it stay a dream. Better to endure what's known than risk losing everything.

Alaric closed the journal, his chest tight. His father's words were heavy with resignation, a stark reminder of the sacrifices made to keep their family whole. Yet, they also fueled the fire in Alaric's heart. He couldn't—wouldn't—let his dreams slip away like his father had.

Flashback: Alaric's Childhood Encounter with Magic

Alaric recalls a memory from when he was seven years old.

The summer evening buzzed with the hum of cicadas. Alaric crouched behind the village well, his small hands gripping the stone as he peered out. The healer moved with deliberate grace, her robes shimmering faintly in the twilight as she tended to the injured shepherd. Her fingers traced glowing patterns in the air—symbols that lingered and pulsed, leaving the air around her tingling with energy.

"What is that?" Alaric had whispered to his mother. "What is she doing?"

"Magic," Elise replied softly, her gaze warm but distant. "Not the kind you'll find here."

Alaric's wide eyes followed every movement, every flicker of light. He didn't understand the symbols, but he knew they meant something. Something important. That night, as the healer disappeared into the shadows of the Alderran Forest, Alaric resolved to understand what she had done, no matter how long it took.

That night, as the village of Caerlyn slept, Alaric stood at the edge of the Alderran Forest, the grimoire in one hand and his father's journal in the other. The stars above seemed brighter, their light cutting through the darkness like tiny beacons.

"I'll come back," he whispered, more to himself than to the world. "But I have to know what's out there."

With one last glance at the quiet village, he stepped into the forest, the weight of both hope and uncertainty pressing on his shoulders. The spark of his childhood wonder had ignited into a flame, guiding him into the unknown.

Chapter 2: The Grand Arcanum

The Grand Arcanum was no mere institution; it was a testament to humanity's boundless ambition. Its spires reached toward the heavens, carved from gleaming crystal and blackened stone, their surfaces alive with shifting glyphs. Alaric Deymorne stood at the threshold, dwarfed by the towering iron gates engraved with scenes of elemental forces clashing and uniting in perfect harmony.

He hesitated. Beyond these gates lay a world of magic he had dreamed of but never touched. The familiar life in Caerlyn felt a thousand miles away. His father's parting words echoed in his mind: "The world isn't as kind as it seems in books, Alaric. Be careful where you tread."

The gates opened silently, as if recognizing the potential in his trembling hands. He stepped forward, the air thickening around him. Every breath buzzed with latent energy, leaving a metallic tang on his tongue. He adjusted the strap of his satchel and tightened his grip on the grimoire tucked within.

Inside, the Nexus Plaza unfolded before him—a sprawling courtyard alive with magic. Each step pulsed faintly beneath his boots as though the ground itself were infused with ley lines. At the plaza's center, the Obelisk of Convergence pierced the sky, its crystalline surface glowing with rhythmic waves of power.

The weight of the Arcanum's grandeur pressed on him. He was not ready. He was just a boy from Caerlyn who had barely learned to harness a spell.

"New blood, huh?"

The voice startled him. A tall boy with tousled blond hair and a smirk stood nearby, arms crossed. "Don't get lost gawking at the obelisk. Orientation's that way."

Alaric mumbled his thanks and hurried to follow the stream of students, his awe tempered by embarrassment.

*****

The halls of the Arcanum were a labyrinth of marble and magic. Crystal sconces cast flickering light that danced in patterns on the walls, their glow shifting hues as students passed.

"Pay attention," snapped an older apprentice as Alaric nearly collided with him.

He stumbled back, muttering an apology. The older student sneered and walked off. Around him, conversations buzzed—names of spells, debates over theories, whispered warnings about instructors.

The murmurs faded when Master Eldaryn entered the hall. The senior mage's presence silenced even the boldest students. His robe shimmered with enchantments, and his staff tapped a steady rhythm as he approached. His sharp eyes scanned the gathered apprentices, landing briefly on Alaric.

"Today, you will prove yourselves," Eldaryn declared. His voice was calm but carried the weight of authority. "Magic demands precision, focus, and discipline. Without these, you will fail—not just here, but in life."

Alaric's stomach tightened as the group followed Eldaryn into the casting chamber.

The Casting Chamber

The circular room was both elegant and unnerving. Its polished marble floor was inscribed with glowing runes, and mirrors lined the walls, reflecting both light and magic.

The apprentices gathered in a hesitant ring as Eldaryn gestured for the first student to step forward.

One by one, they performed. Some succeeded effortlessly, conjuring fire or water with practiced ease. Others faltered, their spells fizzling into smoke or collapsing in sparks.

"Deymorne," Eldaryn called.

Alaric froze. His peers turned to watch, their expressions ranging from mild curiosity to open amusement.

He stepped into the center of the chamber, his hands trembling. The task was simple: summon and sustain a sphere of water.

He closed his eyes, focusing on the spell. He envisioned the tides, their unyielding rhythm, the cold touch of water. Slowly, a bead of liquid formed in the air. It grew, shimmering as it swirled into a perfect sphere.

For a moment, he held it steady. Then his concentration wavered. The sphere burst with a loud pop, drenching him and a few nearby students.

Laughter rippled through the chamber.

Eldaryn's raised hand silenced the room. He approached Alaric, his expression unreadable. "What went wrong?"

"I... I lost focus," Alaric stammered.

"No," Eldaryn said sharply. "You allowed your emotions to interfere. Magic is balance—emotion and logic in perfect harmony. But..." He gestured to the diagrams Alaric had drawn earlier in the session. "Your calculations are impressive. You have the mind of a scholar, Deymorne. However, theory without execution is meaningless."

Alaric nodded, his cheeks burning.

"You will improve," Eldaryn added, his tone softer. "Dismissed."

The Forbidden Library

That night, Alaric couldn't sleep. Eldaryn's critique gnawed at him. His failures were plain, but the flicker of acknowledgment in the master's words kindled a stubborn determination.

He wandered the halls, the Arcanum eerily silent under the glow of its crystal sconces. His steps carried him to the west wing, where the air seemed heavier. The Forbidden Library loomed before him, its iron doors inscribed with runes that pulsed faintly.

He hesitated. This was forbidden territory, the consequences severe. But the weight of his grimoire in his satchel felt like a challenge.

"I have to know," he whispered.

Tracing the runes, he murmured incantations he'd pieced together from stolen glances at ancient texts. The wards resisted, then fell silent as the doors creaked open.

The library was a labyrinth of towering shelves, the air thick with the scent of parchment and something darker. His eyes scanned the spines of books—some bound in leather, others in materials he couldn't name.

One tome caught his attention, its cover etched with a shifting silver sigil. He opened it, and the diagrams within stole his breath.

Ley lines. The veins of magic that coursed through the land, connecting dimensions and powering spells. The pages described their intersections, nexus points of immense energy. But one passage chilled him: "To tamper with ley lines is to unmake the world."

"Do you have a death wish?"

The voice made him jump. He spun around to see Lira, one of the most gifted apprentices, standing in the doorway.

*****

Lira stepped into the room, her piercing blue eyes scanning the shelves. "Breaking into the Forbidden Library? Bold. Stupid, but bold."

"I needed answers," Alaric said defensively.

She raised an eyebrow. "And you thought this was the way to get them? If a professor catches you..."

"They won't," Alaric interrupted. "I can't wait for them to decide when I'm ready. There's too much to learn."

Lira studied him for a moment, her expression unreadable. Then she sighed. "You're reckless, Deymorne. But... maybe you're not entirely wrong."

To his surprise, she began flipping through a nearby tome. For the next hour, they worked in silence, their curiosity forging an unspoken truce.

The weeks that followed were grueling. Alaric poured himself into his studies, struggling to balance his theoretical brilliance with his practical shortcomings. He was ridiculed by some students, admired by others.

Lira's occasional guidance became a lifeline. Though she rarely softened her sharp demeanor, her presence reminded him that he wasn't entirely alone in his relentless pursuit.

One evening, as Alaric stood on the balcony of the Obelisk of Convergence, he looked out at the sprawling landscape below. The ley line diagrams from the forbidden tome lingered in his mind.

"This is just the beginning," he whispered to himself.

And with that, he turned back to the library, determined to uncover more of the secrets the Grand Arcanum sought to hide.

Alaric stumbled back to his dormitory, clutching the grimoire and forbidden tome against his chest. His heart thundered as he replayed the events in his mind—the pulse of the ley line diagrams, the whispered warnings etched into the pages, and Lira's sharp but cryptic comment: "You're reckless, Deymorne. But maybe you're not entirely wrong."

Sleep was impossible. The diagrams seemed burned into his vision, their glowing patterns flashing every time he closed his eyes. Finally, as dawn's light crept through his window, Alaric sat up, retrieved his notebook, and began sketching.

Lines crisscrossed his page, intersecting at points that hummed with invisible energy. He recognized a few of them—the Obelisk of Convergence, the market square of Caerlyn, and a mysterious marking labeled "The Spiral Nexus" near the Alderran Forest. But others were foreign, their locations stretching beyond the known borders of the continent. His fingers itched to understand their significance.

Narrator's Perspective: The Ley Lines' Forgotten Knowledge

The ley lines were older than any written history, their energies woven into the fabric of creation itself. Alaric's understanding of them, rudimentary as it was, placed him among a rare group of individuals who could see the threads of magic connecting the world. But the lines were not merely pathways; they were veins of power, fragile and volatile. For centuries, civilizations had built monuments, temples, and obelisks upon nexus points to harness their energy. Some prospered. Others were consumed.

What Alaric had yet to realize was that his every step within the Arcanum brought him closer to unraveling a truth that many feared to face: the ley lines were not merely tools—they were alive, and they remembered.

The Consequences of Curiosity

"Deymorne!"

Alaric jolted upright as Master Eldaryn's voice rang out across the courtyard. The other students fell silent, their heads swiveling toward the center where Eldaryn stood, his piercing gaze fixed on Alaric. In the master's hands was the tome Alaric had stolen from the Forbidden Library.

The blood drained from Alaric's face.

"Follow me," Eldaryn commanded, his voice as sharp as a blade. The murmurs of the apprentices buzzed like angry hornets as Alaric followed the master into the main tower. The heavy doors swung shut behind them with a resounding thud.

Eldaryn turned, his face a mask of cold fury. "Explain yourself."

"I..." Alaric swallowed hard. "I was searching for answers, Master. I didn't mean any harm."

"You defied the wards of the Forbidden Library," Eldaryn said, his tone measured but dangerous. "Do you understand the gravity of what you've done?"

Alaric hesitated. "The book—it contained information about ley lines. I think they're the key to understanding magic on a deeper level. I had to know."

Eldaryn's expression shifted, a flicker of something—curiosity? Recognition?—crossing his features. He leaned closer. "And what did you find?"

Alaric hesitated again, unsure if honesty would be his salvation or his undoing. Finally, he reached into his satchel and produced the diagram he'd sketched. "This. It shows how the ley lines connect to nexus points. Some of these align with places I've been—or read about. I think they're... alive, in some way."

For a long moment, Eldaryn studied the diagram. When he spoke, his voice was quieter but no less intense. "Ley lines are not a mystery to be trifled with, Deymorne. They are both the foundation of magic and its greatest danger. This knowledge has cost greater men than you their lives. Do not take it lightly."

Alaric nodded, a strange mix of relief and unease settling over him.

Eldaryn sighed, tucking the tome under his arm. "You are reckless. But you are not wrong. Meet me in the casting chamber tomorrow at dawn. If you are so determined to study the ley lines, then you will do so under my supervision."

Flashback: Alaric's Father's Secrets

That night, as Alaric prepared for bed, a memory surfaced—one he had buried deep. He was ten years old, standing in the fields with his father as the sun dipped below the horizon.

"Why don't we ever leave Caerlyn?" Alaric had asked.

His father's hand tightened on the plow. For a moment, Walter's expression darkened. "The world out there... isn't what you think it is, boy. There are things—powerful things—that would tear you apart if you got too close."

Alaric had frowned. "Like what?"

Walter didn't answer, but the way his gaze lingered on the horizon made Alaric shiver. Now, years later, he wondered if his father had known more than he let on.

*****

The next morning, Eldaryn guided Alaric through an advanced casting exercise designed to simulate a nexus point's energy flow. The runes on the chamber floor glowed as Alaric channeled his magic into the pattern, his mind racing with images from the ley line diagrams.

The energy surged through him, wild and untamed. For a moment, he felt everything—the pull of the Obelisk, the hum of the ley lines beneath the Arcanum, the distant pulse of a nexus he had never seen.

And then it collapsed, sending him sprawling to the floor.

"You're too focused on control," Eldaryn said, pulling him to his feet. "Magic is not a beast to be tamed—it is a force to be understood."

Alaric nodded, his determination renewed. He didn't just want to understand magic—he wanted to unlock its secrets, no matter the cost.

After the taxing morning in the casting chamber, Alaric found himself summoned to the Arcanum's Great Library. Unlike the shadowed and forbidden halls he had previously trespassed into, this library was grand and welcoming. Towering shelves stretched toward a ceiling painted with constellations that shimmered faintly, as though alive. Students moved between rows, their robes brushing against the marble floor as they searched for tomes and scrolls.

Eldaryn led him to a secluded alcove at the back of the library. A single table sat beneath an ornate chandelier, and upon it were spread books, loose pages of ancient texts, and several curious artifacts.

"These," Eldaryn began, gesturing to the collection, "are for you. If you are to delve into the mysteries of magic beyond what we teach here, you must understand its many forms."

Alaric's eyes widened as he surveyed the items. "Are these... real?" he asked, barely above a whisper.

"Every one of them," Eldaryn replied. "Handle them carefully. Begin with this."

The master mage handed him a thin, leather-bound tome titled The Principles of Rune Magic. The cover was embossed with an intricate pattern of intersecting circles and lines, each glowing faintly as Alaric ran his fingers over them.

Runes: The Language of Power

Alaric opened the tome, its yellowed pages crackling softly. The text described how runes were more than mere symbols—they were conduits of raw magical energy, each carrying a specific function. One page featured the Rune of Binding, used to trap energy or creatures, and the Rune of Amplification, which could enhance a spell's power.

Beside the descriptions were hand-drawn diagrams showing how to carve the runes into stone, metal, or even flesh. Alaric's heart raced as he imagined the possibilities.

"Rune magic is ancient," Eldaryn explained, his tone reverent. "It predates spoken spells and relies on precision. Even a single misstroke can render a rune useless—or catastrophic."

Alaric nodded, committing the shapes to memory. "Can runes affect the ley lines?" he asked.

Eldaryn hesitated, then said, "Yes. But the consequences of such interference are dire. Some nexus points still bear the scars of rune experiments from centuries past."

Artifacts of Elemental Power

Alaric's attention shifted to a small, crystalline orb sitting atop a bronze pedestal. Its surface swirled with fire-like patterns that flickered and shifted.

"This is the Emberstone," Eldaryn said. "A fragment of raw Fire magic. It draws its power from the Elemental Plane of Fire and can serve as both a weapon and a tool."

Alaric carefully picked up the stone, feeling its warmth radiate through his fingers. The orb pulsed faintly, almost like a heartbeat. "It's alive?"

"In a sense," Eldaryn replied. "Artifacts tied to the elemental planes often carry a fragment of the plane's energy, giving them a semblance of vitality. The Emberstone, for instance, can conjure flames or even summon a Fire Sprite—if the user knows how."

Beside the Emberstone lay a vial of shimmering blue liquid. Its label read Tears of Thalassa.

"What's this?" Alaric asked.

"A potent Water-based potion," Eldaryn said. "It's said to come from the oceanic nexus of Thalassa. One drop can heal grievous wounds or quench the fiercest flames. But beware—it carries the will of the ocean and cannot be controlled easily."

The Creatures of Magic

Among the artifacts, Alaric noticed a parchment displaying detailed sketches of creatures he'd only read about in passing. One depicted a serpentine being with jagged, crystalline scales labeled Shard Serpent. Another showed a large, feline beast with lightning crackling along its fur—Thundercat.

"These creatures," Eldaryn said, tapping the parchment, "are tied directly to the elemental planes. Shard Serpents, for example, dwell in the Plane of Earth and can manipulate gemstones as if they were extensions of their own bodies. Thundercats, meanwhile, are from the Plane of Lightning and can summon storms."

Alaric's gaze lingered on a third sketch—a humanoid figure wrapped in shadows, its eyes glowing like embers. "What is this one?" he asked.

"A Wraith of the Veil," Eldaryn answered grimly. "A being from the Shadow Plane, drawn to areas where ley lines weaken the boundary between dimensions. Wraiths are dangerous, Alaric. Avoid them at all costs."

Paranormal Creatures and Their Mysteries

Eldaryn pulled out another tome, this one bound in black leather with silver lettering that read Paranormal Entities and Their Domains. He flipped to a page depicting a spectral wolf prowling a mist-shrouded forest.

"This," Eldaryn said, "is a Void Hound. It hunts in places where dimensional rifts occur. They are not truly alive but are born of the chaos between planes."

Alaric leaned closer, fascinated. "Can they be stopped?"

"With great difficulty," Eldaryn replied. "Paranormal creatures like these are tied to phenomena beyond our understanding. Even the most skilled mages tread lightly around them."

The Forbidden Texts

Finally, Eldaryn handed Alaric a fragile scroll sealed with a wax sigil bearing the mark of the Arcanum. "This," Eldaryn said, "is a fragment of the Grimoire of Eternal Threads. It is among the rarest texts we possess and speaks of the connection between all magic types—runes, spells, potions, and even creatures."

Alaric broke the seal carefully, his hands trembling. The scroll was filled with densely packed text, interspersed with diagrams of glowing threads weaving through various magical symbols.

"The Eternal Threads," Eldaryn continued, "are believed to represent the flow of magic through all planes of existence. Some call it the Primal Source, from which all ley lines draw their power. Understanding this is the ultimate goal of many scholars. But tread carefully, Alaric. Many who seek such knowledge lose themselves to it."

Flashback Scene: Artifacts

Alaric paused before a low pedestal in the Arcanum's library. Resting on a velvet cushion was a small, red gemstone—the Emberstone. Its surface shimmered faintly, flickering like a captured flame.

"The Emberstone," whispered a soft voice behind him. Alaric turned to see a senior librarian watching him with a faint smile. "A fragment of a nexus conflagration, imbued with the raw energy of fire ley lines. It's said to amplify any spell tied to its element."

"Why is it here and not in use?" Alaric asked, his fingers twitching to touch the gem.

"Because artifacts like this are dangerous, Apprentice. Ley lines and their fragments do not abide control lightly. The last mage who tried to wield the Emberstone alone burned himself from the inside out."

Alaric swallowed hard, feeling the weight of the librarian's warning. Yet, he couldn't look away. The stone seemed to pulse in rhythm with his heartbeat, a reminder of the ley lines' untamed power.

A New Resolve

As the sun dipped below the horizon, Alaric sat alone in the library, surrounded by the treasures Eldaryn had entrusted to him. The Emberstone pulsed softly beside him, its warmth a reminder of the elemental forces he had yet to master. The pages of the texts before him seemed endless, each line a promise of answers—and greater questions.

He picked up the Principles of Rune Magic again, determined to try his hand at carving a basic rune. He chose the Rune of Amplification, tracing its lines carefully onto a shard of wood. The result was crude but functional; when he activated it, the flickering candle beside him flared briefly before settling.

It was a small success, but it ignited something within him—a certainty that he was on the right path.

Narrator's Perspective: The Path Forward

Magic is as infinite as the stars and as unpredictable as the sea. For Alaric, these truths were becoming more tangible with every passing day. But knowledge comes with a cost. The more he learned, the more he glimpsed the dangers hidden beneath the surface.

The Grand Arcanum was a place of learning, but it was also a place of secrets. And as Alaric delved deeper, he was beginning to understand that some secrets were kept hidden for a reason.

*****

Alaric couldn't resist the allure of the Emberstone. Though he'd already spent hours studying its swirling patterns and faint warmth, he longed to understand its power fully. Waiting until the library quieted, he gently cradled the orb in both hands and closed his eyes.

A wave of heat pulsed up his arms, and his thoughts spiraled away as if carried on a scorching wind. The orb's patterns intensified, and faint whispers began to echo in his mind. He glimpsed a barren desert scorched by an unrelenting sun, flames dancing across its surface. Then, with a sudden crack, the Emberstone flared.

The warm, orange glow became a searing blaze. Alaric yelped and dropped the orb onto the table, where it rolled toward the edge before stopping abruptly. The flames did not extinguish. Instead, they flickered, coalescing into the shape of a tiny humanoid figure—a Fire Sprite.

Its eyes glowed like embers as it turned to face Alaric, cocking its head in an oddly inquisitive manner. Then it chittered, a high-pitched sound that made Alaric stumble backward.

"What have you done?" Eldaryn's voice thundered from the doorway. His robes swirled as he strode into the room, raising his staff.

The sprite hissed at the sight of Eldaryn and darted toward a stack of books, setting their edges alight. Eldaryn waved his staff, a spray of water dousing the flames before they could spread further.

"Stay still!" Eldaryn barked at Alaric as he chanted a spell. Threads of blue light encased the sprite, suspending it mid-air. With a flick of his wrist, Eldaryn drew the creature back into the Emberstone, which dimmed once more.

The silence that followed was suffocating.

"Explain yourself," Eldaryn demanded.

"I—I didn't mean to," Alaric stammered. "I was trying to understand its power, and it just... happened."

Eldaryn rubbed his temples. "The Emberstone is not a toy, Deymorne. Its connection to the Elemental Plane of Fire is fragile. If you'd let that sprite loose, it could have razed this entire library."

"I'm sorry," Alaric said, his voice small.

Eldaryn sighed. "Curiosity is admirable, but recklessness is not. You have potential, Alaric, but if you let your ambition outpace your discipline, you'll destroy more than just yourself."

The rebuke stung, but Alaric nodded. He resolved to be more careful—or at least, to hide his experiments better.

The next day, Alaric returned to the casting chamber for his morning lessons. The other apprentices whispered as he entered, word of his mishap with the Emberstone having spread overnight. Among the crowd, one apprentice stood apart—a boy named Kael.

Kael was tall and confident, his robes embroidered with intricate patterns that marked him as a favored student. He smirked as Alaric passed.

"Starting fires in the library, Deymorne?" Kael said loudly. "Didn't think you had it in you."

The others snickered, but Alaric kept his focus on the runes etched into the chamber floor.

"Let's see if you can handle today's trial without burning the place down," Kael added.

The trial was straightforward: summon a protective barrier and sustain it under pressure. Each apprentice took turns stepping into the center of the chamber, where a small magical construct would launch energy bolts at them. Most succeeded with minor faltering.

When it was Alaric's turn, the whispers grew louder.

"Focus," he muttered to himself, stepping into the circle. The construct stirred, its crystalline limbs glowing as it charged the first bolt.

Alaric raised his hands, summoning the protective sphere. It shimmered faintly, holding against the first few strikes. But as the barrage intensified, cracks began to spiderweb across the surface. Alaric gritted his teeth, pouring more energy into the spell.

Finally, the construct paused, its glow dimming. Alaric lowered his hands, his knees weak but his barrier intact. The chamber was silent.

"Not bad," Kael said, stepping forward. "But let me show you how it's really done."

Kael's barrier was flawless, its surface reflecting the energy bolts like polished glass. He ended his trial with a flourish, dismissing his spell with a snap of his fingers. The applause stung more than Alaric cared to admit.

Ley Line Lore

After the trials, Eldaryn called Alaric to his private study. The room was dimly lit, its walls lined with scrolls and ancient maps. At its center stood a large, circular table inlaid with glowing runes.

"Sit," Eldaryn instructed, gesturing to a chair.

Alaric obeyed, his curiosity piqued as Eldaryn spread a map across the table. It was a map of the continent, but unlike any Alaric had seen before. Faint lines of blue and gold crisscrossed the parchment, converging at points marked with elaborate symbols.

"These are the ley lines," Eldaryn said. "The veins of magic that flow through our world. Their power sustains life, magic, and even the natural order."

He tapped one of the nexus points on the map, a location near Caerlyn. "Each nexus holds immense energy. Mages have tried to harness it, but few succeed without catastrophic consequences. You must understand, Alaric—these lines are not tools. They are ancient forces, older than any spell or artifact."

Alaric leaned forward, studying the symbols. "What about the Spiral Nexus? I saw it on a map in the grimoire."

Eldaryn's expression darkened. "The Spiral Nexus is unique. It doesn't align with the natural flow of magic. It's... an anomaly. Some believe it was created, not discovered."

"Created?" Alaric echoed.

Eldaryn nodded. "By whom, or for what purpose, we do not know. But it is dangerous. Stay away from it."

Despite Eldaryn's warnings, Alaric couldn't stop thinking about the Spiral Nexus. That night, he returned to the library, searching for more clues. In the darkest corner of the archives, he found a brittle tome titled The Shattered Veil. Its pages were filled with ominous accounts of mages who had delved too deeply into the ley lines.

One passage caught his attention:

"To tamper with the Spiral Nexus is to court disaster. It is a wound in the fabric of magic, where the natural order frays. Yet, for those who dare, it offers power beyond comprehension."

Alaric's heart raced. Power beyond comprehension. He closed the book, his resolve hardening. He would find the Spiral Nexus. He would uncover its secrets. And he would prove that he was more than just a reckless apprentice.

Narrator's: Historical Role of the Arcanum

The Grand Arcanum was not merely a school; it was a monument to the delicate balance of power in a world dominated by ley lines. For centuries, it had served as both a sanctuary for learning and a fortress against chaos. Kings and queens once sought its counsel, and even now, its influence extended far beyond its crystal walls. But power breeds ambition, and the ley lines—ancient and unpredictable—demanded respect, not mastery. Alaric, like many before him, would soon learn the price of such ambitions.

Narrator's Perspective: The Path Diverges

Magic is a double-edged blade, and those who wield it often find themselves cut by its sharpest edge. Alaric's determination, though admirable, blinded him to the dangers that lay ahead. He sought knowledge, but knowledge, like the ley lines themselves, is unpredictable and unyielding. The Spiral Nexus would test him, not only as a mage but as a person. And the choices he made would echo far beyond the walls of the Grand Arcanum.

Chapter 3: The First Expedition

Alaric sat alone in the Grand Arcanum's vast library, the soft glow of enchanted lamps casting long shadows on the towering shelves. Before him lay a stack of tomes filled with theories on ley lines, but his attention was fixed on the grimoire. Its pages seemed to pulse faintly, as if the book itself were alive and waiting for him to act.

His fingers hovered over the map etched into its centerfold. The glowing ley lines crisscrossed the parchment like veins of light, each intersection marked with intricate symbols. One in particular—a jagged spiral near the northern forests—drew his focus. The symbol wasn't in any of the texts he'd studied, nor did it match the runes in the Grand Arcanum's archives.

"Deymorne," came a sharp voice from behind.

Alaric startled, quickly shutting the grimoire as Master Eldaryn stepped into view. The man's piercing blue eyes scanned the books strewn across the table, his expression unreadable.

"Studying late again, I see," Eldaryn said, folding his arms. "Tell me, do you ever sleep?"

"Not often," Alaric admitted.

Eldaryn's gaze settled on him, his expression softening slightly. "Your thirst for knowledge is admirable, but obsession can blind even the brightest minds. What are you searching for, Deymorne?"

Alaric hesitated. "I think... there's more to ley lines than what the texts say. They're not just pathways for magic—they're connected to something bigger."

"And you believe you're the one to uncover that connection?" Eldaryn asked, his tone skeptical but not dismissive.

"I have to try," Alaric said firmly. "If I don't, who will?"

Eldaryn regarded him for a long moment before nodding. "Very well. But remember this—knowledge is a double-edged sword. Wield it wisely, or it will cut you down."

With that, Eldaryn turned and left, leaving Alaric alone with his thoughts and the pulsing glow of the grimoire.

*****

Two days later, Alaric stood at the gates of the Grand Arcanum, a satchel slung over his shoulder and the grimoire tucked securely within. He had convinced Eldaryn to grant him leave for a field study, citing the need to observe ley line anomalies firsthand. Eldaryn had reluctantly agreed, warning him to be cautious and not to stray too far from known paths.

Lira, a fellow student and one of the few who believed in Alaric's theories, approached him as he adjusted the straps of his satchel.

"Are you sure about this?" she asked, her brow furrowed with concern. "The northern forests aren't exactly known for being friendly."

Alaric offered a small smile. "If it were easy, someone would've done it already."

Lira hesitated, then handed him a small amulet shaped like a crescent moon. "For luck," she said. "And for light, if you need it. Just... don't do anything reckless, okay?"

"I'll be fine," Alaric assured her, though he wasn't entirely certain himself.

With a final glance at the towering spires of the Grand Arcanum, he turned and began his journey.

The northern forests were a stark contrast to the structured elegance of the Grand Arcanum. Towering pines stretched endlessly into the sky, their branches interwoven to form a dense canopy that allowed only slivers of sunlight to filter through. The air was thick with the scent of damp earth and pine needles, and the only sounds were the rustle of leaves and the occasional distant call of a bird.

As Alaric ventured deeper, he felt a strange energy in the air—a faint hum that resonated in his bones. He pulled out the grimoire and studied the map once more. The jagged spiral was close, but the forest's terrain grew increasingly treacherous, with tangled roots and uneven ground slowing his progress.

Hours later, he stumbled upon a clearing where the hum grew louder. At the center stood a large stone obelisk, its surface covered in runes similar to those in the forbidden library. The obelisk pulsed faintly, the glow intensifying as Alaric approached.

He knelt beside it, tracing the runes with his fingers. "This must be a ley line nexus," he murmured. The air around the obelisk felt charged, as though the very fabric of reality was thinner here.

But as he studied the runes, the ground beneath him trembled. The obelisk's glow flickered violently, and a low, guttural growl echoed through the clearing. Alaric spun around to see a creature emerge from the shadows—a hulking beast with eyes that glowed like molten gold.

The Guardian of the Nexus

The creature stepped into the clearing, its form shifting between solidity and shadow. Its claws dug into the earth, and its growl sent a chill down Alaric's spine. He realized it wasn't merely a beast—it was a guardian, likely tied to the ley lines themselves.

Alaric's mind raced. He had read about magical guardians, but nothing in the texts had prepared him for this. Fighting it wasn't an option—he lacked both the skill and the strength. Instead, he raised his hands slowly, hoping to convey that he meant no harm.

"I'm not here to disrupt the nexus," he said, his voice steady despite his fear. "I just want to understand."

The creature paused, its glowing eyes narrowing as if assessing his words. For a moment, the hum of the nexus seemed to synchronize with the beating of his heart. Then, slowly, the creature stepped back, retreating into the shadows.

Alaric let out a shaky breath, his knees weak with relief. Whatever the creature was, it had spared him—for now.

As night fell, Alaric set up camp near the clearing, unable to tear himself away from the nexus. By the light of Lira's amulet, he continued to study the obelisk, carefully sketching the runes and noting their patterns.

When he opened the grimoire, its pages seemed to respond to the proximity of the nexus. New symbols appeared on the map, lines that hadn't been visible before. One led to a symbol resembling a fractured star, far to the west.

"What are you trying to show me?" Alaric whispered, his curiosity burning brighter than ever.

The grimoire offered no answer, but the hum of the nexus seemed almost... expectant, as though it, too, was urging him forward.

Upon his return to the Grand Arcanum, Alaric's findings caused a stir. In a lecture hall filled with students and instructors, he presented his sketches of the nexus and the new lines on the map.

"This proves that the ley lines are more than just magical pathways," Alaric said, his voice filled with conviction. "They're alive, in a way—dynamic and interconnected."

A murmur rippled through the hall. Some students leaned forward, intrigued, while others exchanged skeptical glances. One student, a tall boy named Kael, stood abruptly.

"This is nonsense," Kael said, his tone sharp. "You're basing your theories on a single field study and a grimoire you can barely decipher. You're chasing illusions, Deymorne."

Lira rose in Alaric's defense. "At least he's chasing something worthwhile. What have you contributed, Kael? Another mediocre fireball?"

Laughter broke out among the students, but Alaric felt no triumph. Kael's words stung because there was truth in them. His knowledge was incomplete, and his methods unconventional. But he couldn't let doubt deter him.

The Narrator's Insight: A Spark Ignited

Alaric's journey was far from over. The nexus had revealed only a fraction of the ley lines' mysteries, and the fractured star on the map beckoned him westward. But the challenges he faced were mounting—skepticism from his peers, the dangers of forbidden knowledge, and the ever-present question of what lay at the heart of the ley lines.

For now, he was a student with more questions than answers. But within him burned a spark of determination, a fire that would not be extinguished.

*****

The morning Alaric departed on his second journey, he stood at the edge of the Grand Arcanum's sprawling grounds, adjusting the strap of his satchel and staring at the enchanted Runestone Compass cradled in his hand. It was crude compared to the master-crafted magical artifacts he had seen in the academy's archives, but it was his creation—a small disk of polished stone with etched runes that glowed faintly when he held it.

The compass was more than a guide. It responded to the ley lines, the needle shifting not toward magnetic north but toward the strongest magical current in the area. Alaric had poured hours into its design, channeling everything he had learned about rune-crafting and energy manipulation.

"Let's hope this works," he murmured to himself, holding the compass aloft. The needle quivered, then swung sharply toward the northeast—the direction of the Crystal Glade.

Lira stood nearby, watching him with a mix of concern and curiosity. "You're sure about this?"

"Sure enough," Alaric replied, pocketing the compass. "The glade is a nexus—probably tied to the ley lines. If I can study its energy, I might be able to learn more about how they interact with the world."

Lira frowned. "Just promise me you'll come back in one piece. And don't trust that compass too much—it's not exactly tried and true."

"That's the point of trying," Alaric said with a grin. "See you soon."

With that, he turned and began his journey, the Grand Arcanum fading behind him as he ventured into the unknown.

The Crystal Glade

The journey to the Crystal Glade took Alaric through terrain that grew wilder and more untamed with every step. Fields gave way to dense forests, their shadows stretching long beneath the rising sun. The hum of magic in the air grew stronger as he approached the glade, his Runestone Compass glowing faintly with each passing hour.

By midday, he reached the edge of the glade, stepping into a realm that seemed untouched by time. The trees here were unlike any he had seen before—tall and slender, their bark shimmering like glass. Their leaves glowed faintly, casting dappled patterns of light on the forest floor.

At the center of the glade was a massive crystalline formation, its jagged spires rising from the earth like frozen lightning. The air was thick with energy, and Alaric felt it vibrating in his chest, filling him with a mixture of awe and unease.

He approached the crystal cautiously, his compass glowing brighter with each step. The runes on its surface pulsed in rhythm with the ley line energy, as if resonating with the nexus.

"This is incredible," Alaric whispered, pulling out his grimoire to sketch the scene. The crystal's surface seemed to refract the light of the sun, scattering rainbows across the clearing. Its base was covered in faint markings—runes so ancient they had begun to fade, their purpose lost to time.

As he traced one of the runes with his finger, a sudden pulse of energy surged through the crystal. The ground beneath him trembled, and the light in the glade grew blinding.

When the light subsided, Alaric found himself standing not in the glade, but in a place that defied explanation. The ground beneath him was smooth and glassy, reflecting a sky that shifted between colors—violet, gold, and azure. In the distance, spires of crystal floated, their forms shimmering as if caught between dimensions.

It was a vision, Alaric realized, or perhaps something more—a glimpse into the unknown. The ley lines were not just pathways for magical energy. They were bridges to other realms, threads connecting realities.

As he stood there, a voice echoed in his mind, faint and distant: "The lines are the foundation, the lifeblood. Follow them, and you will find the truth."

The vision faded as quickly as it had come, leaving Alaric back in the glade, his knees weak and his breath uneven. The crystal had dimmed, its energy spent, but the experience left an indelible mark on his mind.

As Alaric set up camp at the edge of the glade that evening, he replayed the vision in his mind. The implications were staggering. If the ley lines truly connected worlds, then their instability could mean more than just disruptions in magic—it could tear the very fabric of reality.

The grimoire sat open beside him, its pages seeming to shift in the firelight. He traced the lines on the map, his finger stopping at a new symbol that had appeared—a fractured circle far to the south.

"What are you trying to show me?" he murmured to the grimoire, half expecting an answer. The book remained silent, but the sense of urgency it instilled in him was unmistakable.

Encounters in the Wild

The next morning, as Alaric prepared to leave the glade, he encountered a group of travelers—a trio of nomadic scholars who had come to study the glade's unique energy. Their leader, a tall woman with silver-streaked hair and a staff adorned with glowing runes, introduced herself as Erynn.

"You're from the Grand Arcanum," she said, eyeing the compass in his hand. "A student, I assume?"

"Alaric," he replied. "And you?"

"We're Seekers of the Undercurrent," Erynn said. "We study the ley lines—not from books, but from the world itself."

Alaric's interest piqued. "What have you learned?"

Erynn's expression darkened. "The ley lines are weakening in some places. Fracturing. If it continues, the damage could be irreversible."

Alaric's thoughts flashed to his vision. "Have you seen... other worlds? Through the lines?"

Erynn hesitated before nodding. "Briefly. But such glimpses come at a cost. The lines are not meant to be crossed lightly."

Her warning stayed with him as they parted ways, her words a reminder of the risks that lay ahead.

The Narrator's Insight: Pathways to the Unknown

Alaric's journey to the Crystal Glade was more than a field study. It was a step toward understanding the true nature of the ley lines—a realization that they were not just energy conduits, but doorways. The compass he had crafted, the grimoire he carried, and the visions he witnessed were all pieces of a puzzle far larger than himself.

But with knowledge came responsibility. The ley lines were not merely paths to be followed; they were the threads holding the world together. And somewhere along those threads, a greater truth awaited—a truth that could either save or destroy everything he knew.

*****

Alaric sat on a smooth stone at the edge of the Crystal Glade, watching the trio of Seekers as they examined the crystalline formation. Erynn crouched near the base, her fingers hovering over the faint runes etched into the surface. The other two Seekers—a lean man with dark, piercing eyes and a younger woman with intricate braids—took readings with strange instruments that emitted soft, rhythmic hums.

"Your Runestone Compass," Erynn said, breaking the silence. "It resonates with the ley lines. Did you craft it yourself?"

"Yes," Alaric said, his tone cautious. "I designed it to detect magical energy flows and anomalies."

"Impressive," she said, nodding. "Though I imagine its readings are inconsistent. The lines don't always follow predictable patterns."

Alaric frowned. "I've noticed that. But I thought ley lines were supposed to be stable."

Erynn stood and crossed her arms. "That's the theory taught in most academies, including your Grand Arcanum. The reality is far more complex. Ley lines are not merely channels for energy—they are alive, in their own way. They shift, react, and even... fracture."

"Fracture?" Alaric asked, his pulse quickening.

The lean man, who had been silent until now, spoke up. "Imagine a riverbed worn thin over centuries. Eventually, the water breaks through, carving a new path—or flooding uncontrollably."

"That's what's happening to the ley lines," Erynn said grimly. "In some regions, the fractures are minor—barely noticeable. In others..." She trailed off, glancing at the crystalline formation. "They create places like this."

Alaric's gaze shifted to the crystal. "You mean the glade exists because of a fractured ley line?"

Erynn nodded. "The energy here is unstable, constantly shifting. It's beautiful, yes, but also dangerous. Prolonged exposure can warp magic, or worse."

Alaric hesitated, his hand brushing the grimoire in his satchel. "Then how do we stop the fractures?"

Erynn exchanged a glance with her companions. "We don't know," she admitted. "We've been studying the phenomenon for years, but the source of the instability eludes us. Some believe it's natural, a consequence of the lines aging over millennia. Others..."

The younger Seeker chimed in, her voice quiet. "Others think it's deliberate."

The words sent a chill through Alaric. "Deliberate? By who—or what?"

"That's the question," Erynn said. "And the answer may lie deeper within the lines themselves."

Later that evening, as the Seekers set up their camp, Alaric returned to the crystalline structure, drawn by a sense of urgency he couldn't explain. The runes at the base of the crystal pulsed faintly, their light flickering in patterns that seemed almost purposeful. Kneeling beside them, he opened the grimoire and compared the markings to the ones on the map.

They didn't match exactly, but there were similarities—enough to suggest a connection. Alaric traced the runes with his finger, feeling the faint vibrations beneath the surface. As he did, the light from the crystal intensified, casting the glade in an ethereal glow.

"What are you trying to tell me?" he muttered, his thoughts racing.

The runes pulsed in a sequence—three short bursts, then a long one. It repeated, over and over, like a heartbeat. Alaric pulled out his compass, watching as its needle spun wildly before settling in a direction that pointed not toward the ley lines, but toward the heart of the crystal.

"Focus, Alaric," he whispered to himself. He began tracing runes in the air, drawing from the knowledge he'd gathered in his studies. The patterns felt intuitive, as if the crystal itself was guiding him. When he completed the final rune, the ground beneath him rumbled, and a section of the crystal's base slid open, revealing a narrow passageway.

Alaric hesitated, glancing back at the Seekers' camp. Part of him wanted to call for their help, but another part—driven by a need to prove himself—urged him forward. Taking a deep breath, he stepped into the passage, the walls of crystal glowing faintly around him.

The Heart of the Nexus

The passage led to a small chamber, its walls covered in runes that pulsed with a soft, golden light. At the center of the room floated a sphere of pure energy, its surface rippling like liquid sunlight. Alaric approached cautiously, the air growing warmer with each step.

The sphere seemed alive, its energy resonating with the grimoire in his satchel. He pulled out the book, and as he opened it, the pages began to glow, their runes shifting and rearranging into a pattern he hadn't seen before.

A voice echoed in his mind, faint but insistent: "The lines are weakening. The fractures must be healed, or the threads will unravel."

Alaric's heart raced. "How? How do I heal them?"

The voice offered no answer, but the runes on the grimoire's page began to pulse in a sequence that matched the sphere's rhythm. Alaric traced the runes in the air, and the sphere's glow intensified. The chamber filled with light, and for a brief moment, he felt as though he were standing at the center of the world, connected to something vast and incomprehensible.

Then, just as suddenly, the light faded, and the sphere dimmed. The chamber was silent once more, but Alaric felt a deep sense of understanding settle over him. The ley lines weren't just pathways—they were threads holding the world together. And something, or someone, was pulling at those threads.

*****

When Alaric emerged from the passage, the Seekers were waiting, their expressions a mix of curiosity and concern.

"What did you find?" Erynn asked, her tone sharp.

Alaric hesitated, then recounted what had happened in the chamber. As he spoke, the younger Seeker's face grew pale.

"The fractures," she said softly. "They're worse than we thought."

Erynn's brow furrowed. "If the ley lines unravel, it won't just disrupt magic. It will destabilize everything—nature, time, reality itself."

Alaric nodded. "And I think... someone is causing it."

The words hung heavy in the air. Erynn's expression hardened, and she placed a hand on Alaric's shoulder.

"If that's true, then you've stepped onto a path far more dangerous than you realize," she said. "The lines are ancient, but they are not invincible. And those who seek to control them will not hesitate to destroy anyone who stands in their way."

Alaric met her gaze, the weight of her words settling over him. He thought of the vision he'd seen in the glade, of the fractured spires and shifting dimensions. The ley lines were more than he'd imagined—and so were the stakes.

"I won't stop," he said quietly. "Not until I understand what's happening."

Erynn smiled faintly. "Good. Just don't lose yourself in the process."

The clearing was alive with energy, the hum of the ley lines growing louder as Alaric approached the nexus. His breath caught as the obelisk at the center of the glade came into view, its fractured surface pulsing faintly with shifting hues of blue and gold. The air felt heavier here, thick with a strange, electric charge that prickled his skin and made the hair on his arms stand on end.

For a moment, he hesitated. The grimoire in his satchel seemed to hum in resonance with the nexus, the faint vibration bleeding through the leather. Alaric felt a tug at the edges of his consciousness—a whisper, not of words, but of emotions: curiosity, wariness, and an undercurrent of something deeper, almost mournful. It was as though the ley lines themselves were aware of his presence, probing his intent.

Do they remember? The thought surfaced unbidden, and with it came a flash of fragmented images: hands etched with glowing runes, a blinding surge of light, and a shattering so profound it echoed in his chest. He stumbled, clutching at the grimoire for balance. The sensation faded as quickly as it had come, leaving behind an unsettling quiet.

Journal Entry: Struggles and Triumphs

Later that evening, as the nexus's glow softened with the arrival of dusk, Alaric sat cross-legged on the grass, his journal open on his lap. The soft scratching of his pen was the only sound in the clearing as he tried to put his thoughts into words:

"The nexus is unlike anything I imagined. The energy here feels alive, as if it's watching me, measuring me. For a moment, I thought I heard... no, felt... something. It's hard to describe. It wasn't a voice, but a presence—ancient and immense. The ley lines aren't just paths for magic; they're something more, something sentient. Do they remember everyone who's touched them? Do they remember every triumph and every failure?

But what do they see in me?

I keep thinking about my father. He must have felt this pull once, the same hunger to understand. But he turned back. I can't. I won't. If I fail, at least I'll know I tried. But the weight of it... it feels heavier than I expected. I wish I could talk to someone who understood. I wish I could talk to him."

He paused, staring at the words until the ink began to blur. With a sigh, he closed the journal and tucked it back into his satchel.

As the last light of the sun dipped below the horizon, the clearing grew eerily still. The obelisk's glow intensified, its fractured surface radiating tendrils of light that coiled and shifted like living things. Alaric stood, drawn closer despite the unease twisting in his gut.

"You should not be here," a voice said, low and resonant, reverberating through the clearing.

Alaric spun around, but the glade was empty. The voice came again, this time from everywhere and nowhere at once. "You walk paths that others have broken. Why?"

A figure began to materialize near the obelisk, coalescing from the light itself. It was humanoid but indistinct, its form shifting like smoke within the confines of its glowing outline. Eyes—if they could be called that—burned with an inner light that seemed to pierce straight through Alaric.

"Who are you?" Alaric managed, his voice trembling.

The entity tilted its head, the motion slow and deliberate. "Who am I? Who are you? A seeker? A thief? Or something worse?"

"I... I'm trying to understand the ley lines," Alaric said. "I want to learn. To help."

The entity's form shimmered, its edges flaring briefly with gold. "Help? The lines have seen your kind before. Builders. Destroyers. You come with questions but bring only ruin."

"That's not what I want," Alaric insisted, stepping forward. "I'm not here to break anything. I just... I need to know the truth."

For a long moment, the entity was silent, its form flickering like a dying flame. Then it spoke again, softer this time. "Truth is not given freely. It is earned. Prove your worth, seeker. But know this: the lines remember, and they will not forgive."

Before Alaric could respond, the entity dissolved into threads of light that rejoined the obelisk. The clearing fell silent once more, the nexus's hum a quiet reminder of the presence that lingered just beyond comprehension.

Alaric lingered in the glade long after the encounter, the entity's words echoing in his mind. The weight of the grimoire felt different now, heavier with the knowledge that he was not alone in seeking the ley lines' secrets—nor in being judged by them.

As he packed his belongings and prepared to leave, he cast one last glance at the obelisk. Its fractured surface glowed faintly, the light steady and watchful.

"I'll prove myself," he said softly, as much to himself as to the unseen presence. "Whatever it takes."

With that, he turned and began the trek back through the forest, the hum of the ley lines fading but never disappearing entirely. Behind him, the nexus pulsed faintly, as if acknowledging his departure—or marking his resolve.

Chapter 4: The Fragile Threads

The Weight of Questions

The halls of the Grand Arcanum felt quieter than usual as Alaric walked them, his mind burdened by the revelations of his last expedition. The vision at the Crystal Glade, the fractured ley lines, and the voice's cryptic warning echoed in his thoughts. The grimoire, tucked securely in his satchel, seemed heavier than it had ever been.

Master Eldaryn's office was on the top floor of the Spire of Knowledge, its wide windows offering a breathtaking view of the sea. As Alaric entered, he found the master standing by one of those windows, his hands clasped behind his back.

"You requested to see me, Deymorne?" Eldaryn asked without turning.

"Yes, Master," Alaric replied. "It's about the ley lines. I believe their fractures are accelerating, and I think... someone might be causing it."

Eldaryn turned, his sharp blue eyes narrowing. "You're certain?"

Alaric hesitated. "Not entirely. But I've seen evidence—corrupted runes, destabilized nexuses—and I encountered a figure manipulating one of the lines. He called himself Veyran."

Eldaryn's expression darkened. "Veyran. That name is not unfamiliar to me."

"You know him?"

"He was a prodigy once," Eldaryn said, his tone heavy. "A student of the Grand Arcanum many years ago. Brilliant, ambitious, and utterly reckless. He believed the ley lines were not just channels of energy but tools to reshape the world. When his experiments endangered others, he was expelled. To hear his name again... it does not bode well."

Alaric felt a chill. "If he's behind the fractures, how do we stop him?"

"That depends on how much you're willing to sacrifice," Eldaryn said. "The ley lines are ancient, their workings only partially understood. To confront someone like Veyran, you must first understand the lines themselves—fully and deeply. That knowledge comes at a price."

"What kind of price?" Alaric asked.

Eldaryn didn't answer directly. Instead, he gestured to the grimoire peeking from Alaric's satchel. "That book chose you for a reason. It will demand much of you before it reveals its secrets. Be prepared for that."

Word of Alaric's latest discoveries spread quickly among the students. The sketches he had shared, the theories he proposed about the ley lines' fragility, had sparked fascination and debate. But not everyone was convinced.

In the practice hall, Alaric faced Kael, his most vocal critic. The two had been paired for a spellcasting exercise, but the tension between them was palpable.

"You really believe these fractures are some grand conspiracy?" Kael scoffed, his tone dripping with derision. "Sounds more like an excuse for your lack of focus in real magic."

Alaric frowned. "This isn't about conspiracies or excuses. I've seen the fractures with my own eyes. They're real, and they're dangerous."

"And yet, the world hasn't collapsed," Kael said, crossing his arms. "Maybe you're exaggerating because it makes you feel important."

"Enough," snapped Lira, who had been practicing nearby. She stepped between them, her gaze sharp. "At least Alaric is trying to do something meaningful. What have you done lately, Kael? Perfected another fireball?"

Kael's jaw tightened, and he stalked away without another word. Alaric sighed, turning to Lira. "Thanks."

"Don't thank me," she said, her tone softer. "Just make sure you prove him wrong."

Consulting the Seekers

That evening, Alaric slipped out of the Grand Arcanum and made his way to the Seekers of the Undercurrent, who had set up a temporary camp near a minor ley line nexus. The camp was simple—tents arranged in a circle, with magical wards shimmering faintly around the perimeter.

Erynn greeted him with a nod, her silver-streaked hair catching the firelight. "Back so soon, Deymorne? I thought your academy would keep you busy."

"It has," Alaric admitted. "But I need your help. I've found evidence that someone is tampering with the ley lines—deliberately."

Erynn's expression darkened. "Tampering how?"

Alaric described the corrupted runes he had seen and his encounter with Veyran. As he spoke, the other Seekers gathered around, their faces grave.

"This aligns with some of our findings," Erynn said when he finished. "The fractures aren't natural. We've detected signs of interference—artifacts embedded near nexuses, designed to destabilize their energy flows. Whoever is doing this is using methods we don't fully understand."

"Do you think they're trying to break the lines completely?" Alaric asked.

"It's possible," Erynn said. "Or they might be trying to redirect the energy for their own purposes. Either way, it's a threat we can't ignore."

One of the younger Seekers, a boy named Ren, spoke up. "If the lines collapse, they'll take everything with them—magic, nature, even the fabric of reality."

Erynn nodded. "The ley lines aren't just pathways. They're the threads holding our world together. If they unravel..." She let the sentence hang, the unspoken consequences clear.

A Glimpse into the Grimoire

That night, back at the Grand Arcanum, Alaric sat by his window, the grimoire open on his lap. Its pages glowed faintly in the moonlight, the runes shifting as if alive. He traced his fingers over the map, watching as a new symbol appeared—a spiral within a circle, glowing softly near the western mountains.

The book felt warmer in his hands, as though responding to his thoughts. He closed his eyes, letting the grimoire's energy wash over him. Images began to form in his mind—flashes of shattered landscapes, rifts opening in the sky, and ley lines snapping like frayed threads.

In the vision, he saw Veyran standing at the center of a nexus, his hands outstretched as raw energy swirled around him. The voice from the Crystal Glade returned, faint but insistent: "The lines are breaking. Only the threads of knowledge can mend them."

Alaric awoke with a start, his heart pounding. The grimoire's glow had faded, but the symbol remained etched in his mind.

*****

The next morning, Alaric shared his findings with Master Eldaryn and the Seekers. Together, they pieced together a grim theory: Veyran wasn't just tampering with the ley lines—he was trying to rewrite them. By disrupting their natural flows, he could bend the world to his will, creating a reality shaped by his desires.

"This isn't just about magic," Erynn said, her voice heavy. "This is about control. If Veyran succeeds, he'll hold the threads of existence in his hands."

"And if we fail to stop him?" Alaric asked.

Erynn's gaze was steady. "Then the world as we know it will cease to exist."

Ley Line Mechanics: Consulting Eldaryn and the Seekers

The Spire of Knowledge felt colder than usual as Alaric entered Master Eldaryn's study. The chamber's tall, arched windows framed the stormy sea, their glass etched with shifting runes that reflected the ebb and flow of magical energy. Bookshelves lined the walls, stacked with ancient tomes and scrolls that seemed almost to hum with latent power.

Eldaryn sat at his desk, his fingers steepled beneath his chin as he studied Alaric's expression.

"You've been restless, Deymorne," Eldaryn said, his voice even but probing. "What troubles you?"

Alaric hesitated, pulling the grimoire from his satchel and placing it on the desk. The book's cover shimmered faintly, the swirling patterns of its runes shifting under the room's light.

"I've seen things, Master," Alaric began, his voice steady despite the weight of his words. "Visions through the ley lines. I believe the fractures are worsening, and... I think someone is causing it."

Eldaryn's sharp gaze locked onto Alaric's. "And what makes you believe this?"

Alaric opened the grimoire to a page marked by a glowing spiral. "I've found corrupted runes at nexus sites—runes that disrupt the ley lines' energy flow. They don't match any of the patterns we've studied. And during my last expedition, I encountered a man who called himself Veyran. He was manipulating a nexus deliberately."

Eldaryn's expression darkened. He stood and walked to the window, his hands clasped behind his back. "Veyran," he murmured, the name heavy with unspoken meaning. "Do you know what he seeks?"

"He mentioned reshaping the world," Alaric replied. "He believes the ley lines are tools for control."

Eldaryn sighed, his voice tinged with both anger and sorrow. "Ley lines are not tools, Deymorne. They are the lifeblood of our reality—the threads that hold magic, nature, and even time in balance. If they fracture completely, the consequences will be... unimaginable."

Alaric leaned forward. "Then we have to stop him. We have to repair the fractures."

Eldaryn turned, his expression grave. "That may not be possible. The ley lines are ancient, their true nature only partially understood. To tamper with them further could risk unraveling everything."

"Then what should I do?" Alaric asked, frustration creeping into his voice.

"Learn," Eldaryn said firmly. "Study the lines as deeply as you can. The answers lie within them—but tread carefully, Deymorne. Knowledge can be as dangerous as ignorance."

The Seekers' Camp: Elemental Magic and Beings

Alaric found the Seekers of the Undercurrent near a bubbling hot spring in the Verdant Expanse, a region of rolling hills and thick forests alive with vibrant magic. Their camp was nestled in a grove of ancient oaks, their bark glowing faintly with green runes. Erynn greeted him with a nod, her silver-streaked hair catching the sunlight.

"You've returned," she said. "Does the Grand Arcanum have answers?"

"More warnings than answers," Alaric replied, his tone dry. "But I need to learn more. I need to understand the ley lines before it's too late."

Erynn gestured for him to follow her. The Seekers were gathered around a large stone table, its surface etched with a detailed map of the ley lines. Nearby, elemental beings moved gracefully among the tents—small sylphs with translucent wings flitted through the air, while squat salamanders basked near the fire pit, their molten bodies radiating heat.

"These beings," Alaric said, watching a sylph spiral upward in a gust of wind. "They're tied to the ley lines, aren't they?"

"Indeed," Erynn said. "Elementals are the natural expressions of the lines' energy. Each nexus nurtures its own unique ecosystem, shaped by the dominant element of the ley line in that region."

As they spoke, a Sand Ferret—a creature resembling a golden mongoose with shifting, grain-like fur—emerged from a tent, carrying a bundle of scrolls in its tiny claws. It paused to study Alaric with its gleaming eyes before darting away.

"Fascinating," Alaric murmured. "If the ley lines fracture, what happens to them?"

"They'll fade," Erynn said simply. "Or worse, become corrupted."

Her words weighed heavily on him as he approached the map. "What do you know about Veyran?"

"Not much," she admitted. "But we've found evidence of his interference. Artifacts embedded in nexuses, designed to destabilize them. He's deliberate, methodical. If we don't stop him soon, the fractures will spread beyond our ability to contain them."

A Vision of the Ley Lines

That night, Alaric sat alone by the campfire, the grimoire open on his lap. Its pages glowed faintly in the flickering light, and as he traced a rune on the map, the world around him seemed to fade.

He found himself standing in a vast, empty plain, the sky above him a shifting canvas of light and color. Threads of golden energy crisscrossed the ground, pulsing with rhythmic vitality. These were the ley lines in their purest form—unbroken, harmonious.

But as he watched, one of the threads darkened, its light dimming until it snapped. The ground beneath it cracked, and a jagged chasm spread outward, consuming the other threads in its path.

Alaric turned, and there stood Veyran, his figure shrouded in shadows. His eyes glowed with an unnatural light, and his voice echoed like a thunderclap: "The old order must fall to make way for the new. You cannot stop what is already in motion."

The vision shattered, and Alaric awoke with a gasp. The grimoire's pages were blank, the glow extinguished, but the fear in his chest lingered.

*****

Back at the Grand Arcanum, Alaric shared his findings with Lira. They sat on a low stone wall overlooking the academy gardens, the evening breeze carrying the scent of blooming flowers.

"Veyran is more dangerous than I thought," Alaric said, his voice low. "He's not just tampering with the ley lines—he's trying to rewrite them entirely."

Lira frowned. "And what happens if he succeeds?"

"The world won't survive it," Alaric said bluntly. "The fractures will consume everything."

Lira placed a hand on his arm. "Then you have to stop him."

Alaric met her gaze, the determination in her eyes mirroring his own. "I will. But I can't do it alone."

"You won't have to," she said softly. "Just don't lose yourself in the process, Alaric. I'm worried about you. This obsession... it's consuming you."

He hesitated, then nodded. "I know. But if I don't see this through, no one else will."

Later that week, Alaric returned to a minor nexus site in the Shattered Vale, a desolate region where fractured ley lines had warped the landscape into jagged cliffs and swirling mists. The air buzzed with erratic energy, and the ground beneath his feet felt unstable.

Near the nexus, he found a corrupted rune etched into the stone—a jagged mark that radiated a sickly, pulsating light. It didn't match any magical patterns he'd studied, but its presence was unmistakable: someone had placed it there deliberately.

As he reached to study it, the ground trembled, and an Earth Golem emerged from the nexus, its massive form towering above him. Its eyes glowed with the same sickly light as the rune, and it lumbered toward him with a low, guttural roar.

Alaric scrambled to trace a protective rune in the air, his heart pounding. The grimoire's pages fluttered in the wind, offering him guidance. He channeled the ley line's energy into a stabilizing spell, and the rune on the golem's chest shattered. The creature collapsed into a pile of rubble, but the experience left him shaken.

As he stood there, breathing heavily, he realized just how far Veyran was willing to go to destabilize the ley lines—and just how unprepared he was to face him.

Alaric knelt beside the remains of the Earth Golem, his hands trembling as he traced the lines of the corrupted rune. The air was thick with residual magic, a pungent mixture of metallic tang and burnt ozone. The shattered fragments of the golem's core—a jagged crystal infused with the sickly light—still pulsed faintly, radiating unease.

"This isn't natural," he muttered, pulling the grimoire from his satchel. The book's pages fluttered open, almost as if responding to the energy in the air. A new series of runes appeared on the map, glowing faintly in a spiral pattern near the Shattered Vale.

"What are you trying to show me?" Alaric murmured.

The runes seemed to pulse in reply, their rhythm aligning with the lingering energy from the corrupted rune. It was as if the grimoire was guiding him—not just to understand the fractures but to uncover their origin. He snapped the book shut and stood, determination hardening his features.

"I'm not done here," he said to himself, his voice steady despite the lingering tremor in his hands.

*****

When Alaric returned to the Grand Arcanum, the air of skepticism surrounding him had only deepened. Whispers followed him through the halls as students cast sidelong glances, their expressions ranging from curiosity to outright disdain. Kael, as always, was the loudest voice of dissent.

"You're playing with forces you don't understand, Deymorne," Kael said, his tone sharp as he confronted Alaric outside the practice hall. "First it's corrupted runes and broken ley lines, and now you're tangling with rogue mages? You're going to get yourself—and probably the rest of us—killed."

"I'm trying to prevent that," Alaric shot back. "The ley lines are fracturing, Kael. If we don't act now, the consequences will be far worse than anything Veyran can do."

"And you think you're the one to fix it?" Kael scoffed. "You can barely stabilize a basic construct. What makes you think you're qualified to handle something this big?"

Alaric's jaw tightened, but before he could respond, Lira stepped between them.

"Enough," she said, her voice firm. "Alaric is doing something that matters, Kael. Maybe instead of tearing him down, you should try contributing for once."

Kael glared at her, then at Alaric, before storming off. Lira turned to Alaric, her expression softening.

"He's not entirely wrong, you know," she said quietly. "You're taking a lot on yourself. Just promise me you won't try to carry it alone."

Alaric nodded, his resolve unwavering. "I promise."

Encounter with Elementals

Later that week, Master Eldaryn sent Alaric to the Verdant Expanse to observe a ley line that had begun to exhibit unstable patterns. It was a test, one that Eldaryn framed as a learning exercise but that Alaric suspected was meant to keep him out of trouble.

The Verdant Expanse was alive with magic, its lush forests humming with energy. Sylphs flitted among the trees, their translucent forms weaving through branches with effortless grace. Nearby, Salamanders lounged on sunlit rocks, their molten bodies casting faint heatwaves into the air.

As Alaric approached the nexus, a creature emerged from the undergrowth—a Fire Praying Mantis, its obsidian exoskeleton gleaming with streaks of molten red. It moved with fluid precision, its forelegs crackling with sparks of energy as it studied Alaric with unblinking eyes.

Alaric froze, his hand instinctively going to the grimoire. The creature didn't attack, but its presence was a warning. This was its domain, shaped and sustained by the ley line's energy. Any disruption would be met with force.

"I'm not here to harm you," Alaric said softly, holding his hands up in a gesture of peace. "I just want to understand."

The mantis clicked its mandibles but made no move to strike. Alaric took a cautious step forward, tracing a rune in the air that pulsed with calming energy. The creature tilted its head, then retreated into the foliage, its molten glow fading into the shadows.

Alaric let out a shaky breath and knelt beside the nexus, its glowing runes pulsing in time with the ley line's rhythm. He opened the grimoire, its pages shifting to reveal a diagram of interconnected runes.

"This is different," he murmured, comparing the diagram to the runes on the nexus. The pattern was similar but not identical—almost as if someone had altered it. His heart sank as he realized what it meant: Veyran's tampering wasn't limited to corrupted runes. He was actively reshaping the ley lines' structure.

That night, as Alaric camped beneath the canopy of glowing leaves, the grimoire pulsed with a faint, insistent light. When he opened it, the pages revealed a new vision—a fractured ley line nexus bathed in an unnatural red glow. Veyran stood at its center, his hands wreathed in spiraling energy.

"You see the cracks," Veyran's voice echoed, as though he were speaking directly to Alaric. "But do you understand what they mean? The old order is failing. The ley lines are no longer enough to sustain this world. A new structure must emerge, one that bends to my design."

The vision shifted, showing the aftermath of a ley line's collapse—a desolate wasteland where nothing lived, the air thick with ash and silence. Alaric's stomach churned, his resolve hardening further.

"I won't let this happen," he said aloud, his voice steady despite the fear clawing at his chest. "Not while I can stop it."

Returning to the Grand Arcanum, Alaric spent hours in the library, poring over ancient texts and cross-referencing them with the grimoire. He documented elemental patterns, charted ley line anomalies, and recorded every detail about the creatures he encountered. But with each discovery came a growing weight of responsibility.

Lira found him there late one evening, surrounded by stacks of books and half-finished notes. She pulled up a chair beside him, her expression a mix of concern and admiration.

"You're pushing yourself too hard," she said gently. "You can't do this alone, Alaric. Let us help you."

"I appreciate that," he said, not looking up from his notes. "But I have to figure this out. If I don't..."

"You don't have to bear the weight of the world on your shoulders," she said, placing a hand on his arm. "We're in this together. Remember that."

Her words lingered with him long after she left, a reminder that even the strongest ambitions needed the grounding of connection.

Chapter 5: The Spiral Nexus

The grimoire pulsed with faint light, bathing the cramped dormitory in a pale, otherworldly glow. Alaric sat hunched at his desk, his fingers tracing the intricate map etched into the book's pages. A jagged spiral, glowing faintly at the northern edge of the map, seemed to flicker in sync with the thudding of his heart. Around the spiral, runes rearranged themselves like a shifting puzzle, forming cryptic phrases in a language he was slowly learning to decipher.

"When the lifelines cross, balance breaks. Repair the spiral, or worlds will fracture."

The words hung heavy in the air, their meaning unclear but urgent. The weight of responsibility pressed on Alaric's shoulders. He had heard Eldaryn's warnings—about the ley lines, the dangers of meddling with forces older than humanity itself—but he couldn't ignore what he had seen. The fractures in the ley lines weren't natural. Someone, or something, was tampering with them. And the Spiral Nexus seemed to be at the heart of it all.

Alaric leaned back in his chair, staring at the flickering candle on his desk. His mind swirled with questions. Why had the grimoire chosen him? Why did the ley lines seem to respond to him in ways they didn't with others? And most importantly, could he truly fix what was breaking?

The knock at the door startled him. Before he could answer, the door creaked open, and Lira stepped in. Her dark eyes, sharp with worry, flicked from the packed satchel on his bed to the glowing grimoire on the desk.

"You're leaving," she said flatly.

"I have to," Alaric replied, closing the grimoire. "The Nexus is destabilizing. If I don't act now—"

"Someone else will," Lira interrupted, stepping closer. "Someone more experienced. More prepared."

"There's no time to wait for the council or the Seekers to debate," Alaric said, his voice rising. "If we let this go unchecked, the damage could spread across the ley lines. I can't just sit here."

"You don't even know what you're walking into," Lira shot back. Her gaze softened, and she stepped closer. "Alaric, you're brilliant, but you're reckless. This isn't just another experiment in the casting chamber. It's dangerous—lethal."

"I know," Alaric said quietly, his frustration giving way to resolve. "But I can't ignore it, Lira. The grimoire chose me for a reason."

Lira's expression faltered, and after a long pause, she reached up to remove a small silver amulet from her neck. She pressed it into Alaric's hand, her voice quiet. "Fine. But take this. It's enchanted—light in the dark, protection when you need it most."

Alaric stared at the crescent-shaped charm, its surface etched with delicate runes. "Lira, I—"

"Don't argue with me," she said firmly. "Just promise me you'll come back."

"I promise," he said, slipping the amulet into his satchel. "Thank you."

She lingered for a moment, as though she wanted to say more, before turning and leaving without another word. Alaric watched the door close, his resolve hardening. The path ahead was uncertain, but it was his to walk.

*****

The northern forests loomed ahead, their dense canopy casting a shadowy gloom over the winding path. Alaric clutched the Runestone Compass in one hand, the grimoire secured in his satchel. The compass's needle spun erratically, responding to the fluctuating energy in the air. The hum of the ley lines grew stronger with each step, a low vibration that resonated in his chest.

The flora around him became stranger the deeper he ventured. Trees twisted unnaturally, their trunks splitting into jagged, glowing veins that pulsed with faint light. Luminescent fungi carpeted the ground, and vines with shimmering, iridescent leaves coiled around the warped trunks. Small, glowing insects flitted through the air, their trails leaving faint streaks of light.

As he stepped over a gnarled root, the ground beneath him shifted. Alaric stumbled, catching himself against a tree. A low, guttural growl echoed through the forest, and he froze, his heart pounding. A shadow moved between the trees, too fast to follow.

The creature emerged slowly, its translucent body glowing faintly. It resembled a great feline, but its limbs were elongated, and its faceted eyes glimmered like gemstones. The beast sniffed the air, its glowing gaze locking onto Alaric. It let out a low growl, its body tensing as though ready to pounce.

Alaric reached into his satchel, his hand brushing against Lira's amulet. He whispered an incantation, and the charm flared with light. The beast recoiled, letting out a sharp screech before retreating into the shadows.

Alaric exhaled shakily, clutching the amulet. The hum of the ley lines pulled him forward, and he pressed on, his steps quickening.

The clearing opened before him suddenly, and Alaric stopped in awe. The Spiral Nexus towered at its center—a jagged spire of crystal surrounded by swirling ley lines. Threads of blue, gold, and crimson energy danced around it, crackling and surging like lightning. The ground around the spire was fractured, glowing fissures spreading outward in chaotic patterns.

Alaric stepped into the clearing, the hum of the ley lines rising to a deafening pitch. The grimoire in his satchel began to glow, and he pulled it out. Its pages flipped open on their own, revealing diagrams and instructions he hadn't seen before.

"Align the strands, steady the weave, but disturb not the spiral's core."

He knelt beside one of the glowing fissures, tracing the runes etched into the ground. They were jagged and chaotic, unlike any he had seen before. Someone had been tampering with the Nexus.

Nearby, a glint of metal caught his eye. He reached for it, pulling a small sigil from the dirt. The circular emblem was etched with dark runes that seemed to writhe under his gaze. Its energy was discordant, clashing with the natural rhythm of the ley lines.

"Who could have done this?" he murmured, dread coiling in his stomach.

*****

A surge of energy erupted from the Nexus, and the clearing was flooded with blinding light. When the brilliance subsided, a towering figure stood before him. The ley line guardian was a being of shifting shadows and light, its form constantly in flux. Its glowing eyes burned with an intensity that made Alaric's breath catch.

"Why have you come here, mortal?" the guardian demanded, its voice like rolling thunder. "The Spiral Nexus is not yours to disturb."

Alaric stood, clutching the grimoire tightly. "The ley lines are fracturing. Someone has tampered with this Nexus. If I don't act, the damage could spread."

The guardian's gaze narrowed. "You speak of what you do not comprehend. The ley lines are not merely conduits—they are the lifeblood of existence. Tampering with their flow invites ruin."

"I'm not here to destroy," Alaric said firmly. "If there's a way to fix this, I'll find it."

The guardian loomed closer, its presence suffocating. "Beware, seeker. Knowledge is a burden, and power demands a price. The threads you seek to mend may unravel your own fate."

Before Alaric could respond, a voice rang out behind him. "Of course you'd be here, Deymorne."

Alaric turned to see Kael stepping into the clearing, his staff glowing faintly. The older apprentice's expression was smug, his tone dripping with disdain. "Always sticking your nose where it doesn't belong."

"I don't have time for this, Kael," Alaric said, his frustration mounting. "The Nexus is destabilizing. If I don't act—"

"You'll make it worse," Kael interrupted, stepping closer. "You're reckless. Always have been. Do you even understand what you're dealing with?"

Alaric clenched his fists. "At least I'm trying. What are you doing, Kael? Standing on the sidelines, waiting to criticize?"

The argument escalated, their voices echoing through the clearing. The ley lines pulsed violently, and the ground trembled beneath them.

*****

Ignoring Kael's protests, Alaric focused on the grimoire's instructions. He knelt and began carving runes into the ground, chanting the stabilization spell. Energy surged around him, the Nexus flaring with light. His vision blurred as he was pulled into a fragmented realm of floating islands and swirling energy.

He saw fractured worlds colliding, their boundaries bleeding into one another. At the center of the chaos stood a shadowy figure, its hands manipulating the ley lines like threads on a loom. The figure turned toward Alaric, its glowing eyes filled with malevolence.

The vision ended abruptly, leaving Alaric gasping for breath. The Nexus stabilized momentarily before flaring again, its chaos renewed.

Exhausted and battered, Alaric stumbled back to the Grand Arcanum. He recounted his experience to Eldaryn, describing the tampering at the Nexus and the shadowy figure in his vision. The master mage's expression was grim.

"You've seen much, Deymorne," Eldaryn said finally. "But you've also placed yourself in grave danger. The ley lines are not a puzzle to solve—they are the lifeblood of our world. Tread carefully."

That night, Alaric sat alone in his dormitory, the grimoire pulsing faintly beside him. A new mark had appeared on the map—a fractured circle to the south. Despite his exhaustion, determination burned within him.

The Spiral Nexus was only the beginning.

Alaric sat cross-legged on the cold stone floor of his dormitory, unable to sleep. The events at the Spiral Nexus replayed in his mind like a haunting melody. The shadowy figure he had seen in his vision—its ominous presence and manipulative gestures—lingered at the edges of his thoughts. Each flicker of the grimoire's faint glow seemed to whisper new questions.

He opened the grimoire once more, flipping to the page where the Spiral Nexus map had been etched. But something had changed. A new symbol now pulsed faintly on the map, far to the south—a fractured circle surrounded by faint runes. Alaric's breath caught in his throat as he traced its edges with his finger. The grimoire responded, the ink shifting beneath his touch to reveal fragments of text.

"The strands converge... Seek the veiled maker... Beware the price."

The fragmented words only deepened the mystery. What was the price? And who—or what—was the veiled maker? Alaric clenched his fists. He couldn't stop now. Whatever tampering had destabilized the ley lines wasn't over. The figure he had seen was a part of this puzzle, and the new mark on the map promised another lead.

But first, he needed answers—and allies.

*****

The morning sun cast long shadows across the Grand Arcanum's spires as Alaric approached Eldaryn's private study. The master mage's chambers were a labyrinth of shelves, scrolls, and ancient artifacts, each buzzing faintly with latent magic. Eldaryn sat at his desk, scribbling notes into an oversized tome. He glanced up as Alaric entered, his sharp blue eyes narrowing.

"Deymorne," Eldaryn said, his tone measured. "You've returned earlier than I expected. I assume you have more to share about your escapade."

Alaric hesitated, then placed the sigil he had found at the Spiral Nexus on Eldaryn's desk. "I found this embedded near the Nexus. It doesn't belong there, does it?"

Eldaryn's gaze sharpened. He picked up the sigil, examining the dark, writhing runes etched into its surface. "No, it doesn't. This is the work of the Veiled Order."

"The Veiled Order?" Alaric echoed, leaning closer.

Eldaryn sighed, setting the sigil down. "An ancient faction that sought to manipulate the ley lines for their own ends. They believed that by destabilizing the lines, they could harness raw power and reshape the world as they saw fit. Most of their members were wiped out centuries ago, but their influence lingers."

Alaric's pulse quickened. "I saw someone—something—in a vision while stabilizing the Nexus. A figure manipulating the ley lines. Could it be them?"

Eldaryn's expression darkened. "It's possible. But if the Veiled Order has returned, you're in far greater danger than you realize. Their experiments with the ley lines were catastrophic, and their methods... unrelenting."

"What do I do?" Alaric asked, his voice steady despite the fear gnawing at him.

"You prepare," Eldaryn said gravely. "And you tread carefully. The ley lines are volatile enough without you throwing yourself into every Nexus you find."

Alaric nodded, though his resolve only deepened. He wasn't about to abandon the path now.

Word of Alaric's encounter at the Spiral Nexus spread quickly through the Grand Arcanum. Whispers followed him in the halls, students shooting him curious or wary glances. Some praised his bravery, while others dismissed him as reckless.

Kael was firmly in the latter camp.

"You're a fool, Deymorne," Kael sneered as they passed in the Nexus Plaza. The plaza's central obelisk cast a long shadow over the crowd of apprentices gathered there. "Running off to play hero while the rest of us study like actual mages."

Alaric stopped, his jaw tightening. "At least I'm doing something. What have you done lately, Kael? Perfected your smug smirk?"

Kael's face twisted with anger. "What I've done is avoid getting people killed. You can't even stabilize a Nexus without dragging the ley lines further into chaos."

Alaric stepped closer, his voice low but fierce. "If you're so confident in your superiority, why don't you come with me next time? Show me how it's done."

Kael scoffed, though there was a flicker of hesitation in his eyes. "I wouldn't waste my time."

As Kael walked away, Alaric felt the weight of their rivalry settle heavier than ever. But the exchange had sparked an idea. Kael's taunts might have stung, but he wasn't entirely wrong. If Alaric was to continue his journey, he needed more than determination—he needed a team.

That evening, Alaric sought out Lira in the library. She was seated in a secluded corner, poring over a thick tome of elemental runes. When he approached, she looked up, her expression guarded.

"I need your help," Alaric said without preamble.

Lira closed her book and crossed her arms. "Help with what? Getting yourself killed faster?"

"I'm serious," Alaric said, pulling up a chair. "The Spiral Nexus was just the beginning. The grimoire's map shows another mark—south of here. And Eldaryn thinks the Veiled Order might be involved."

Lira's eyes widened. "The Veiled Order? That's... not good."

"Exactly," Alaric said. "And if they're behind this, I can't face it alone. I need someone I trust. Someone who won't back down when things get dangerous."

Lira studied him for a long moment before sighing. "You really don't know when to quit, do you?"

"Is that a yes?"

She rolled her eyes but nodded. "Fine. But if we're doing this, we're doing it smart. No more solo heroics."

Alaric smiled. "Deal."

The journey south began under clear skies, but the terrain quickly grew harsher as they approached the ley line anomaly. The Runestone Compass guided them through dense forests, rocky ridges, and ancient ruins overgrown with vines. Each step brought new challenges—wild magic storms that bent the laws of physics, treacherous terrain, and strange creatures drawn to the ley lines' unstable energy.

Lira proved invaluable, her mastery of elemental magic allowing them to navigate obstacles that might have stopped Alaric alone. When a swarm of shadow-beetles descended on them in the ruins of an old watchtower, she conjured a wave of flame to drive them back, her focus unshaken even as the creatures swarmed around her.

"Remind me why I agreed to this again?" she muttered as they made camp that evening.

"Because you secretly enjoy saving my life," Alaric replied with a grin.

She smirked but didn't argue.

The Southern Nexus

When they finally reached the southern mark on the grimoire's map, the sight before them took their breath away. The Nexus was hidden within a sprawling canyon, its walls carved with ancient runes that glowed faintly in the dim light. At its center stood a massive crystal spire, its surface fractured and pulsing with unstable energy.

"This is worse than the Spiral Nexus," Lira said, her voice tinged with unease.

Alaric nodded. The ley lines here were in complete disarray, their energy spiraling out of control. He could feel the pressure in the air, the raw power threatening to rupture at any moment.

As they approached, Alaric noticed something embedded in the crystal—a sigil identical to the one he had found before. But this one was larger, its runes glowing with dark energy.

"Lira," he said quietly. "This is it. Proof of the Veiled Order's tampering."

Before she could respond, the Nexus flared violently, and a figure emerged from the swirling energy. It was cloaked in shadow, its form shifting and indistinct. But its presence was undeniable.

"You should not have come here," the figure said, its voice cold and hollow. "The ley lines are not yours to protect."

Alaric stepped forward, his heart pounding. "And they're not yours to destroy."

The shadowy figure loomed before Alaric and Lira, its form flickering like a candle in the wind. Tendrils of energy snaked out from the Southern Nexus, wrapping around its shifting body as if it drew power from the chaos.

"You should not have come here," the figure repeated, its voice a blend of cold finality and an almost human sorrow.

Alaric clenched his fists, stepping protectively in front of Lira. "Who are you? What do you want with the ley lines?"

The figure tilted its head, a motion eerily deliberate and unnatural. "I am no one. I am many. And I do not want the ley lines. I am their guardian, their warden, their breaker."

"That makes no sense," Lira shot back, fire flickering in her palms. "A guardian wouldn't shatter what they're supposed to protect. The Nexus is collapsing because of you!"

The figure's form rippled, the energy around it growing unstable. "You cannot understand. What is broken must break further before it can heal."

"That's a lie," Alaric said sharply, taking a step closer. The sigil embedded in the Nexus caught his eye again, its dark runes pulsing faintly. "You placed that sigil there, didn't you? You're the reason the ley lines are fracturing!"

The shadow shifted but did not respond.

"Why?!" Alaric pressed, his voice rising. "What are you trying to do?"

The figure let out a sound that could have been a sigh or a growl. "You will not stop what is inevitable. The fabric weakens, and the threads must be rewoven."

Before either of them could respond, the figure dissolved into the air, leaving only a faint hum of residual energy. The Nexus remained volatile, its fractured spire sending out dangerous arcs of magic.

Lira broke the tense silence. "What in the nine realms was that supposed to mean? 'Rewoven threads'? Is this thing trying to fix the ley lines by breaking them?"

"If that's fixing, I'd hate to see what breaking looks like," Alaric muttered, his gaze lingering on the sigil. "But it's not just a creature. It's intelligent. And I don't think it's working alone."

*****

Back at their camp, Alaric and Lira carefully studied the sigil Alaric had pried from the Nexus. It lay between them on a flat rock, glowing faintly with its dark runes. Alaric had sketched its pattern into his notebook, each rune meticulously copied. Now, he combed through the grimoire for anything that might resemble its strange markings.

"This one," he said, pointing to a rune near the edge of the sigil. "It looks like a corruption of a stabilization rune. But it's... wrong. The angles are sharper, and there's an inversion here that shouldn't be possible."

Lira leaned closer, her brow furrowed. "And this one," she said, pointing to a different rune near the center. "It's similar to a summoning glyph. But if that's the case, what was it summoning?"

Alaric shook his head. "Not summoning. Redirecting. Look at the ley lines around the Nexus. They're all pulling toward this point. Whatever this sigil is doing, it's siphoning ley line energy—but not just here. It's connected to something larger."

Lira's eyes widened. "You think there are more of these?"

Alaric nodded grimly. "The figure we saw—it called itself a guardian, but it's clearly tampering with the ley lines on purpose. If there are other sigils at other Nexuses, the entire system could be at risk."

Lira sat back, her arms crossed. "So now we're hunting sigils and shadowy figures. Wonderful. What's next? A secret society plotting to reshape the world?"

"That's not far off," Alaric admitted. He hesitated before continuing. "Eldaryn told me about the Veiled Order. They've been gone for centuries, but this sigil matches their techniques. I think they're back."

Lira let out a low whistle. "The Veiled Order. As in the 'mad mages who nearly broke the world' Veiled Order?"

Alaric nodded. "If they're behind this, we need to find proof. And fast."

The Whispering Ruins

The following day, their journey took them to a site marked in the grimoire—a set of ancient ruins near a ley line nexus. The ruins, hidden deep within the forest, were shrouded in mist that clung to the ground like a living thing. Massive stone pillars jutted out from the earth, their surfaces covered in moss and etched with runes that flickered faintly in the dim light.

"This place feels... wrong," Lira said, her voice barely above a whisper. Her hand rested on the hilt of her dagger, her eyes scanning the shadows.

Alaric nodded, his compass quivering in his hand. "The ley lines are strong here. Stronger than they should be. Whatever's happening, this place is tied to it."

As they stepped deeper into the ruins, a faint whispering sound reached their ears. It was indistinct, like voices carried on the wind, but it sent a chill down Alaric's spine.

"Do you hear that?" he asked, his voice hushed.

Lira nodded. "I don't think we're alone."

They followed the sound to a central chamber where the remains of an ancient altar stood. At its center lay another sigil, this one larger and more intricate than the one Alaric had found at the Nexus. The air around it shimmered with energy, and the whispers grew louder.

Alaric approached cautiously, his eyes locked on the sigil. "It's the same pattern. But this one's active."

"Active how?" Lira asked, her tone tense.

Before Alaric could answer, the sigil flared with light, and the whispers coalesced into a single voice.

"Who dares disturb the threads?"

Alaric and Lira staggered back as the air in the chamber grew thick with energy. A spectral figure emerged from the sigil, its form flickering between human and monstrous.

"Another one," Lira muttered, flames sparking at her fingertips.

The figure's hollow eyes locked onto Alaric. "You meddle in matters beyond your understanding. The threads must be broken to be rewoven."

Alaric took a step forward, his voice steady. "The threads are breaking because of you. You're destabilizing the ley lines, endangering everyone. Why?"

The figure's form flickered. "Balance must be restored. The old weave is flawed. A new pattern must emerge."

"Who are you working with?" Alaric demanded. "Is this the Veiled Order?"

The figure's gaze darkened. "The Veiled Order serves the weave. As do you, whether you realize it or not."

Before Alaric could press further, the figure dissolved into light, leaving the sigil pulsing faintly. The whispers faded, and the chamber fell silent.

Alaric knelt beside the sigil, his hands trembling as he traced its runes. "It's the same inversion. And this center glyph—it's a trigger point. They're not just redirecting the ley lines. They're—"

"Rewriting them," Lira finished, her voice quiet.

Alaric looked up at her, his expression grim. "If they rewrite enough of the ley lines, they could reshape the flow of magic entirely. Control it. Destroy it."

Lira's face paled. "And that's their goal? To destroy magic?"

"Or remake it in their image," Alaric said, his voice hollow. "Either way, it's dangerous. We need to find their next target before they do."

As they left the ruins, Alaric couldn't shake the feeling of being watched. The forest seemed darker, the air heavier. He glanced over his shoulder repeatedly, but there was nothing—only the faint hum of the ley lines beneath his feet.

"You keep looking back," Lira said, her tone cautious. "You think they're following us?"

Alaric nodded. "If they know we're onto them, they won't let us keep digging."

Lira smirked, though it didn't reach her eyes. "Good. Let them try. I've got plenty of fire left."

The ley lines were more than simple conduits of magic; they were the lifeblood of the world, an invisible web connecting realms, elements, and even time. Alaric had always marveled at their intricacy during his studies, but seeing them destabilized in person was like witnessing an open wound in reality.

As he and Lira trekked deeper into the wilderness, he couldn't help but reflect on what Eldaryn had taught him: "The ley lines are not merely power. They are memory, intention, and balance. To tamper with them is to rewrite the story of the world."

"Why would the Veiled Order want to rewrite magic itself?" Lira asked, as though reading his thoughts. Her voice cut through the eerie silence of the forest, where even the birds seemed afraid to sing.

"They're zealots," Alaric replied, though his tone betrayed doubt. "If they're anything like the stories, they believe the current flow of magic is flawed—too chaotic, too free. They want to control it. Shape it into something... obedient."

Lira glanced at him, skepticism flickering across her face. "And you think they're right?"

Alaric hesitated. He hated admitting it, but part of him understood the temptation. The ley lines were unpredictable, their magic often manifesting in dangerous, uncontrollable ways. Could they be improved? Refined? Or was that hubris speaking?

"I don't know," he said finally. "But I do know this. If the Veiled Order succeeds, it won't be balance they create. It'll be domination."

Their journey brought them to Andryth, an abandoned city steeped in magical history. Once a bustling hub of arcane innovation, it had been reduced to crumbling stone and haunting echoes. The ley lines here were unusually potent, pulsing beneath the cracked cobblestones like a heartbeat.

Alaric paused in the shadow of a massive archway, its keystone engraved with intricate glyphs that shimmered faintly in the dim light. "This place was a ley line nexus," he said, his voice reverent. "One of the largest in the region."

"And now it's a ghost town," Lira replied, her voice tinged with unease. "What happened here?"

"Ley line experiments," Alaric said, stepping cautiously into the ruins. "When Andryth's mages tried to harness the lines' power for massive spells, they overreached. The resulting backlash destroyed the city and destabilized the surrounding area for decades."

"And now someone's trying to do it again," Lira said darkly. She placed a hand on a crumbling wall, where faint scorch marks told stories of long-past destruction.

The air here was thick with residual magic, the kind that lingered after catastrophic spells. Alaric knelt by a broken fountain at the center of the plaza, examining the ley lines' faint glow beneath the stones.

"The pattern is wrong," he murmured, tracing the lines with his fingertips. "It's been... disrupted. Whoever tampered with the Nexus is using places like this to amplify their work."

Lira crouched beside him, her sharp eyes scanning the glyphs. "Amplify how?"

"Imagine the ley lines as threads in a tapestry," Alaric explained. "A single tear can unravel a small section. But if you pull at specific points—nexuses like this one—you can destabilize the whole weave."

"So Andryth was just a test," Lira said, realization dawning. "They're not done."

Alaric nodded grimly. "Not even close."

As night fell, they made camp within the ruins. The crumbling walls offered little protection from the biting wind, but Alaric found solace in the ancient tomes and scrolls scattered throughout the remnants of Andryth's libraries. By the flickering light of their campfire, he poured over a decayed manuscript, its pages barely legible.

"What are you looking for?" Lira asked, her voice muffled by the scarf she had wrapped tightly around her face.

"Anything about the Veiled Order," Alaric replied, holding a brittle page up to the light. "They left behind traces, but no one's ever pieced together their full story."

"What if the story isn't what you think it is?" Lira asked. "What if they weren't zealots but... something else?"

Alaric looked up at her, intrigued. "Go on."

She hesitated, choosing her words carefully. "What if they weren't trying to control the ley lines? What if they were trying to stop something? Something bigger."

The idea struck Alaric like a thunderclap. "You're suggesting the Veiled Order might've been... right?"

"Not entirely," Lira said quickly. "But maybe their actions weren't just about power. Maybe they saw something in the ley lines no one else did. A flaw—or a threat."

Alaric stared at her, the gears in his mind turning. If that were true, then everything he thought he knew about the Veiled Order—and the ley lines themselves—was wrong.

Later that night, unable to sleep, Alaric studied the grimoire's map by the light of the campfire. The intricate web of ley lines stretched across the page, their intersections marked by glowing nexuses. He traced a finger along their paths, noticing for the first time a subtle pattern.

"These lines," he murmured to himself. "They're not random."

"What?" Lira asked, sitting up from her bedroll.

Alaric turned the grimoire toward her. "Look at the nexuses. They're arranged in a spiral, converging toward a single point. This isn't just a map of the ley lines. It's a blueprint."

"For what?" Lira asked, leaning closer.

"I don't know yet," Alaric admitted. "But if the Veiled Order was following this pattern, it means they weren't just tampering with the ley lines. They were building something."

*****

The next morning, their exploration of the ruins led them to a massive underground chamber hidden beneath Andryth. The chamber was dominated by an enormous, ancient device—a complex lattice of crystal, metal, and stone that pulsed faintly with dormant magic. It was unlike anything Alaric had ever seen.

"What is this?" Lira whispered, awe and fear mingling in her voice.

Alaric approached the apparatus cautiously, his fingers brushing against its cold surface. "It's... a ley line amplifier. But on a scale I didn't think was possible."

"You mean this thing could control the ley lines?" Lira asked, her eyes wide.

"Not just control," Alaric said, his voice hushed. "Reshape them. Reweave the entire network."

He stepped back, his mind racing. If the Veiled Order had built this device, it explained their ability to manipulate the ley lines so precisely. But it also meant they had been far more advanced—and dangerous—than anyone realized.

"We need to disable this," Lira said, her voice firm. "If the Order is still out there, they'll come back for it."

Alaric nodded, but a part of him hesitated. The apparatus was ancient, a relic of unimaginable power. Destroying it felt like erasing a piece of history. But leaving it intact risked catastrophe.

Before they could act, the apparatus flared to life, its crystals glowing with sudden intensity. The ley lines beneath their feet pulsed violently, and a low, resonant hum filled the chamber.

"They know we're here," Alaric said, his voice tight.

The hum from the ley line apparatus grew louder, reverberating through the chamber. Crystals embedded in the machine's lattice began to pulse in rhythm, each one glowing a different hue—brilliant reds, deep blues, and shimmering golds. The vibrations in the air were so intense that Alaric could feel them in his chest.

"This isn't a coincidence," Lira said, drawing her dagger. "Something—or someone—is activating it."

Alaric's mind raced as he circled the massive construct, his hands brushing against its cold, alien surface. Runes etched into the metal frame began to light up, flowing like liquid fire. It wasn't just an amplifier; it was a mechanism designed to interact directly with the ley lines.

"They're drawing power from the Nexus," Alaric said, his voice tinged with awe and dread. "But why now?"

The grimoire in his satchel began to glow faintly, its warmth seeping through the fabric. He pulled it free, the pages flipping open on their own. A new diagram appeared, one that resembled the apparatus before them. At its center was a warning written in jagged, angular script: When the strands converge, the spiral will break.

"This thing isn't just tampering with the ley lines," Alaric realized, his eyes widening. "It's forcing a convergence—a collapse."

"Then we stop it," Lira said firmly. "Before it takes us with it."

*****

As Lira searched for a way to disable the apparatus, the temperature in the chamber plummeted. A faint mist began to seep from the walls, and the air grew heavy with an unnatural chill.

"Alaric," Lira said, her voice tense. "Do you feel that?"

He turned to respond, but his words caught in his throat. The shadowy figure from the Nexus emerged from the mist, its form flickering and shifting. It moved with unnatural grace, its hollow eyes locked on Alaric.

"You meddle again," it said, its voice echoing as though spoken by many. "The threads must be rewoven. You cannot stop what has already begun."

Alaric took a step forward, summoning his courage. "What are you trying to accomplish? Breaking the ley lines won't fix anything—it'll destroy everything."

The figure's form rippled, its edges dissolving like smoke. "You speak of destruction because you cannot see beyond the present. The old weave is flawed. A new pattern must emerge."

Lira stepped between Alaric and the figure, flames crackling in her palm. "Save your cryptic speeches. We're shutting this thing down, whether you like it or not."

The figure's gaze flicked to her, and for a moment, the mist thickened, coiling around her legs like serpents. But Lira didn't flinch. The flames in her hand flared brighter, pushing the mist back.

"Fools," the figure hissed. "You fight against the inevitable."

As the figure dissolved into the mist, Alaric turned his attention back to the apparatus. He traced the glowing runes, his mind racing to decipher their meaning. The machine wasn't just active—it was accelerating the ley line collapse. If they didn't act quickly, the entire region could be thrown into chaos.

"Here!" Lira called from the far side of the chamber. She had found a panel in the apparatus's base, its surface covered in intricate glyphs. "This looks like a control point."

Alaric joined her, his eyes scanning the runes. He recognized some of the symbols as stabilizing glyphs, but they had been corrupted, their edges jagged and uneven.

"It's like someone twisted the original design," he said, frowning. "They've inverted the flow, turning it into a siphon."

"Can you reverse it?" Lira asked, her voice tight with urgency.

"I think so," Alaric replied, though doubt crept into his tone. "But if I get it wrong—"

"We don't have time for 'if," Lira interrupted. "Just do it."

Alaric nodded, drawing a piece of chalk from his satchel. He knelt by the panel, carefully sketching over the corrupted runes with stabilizing sigils. Each stroke of chalk glowed faintly as he worked, the apparatus's hum fluctuating in response.

As he finished the final glyph, the apparatus shuddered violently. The crystals dimmed for a moment, then flared with blinding light. The hum reached a deafening pitch before cutting off entirely, leaving the chamber in silence.

"Did we stop it?" Lira asked, her voice barely above a whisper.

Before Alaric could answer, the ground beneath them rumbled, and a fissure opened in the floor. A surge of energy erupted from the ley lines below, sending them both sprawling.

*****

When Alaric opened his eyes, he wasn't in the chamber anymore. He stood in a void, surrounded by swirling tendrils of light that pulsed with the rhythm of the ley lines. Fractured images flashed around him—cities crumbling into dust, skies torn apart by storms of raw magic, and a figure standing at the center of it all.

The shadowy figure was clearer now, its features sharpening into something almost human. Its voice echoed in Alaric's mind. "You see the threads unraveling, but you do not see the loom."

"What do you mean?" Alaric demanded, his voice trembling. "Who are you?"

The figure raised a hand, and the tendrils of light coiled around it like living threads. "I am a weaver. The old pattern is failing. You cling to it out of fear, but fear will not save you."

"Destroying the ley lines won't save us either," Alaric countered. "You're playing with forces you don't understand."

The figure's gaze darkened. "It is you who does not understand. The loom cannot stop. The weave cannot pause. Choose your place in the new pattern—or be unraveled."

Before Alaric could respond, the vision shattered, and he was back in the chamber.

Alaric sat up, his head pounding. Lira was beside him, her expression a mix of relief and frustration.

"You're alive," she said, helping him to his feet. "Barely."

"What happened?" Alaric asked, his voice hoarse.

"You tell me," Lira replied. "One second the apparatus is going haywire, the next it shuts down and you're out cold. Did you see something?"

Alaric hesitated, the shadowy figure's words still echoing in his mind. "It's... complicated. But I think I know what they're trying to do."

"Care to share with the class?" Lira asked, crossing her arms.

"They're not just breaking the ley lines," Alaric said. "They're trying to remake them. To create a new system of magic, one that follows their rules."

"And what happens to the rest of us while they're 'rewriting the rules'?" Lira asked darkly.

Alaric shook his head. "Nothing good."

As they left the chamber, the ley lines beneath Andryth pulsed faintly, their energy stabilizing but still fragile. Alaric's thoughts churned with possibilities. If the Veiled Order's goal was to reweave the ley lines, it meant they had access to knowledge and power far beyond what anyone in the Grand Arcanum understood. But it also meant they were vulnerable—every weave had a weak thread.

"We need to find the next Nexus," Alaric said as they emerged into the cold morning light. "If we can figure out where they're working from, we might be able to stop them."

Lira raised an eyebrow. "You're assuming there's only one more Nexus. What if this is just the beginning?"

Alaric tightened his grip on the grimoire. "Then we find every thread they've tampered with and cut them loose."

The journey ahead was daunting, but Alaric felt a fire burning in his chest. The Veiled Order had underestimated him, and he wasn't about to let their vision for a rewritten world come to pass.

Beneath Andryth: The Forgotten Chamber

The chamber beneath Andryth was a symphony of silence and tension, broken only by the faint hum of residual ley line energy. Every step Alaric and Lira took echoed against the ancient stone walls, as though the ruins themselves disapproved of their presence. The air was thick with the scent of damp earth and old magic—a sharp tang that made the hairs on Alaric's arms stand on end.

The ley line apparatus stood at the center of the cavern, a monument to both ingenuity and hubris. Its lattice of crystal and metal spiraled upward like a twisted tower, jagged and beautiful in its imperfection. Crystals embedded within the framework glimmered faintly, their light uneven, as if struggling against some unseen force. Alaric couldn't help but marvel at the craftsmanship—each piece was carved with precision, its runes so intricate they seemed almost alive.

"What do you think this place was?" Lira asked, her voice hushed as though speaking louder might disturb the ghosts of Andryth.

"A workshop, maybe," Alaric replied, running his hand along the smooth surface of the apparatus. "A place where the mages of Andryth studied the ley lines. But this..." He gestured to the apparatus, its faint glow casting eerie shadows on the walls. "This is beyond anything I've read about."

He crouched by one of the lower crystal nodes, studying the runes etched into its surface. They were familiar yet foreign, like an ancient dialect of the stabilization sigils he had learned at the Grand Arcanum. But these symbols were twisted, their edges jagged and harsh.

"These runes," Alaric murmured, tracing one with his finger. "They're meant to stabilize ley lines, but someone's corrupted them. Inverted the flow."

Lira knelt beside him, her dagger glinting faintly in the apparatus's light. "Corrupted how?"

"Think of the ley lines as a river," Alaric explained. "Normally, spells like this create dams to regulate the flow. But these... they're like whirlpools. They don't just stop the energy—they twist it, pull it in."

"And what happens when they pull in too much?" Lira asked, her tone grim.

Alaric didn't need to answer. The damage to Andryth's ruins spoke for itself.

Flashback: Lessons from Eldaryn

The sight of the apparatus brought memories rushing back—lessons in the Grand Arcanum's lecture halls, Eldaryn pacing before a class of eager apprentices. Alaric could almost hear his mentor's voice, measured and authoritative.

"The ley lines are not mere tools," Eldaryn had said, his piercing gaze sweeping the room. "They are the veins of our world, carrying magic and life. To tamper with them recklessly is to gamble with existence itself."

He had conjured a simple illusion, a shimmering web of light hovering over his desk. "Each strand in this web represents a ley line. Notice how they intersect, creating nexuses—points of immense power. These are not to be trifled with. Disturb one nexus, and you risk destabilizing the entire network."

A younger Alaric had raised his hand, his curiosity outpacing his caution. "But what if someone could control the ley lines? Use them to create new forms of magic?"

Eldaryn's expression had hardened. "Control is an illusion, Deymorne. The ley lines are not yours to shape. Those who try to dominate them inevitably find themselves consumed."

The memory faded, leaving Alaric with a hollow ache in his chest. He understood Eldaryn's warning now more than ever, but the temptation to understand, to explore, was a force he couldn't ignore.

The Creatures of Andryth

Their exploration of the chamber was interrupted by a low, guttural growl that echoed through the cavern. Alaric and Lira froze, their hands instinctively reaching for their weapons.

The growl came again, accompanied by the soft scrape of claws against stone. From the shadows emerged a creature unlike anything Alaric had seen—a hunched, feline shape with glowing eyes that burned like embers. Its translucent skin shimmered faintly, revealing veins of raw magic coursing through its body.

"Ley-beasts," Alaric whispered, his voice tinged with both awe and fear. He had read about such creatures in the Arcanum's archives—beings born from ley line surges, their forms shaped by the chaotic energy of fractured magic.

The ley-beast prowled closer, its movements unnervingly fluid. Its eyes fixed on the apparatus, as though drawn to its energy. Alaric held his breath, his grip tightening on the grimoire.

"Do they attack?" Lira asked, her voice low.

"They're unpredictable," Alaric replied. "But if the ley lines here are unstable, it might be—"

Before he could finish, the creature let out a piercing shriek, its body surging toward the apparatus. Lira reacted instantly, hurling a bolt of flame that exploded against the beast's flank. It staggered but didn't retreat, its form flickering like a mirage.

"Great," Lira muttered. "It doesn't burn."

Alaric flipped open the grimoire, scanning its pages desperately. "Ley-beasts are resistant to elemental magic," he said. "But they're vulnerable to disruption. We need to destabilize it."

"How?" Lira demanded, dodging as the creature lunged toward her.

"Distract it!" Alaric shouted, his fingers tracing a glyph on the grimoire's page. He muttered an incantation, his voice trembling with effort. The spell took shape—a shimmering orb of blue light that pulsed in his palm.

The ley-beast turned toward him, its gaze locking onto the orb. With a flick of his wrist, Alaric hurled the orb at the creature. It struck its chest, exploding in a burst of radiant energy. The ley-beast let out a final, mournful cry before dissolving into a cloud of shimmering mist.

Lira lowered her dagger, breathing heavily. "Next time, lead with that."

*****

After the encounter, Alaric and Lira resumed their examination of the chamber. In one corner, they found a collection of ancient artifacts—crystals, amulets, and fragments of what appeared to be enchanted weapons. Each item hummed faintly with latent power, their auras varying in intensity.

"This is Andryth's legacy," Alaric said, lifting a small, jagged crystal from the pile. Its surface was etched with runes similar to those on the apparatus. "These artifacts were created to interact with the ley lines. They might even predate the apparatus."

Lira picked up a tarnished amulet, its chain broken. The central gem glowed faintly, its light pulsating in time with the ley lines beneath their feet. "This one's still active," she said, holding it out to Alaric.

He examined the amulet closely, his brow furrowing. "It's a ley attunement charm. It could help us track disruptions in the ley lines. Or..." He hesitated, glancing at Lira. "It could amplify them."

Her expression hardened. "We're not using it unless we know exactly what it does."

"Agreed," Alaric said, slipping the amulet into his satchel. "But if we're going to stop whoever's behind this, we'll need every tool we can get."

The discovery of the apparatus and the artifacts only deepened the mystery. As they prepared to leave the chamber, Alaric felt a strange pull in the air—a subtle yet insistent tug that seemed to draw him toward the ley lines' convergence beneath Andryth.

He paused, his hand resting on the apparatus. The grimoire's map had shown a spiral pattern connecting the nexuses, but now he wondered if there was more to the design. The pattern wasn't random—it was deliberate, like a loom weaving threads into a tapestry.

"What if this isn't just about the ley lines?" Alaric murmured, more to himself than to Lira.

"What do you mean?" she asked.

Alaric turned to her, his expression thoughtful. "What if the Veiled Order isn't just rewriting magic? What if they're rewriting reality?"

Lira stared at him, her eyes narrowing. "Then we're going to need a lot more than chalk and a grimoire to stop them."

The Spiral Nexus stood before Alaric, a swirling maelstrom of light and shadow suspended in a frame of cracked, ancient stone. Its presence was overwhelming, both beautiful and terrifying. The nexus pulsed with energy, threads of magic twisting outward like tendrils seeking purchase in the air. The hum of the ley lines resonated in Alaric's chest, a rhythm that felt at once alien and achingly familiar.

He took a hesitant step forward, clutching the grimoire tightly. The runes on its cover seemed to glow faintly, mirroring the nexus's pulsations. Eldaryn stood several paces behind him, his face a mask of grim determination.

"Do not linger too long," Eldaryn warned. "The Spiral Nexus is not kind to wanderers. Its power is as destructive as it is alluring."

Alaric nodded, though his eyes remained fixed on the nexus. He reached out tentatively, feeling the air grow heavier as his fingers brushed the edge of the nexus's aura. The sensation was electrifying, a jolt that sent shivers down his spine.

Journal Entry: Fear and Reflection

Later that night, as the Spiral Nexus loomed in the distance, Alaric sat by the light of a small, flickering flame. His journal lay open before him, the quill in his hand trembling slightly as he began to write:

The Spiral Nexus is unlike anything I've ever seen. Its beauty is deceptive, like a flame that draws a moth only to consume it. I felt its power today—alive, ancient, and utterly indifferent to me. For a moment, I thought I heard something. A whisper? A song? I'm not sure. But it wasn't welcoming.

Eldaryn's warnings ring in my ears. He says the nexus remembers, that it bears the scars of every mage who's tried to harness its energy. I wonder if it remembers him. He hasn't said as much, but I can see it in his eyes: this isn't his first time standing before the Spiral Nexus. Did he fail? Did he lose someone? Or is he simply afraid I will repeat his mistakes?

The ley lines feel different here. They're not just currents of magic—they're something more. I can feel them pulling at me, testing me. And I'm afraid. Afraid of what I might become if I let them in. Afraid of what I might do if I can't control them.

He paused, staring at the words as the ink dried. With a sigh, he closed the journal and placed it beside him. The fire crackled softly, its light a feeble shield against the shadows of the night.

Perspective Shift: Eldaryn's Reflection

From a distance, Eldaryn watched Alaric. The boy was ambitious, curious, and dangerously naive. He reminded Eldaryn of himself—a memory that was both a comfort and a curse.

Eldaryn's gaze drifted to the Spiral Nexus, its chaotic energy illuminating the landscape in erratic pulses. It was an anomaly, even among the ley lines. He had stood in this very spot years ago, full of hope and arrogance. He had believed he could tame the nexus, bend its power to his will.

But the nexus had shown him the truth.

The memory surfaced unbidden: the tendrils of light twisting around him, the hum of the ley lines growing deafening, and then the fracture. The energy had surged out of control, claiming lives and leaving Eldaryn broken in more ways than one. He had survived, but not without scars—both visible and hidden.

"Do you sense it, too?" Eldaryn whispered, his voice barely audible over the nexus's hum. "Do you see the same flaws in him that you saw in me?"

The nexus seemed to pulse in response, its light dimming briefly before flaring brighter. Eldaryn's jaw tightened. It was as if the nexus were laughing at him, mocking his failure and daring him to try again.

Perspective Shift: The Nexus Entity

Deep within the Spiral Nexus, a fragment of consciousness stirred. It was not a mind in the way mortals understood, but an awareness born of centuries of existence. It felt the approach of the young mage, his curiosity and fear like faint ripples across a vast ocean.

Another seeker, it thought, though the concept of thought was alien to its nature. They come and they fall. Always seeking, always breaking.

The nexus did not hate them. It could not hate. But it remembered. It remembered the hands that had reached for its power, the voices that had spoken its name, the lives that had unraveled in its embrace. It remembered the man who now stood behind the boy, his presence a familiar echo of past mistakes.

He failed, the nexus mused, its light shifting in rhythm with its awareness. Will the boy fail, too? Or will he see? Will he listen?

The nexus reached out, a tendril of energy brushing against the boy's mind. It whispered, not in words but in sensations—images of a world torn apart, of magic unleashed and uncontrolled, of a silence that followed. It showed him what could be, not as a warning, but as a possibility.

A Moment of Resolve

Alaric shuddered as the vision faded. He staggered back, clutching his head as the hum of the ley lines grew louder. For a moment, he thought he might collapse.

"Alaric," Eldaryn's voice cut through the haze, firm and steady. "What did you see?"

Alaric opened his eyes, the nexus's light reflected in their depths. "It's alive," he said, his voice trembling. "It's not just power. It's something more. It's... waiting."

Eldaryn placed a hand on his shoulder. "And what will you do now that you know?"

Alaric straightened, his grip on the grimoire tightening. "I'll learn. I'll prove I'm worthy."

Eldaryn's expression softened, though his eyes remained wary. "Then we must tread carefully. The Spiral Nexus does not forgive recklessness. Remember that."

As they turned away from the nexus, its light pulsed once more, as if in acknowledgment of the boy's resolve. Behind them, the ley lines hummed softly, their rhythm unchanging but full of unspoken promise.

The spiral runes etched into the ancient walls pulsed faintly, their light dimming as Alaric and Lira stepped into the stillness of the cavern. The air was heavy, laden with the unmistakable hum of ley line energy—steady, yet unnervingly irregular.

"This place feels... wrong," Lira murmured, her hand resting on the hilt of her blade. Her sharp eyes scanned the chamber, where cracks in the stone seemed to emit a faint, unnatural glow.

"It's not the Nexus itself," Alaric replied, his voice tinged with unease. He knelt beside one of the glowing cracks, his fingers tracing its jagged edges. "The ley lines are trying to adjust, but something is interfering with their rhythm. It's like the energy is being redirected—or disrupted."

He opened the grimoire at his side, its pages flickering to reveal diagrams of rune patterns tied to ley line stabilization. His eyes narrowed as he compared the script on the walls to the symbols on the page. At first glance, they seemed harmonious, but on closer inspection, faint etchings overlapped the original designs—markings that didn't belong.

"These aren't natural," Alaric said, gesturing to the overlapping runes. "Someone's been here. These marks—they're deliberate."

"Could it be the Veiled Order?" Lira asked, her voice sharp.

Alaric hesitated. He had read of their exploits in the Grimoire of Eternal Threads—accounts of their attempts to manipulate ley lines for their own ends. If these were indeed their marks, then this was no ordinary interference.

"Maybe," he admitted, his tone grim. "But if they've tampered with the ley lines here, it means this Nexus is more significant than we realized."

Flashback: Ley Line Anomalies

The faint glow of the chamber's runes blurred, giving way to a memory. Alaric found himself standing once again in the Grand Arcanum, poring over a ley line map that spanned an entire wall. His mentor, Eldaryn, stood at his side, pointing to a cluster of fractures in the northern regions.

"These anomalies are recent," Eldaryn had said, his voice low and measured. "The ley lines in this area have always been volatile, but this... this is different."

"What caused them?" Alaric had asked, his younger voice filled with curiosity.

"No one knows," Eldaryn had replied. "But the pattern—" He gestured to the fractures that spiraled outward from a single point. "It's not random. Someone, or something, is pulling at the threads. Be cautious, Alaric. Not all who study the ley lines seek to preserve them."

The memory faded, replaced by the dim light of the cavern. Alaric clenched his fists, his mentor's warning now more relevant than ever. The overlapping runes on the walls were no accident; they were evidence of the Veiled Order's deliberate meddling.

Flashback: The Veiled Order's Cryptic Runes

As Alaric adjusted the light from his grimoire, a memory surfaced—his first encounter with the Veiled Order's marks.

It had been years ago, during his studies at the Arcanum. He had stumbled upon an abandoned ley line node deep in the mountains. The energy there had been chaotic, its flow erratic. Upon closer inspection, he had discovered runes carved into the surrounding rocks—jagged symbols that defied the natural harmony of magic.

He had shown sketches of the runes to Eldaryn, who had gone pale at the sight.

"These are forbidden," his mentor had said, his tone urgent. "They bend the ley lines to the caster's will, forcing them to break their natural rhythm. Alaric, promise me you'll never try to replicate them. They are a poison to the ley lines."

Returning to the present, Alaric felt a cold dread as he studied the overlapping runes on the cavern walls. The similarities to the Veiled Order's forbidden symbols were undeniable. Whoever had left them here wasn't just tampering with the ley lines—they were attempting to rewrite their structure.

"This isn't just interference," he said aloud, his voice steady despite the growing tension. "It's a deliberate attempt to destabilize the Nexus."

"What do we do?" Lira asked, her eyes scanning the chamber for any sign of danger.

"We find the source," Alaric replied, closing his grimoire with a decisive snap. "And we stop it before it's too late."

As they pressed deeper into the cavern, the hum of the ley lines grew louder, their rhythm increasingly erratic. The faint glow of the overlapping runes seemed to pulse in time with the fractures, guiding them toward the heart of the disturbance—and the answers they sought.

The hum of the ley lines grew louder, their rhythm discordant and fractured, as Alaric and Lira delved deeper into the Spiral Nexus. The air grew heavier with each step, carrying the weight of countless intertwined threads of energy struggling against unseen forces. Alaric's grimoire pulsed faintly in his satchel, as though resonating with the imbalance.

"It's like the ley lines are screaming," Lira murmured, her voice barely audible over the cacophony.

"They are," Alaric replied, his expression grim. "And someone's been listening."

Ahead, a faint glow illuminated the cavern's narrowing path. The corrupted runes that had marked their way through the Spiral Nexus now grew larger and more erratic, their jagged lines pulsating with a dark energy. Each step brought them closer to the heart of the disturbance, but also deeper into its chaos.

"What do you think we'll find?" Lira asked, clutching her amulet tightly.

"Answers," Alaric said, though his tone carried no certainty. "And maybe the source of all this."

As they rounded a corner, the path opened into a vast chamber dominated by a strange apparatus of crystal and metal, its surface crawling with glowing runes. The energy it emitted was both mesmerizing and repellent, a force that seemed to pull at their very essence.

"It's a convergence point," Alaric said, his breath catching. "The ley lines are being drawn here—twisted and forced into this... thing."

Lira stepped closer, her eyes narrowing. "The Veiled Order?"

Alaric nodded. "It has to be. No one else could create something this destructive."

The apparatus pulsed once, sending a ripple of energy through the chamber. The ground beneath them trembled, and the air grew thick with static.

Lira drew her blade. "Whatever it is, it's not stopping us."

With a shared look of resolve, they stepped forward, ready to confront the chaos.

Narrator: Historical Context of the Spiral Nexus

The Spiral Nexus was not born of nature but of necessity, forged in the crucible of desperation. Ancient mages—scholars, visionaries, and, perhaps, fools—came together during an era known only as the Breaking, a time when the ley lines, the very veins of magic, began to fracture. Their collapse sent waves of chaos across the realms: cities crumbled as gravity unraveled, rivers reversed their courses, and entire forests turned to stone overnight. The earth itself seemed to rebel, rejecting the balance that had sustained it for millennia.

To halt the destruction, these mages constructed the Spiral Nexus at the heart of the ley line network, a convergence point where magic could be stabilized and redirected. It was an audacious undertaking, requiring the sacrifice of lifetimes and the bending of natural laws. Yet, while the Spiral Nexus restored balance, it also became a paradox. It was both a savior and a prisoner, tethered to the chaotic forces it sought to contain.

Over the centuries, the Spiral Nexus became shrouded in myth. Some said it whispered to those who approached, revealing the truths of creation—or driving them mad. Others claimed it held memories of the Breaking, etched into its shifting threads. One thing was certain: those who tampered with it risked not only their lives but the very fabric of existence.

Flashback: Eldaryn's Earlier Encounters with the Spiral Nexus

Eldaryn's sharp green eyes softened, his gaze distant as if peering into a memory he wished to forget. "I was younger then," he began, his voice low but steady. "I thought the ley lines were tools—raw energy waiting to be shaped. And the Spiral Nexus? I believed it was my proving ground. A place to master the untamable."

Alaric leaned forward, the weight of the older mage's words pressing on him. "What happened?"

Eldaryn sighed, holding out his hands. Even in the dim light of the chamber, faint scars were visible, jagged and pale against his weathered skin. "I underestimated it. The ley lines aren't just streams of energy—they're alive. They remember. And they do not take kindly to arrogance."

The memory unfolded vividly in Eldaryn's mind. He stood in the Nexus Chamber, surrounded by swirling tendrils of light and shadow. The air buzzed with energy, a symphony of hums and whispers that seemed to speak directly to his thoughts. With his crystalline staff raised high, he attempted to bind the threads of magic into a stronger weave, pulling on their power with all the precision he could muster. For a fleeting moment, it seemed to work. The Nexus threads steadied, glowing brighter as they aligned.

But then the ley lines resisted.

"It was like trying to hold the wind in your hands," Eldaryn continued, his voice tightening. "They rebelled against me—no, against my hubris."

The room had erupted into chaos. Tendrils of raw energy lashed out, one striking his staff and shattering it into fragments. Another wrapped around his arm, searing his flesh with an unholy heat. The air turned thick, choking him with its intensity. Eldaryn had barely escaped, staggering through the Nexus Chamber's gates as the threads snapped back into their chaotic dance.

"The scars healed," he said, gesturing to his hands, "but the lesson didn't fade. The ley lines are not ours to command. At best, they permit our touch. At worst..." He trailed off, shaking his head. "At worst, they unmake us."

Alaric stared, his breath shallow. He had always thought of magic as something to master, to shape. But in that moment, he saw it as Eldaryn did: a force older and greater than any one mage, powerful enough to create worlds—and destroy them.

Chapter 6: Convergence and Chaos

Alaric sat cross-legged on the cold stone floor of the chamber beneath Andryth, the remnants of the ley line apparatus looming above him like a broken giant. The air was heavy with magic, the energy still pulsing faintly through the crystals embedded in the machine's lattice. His hands trembled as he turned the pages of the grimoire, its ink shifting into new diagrams that made his stomach twist. The apparatus was merely a fragment of a far greater scheme.

The runes he had sketched from the corrupted sigils on the apparatus danced in his mind. They were not just symbols of disruption—they were part of a deliberate system designed to amplify instability. Alaric leaned against the wall, his exhaustion weighing him down. The grimoire's pages glowed faintly, revealing a new mark on its map. The Spiral Nexus.

"Another one?" Lira's voice broke through his thoughts as she leaned against a nearby column, her arms crossed. She looked as tired as he felt. "Are we just going to chase these things forever?"

Alaric didn't answer immediately. He closed the grimoire and exhaled slowly, staring at the fractured crystals around them. "I don't think we have a choice. If we don't act, these fractures will get worse. The ley lines—everything—will collapse."

Lira stepped closer, her tone softening. "And if we're wrong? If we can't fix this?"

"We have to try," Alaric said firmly. He opened his satchel and pulled out his journal, jotting down his observations about the apparatus. He sketched the corrupted runes and detailed how they siphoned energy from the ley lines, cross-referencing them with diagrams from the grimoire. The fractured circle in the grimoire map pulsed faintly, pointing him toward the Spiral Nexus.

"I'll keep tracking the patterns," he added, his voice steady despite the knot in his chest. "But this is bigger than us. We need help."

Lira hesitated, then nodded. "The Grand Arcanum?"

Alaric looked up at her, conflicted. "Eventually. But first, I need to see the Spiral Nexus for myself. If we can stabilize it, maybe we'll have something concrete to bring back to them."

"Then let's get moving," Lira said, though the tension in her voice betrayed her unease. "This place is giving me the creeps."

*****

The path to the Spiral Nexus was unlike anything Alaric had encountered. The grimoire's map led them through landscapes warped by the ley lines' instability. Dense forests twisted into labyrinths, their trees contorted into unnatural shapes. Streams of molten earth cut through frozen lakes, the elements clashing in chaotic harmony.

One night, as they made camp beneath a sky streaked with auroras of unnatural colors, Alaric sat with the grimoire open on his lap. He experimented with runes, his chalk etching symbols into flat stones he had collected along the way. His Runestone Compass sat beside him, its needle spinning erratically as it responded to the ley lines' turbulent energy.

"What are you working on now?" Lira asked, leaning against a fallen log.

"Containment runes," Alaric replied, holding up a stone etched with an intricate spiral. "The apparatus back in Andryth—its crystals amplified the ley lines' energy. I'm trying to create something that does the opposite. A way to store excess energy temporarily and redistribute it safely."

Lira frowned. "Like a magical capacitor?"

"Exactly," Alaric said, a small smile tugging at his lips. "If I can stabilize the ley lines around the Spiral Nexus, even for a moment, we might be able to figure out what's causing the imbalance."

"And if it doesn't work?" Lira asked, her tone cautious.

Alaric looked at the swirling auroras overhead, his smile fading. "Then we'll find another way."

When they arrived at the Spiral Nexus, the sheer scale of it took their breath away. The nexus was a massive vortex of energy, with threads of blue, red, and gold magic spiraling into a singular point above a jagged crystalline spire. The ground around the spire was cracked and scorched, with patches of vegetation frozen in ice or consumed by flames.

Alaric knelt by a fissure in the ground, his fingers brushing against the charred soil. The energy here was chaotic—more than just unstable. It was alive, responding to the imbalance with violent discharges of elemental magic. The air smelled of ozone and sulfur, and the temperature fluctuated wildly between searing heat and bone-chilling cold.

"This is worse than I imagined," Alaric said, his voice barely audible over the hum of the nexus.

"What's causing it?" Lira asked, standing beside him.

Alaric opened the grimoire, flipping to a page filled with diagrams of ley line intersections. "The energy flows here are out of balance. There's too much air and fire energy—too much heat and motion. It's overwhelming the system."

"Can you fix it?" Lira asked, her tone sharp with urgency.

"Maybe," Alaric said, his eyes scanning the environment. He pointed to a cluster of metallic minerals jutting from the ground nearby. "Those might work as conductors. If I can redistribute the energy, I might be able to stabilize the flow temporarily."

Alaric worked methodically, carving runes into the metallic minerals and arranging them in a circle around the nexus. Each rune corresponded to an element—water to cool the fire, earth to ground the air. He used his Runestone Compass to align the runes with the ley lines, the needle finally stabilizing as he completed the circle.

"This might work," Alaric muttered, his hands shaking as he etched the final rune. He stepped back, clutching the grimoire. "Lira, be ready to run if this goes wrong."

"You're really selling this plan," Lira said, though her attempt at humor couldn't mask her nervousness.

Alaric began the incantation, his voice steady despite the energy swirling around him. The runes glowed faintly, their light spreading through the minerals and into the ground. For a moment, the nexus's chaotic energy seemed to calm, its spiraling threads aligning into a harmonious flow.

But then the ground shook violently, and a surge of energy erupted from the nexus. A portal formed above the crystalline spire, its edges shimmering with an eerie light. Through the portal, Alaric glimpsed a barren world—an endless expanse of cracked earth and gray skies, with ley lines reduced to faint, lifeless scars.

"This isn't right," Alaric said, his voice shaking. "The balance is still off."

The portal flickered, and a creature emerged—an elemental fragment of pure plasma. It hovered before them, its form constantly shifting between fire, air, and electricity. It moved with purpose but without intelligence, reacting to the energy around it like a living flame.

"Alaric," Lira said, her voice tight with fear. "What is that?"

"An elemental fragment," Alaric said, his eyes locked on the creature. "It's a byproduct of the imbalance—a manifestation of excess energy."

The fragment turned toward them, its crackling energy growing more intense. Alaric reached for his satchel, pulling out one of the containment runes he had crafted. He hurled the stone at the fragment, the rune activating in a burst of blue light. The fragment writhed, its energy dimming before it dissolved into a harmless wisp of smoke.

*****

As the portal closed and the nexus began to stabilize, Alaric sat on the ground, his exhaustion catching up to him. He opened his journal, his hands shaking as he documented the experiment's results and the glimpse into the barren world.

"What did you see?" Lira asked, sitting beside him.

"A world without ley lines," Alaric said quietly. "A world where the balance was lost. It was lifeless. Empty."

Lira placed a hand on his shoulder. "And that's what we're fighting to prevent."

Alaric nodded, though his mind was racing. The nexus was stable for now, but the fractures were spreading. The grimoire's map showed other marks—other nexuses in danger. And the shadow of the Veiled Order loomed over it all.

"We need to go back to the Grand Arcanum," Alaric said finally. "This is bigger than us. If we don't act soon, the whole system will collapse."

Lira nodded. "Then let's not waste any time."

The Grand Arcanum: Ripples of Chaos

The journey back to the Grand Arcanum was fraught with tension. Even as they left the Spiral Nexus behind, Alaric and Lira could feel the unstable energy coursing through the ley lines. The Runestone Compass in Alaric's hand quivered constantly, its needle flickering between directions like a frightened animal.

"This isn't over," Alaric murmured, glancing at the faintly glowing grimoire in his satchel. Its mark of the Spiral Nexus remained dim, but the other nexuses were beginning to pulse faintly on the map. "Whatever we did, it's only a temporary fix."

Lira gave him a sideways look. "And what happens when the fix fails?"

Alaric didn't answer. He didn't need to.

When they arrived at the Grand Arcanum, the campus was buzzing with activity. Apprentices and professors alike whispered in hushed tones, their faces pale with concern. The disturbances in the ley lines had not gone unnoticed.

Alaric and Lira barely had time to catch their breath before they were summoned to the council chamber. The room was vast, its high domed ceiling adorned with frescoes depicting the origins of the ley lines. Eldaryn stood at the head of a long table, his piercing gaze fixed on Alaric as they entered.

"You've caused quite the stir, Deymorne," Eldaryn said, his voice calm but heavy with expectation.

Alaric swallowed hard, stepping forward. "Master Eldaryn, we stabilized the Spiral Nexus—at least temporarily. But the imbalance isn't isolated. The fractures are spreading."

Eldaryn gestured for him to continue. Alaric retrieved his journal, laying it open on the table to show his sketches and notes. "The Spiral Nexus had an overabundance of air and fire energy. I used conductive materials and containment runes to redistribute the flows, but it wasn't enough. The grimoire—"

At the mention of the grimoire, a murmur rippled through the room. Eldaryn's eyes narrowed. "This grimoire of yours... Is it the same one that led you to the apparatus in Andryth?"

"Yes," Alaric admitted. "It's been guiding me, revealing marks on the map—nexuses in danger. If we don't act, the entire ley line network could collapse."

Kael, seated near the back of the room, scoffed loudly. "And we're supposed to trust this... magical book? Or your ability to interpret it? Last I checked, you nearly caused a rupture at the Spiral Nexus."

Alaric bristled. "I stabilized the Nexus! Without my actions, the damage would have been catastrophic."

Kael leaned forward, his smirk sharp. "Or perhaps it was your meddling that caused the imbalance in the first place."

"Enough," Eldaryn said sharply, silencing the room. He turned to Alaric, his expression unreadable. "You've uncovered something significant, but your actions have also raised questions. There will be a formal review of your methods and findings."

After the council adjourned, Alaric found himself sitting alone in the Arcanum's central library. The soft glow of enchanted lamps illuminated rows of ancient tomes, their spines bearing the faded symbols of long-forgotten authors. He stared at the grimoire on the table before him, its pages open to the pulsing map.

The fractured circle near the Spiral Nexus still lingered, but another mark had begun to pulse faintly—a distant nexus in the eastern mountains. The weight of it all pressed heavily on his chest.

"You look like you've aged a decade," Lira said, sliding into the chair across from him. She placed two steaming mugs of tea on the table. "Here. Drink."

Alaric picked up the mug, the warmth grounding him. "Thanks."

Lira sipped her tea, watching him closely. "What's the plan?"

Alaric hesitated. "I don't know yet. If the council decides to block me from acting, I'll have to go alone. But this isn't just about me. The fractures are spreading faster than I thought."

Lira raised an eyebrow. "And Kael? He won't stop until he discredits you."

"Let him try," Alaric said, though his voice lacked conviction.

Lira leaned closer. "I did some digging while you were at the council. Kael's family owns one of the largest ley crystal mining operations in the region. If the ley lines destabilize, their business will boom. Artificial instability means higher demand for stabilizing crystals."

Alaric's grip tightened on the mug. "He's profiting from the collapse?"

"It's just a theory," Lira said. "But it explains why he's so eager to shut you down."

The Eastern Nexus: Natural Anomalies

The journey to the eastern mountains was grueling. Alaric and Lira traversed dense forests, rocky cliffs, and treacherous terrain where the ley lines' instability was evident in the environment. The air grew thinner as they ascended, and the weather shifted unpredictably—one moment blistering heat, the next a sudden hailstorm.

"This place feels... wrong," Lira said, her voice barely audible over the howling wind. "Like the elements are fighting each other."

Alaric nodded. The eastern nexus was unlike anything he had encountered before. The ley lines converged in a violent vortex, creating a tear in the natural flow of energy. Streams of fire and air clashed with bursts of water and earth, creating an environment that was both beautiful and deadly.

"This imbalance isn't just affecting the ley lines," Alaric said, studying the grimoire's diagrams. "It's destabilizing the entire region. Look at those cliffs."

Lira followed his gaze. Massive cracks ran through the mountainside, and chunks of rock occasionally broke free, tumbling into the abyss below. The ground beneath their feet rumbled faintly, as though warning them of the chaos to come.

*****

As they approached the nexus, the energy in the air became almost unbearable. Sparks of plasma crackled around them, and the very air seemed to vibrate with tension. Alaric paused, his Runestone Compass spinning wildly.

"We're close," he said, his voice tight with focus. "But something's... off."

Before Lira could respond, a sudden burst of light erupted from the nexus. A being of pure plasma emerged, its form shifting between humanoid and amorphous. It radiated heat and electricity, its movements erratic but purposeful.

"Another elemental fragment," Alaric muttered, pulling out one of his containment runes. "But this one's stronger."

The fragment let out a high-pitched screech, sending a bolt of lightning toward them. Lira raised a shield of flame, deflecting the attack but staggering under the force.

"Tell me you have a plan!" she shouted.

Alaric hurled the containment rune, its activation circle glowing blue as it latched onto the fragment. The fragment writhed, its energy dimming slightly, but it wasn't enough.

"We need to redirect the energy!" Alaric shouted, flipping through the grimoire. "If we can ground it—"

"Ground it? With what?" Lira demanded.

Alaric scanned the environment, his gaze landing on a cluster of quartz crystals jutting from the ground. "Those! Quartz is a natural conductor—it can absorb and redirect the energy."

Together, they worked to inscribe grounding runes onto the crystals, using chalk and the grimoire's instructions. The fragment lashed out repeatedly, but each bolt of energy was drawn toward the quartz, dissipating harmlessly.

Finally, the fragment dissolved into a harmless wisp of light, leaving the nexus quiet but still unstable.

As Alaric approached the nexus, the energy pulsing from it began to warp his vision. Images flashed before his eyes—a barren world of ash and shadow, where the ley lines lay dormant and dead.

He saw towers of crystal siphoning the last remnants of energy, their creators long gone.

A voice echoed in his mind, hollow and ancient. "The weave is fragile. Restore it, or suffer the same fate."

When the vision ended, Alaric stumbled back, gasping for breath. Lira caught him before he fell. "What did you see?"

"A warning," Alaric said, his voice trembling. "Our world is on the same path as theirs. If we don't act, it'll all end."

The Eastern Nexus pulsed like a living thing. Alaric felt its energy in his bones, each fluctuation a jarring vibration that disrupted his thoughts. Unlike the Spiral Nexus, this site was more volatile. The elemental imbalance here was visible in the chaotic interplay of forces: gouts of fire erupted from fissures, only to be doused by sudden downpours, while gusts of wind tore at the cliffs, dislodging boulders that tumbled into rivers carving new paths through the rock.

Alaric crouched at the edge of the nexus's epicenter, sketching diagrams in his journal. The energy flows were unlike anything he had encountered. Where the Spiral Nexus had shown imbalances in air and fire, this nexus seemed to lack any stable patterns. Its energy fields twisted unpredictably, intersecting and repelling each other like magnets forced together.

"This isn't just an imbalance," Alaric murmured. "It's chaos."

Lira watched from a safer distance, her arms crossed. "Isn't that what you were expecting?"

"Not like this," Alaric replied, flipping to a page in the grimoire. Its diagrams revealed swirling patterns that vaguely mirrored what he observed, but the annotations described chaos as potential, not disorder. "This is something else entirely. It's like the nexus has become self-organizing. The energy flows aren't random—they're adapting."

"Adapting to what?" Lira asked, stepping closer despite the volatile winds.

Alaric pointed to a cluster of crystalline formations growing from a nearby fissure. The crystals were jagged and irregular, glowing faintly with energy. "To its environment. Those crystals are a byproduct of the chaos magic. They're growing in response to the elemental forces, almost like they're alive."

He approached the crystals cautiously, his Runestone Compass spinning wildly as he drew nearer. The compass needle aligned briefly, then snapped back into its erratic rotation. Alaric crouched and placed his hand near the crystals. They radiated heat, but instead of a steady warmth, the temperature fluctuated wildly—hot, then cold, then back again.

Chaos and the Science of Magic

As Alaric examined the crystals, he couldn't help but think back to his studies at the Grand Arcanum. Chaos magic had always been an enigma, dismissed by many as an unpredictable and dangerous force. But Alaric had always seen it differently. Chaos, he believed, wasn't the absence of order—it was the foundation of change, a catalyst for evolution.

"These crystals are amplifiers," Alaric said, his voice tinged with excitement. "They're absorbing the chaos energy and storing it, like capacitors in an electrical circuit."

"And what happens when they're full?" Lira asked, her tone wary.

"They release it," Alaric replied, standing and pointing to the fissures. "That's what's causing the elemental surges. The crystals discharge their energy into the environment, creating these extreme weather patterns."

Lira frowned. "So, what's your plan? Pluck the crystals out and hope the nexus calms down?"

"Not exactly," Alaric said, pulling a piece of chalk from his satchel. "I need to map the flow of energy through the crystals and the nexus itself. If I can create a feedback loop, I might be able to stabilize the chaos."

"Feedback loop?" Lira echoed. "That sounds... risky."

"It is," Alaric admitted. "But chaos magic thrives on unpredictability. The key is to guide it, not control it. If I can set up a self-regulating system, the nexus might stabilize itself."

Lira sighed. "Fine. But if this backfires, I'm not cleaning up the mess."

*****

Alaric worked quickly, inscribing runes onto flat stones and arranging them around the nexus in a spiral pattern. Each rune corresponded to an elemental force, with specific symbols representing fire, water, air, and earth. He used his Runestone Compass to align the runes with the nexus's chaotic energy flows, recalibrating their positions until the compass needle steadied.

"This is incredible," Alaric muttered as he worked. "The chaos energy behaves like plasma—highly reactive, influenced by magnetic and electrical fields. It's like the nexus is its own miniature star."

"Let's just hope it doesn't go supernova," Lira muttered, keeping an eye on the swirling energy above them.

Once the runes were in place, Alaric retrieved a shard of one of the chaos crystals and placed it at the center of the spiral. The crystal's glow intensified, its jagged edges refracting the nexus's energy into a kaleidoscope of colors. Alaric began the incantation, his voice steady as he channeled his focus into the runes.

The energy flows around the nexus shifted, the chaotic surges slowing as the runes began to glow. The spiral pattern created a feedback loop, redirecting excess energy into the crystals while maintaining the nexus's natural flow.

"It's working," Alaric said, a note of triumph in his voice.

But as the energy stabilized, the ground beneath them trembled. A faint crackling sound echoed through the air, and Alaric looked up to see a shimmering portal forming above the nexus. The portal's edges were jagged, its interior a swirling void of light and shadow.

"What did you do?" Lira demanded, backing away from the portal.

"I don't know!" Alaric shouted, shielding his eyes from the portal's brilliance. "The nexus must be drawing energy from somewhere else!"

The portal stabilized, revealing a fractured world on the other side. Alaric could see vast wastelands of cracked earth and jagged cliffs, the air shimmering with heat. In the distance, towers of crystal rose like skeletal spires, their surfaces glowing faintly.

"This isn't our world," Alaric said, his voice barely above a whisper. "It's... something else. A dimension where chaos magic has run unchecked."

Before Lira could respond, a figure emerged from the portal. It was humanoid in shape but composed entirely of shifting light and shadow, its form constantly breaking apart and reassembling. The figure's presence radiated power, and its voice echoed in their minds.

"You meddle in forces you do not comprehend," the figure said, its tone both cold and commanding. "The weave of your world is unraveling, and you are its thread."

Alaric stepped forward, his curiosity outweighing his fear. "Who are you? What is this place?"

The figure tilted its head, its form flickering. "I am a remnant of a world consumed by chaos. Your actions mirror those of my creators, who sought to control what cannot be controlled."

Alaric's mind raced. "Then help us. Tell us how to fix it."

The figure's form began to dissolve, its voice fading. "Balance cannot be forced. It must be found."

As the figure vanished, the portal began to collapse. Alaric and Lira scrambled back as the nexus surged, the feedback loop straining against the chaos energy. With a final burst of light, the portal closed, leaving the nexus quiet but far from stable.

Reflection and Resolve

Back at their camp, Alaric sat by the fire, his journal open on his lap. He sketched the portal and the figure, his mind replaying the encounter over and over.

"What do you think it meant?" Lira asked, breaking the silence.

"Balance," Alaric said, his voice thoughtful. "The chaos magic isn't inherently destructive. It's... reactive. Adaptive. If we can guide it toward equilibrium, we might be able to repair the ley lines."

Lira nodded slowly. "And if we can't?"

Alaric looked at the grimoire, its map glowing faintly with new marks. "Then we'll face whatever comes next. But one thing's clear—this isn't just about stabilizing nexuses anymore. The whole system is unraveling."

He closed the journal, determination hardening in his expression. "We need to understand the chaos, not fight it. And that starts with the next mark."

Chapter 7: Laws of Chaos and Order

As Alaric and Lira descended from the nexus site, the weight of their discoveries pressed heavily upon them. The chaotic interplay of elemental forces they had witnessed was no longer just a localized anomaly—it was a symptom of a far greater unraveling. The ley lines were not merely sources of magic; they were bound by the same fundamental principles that governed the natural world. Their disturbances mirrored the chaos that occurred when universal laws were pushed to their limits.

That night, Alaric sat by the campfire, his grimoire and journal spread before him. The stars overhead were unusually bright, their constellations subtly distorted—a sign, perhaps, of the dimensional instability caused by the fractures. He dipped his quill into ink and began a new journal entry, his thoughts racing as he tried to reconcile magic with the principles he had studied at the Grand Arcanum.

Journal Entry: The First Laws of Chaos and Order
Newton's First Law of Motion (Inertia):

The nexus behaves like a closed system, maintaining its chaotic state until an external force—my containment runes—acted upon it. The energy flows resisted stabilization, demonstrating that chaos, like inertia, perpetuates itself unless interrupted.

Newton's Second Law of Motion (F = ma):

The force required to redirect the nexus's energy depended on the "mass" of its chaotic flows (its intensity and volume) and the rate at which I attempted to change them. Larger surges of energy required more powerful runes to counteract the flow, proving that even magic adheres to the principle of proportionality.

Newton's Third Law of Motion (Action-Reaction):

For every rune I inscribed to stabilize an elemental force, the nexus reacted with an equal and opposite burst of energy. The feedback loop I created was an attempt to harness this principle—redirecting the reaction into a controlled flow instead of allowing it to spiral out of control.

The Nature of Gravitational Magic

The next morning, as the sunlight filtered through the dense forest canopy, Alaric examined one of the jagged chaos crystals he had collected from the nexus. He noticed that the crystal, when placed near his compass, caused the needle to deflect slightly, as though exerting its own gravitational pull.

"Gravity," Alaric murmured, holding the crystal up to the light. "It's not just mass that attracts mass—it's energy too. These crystals are dense with chaotic energy, and they're warping the ley lines around them."

Lira raised an eyebrow. "Are you saying magic can mimic gravity?"

"Not mimic," Alaric corrected. "It is gravity—or at least a version of it. The ley lines are like spacetime, bending and twisting around powerful sources of energy. The more energy concentrated in one place, the greater the distortion."

He jotted another entry into his journal.

Journal Entry: The Law of Universal Gravitation in Ley Magic

The attraction between chaos crystals and nearby energy fields resembles the gravitational pull between masses. Their influence increases with proximity and intensity, creating "wells" in the ley lines that draw in elemental forces. The nexus's chaotic vortex may have formed because of an overconcentration of energy, much like how black holes distort spacetime.

Heat, Entropy, and the Nexus

As they continued their journey, Alaric began to notice patterns in the environmental anomalies caused by the ley line disturbances. In one valley, the air was stiflingly hot, with geysers of steam erupting from fissures in the ground. In another, frost coated the trees, and the streams had frozen solid despite the summer season.

"It's like the elements are fighting for dominance," Lira observed as they trudged through a patch of ice-crusted underbrush.

"Or they're trying to reach equilibrium," Alaric replied. He stopped to examine a patch of frost that had formed in a spiral pattern. "The first law of thermodynamics says energy can't be created or destroyed—it only changes forms. The ley lines are trying to redistribute their excess energy, but the chaos magic is preventing them from doing it efficiently."

He added another entry to his journal.

Journal Entry: Thermodynamics and Ley Lines

First Law: The energy surges in the ley lines aren't disappearing—they're transforming into chaotic elemental phenomena. Fire becomes heat, air becomes storms, and water becomes ice. Magic is bound by the same conservation principles as physical energy.

Second Law: The increasing entropy in the ley lines mirrors the natural tendency of systems to move toward disorder. The more unstable the nexus becomes, the harder it is for the system to restore balance.

Third Law: As the chaos approaches absolute zero (a fully stabilized state), the ley lines' entropy should reach a minimum. But the fragments of chaos magic may be preventing this stabilization, creating endless feedback loops of instability.

Harnessing Electromagnetic Principles

The duo's journey brought them to a desolate plateau, where jagged rocks jutted out of the earth like broken teeth. The air was charged with static electricity, and faint arcs of lightning flickered between the stones.

"This place feels alive," Lira muttered, her voice tinged with unease.

"It's the magnetic fields," Alaric said, holding up his compass. The needle spun wildly before snapping to a new alignment. "The ley lines here are generating electromagnetic currents."

He reached into his satchel and retrieved a coil of copper wire—a tool he had brought for his experiments. Wrapping the wire around one of the chaos crystals, he held it up to the lightning. The crystal glowed faintly, and the wire began to hum.

"Faraday's Law," Alaric said, his voice filled with wonder. "Changing magnetic fields create electric fields. If I can harness this effect, I might be able to create a stabilizing barrier."

"You're making a magical Faraday cage?" Lira asked.

"Exactly," Alaric said, sketching a diagram in his journal.

Journal Entry: Electromagnetic Magic

The ley lines generate electromagnetic fields that interact with nearby materials. By wrapping conductive materials (e.g., copper) around chaos crystals, I can harness these fields to create stabilizing barriers. This technique could protect nexuses from external disruptions while allowing natural energy flows to continue.

Quantum Chaos and the Uncertainty Principle

As the ley lines grew more unstable, Alaric began to notice an unsettling phenomenon. Objects near the nexuses seemed to flicker between states, their positions and shapes shifting subtly when viewed from different angles.

"It's like they're not fully here," Lira said, watching a rock that appeared to blur and sharpen in the corner of her vision.

"Quantum uncertainty," Alaric muttered, flipping through the grimoire. "The ley lines are destabilizing the fabric of reality itself. Particles—matter, magic, everything—are behaving like waves, their positions and states becoming probabilistic."

He added another entry to his journal.

Journal Entry: Quantum Chaos in Magic

The disturbances in the ley lines mirror quantum phenomena:

Wave-Particle Duality: Magic behaves both as a tangible force (waves) and a localized effect (particles).

Uncertainty Principle: The chaotic energy makes it impossible to precisely measure both the position and flow of magic within a nexus.

Entanglement: Disruptions in one nexus affect others across vast distances, suggesting a deep interconnectedness.

That night, as they camped beneath a sky streaked with auroras of chaotic magic, Alaric stared at the grimoire's map. The eastern nexus glowed faintly, but two more marks had begun to pulse—one far to the north, the other deep beneath the sea.

"This isn't just a crisis," Alaric said, his voice filled with quiet determination. "It's a system-wide collapse. If we don't restore balance soon, the ley lines won't just destabilize—they'll tear our world apart."

Lira placed a hand on his shoulder. "Then let's make sure that doesn't happen."

Alaric nodded, his resolve hardening. He would continue to study the nexus patterns, refining his understanding of the laws that governed both magic and the natural world. Chaos was not his enemy—it was a force to be understood, harnessed, and, ultimately, balanced.

*****

Alaric stood at the edge of the Crystal Glade, a place of breathtaking beauty hidden deep within a mist-shrouded forest. Towering crystals, some as tall as ancient oaks, jutted from the ground in irregular patterns. Their surfaces shimmered with internal light, each crystal pulsing in sync with the ley lines beneath his feet. The hum of magic resonated in the air, a low-frequency vibration that seemed to harmonize with his very heartbeat.

"This is the purest form of a nexus," Alaric murmured, kneeling beside a cluster of smaller crystals. He ran his fingers over their smooth surfaces, feeling the energy coursing through them like the current of a mighty river. "The ley lines converge here without chaos, creating a balance that sustains the entire glade."

Lira stood a few paces away, her gaze sweeping the crystalline forest. "It's beautiful, but it feels... fragile. Like one wrong step could break it."

Alaric nodded. "That's why nexuses like this are so rare. They're naturally self-regulating, but even a slight disruption in the ley lines could destabilize the entire area."

He pulled out his journal and began sketching the crystalline formations, annotating his observations.

Journal Entry: The Crystal Glade

The Crystal Glade is a natural nexus where the ley lines converge in perfect harmony. The crystals act as conduits and stabilizers, channeling elemental energies into a balanced flow. Their structure appears to follow geometric principles, resembling fractals in nature.

Physical Properties: The crystals are composed of an unknown material that resembles quartz but exhibits unique refractive properties.

Energy Conduction: The crystals amplify and distribute ley line energy, creating a localized equilibrium.

Theoretical Applications: If harnessed correctly, these crystals could serve as templates for stabilizing chaotic nexuses elsewhere.

Fireheart Mountain: The Nexus of Destruction

The ascent to Fireheart Mountain was grueling. The air grew hotter with every step, and the rocky terrain was riddled with fissures spewing jets of flame. The mountain's peak glowed ominously, a beacon of raw, unbridled power. Alaric and Lira approached cautiously, their Runestone Compass vibrating wildly.

"This nexus isn't just unstable—it's explosive," Alaric said, wiping sweat from his brow. "The fire energy here is overwhelming, completely drowning out the other elements."

As they neared the summit, a massive burst of flame erupted from the ground, forcing them to dive for cover. When the smoke cleared, they saw creatures emerging from the fissures—small, humanoid beings made of living flame. Their eyes burned with an intense orange glow, and they moved with the erratic energy of a wildfire.

"Flame Sprites," Alaric whispered. "Manifestations of pure fire energy. They're drawn to the chaos here."

The sprites didn't seem hostile, but their presence made the environment even more volatile. Alaric studied their movements, noting how they seemed to gravitate toward the fissures.

"The sprites are amplifying the energy surges," Alaric observed. "If we can redirect them—"

A sudden roar interrupted him. From the summit of the mountain emerged a colossal figure, its body wreathed in flames. It was a Fire Lord, a being of immense power from the Plane of Fire.

"We need to leave," Lira said urgently, pulling Alaric to his feet.

Journal Entry: Fireheart Mountain

Fireheart Mountain is a destructive nexus dominated by fire energy. The presence of Flame Sprites and a Fire Lord suggests a direct link to the Plane of Fire.

Energy Imbalance: The overabundance of fire energy creates chaotic surges, threatening the mountain's stability.

Plane Interaction: The Fire Lord's appearance indicates that the nexus acts as a gateway to the Elemental Plane of Fire.

Containment Strategy: Redirecting Flame Sprites to less volatile fissures could mitigate energy surges.

*****

The Abyssal Chasm was a vast rift in the earth, its depths obscured by a swirling mist that seemed to pulse with unnatural light. Alaric and Lira stood at its edge, peering into the void.

"This nexus feels... different," Alaric said, his voice tinged with unease. "It's not just elemental energy—it's something deeper. Dimensional."

As he spoke, the mist began to shift, revealing faint shapes moving within. Serpentine forms coiled and writhed in the depths, their translucent bodies shimmering like moonlight on water.

"Ethereal Serpents," Lira said, her voice hushed. "Guardians of dimensional rifts. They'll attack anything they perceive as a threat."

Alaric retrieved his Runestone Compass, its needle pointing directly into the chasm. "This nexus is a dimensional crossroad. The ley lines here connect not just places but planes."

He flipped open the grimoire, its pages shifting to reveal new diagrams. "This chasm might be part of the Astral Bridge—a network of pathways between dimensions. If we can understand its structure, we might be able to stabilize dimensional nexuses."

Journal Entry: The Abyssal Chasm

The Abyssal Chasm is a dimensional nexus guarded by Ethereal Serpents. Its energy flows are more complex than elemental nexuses, involving interdimensional currents.

Dimensional Pathways: The ley lines here act as conduits between planes, creating potential gateways.

Guardians: Ethereal Serpents maintain the rift's integrity, attacking intruders to preserve balance.

The Astral Bridge: This nexus may be part of a larger system connecting the Elemental Planes and other dimensions.

While mapping the ley lines near the chasm, Alaric discovered a hidden valley where fire and ice coexisted in perfect harmony. Fiery geysers erupted beside frozen lakes, and the air alternated between warm gusts and chilling breezes.

"This valley is a paradox," Alaric said, his breath visible in the cold air. "Fire and ice should cancel each other out, but here they coexist."

He studied the ley lines, noting how they formed a unique pattern—a double helix of fire and water energy. "The ley lines aren't opposing each other—they're intertwined. It's a self-regulating system."

As he explored further, Alaric stumbled upon an ancient altar carved from obsidian and ice. Runes covered its surface, glowing faintly with alternating red and blue light. He recognized some of the symbols from the grimoire.

"This altar was created to maintain the valley's balance," Alaric said. "It's an example of how ancient civilizations used ley lines to harmonize opposing forces."

Journal Entry: The Hidden Valley

The Hidden Valley is a unique nexus where fire and ice coexist in harmony. Its energy flows demonstrate the potential for balance in chaotic systems.

Interwoven Ley Lines: The double-helix pattern stabilizes conflicting elements, creating a self-sustaining equilibrium.

Ancient Altar: The runes on the altar suggest advanced knowledge of ley line manipulation.

Applications: This system could serve as a model for stabilizing other nexuses.

The Astral Bridge and the Plane of Fire

After weeks of study, Alaric returned to the Abyssal Chasm with a new plan. Using runes inspired by the altar in the Hidden Valley, he created a stabilizing circle around the rift. The Ethereal Serpents observed him warily but did not interfere.

When the runes activated, the rift stabilized, forming a clear portal. Alaric stepped through, finding himself in the Plane of Fire. The air was blisteringly hot, the sky a roiling sea of flame. Rivers of molten lava crisscrossed the landscape, and towering obsidian spires rose from the ground.

He encountered Flame Sprites and a Fire Lord, learning that the Plane of Fire was a realm of constant creation and destruction. Its energy was raw and unbridled, but Alaric saw patterns within the chaos—cycles of renewal that mirrored the ley lines' flows.

Journal Entry: The Plane of Fire

The Plane of Fire is a realm of intense elemental energy, governed by cycles of creation and destruction. Its connection to the ley lines influences nexuses like Fireheart Mountain.

Elemental Forces: Fire energy here is self-sustaining, feeding on its own cycles.

Dimensional Influence: The Plane of Fire's proximity to nexuses explains their volatility.

Insights: Understanding these cycles could help stabilize fire-dominated nexuses.

The Fire and Ice Valley

The hidden valley stretched before Alaric and Lira like a vision torn from myth. Jagged spires of obsidian jutted skyward alongside frozen waterfalls, their icy surfaces shimmering in the golden light of an unseen sun. Fiery geysers erupted at irregular intervals, sending streams of steam billowing into the air where they collided with glacial winds. The clash of elements created an otherworldly symphony—a hiss of steam, a crackle of fire, and the low groan of shifting ice.

"This place shouldn't exist," Lira murmured, her breath visible as she pulled her cloak tighter. "Fire and ice... they're supposed to destroy each other."

"And yet, here they are," Alaric replied, his voice filled with awe. He crouched by a pool of molten lava that bordered a frozen pond, dipping a finger into the cold water. "Look at this—the heat from the lava isn't melting the ice, and the cold from the pond isn't freezing the lava. The forces are in perfect balance."

The air itself seemed alive, charged with the opposing forces of fire and ice. Alaric could feel the ley lines beneath his feet, their currents intertwining like twin serpents, neither dominating the other. He pulled out his Runestone Compass, which glowed faintly as it aligned with the valley's unique energy.

"This valley is a nexus," Alaric said, standing. "But it's unlike any other I've seen. The ley lines here aren't chaotic or destructive—they're harmonized."

Lira gave him a wary look. "And what happens if that harmony breaks?"

Alaric glanced at the crystalline altar in the center of the valley, its obsidian and ice surfaces glowing faintly with alternating red and blue light. "That's what the altar is for. It's maintaining the balance."

*****

The altar stood at the heart of the valley, a monolith of obsidian entwined with frozen, translucent ice. Runes etched into its surface glowed faintly, their colors shifting between fiery orange and icy blue. Alaric approached cautiously, his journal open as he sketched its intricate patterns.

"This craftsmanship..." Alaric murmured, running his fingers over the runes. "It's ancient, but not crude. Whoever built this understood the ley lines better than anyone at the Grand Arcanum."

Lira crouched beside him, studying the runes with a frown. "These symbols—they're similar to the containment runes you've been using, but they're more complex. Do you think they could work for other nexuses?"

"Possibly," Alaric said, tracing one of the symbols. "These runes don't just contain energy—they redistribute it. They're designed to sustain equilibrium, not suppress chaos."

As he studied the altar, Alaric felt a strange resonance in the air. The valley's energy seemed to respond to the altar's presence, its fiery and icy forces drawn toward it in delicate balance. He added a new entry to his journal, annotating the runes and theorizing how they might be adapted for other nexuses.

Journal Entry: The Altar of Harmony

The altar in the Fire and Ice Valley is a masterwork of ley line manipulation, balancing opposing elemental forces.

Runic Patterns: The runes inscribed on the altar redistribute energy, maintaining equilibrium between fire and ice.

Ley Line Interaction: The altar acts as both a conduit and regulator, ensuring that neither element overwhelms the other.

Applications: These principles could be adapted for chaotic nexuses, provided the runes are calibrated to the specific elements involved.

The Crystal Spiders

As Alaric and Lira continued their exploration, they encountered a new inhabitant of the valley: crystalline spiders that shimmered like living jewels. The creatures ranged in size from small as a hand to as large as a horse, their translucent bodies refracting light into rainbows.

One of the smaller spiders scuttled toward them, its movements graceful despite its rigid, crystalline form. Its many legs clicked softly against the icy ground as it tilted its faceted head, observing them with eyes that glowed faintly.

"Don't make any sudden moves," Alaric whispered, holding out a hand to signal Lira to stay still. "I think it's curious, not hostile."

The spider approached cautiously, its legs moving with an almost mechanical precision. Alaric crouched, his heart pounding as he extended his hand. To his surprise, the spider brushed its body against his palm, its surface cool and smooth like polished quartz.

"They're drawn to the ley lines," Alaric said, watching as the spider scuttled away toward a nearby geyser. "Their bodies must act as conduits for the valley's energy."

Lira exhaled slowly, lowering her dagger. "They're beautiful. But if one of those horse-sized ones decides we're a threat, I'm not sticking around."

The Plane of Fire

Days later, Alaric and Lira returned to the Abyssal Chasm, where the stabilized portal shimmered faintly. Alaric's preparations had taken weeks of careful study, but now he was ready. With Lira watching his back, he stepped through the portal into the Plane of Fire.

The heat was immediate and oppressive, like stepping into a blazing furnace. The ground beneath his feet was blackened rock, crisscrossed by rivers of molten lava. The sky above was a roiling sea of flame, its light casting long, flickering shadows.

Flame Sprites darted through the air like fireflies, their bodies leaving trails of sparks. Nearby, a massive obsidian spire rose from the ground, its surface glowing with veins of molten energy.

"This place is alive with fire magic," Alaric said, his voice hoarse from the heat. "But it's not chaotic. It's... purposeful."

As they approached the spire, a deep rumble shook the ground. From the base of the spire emerged a Fire Lord, its massive form wreathed in flames. The being towered over them, its molten eyes glowing with ancient intelligence.

"Why do you trespass in my domain?" the Fire Lord boomed, its voice like an erupting volcano.

Alaric stepped forward, bowing slightly. "We seek knowledge. The ley lines in our world are destabilizing, and we believe your plane holds the answers we need to restore balance."

The Fire Lord regarded him for a long moment, its flames flickering. "Knowledge comes at a cost. If you wish to learn, you must prove your worth."

The Plane of Water

After surviving the Fire Lord's trial—a test of endurance and willpower—Alaric and Lira journeyed to the Plane of Water through another stabilized portal. The transition was jarring, the searing heat of the Plane of Fire replaced by the cool embrace of an endless ocean.

They stood on a coral reef that seemed to float in the middle of the sea. Above them, the water shimmered with the light of an unseen sun, and below, the depths were alive with bioluminescent creatures. Schools of glowing fish darted past, their movements synchronized like a single organism.

As they ventured deeper into the plane, they encountered Mist Elementals—ethereal beings that swirled like living clouds. Their forms were fluid and ever-changing, their voices a soft whisper that carried hints of ancient wisdom.

"We must tread carefully," Alaric said, watching as one of the elementals drifted closer. "These beings are tied to the ley lines, just like the Flame Sprites. If we disturb them—"

A deep roar echoed from the depths, and the water trembled. From the darkness below emerged a Leviathan, its massive form dwarfing the reef. Its eyes glowed like twin suns, and its scales shimmered with iridescent light.

"We've got company," Lira muttered, gripping her dagger.

Alaric took a deep breath, raising his hands. "We mean no harm," he called out, his voice steady despite his fear. "We seek only to understand."

The Leviathan regarded them for a moment before diving back into the depths, its presence leaving a trail of calm water in its wake.

Flashback: Journal Entry from an Ancient Mage

Excerpt from the Journal of Magister Valareth, Year 746

The ley lines are not mere rivers of energy—they are the threads of existence itself. To manipulate them is to touch the soul of creation. Yet, as I record this, I am haunted by the specter of my failure.

It began with a single fracture, a subtle disruption in the Spiral Nexus. The balance faltered, and Chaos seeped into the threads. At first, it was subtle—anomalies in the flow of time, storms that raged without end. But as the ley lines frayed, the anomalies became catastrophes. Whole cities were swallowed by the earth, their people screaming as the ground turned to shadow beneath their feet.

I tried to restore the balance. I failed.

Chaos is not the absence of Order; it is its adversary, a force that reacts violently to control. To force Chaos into submission is to ensure ruin. To guide it, however, is to court salvation.

Eldaryn on Chaos vs. Order

Eldaryn leaned against the ancient oak, his gaze fixed on the distant horizon where the Spiral Nexus pulsed faintly, a distant star in the twilight. "Chaos and Order," he began, his voice calm yet tinged with weariness. "They are not enemies. They are siblings, forever at odds, yet forever entwined."

Alaric frowned. "But if we stabilize the ley lines, won't that mean eliminating Chaos?"

"No," Eldaryn replied, shaking his head. "To stabilize the ley lines is not to destroy Chaos, but to embrace it. Chaos thrives in imbalance, but without it, Order stagnates. Magic itself is a testament to their coexistence—a wild force shaped by intent. The moment you try to silence Chaos completely, you risk silencing magic itself."

Lira, perched on a nearby boulder, folded her arms. "So how do we find balance?"

Eldaryn smiled faintly, his eyes shadowed with memories. "By listening. The ley lines will tell us what they need, if we are humble enough to hear them."

Chapter 8: Bridges Between Worlds

The Leviathan's retreat left an eerie silence over the reef. The gentle sway of the coral and the faint glow of bioluminescent fish returned, but the memory of the colossal creature's presence lingered in Alaric's mind. He scribbled hastily in his journal, documenting its immense form and the strange aura of intelligence it exuded.

Lira paced nearby, her boots splashing softly in the shallow water. "That thing could've swallowed us whole," she said, her voice still shaky. "Why didn't it?"

Alaric paused, his quill hovering over the page. "It sensed our intent. Or maybe... it wanted us to learn something."

"Learn what? How close we can get to being eaten?" Lira shot back, though the tension in her tone softened when Alaric chuckled.

"Not exactly," he said, closing his journal and standing. "The Leviathan didn't act out of malice. It's a guardian, tied to the nexus between our world and this one. If the ley lines collapse, creatures like that might spill into our realm—and it's unlikely they'd be so benevolent."

Lira frowned, crossing her arms. "So, you're saying we just got a glimpse of what happens if we fail?"

"Exactly," Alaric replied. "And we need to make sure it doesn't come to that."

The portal back to the Abyssal Chasm shimmered faintly, its edges rippling like water. Stepping through, Alaric felt the familiar pull of dimensional magic, a sensation like being stretched and compressed at the same time. He stumbled slightly as they emerged back into the chasm, the cool air a sharp contrast to the elemental planes they had visited.

The Ethereal Serpents circled above them, their translucent forms undulating like ribbons of light. Alaric and Lira moved carefully, avoiding sudden movements that might provoke the creatures.

"We've seen two planes now," Lira said, her voice low. "Fire and Water. But what about the others? Earth, Air, and whatever else might be out there?"

Alaric nodded thoughtfully. "Each plane must connect to our world through a nexus. The ley lines act as bridges, linking dimensions. If we stabilize our ley lines, we can prevent more rifts from opening—and keep these planes separate."

He glanced at his Runestone Compass, which vibrated faintly in his hand. The needle pointed toward the horizon, where a faint glow marked their next destination. "But first, we need to map out the rest of the nexuses."

The Astral Bridge

Days later, Alaric and Lira stood before a massive archway carved into the side of a mountain. The structure shimmered faintly, its surface inscribed with runes that pulsed with a soft, silver light. The air around it buzzed with energy, and the ley lines beneath their feet thrummed like a heartbeat.

"This must be the Astral Bridge," Alaric said, his voice filled with awe. "A gateway connecting all the nexuses."

The runes on the archway shifted as they approached, rearranging themselves into a language Alaric recognized from the grimoire. He reached out cautiously, his fingers brushing against the cool surface of the arch. The instant he made contact, the runes flared brightly, and the space within the arch transformed into a swirling vortex of light and shadow.

Lira stepped back instinctively, drawing her dagger. "Are we sure we want to go through that?"

"We don't have a choice," Alaric replied, his voice steady despite the nervous energy coursing through him. "If the Astral Bridge connects the nexuses, it might hold the key to stabilizing the ley lines."

Taking a deep breath, he stepped through the vortex. The sensation was disorienting, a kaleidoscope of colors and sounds that seemed to pull him in every direction at once. When the sensation passed, he found himself standing on a vast expanse of shimmering light, the ground beneath him a translucent bridge suspended in an endless void.

As They Cross the Astral Bridge

The shimmering expanse of the Astral Bridge stretched before them, its translucent surface pulsing faintly beneath their feet. Each step sent ripples of light cascading outward, as though the bridge itself were alive.

Alaric paused, a hand brushing the edge of the barrierless path. A strange sensation stirred within him—a low hum that seemed to emanate from his chest, resonating with the rhythm of his heartbeat. It wasn't sound, not in the traditional sense, but a vibration that flowed through his veins, weaving into his thoughts.

He stumbled slightly, his vision blurring. Golden threads stretched across an infinite void, weaving intricate patterns that seemed to shift and pulse in time with an unseen rhythm. They formed rivers, fractals, and spirals—then splintered and frayed, edges unraveling like an ancient tapestry on the verge of collapse.

"Do you feel that?" he murmured, turning to Lira.

She stopped, her gaze fixed ahead. The mist surrounding the bridge swirled in unnatural patterns, as if drawn to her presence. Her lips parted, and her voice was soft, almost reverent. "I've felt this before... It's like... the air is calling to me."

Alaric raised an eyebrow. "Calling? You've never mentioned this."

She hesitated, her fingers brushing the mist. "I thought it was just dreams. But now... I'm not so sure." The mist coiled around her hand like a living thing, and for a moment, her eyes seemed to glow faintly.

"Lira..." Alaric began, but his words were interrupted by a voice echoing across the bridge.

The voice was young yet heavy with wisdom, its tone playful but laced with an edge. "You're walking into a web, seeker."

Alaric and Lira turned sharply. A boy in black stood at the edge of the bridge, his dark eyes reflecting the glowing threads below. He wore a skull emblem on his chest, and his grin was equal parts mischievous and knowing.

"Who are you?" Lira demanded, stepping in front of Alaric.

"Pecos," the boy replied, bowing theatrically. "A friend of the ley lines—or what's left of them. The Spiral Nexus isn't just a wound, you know. It's a trap. And they're waiting for you."

Alaric's chest tightened. "They? The Veiled Order?"

Pecos' grin widened, but he said nothing. Instead, he pointed to the threads of light below the bridge. "Watch closely, seeker. The Spiral Nexus isn't just fraying—it's bleeding. And the more you meddle, the closer you'll come to unravelling everything."

As the vision of Pecos faded, Alaric's thoughts were drawn back to his last encounter with Kael. His rival's voice echoed in his mind, sharp with accusation.

"You think you're the only one who's ever questioned the texts?" Kael had snapped, his hands gripping the edge of a casting table. "You're not special, Deymorne. But you are dangerous. Poking at ley lines like they're harmless toys? You'll tear the world apart before you find the answers you're looking for."

Phelipandro's Return

A burst of light illuminated the bridge ahead, and Phelipandro appeared, its platinum feathers glowing like starlight. The ley line guardian's voice resonated in their minds, calm yet urgent.

"The ley lines are fraying," it said, its wings spreading to reveal threads of light that danced across its form. "Every fracture weakens the threads that bind dimensions. You must act quickly, Alaric. But beware—others seek the Spiral Nexus for their own ends. Their desires will unravel far more than magic."

Lira stepped forward, her brow furrowed. "What can we do?"

Phelipandro regarded his, its glowing eyes softening. "The ley lines do not merely need fixing. They need understanding. Each trial you face will reveal a truth, a fragment of their will. Only then can you restore balance."

Setting the Stage for the Trials

As the bridge stretched into the distance, Alaric and Lira exchanged a glance. The weight of the ley lines' sentience, the warning of Pecos, and Phelipandro's guidance settled over them like a shroud.

"This is bigger than just us," Alaric said quietly, his voice tinged with both awe and fear. "If the ley lines are alive, then every choice we make matters. Every step."

"And every mistake," Lira added, her voice steady despite the unease in her eyes.

Together, they took the next step forward, the mist parting to reveal the path to the Elemental Trials. The bridge pulsed beneath them, as if urging them onward.

The silence of the Astral Bridge pressed against Alaric and Lira like an invisible shroud as they moved forward. The ley lines' hum deepened, threading into their thoughts with growing intensity. Alaric felt it now—more than ever. It wasn't just energy; it was intention.

"Phelipandro," he began, his voice faltering as the goose-formed entity glided beside them. "If the ley lines are alive, why would they allow themselves to be fractured? Why not protect themselves?"

Phelipandro tilted its head, a faint glimmer of light tracing the edges of its platinum feathers. "The ley lines are not invulnerable, seeker. Their will is strong, but their existence is interconnected with all realms, all dimensions, and all life. They allow interaction and even exploitation to preserve the balance of creation."

Lira frowned. "That sounds... dangerous. They're putting themselves at risk."

Phelipandro turned its glowing gaze to her. "That is the nature of balance, child. The ley lines give freely, but when their will is ignored, chaos ensues. Your kind," it glanced pointedly at Alaric, "has long sought to harness their power without regard for harmony. The fractures are a result of such hubris."

Alaric's steps slowed. The words pierced him in a way he hadn't expected. He had always thought of magic as a puzzle to solve, a force to understand and control. The idea that it had agency—that it could resist—upended everything he knew.

"But if they're alive," he said carefully, "how do we... fix this? How do you 'heal' something that can think for itself?"

*****

"The nexuses," Phelipandro explained, "are anchors. Where the ley lines intersect, their energy pools, stabilizing the threads of existence. These points form nexuses, each attuned to a specific aspect of the multiverse—time, elements, emotion, and more."

Alaric nodded slowly, mentally cataloging the explanation. "And the Spiral Nexus?"

"The Spiral Nexus is unique," Phelipandro replied. "It is not an anchor. It is a convergence—a focal point where all ley lines meet and spiral outward into infinity. It binds the dimensions together. But its power is also its weakness. A fracture there ripples across every realm, magnifying the chaos."

"So the Veiled Order is targeting it," Lira said, her jaw tightening. "They're using the fractures to destabilize it."

"They seek control," Phelipandro confirmed, its tone grave. "But the Spiral Nexus cannot be controlled. It can only be balanced. And to restore that balance, you must first prove yourselves worthy."

As they walked, the mist around the bridge thickened, curling into shapes that whispered and flickered like distant memories. Lira slowed, her eyes narrowing.

"Do you see that?" she whispered, pointing to a figure just ahead—a shadowy outline that seemed to dance within the fog. It was small, childlike, and moved with unnatural fluidity.

Phelipandro glided to her side, its gaze fixed on the shape. "Ayiyi Mones," it said softly. "A guardian of innocence and perception. It is drawn to you, child."

Lira blinked. "Me? Why?"

"Perhaps it sees a reflection of itself," Phelipandro said cryptically. "Or perhaps it recognizes your potential."

The shadow stepped closer, resolving into a small child with luminous eyes and a wide, mischievous smile. It giggled—a sound that seemed to echo through the ley lines themselves.

"You're funny," the child said, pointing at Lira. "You don't know what you are yet."

Lira frowned. "What I am?"

Ayiyi Mones giggled again, spinning in place as the mist swirled around it. "You'll find out. But you have to listen. The air knows. The water knows. They're waiting for you."

The words struck something deep within her—a sensation she couldn't quite name but had felt before. It was like the pull of the ocean's tide or the rush of wind before a storm. She glanced at Alaric, who was watching intently.

"We don't have time for riddles," she said firmly, though her voice wavered slightly. "What do we need to do?"

The child tilted its head, its smile fading slightly. "Fix the broken pieces," it said. "But remember—they don't all want to be fixed."

The mist swirled violently as Ayiyi Mones vanished, and a new figure appeared—a man this time, dressed in black with a skull embroidered on his cloak. His eyes gleamed with a dark, knowing light.

"Pecos," Alaric murmured. He recognized the name from Phelipandro's earlier warnings.

"You're bold, seeker," Pecos said, his voice calm yet cutting. "But boldness won't save you. The Spiral Nexus is a wound, yes—but it's also a test. And not everyone passes."

"We're not looking to pass a test," Alaric replied. "We're trying to restore the ley lines."

Pecos laughed, a sharp, biting sound. "Restore them? Do you even know what that means? The ley lines have their own will, boy. Some fractures run deep because they want to. Not all broken things should be mended."

Alaric's jaw tightened. "If the Spiral Nexus fails, everything fails. Surely you don't want that."

Pecos stepped closer, his gaze piercing. "Do not presume to know what I want, seeker. The Spiral Nexus is not yours to fix. It's yours to understand. Fail that, and you'll only make the fractures worse."

As Pecos faded into the mist, Alaric felt the bridge begin to shift beneath their feet. The path ahead splintered into multiple threads, each one glowing with a different elemental hue.

Phelipandro spread its wings, its feathers catching the light. "The ley lines require proof of your understanding, seeker. Each trial ahead corresponds to a nexus plane. Only by facing these trials will you gain the knowledge needed to approach the Spiral Nexus."

Alaric exchanged a glance with Lira, her expression a mix of determination and unease. The mist swirled around them, the threads of light stretching into the unknown.

"Are you ready?" he asked quietly.

Lira took a deep breath, her hand brushing the mist once more. "Ready or not, we don't have a choice."

Together, they stepped forward, the threads of the ley lines pulsing beneath their feet like a heartbeat.

Chapter 9: The Trial of Earth

Into the Earth Nexus

The air thickened as the shimmering expanse of the Astral Bridge dissolved into rugged terrain. Massive stone pillars rose like jagged teeth from the earth, their surfaces etched with glowing runes that pulsed in a slow, steady rhythm.

Alaric's gaze darted to the intricate patterns, his fingers brushing a nearby pillar. "These are ancient, far older than the Grand Arcanum's records. The precision of these runes... it's like they weren't carved but grown."

"Or breathed into existence," Lira added. She crouched low, pressing her fingers into the soil. "It's alive, Alaric. The ground is breathing."

Alaric frowned, kneeling to inspect the runes more closely. His fingers traced a line of glyphs that seemed to shimmer under his touch. "Alive or not, something here doesn't want us to pass. These runes are defensive, layered to repel or entrap intruders."

"Let's hope they don't decide to turn on us," Lira said, straightening. Her gaze shifted to the labyrinth ahead, where paths twisted into a network of ever-shifting walls. The faint glow of crystalline veins provided the only light, casting eerie shadows.

"Stick close," Alaric said, flipping through his grimoire. He sketched a rune in the air, its golden lines lingering like smoke. "This will help stabilize the ground, but it won't hold forever."

"Good," Lira replied, stepping forward. "Because something tells me we're not alone here."

The Labyrinth Awakens

The first hour was tense but uneventful. Alaric's stabilization runes glowed faintly with each step, holding the labyrinth's shifting walls at bay. Yet the deeper they ventured, the more erratic the movements became. The ground trembled with increasing intensity, and the air grew colder.

"Something's wrong," Alaric muttered, his voice low. "The labyrinth is resisting. It's like it's learning to counter my runes."

Before Lira could respond, a deep, guttural growl echoed through the cavern. The sound reverberated through the walls, sending dust cascading from above.

"What was that?" Lira whispered, her hand instinctively gripping the hilt of her blade.

"Trouble," Alaric said grimly, flipping through his grimoire. He began inscribing runes on the ground, their golden light flaring brighter than before.

The growl came again, louder this time. From the shadows emerged two massive Earth Golems, their bodies forged from stone and crystal. Molten orange light glowed in their eyes as they lumbered forward, their footsteps shaking the ground.

"Lira, keep them busy!" Alaric shouted, his hands moving in a blur as he etched containment sigils into the ground. "I need time to immobilize them!"

"Busy, huh? Sure, I'll just ask them to tea," Lira muttered, unsheathing her blade. She darted forward, her movements quick and precise. The first golem swung its massive arm, but she rolled under the attack, slashing at its leg. Her blade struck the crystalline seam near its knee, sending shards flying.

"Alaric, their weak points are in the crystals!" she called out, dodging another swing.

"Got it!" Alaric replied, his containment sigil complete. The rune flared, and the ground beneath the nearest golem rippled, swallowing its legs and rooting it in place. The creature roared, struggling against the magical bind.

The second golem turned its attention to Alaric, its molten eyes narrowing. It raised both arms, slamming them down with earth-shaking force. Alaric barely leapt aside, the impact sending a shockwave that cracked the ground.

"Lira, now would be a great time to finish that one!" Alaric yelled, scrambling to his feet.

Lira sprang onto the immobilized golem, her blade flashing as it struck the crystal embedded in its chest. The crystal shattered with a deafening crack, and the golem collapsed, its body crumbling into rubble.

"On it!" she shouted, charging toward the second golem. Alaric, recovering his balance, quickly sketched a rune of force. The sigil crackled with energy as a bolt of golden light shot forth, striking the golem's chest and exposing its core.

Lira seized the opportunity, her blade slicing clean through the glowing crystal. The second golem faltered, then toppled with a thunderous crash.

As the dust settled, Alaric leaned against a wall, catching his breath. "Please tell me that was the last of them."

"Don't count on it," Lira replied, her eyes scanning the shifting walls ahead. "This place feels like it's just getting started."

A Test of Perception

As they ventured deeper, the labyrinth grew darker, the crystalline veins dimming until only faint pulses of light remained. The air was heavy, each step echoing with a low vibration that seemed to resonate within their bones.

"It's guiding us," Lira said, pausing to kneel on the ground. She closed her eyes, her hands pressed flat against the earth. "There's a rhythm to it... a pattern. It's like... a heartbeat."

Alaric watched her, his brow furrowed. "You're saying the labyrinth is alive?"

"Not alive exactly," she replied, her voice distant. "But aware. It's reacting to us."

Before Alaric could respond, a faint chuckle echoed through the chamber. He spun around, his heart racing. "Who's there?"

From the shadows stepped a figure—a boy dressed in black with a skull emblem on his chest. His dark eyes glinted with amusement, and his grin was sharp and unsettling.

"Pecos," the boy said, his tone light but laced with menace. "At your service."

"Great," Alaric muttered, his grip tightening on his grimoire. "Another cryptic guardian."

"Cryptic?" Pecos smirked, leaning against a nearby pillar. "You wound me, seeker. I'm just here to help. The labyrinth doesn't care about strength, you know. It cares about understanding."

"And if we don't understand?" Lira asked, her tone wary.

"Then you'll never leave," Pecos replied simply. He gestured to two paths that had appeared behind him—one glowing faintly green, the other shrouded in darkness. "Two paths. Two choices. One leads closer to the nexus, the other... to something less pleasant."

Alaric exchanged a glance with Lira. "What's the catch?"

Pecos's grin widened. "No catch. Just a test. But choose wisely."

The Nexus Heart

The path they chose led them to a vast chamber, its walls lined with glowing crystals that pulsed like living veins. In the center, a massive thread of light twisted upward, entwined with ancient roots that glowed faintly green.

"This must be the heart of the nexus," Alaric said, awe filling his voice.

Lira stepped forward, her hand outstretched. The thread pulsed in response, its light growing brighter. "It's alive," she murmured. "And it's listening."

Before they could approach further, the ground trembled violently. From the shadows emerged an Earth Guardian, its body a towering mass of stone and glowing crystal. Intricate runes adorned its form, and its amber eyes burned with intensity.

"This is it," Alaric said, flipping through his grimoire. "The final test."

The battle was brutal. Alaric used his runes to create barriers and deflect attacks, while Lira danced around the guardian's massive strikes, her blade seeking out its crystalline weak points. Each hit sent shockwaves through the chamber, the walls threatening to collapse.

With a final coordinated effort, Alaric unleashed a concentrated burst of magical force, cracking the guardian's chest crystal. Lira leapt forward, driving her blade into the exposed core. The guardian roared one last time before crumbling into rubble.

The nexus thread pulsed brighter, enveloping the chamber in a soft glow. The air grew calm, and the labyrinth stilled.

"You've proven yourselves," a voice echoed—Pecos, now appearing as an older man. "But this is only the beginning."

Resolution

As they left the labyrinth, Alaric and Lira reflected on the trial's lessons. The jade amulet they found now glowed faintly, a symbol of their connection to the ley lines.

"The labyrinth wasn't just a challenge," Alaric said. "It was trying to teach us something."

"And I think we're starting to understand," Lira replied, her voice steady.

Ahead, the path to the Air nexus stretched into the distance, the winds howling faintly.

"Ready for the next one?" Alaric asked.

Lira smiled, her hand brushing the jade amulet. "Let's find out."

The glow of the jade amulet bathed Alaric's fingers as he inspected its intricate carvings. The runes on its surface shifted faintly, alive with energy that pulsed in time with the rhythmic vibrations of the nexus thread.

"This isn't just a key," Alaric murmured, tilting the amulet to catch the shifting light. "It's attuned to the ley lines."

"Attuned how?" Lira asked, stepping beside him. Her gaze lingered on the thread of light entwined with the ancient roots at the chamber's center.

"It's responding to the thread," Alaric said, his brow furrowing. "Like it's part of the same system. These runes... they're designed to amplify stabilization magic, but they're incomplete. If I could decipher the rest, I might be able to—"

The ground shuddered violently beneath them, cutting him off. The light of the nexus thread flared, illuminating the chamber with a brilliant green glow. The roots around it pulsed as though alive, coiling tighter around the thread.

"What's happening?" Lira demanded, drawing her blade.

"It's reacting to us," Alaric said, his voice tight. "We must have triggered something."

From the far side of the chamber, the rubble of the fallen Earth Guardian began to stir. Shards of stone and crystal floated upward, coalescing into a new form. This creature was smaller but more agile, its jagged limbs snapping into place with deadly precision.

Alaric cursed, fumbling for his grimoire. "Another one? The labyrinth doesn't know when to quit."

"This one's different," Lira said, her eyes narrowing. She stepped forward, blade at the ready. "Stay back—I'll keep it occupied. Figure out what's wrong with the thread."

"Got it," Alaric said, flipping through the grimoire. The pages fluttered, glowing faintly as he chanted under his breath. Golden sigils formed in the air around him, weaving into a protective barrier.

The creature lunged, its movements sharp and deliberate. Lira barely had time to raise her blade before it struck, its crystalline claws raking against the stone floor where she had stood moments before.

"You're faster than the last one," she muttered, rolling to her feet. She darted forward, aiming for the glowing crystal at its chest, but the creature twisted away with inhuman speed.

It retaliated with a sweeping strike, forcing her to leap back. The edge of its claw grazed her arm, leaving a shallow cut.

"Lira, keep it distracted!" Alaric called, his focus on the nexus thread. He traced the shifting runes on the jade amulet, his mind racing to piece together their meaning. "These patterns—they're a stabilization matrix. If I can finish it, I might be able to calm the thread."

"Then do it faster!" Lira snapped, blocking another attack. Her blade clashed against the creature's crystalline arm, sending sparks flying. She spun, using her momentum to drive the blade into its side. The strike chipped away at the crystal, but the creature barely faltered.

It roared, its molten eyes glowing brighter as it lashed out with both arms. Lira ducked, the force of the attack sending a shockwave through the chamber. She stumbled, her foot catching on loose rubble.

The creature lunged, its claws poised to strike.

"Enough!" Alaric shouted, slamming the jade amulet into the ground. The runes on its surface flared, and a wave of energy rippled outward. The creature froze mid-strike, its limbs trembling as the light of the nexus thread pulsed in rhythm with the amulet.

"What did you do?" Lira asked, scrambling to her feet.

"I synchronized the amulet with the thread," Alaric said, his voice strained. Sweat dripped from his brow as he held the amulet in place. "It's temporarily stabilizing the nexus—but I can't hold it for long."

The creature roared again, breaking free of the energy's grip. It turned its glowing eyes on Alaric, its movements erratic as if the stabilization had weakened its form.

"Lira, the crystal in its chest," Alaric said, his voice tight. "That's its anchor. Destroy it now!"

Without hesitation, Lira charged forward. The creature swung its arm to intercept her, but she ducked under the blow, her blade flashing as it struck the crystal dead center. The impact sent a sharp, ringing sound through the chamber, and cracks spiderwebbed across the creature's body.

With a final roar, the guardian shattered, its pieces falling lifelessly to the ground.

The chamber fell silent except for the steady hum of the nexus thread. Lira approached Alaric, her blade still in hand. "Is it over?"

"For now," Alaric replied, his hands still pressed against the jade amulet. "But the thread isn't fully stabilized. The roots are constricting it, interfering with its natural flow."

"What do we do?" Lira asked, kneeling beside him.

Alaric hesitated, his eyes scanning the runes on the amulet. "If I can attune the amulet to the thread's energy, it should loosen the roots' grip. But it'll take precise calibration—and I'll need your help."

Lira nodded. "Tell me what to do."

"Place your hands on the thread," Alaric instructed. "You have a stronger connection to the ley lines than I do. If you focus, you might be able to guide the energy flow."

Lira hesitated, her gaze flickering to the glowing thread. "What if it doesn't work?"

"It will," Alaric said firmly. "I trust you."

Taking a deep breath, Lira reached out. Her hands trembled as they made contact with the thread, but the moment she touched it, a wave of warmth surged through her. The vibrations she had felt earlier intensified, resonating through her entire body.

"It's... alive," she whispered. "I can feel it."

"Good," Alaric said, his voice steady. "Now, guide it. Imagine the energy flowing freely, like a river breaking through a dam."

Lira closed her eyes, focusing on the vibrations. Slowly, the roots around the thread began to loosen, their glow dimming as the thread's light grew stronger.

"It's working," Alaric said, his relief evident. "Keep going."

When the last root fell away, the nexus thread pulsed brightly, its energy stabilizing. The jade amulet in Alaric's hand grew cool, its runes fading.

"It's done," Alaric said, leaning back with a sigh. "The nexus is stable—for now."

Lira stepped away from the thread, her expression unreadable. "That was... different. It wasn't just a trial. It felt like the nexus was trying to tell us something."

The grinding of stone against stone reverberated through the cavern as Alaric and Lira faced the Earth Golem, its massive form towering over them. The creature's emerald eyes glowed with the raw energy of the ley lines, pulsating in rhythm with the shifting earth beneath their feet. Each step it took sent tremors through the ground, dislodging chunks of rock from the cavern walls.

Alaric tightened his grip on his staff, his mind racing to recall the stabilization rune sequence he had used earlier. But the labyrinth's adaptation had rendered his previous attempts futile. He stole a glance at Lira, who was already forming a barrier of energy between them and the advancing Golem. Her usually confident demeanor was now tinged with doubt.

"It's learning," Alaric muttered. "Every time we use magic, the labyrinth adapts. We need to outthink it."

"Outthink a labyrinth? Brilliant," Lira snapped, sweat beading on her forehead as she maintained the barrier. "Any genius ideas, or are you just going to narrate our demise?"

Alaric ignored her sarcasm and dropped to one knee, pressing his palm to the cavern floor. He could feel the ley lines—fractured, chaotic, and alive. The Golem wasn't just a guardian; it was a manifestation of the labyrinth itself, a sentinel created to protect the Earth Nexus.

"It's drawing power directly from the ley lines," Alaric said, his voice steady despite the chaos. "If we disrupt the flow, we can weaken it."

Lira cast him a skeptical glance. "And how do you plan to disrupt something ancient and alive?"

"By making it unstable," Alaric replied. He began sketching a rune in the dirt, his movements precise despite the shaking ground. "I'll create a feedback loop. It won't destroy the ley lines, but it might confuse the Golem long enough for us to reach the Nexus."

Lira hesitated, then nodded. "Fine. Just tell me what you need me to do."

"Keep it distracted," Alaric said, his voice tinged with urgency. "And stay alive."

With a grim smile, Lira dispelled her barrier and surged forward, her twin blades shimmering with energy. She darted around the Golem with practiced agility, her strikes carving shallow grooves into its stony exterior. The creature roared, its massive arms swinging in wide arcs, but Lira's nimbleness kept her just out of reach.

Meanwhile, Alaric completed the rune sequence, his fingers tracing the final line with deliberate care. The symbols glowed faintly, their energy resonating with the fractured ley lines beneath the cavern. He pressed his hand to the center of the rune, channeling his magic into it.

The effect was immediate. The ground beneath the Golem trembled violently, cracks spiderwebbing outward as the feedback loop disrupted the ley lines' flow. The creature staggered, its glowing eyes flickering as it struggled to maintain its form.

"It's working!" Lira shouted, dodging another swing. "Whatever you're doing, keep at it!"

But Alaric knew the effect wouldn't last. The feedback loop was unstable by design, a temporary reprieve at best. "We need to move!" he called to Lira. "The Nexus is just ahead!"

Lira nodded and broke into a sprint, her blades still glowing as she slashed at the Golem's legs to slow its pursuit. Alaric followed, his heart pounding as the unstable ground shifted beneath him. The glowing aura of the Earth Nexus came into view, a swirling vortex of green and gold light that seemed both inviting and forbidding.

The Golem let out a deafening roar, its form destabilizing as the feedback loop continued to disrupt the ley lines. Chunks of its body crumbled away, but it still pursued them with relentless determination. Alaric and Lira reached the Nexus just as the creature's massive hand swiped at them, narrowly missing by mere inches.

Standing before the Nexus, Alaric felt the overwhelming power of the ley lines coursing through it. He could see the intricate patterns of energy weaving together, their harmony disrupted by the labyrinth's chaotic influence.

"What now?" Lira asked, her voice breathless but steady.

Alaric raised his staff, his mind racing. "We stabilize it," he said. "If we can restore balance to the ley lines here, it should weaken the labyrinth's control over the Nexus."

"And how do we do that?"

"Together."

Lira hesitated, then placed her hands over his on the staff. The two of them began channeling their magic into the Nexus, their energies merging as they worked to synchronize with the ley lines. The process was grueling, the chaotic energy resisting their efforts at every turn. But slowly, the patterns began to stabilize, the fractured lines weaving back together into a cohesive flow.

The Golem, now barely holding its form, let out one final roar before collapsing into a heap of inert stone. The ground beneath the Nexus ceased its tremors, and the swirling vortex of light grew calm and steady.

Alaric and Lira stepped back, their breaths heavy as they surveyed their work. The Earth Nexus now glowed with a serene energy, its power no longer tainted by the labyrinth's chaos.

"We did it," Lira said, a hint of disbelief in her voice.

Alaric managed a weak smile. "Barely."

But their relief was short-lived. As the Nexus stabilized, a faint hum filled the cavern, growing steadily louder. A figure emerged from the shadows, their presence radiating authority and menace. Pecos, their enigmatic guide, stood before them, his eyes fixed on the Nexus.

"Impressive," Pecos said, his voice smooth but laced with something unspoken. "You've proven yourselves worthy—for now."

Lira stepped forward, her blades still drawn. "What do you want, Pecos?" she demanded.

Pecos smirked. "To ensure you understand the stakes," he said. He gestured to the Nexus. "This is just one piece of the puzzle. The Spiral Nexus... it will test you in ways you cannot imagine. And failure there will mean far more than your lives."

Alaric frowned, his grip on his staff tightening. "What do you know about the Spiral Nexus?"

Pecos's expression grew serious. "Enough to know that your journey is far from over. The ley lines are not just a source of power; they are the lifeblood of this world. And they are unraveling. Every step you take brings you closer to the truth—and to the sacrifices that truth demands."

With that, Pecos turned and disappeared into the shadows, leaving Alaric and Lira alone before the glowing Nexus. They exchanged a glance, the weight of his words settling over them.

"Do you think he's right?" Lira asked quietly.

Alaric didn't answer immediately. He looked at the Nexus, its steady glow a reminder of their victory—and of the challenges still ahead. "I don't know," he admitted. "But we can't stop now. The Spiral Nexus... we have to reach it. For the ley lines. For everyone."

Lira nodded, her resolve hardening. "Then let's make sure we're ready."

As they turned to leave the cavern, the Earth Nexus pulsed gently, its energy a silent acknowledgment of their efforts. But the faint hum in the air—a reminder of the labyrinth's ever-present danger—lingered, echoing in their minds as they prepared for the trials yet to come.

Chapter 10: The Trial of Air

The Earth Nexus lay behind them, its once-fractured energy now stable, its pulse rhythmic and steady. The jade amulet in Alaric's hand felt cold, its runes dormant. He turned it over, the intricate carvings catching the dim light of the fading labyrinth.

"We stabilized it," Alaric murmured, though his voice held no triumph. His brow furrowed as he stared at the nexus thread's faint glow in the distance. "But the ley lines didn't just accept us. They... tested us."

"They're not tools," Lira said quietly. She leaned against a crystalline wall, her hand absently tracing the shallow cut on her arm from the Earth Guardian. "Maybe they never were."

Alaric sighed, closing his grimoire. "If the nexuses are alive, then every fracture we mend is as much negotiation as repair. But there's something else at play here."

The air around them began to shift, the temperature dropping sharply. Alaric's vision blurred, and the jade amulet pulsed faintly in his grip. His surroundings darkened, the labyrinth dissolving into a swirl of shadow and flame. Voices echoed, faint at first, then growing louder.

Alaric stood in a vast, dark chamber, its walls inscribed with glowing runes that pulsed like dying embers. In the center, a figure clad in flowing robes argued with a group of shadowed silhouettes. Their faces were obscured, but their voices carried a chilling conviction.

"The ley lines are shackled," the robed figure said, slamming a staff into the ground. "They bind us to the whims of nature, limiting our potential. If we rewrite their structure, we can control the flow of magic, shape reality to our will."

"And risk collapsing the Spiral Nexus?" one of the shadows hissed. "The threads that hold this world together are not meant to be tampered with!"

The robed figure turned sharply, their voice sharp and cold. "You cling to balance like a crutch. Progress demands sacrifice. The ley lines are tools, not masters."

The vision shifted, the chamber dissolving into chaos. Cracks formed in the walls, spilling radiant light and shadow. The ley lines themselves seemed to writhe in pain, their threads fraying and snapping. A voice boomed through the chaos, its words indistinct but heavy with warning.

"Alaric!" Lira's voice broke through the vision, pulling him back to the labyrinth. He staggered, clutching the amulet as its glow faded.

"What did you see?" she asked, her eyes wide with concern.

Alaric swallowed hard. "The Veiled Order... they don't just want to use the ley lines—they want to rewrite them. To reshape magic itself."

"And the Spiral Nexus?" Lira pressed.

"They know it's dangerous," Alaric said, his voice low. "But they think it's worth the risk."

The air grew colder as they approached the next nexus, the faint sound of wind howling through unseen corridors. Pecos was waiting for them, leaning against a jagged stone pillar. This time, he appeared older—closer to Alaric's age, his dark eyes gleaming with mischief.

"Well, well," Pecos drawled. "You survived the Earth Nexus. Congratulations. But don't get too comfortable."

Alaric glared at him. "We don't have time for your games. What's the next trial?"

Pecos smirked, stepping closer. "Patience, seeker. The Air Nexus will test more than your strength or knowledge. It will test your loyalty."

Lira stiffened. "Loyalty to what?"

"To each other," Pecos said, his grin fading. His gaze turned serious, his voice softening. "The Air Nexus doesn't care about power or skill. It cares about trust. Fail that, and it won't just reject you—it will destroy you."

"Why are you telling us this?" Alaric demanded, his fists clenching. "What do you gain from helping us?"

Pecos tilted his head, his grin returning. "Who said I'm helping? Consider it... a warning."

With that, Pecos faded into the shadows, leaving Alaric and Lira alone.

The entrance to the Air Nexus loomed ahead, a swirling vortex of wind and light suspended in midair. Alaric knelt by the edge, sketching runes in the dirt while flipping through his grimoire.

"The gravitational shifts will be unpredictable," he muttered, jotting down notes. "I'll need to design runes to anchor us, but they'll have to adjust dynamically to the flow of the winds."

Lira paced nearby, her arms crossed. She stopped suddenly, staring at the vortex. "It's calling to me," she said softly.

Alaric looked up. "What do you mean?"

Lira hesitated, her hand brushing against the jade amulet she now wore. "It's like the Earth Nexus. I can feel... something. A rhythm. A pull."

Alaric frowned, studying her. "You might be more connected to the ley lines than we realized."

"Or more connected than I want to be," Lira muttered. She shook her head, refocusing. "What do you need me to do?"

Alaric handed her a small vial of glowing liquid. "Place this on the nexus's outer edge. It'll stabilize the wind long enough for me to adjust the runes."

Lira nodded, taking the vial. "Let's hope this works."

As they prepared to enter the vortex, a familiar voice rang out.

"Deymorne!" Kael's sharp tone cut through the air.

Alaric turned to see his rival approaching, his robes torn and his expression furious. "Kael? What are you doing here?"

"Cleaning up your mess," Kael snapped, gesturing to the swirling vortex. "Do you have any idea how unstable the ley lines have become since you started meddling? You're making things worse."

Alaric stepped forward, his jaw tight. "I'm stabilizing them. The nexuses were already fractured."

"And you think you're the one to fix them?" Kael sneered. "You're reckless. The ley lines need balance, not brute force."

Their argument escalated, Kael's accusations stoking Alaric's frustration. In a moment of anger, Kael reached into his bag and hurled a crystal into the vortex. The winds surged violently, the vortex expanding and destabilizing.

"What did you do?" Lira shouted as the ground trembled.

"Showing you what happens when you interfere!" Kael spat before disappearing into the shadows.

The Air Nexus: Trial of Trust

The vortex expanded, pulling Alaric and Lira into its chaotic center. They found themselves suspended in an inverted tornado, the ground far below and the sky above twisting unnaturally.

Gravity shifted unpredictably, sending them tumbling. Alaric managed to stabilize himself with a hastily drawn rune, but Lira was thrown further into the storm.

"Lira!" Alaric shouted, sketching another rune to anchor himself before leaping after her.

The storm elemental emerged from the vortex's core, a massive, shifting entity of wind and light. It roared, its chaotic energy threatening to tear them apart.

"We have to calm it!" Alaric yelled, his voice barely audible over the howling winds. "Focus on the rhythm of the storm—it's alive!"

Lira closed her eyes, letting the winds guide her. She reached out, her movements synchronized with the elemental's shifting form. Slowly, the storm began to stabilize, its energy resonating with her touch.

Alaric used the moment to complete a binding rune, anchoring the elemental's chaotic energy to the jade amulet. The vortex began to shrink, its violent winds fading into a gentle breeze.

As the Air Nexus stabilized, Alaric and Lira collapsed on the now-solid ground. Alaric pulled out his journal, documenting the encounter.

"The storm elemental was not inherently chaotic," he wrote. "It reflected the instability of the ley lines, its actions mirroring the fractures in the nexus. Creatures like this are a natural extension of the ley lines, not separate entities."

Lira glanced over his shoulder. "What does that mean for the next trials?"

Alaric closed the journal, his expression grim. "It means the ley lines aren't just testing us. They're teaching us."

Ahead, the path to the next nexus stretched into the distance, its faint glow illuminating the way forward.

"Ready?" Lira asked, standing.

Alaric nodded, the jade amulet pulsing faintly in his hand. "Let's see what's next."

The Air Nexus pulsed faintly now, but the storm elemental still loomed, its body twisting unpredictably between torrents of wind and flickers of light. As the vortex settled slightly, Alaric could see its core—a spinning crystalline shard suspended within the maelstrom.

Lira took a cautious step forward, her hand gripping the jade amulet around her neck. "It's not attacking. Not yet."

"That doesn't mean it won't," Alaric said, flipping through his grimoire. "The core... it's resonating with the ley lines, just like the Earth Nexus thread. We need to stabilize it."

The elemental's roar cut through the air, its body surging toward them. Lira darted back, her reflexes barely keeping her ahead of the attack. Alaric sketched a quick rune in the air, the golden lines expanding into a protective barrier that deflected the elemental's next strike.

"Not inherently chaotic, huh?" Lira shouted, her voice strained as she kept moving.

"It's reacting to us," Alaric said, his voice tight. "We're intruding."

The elemental shifted, its form flickering. In an instant, its limbs elongated into sharp tendrils of light, striking the ground around them. The force shattered the floor into fragments that floated in the unstable gravity field, creating an obstacle course of drifting platforms.

"Lira, get to the core!" Alaric yelled, his eyes scanning the environment for a stable path. "I'll keep it distracted."

"Distracted?" Lira glanced back as the elemental turned its glowing eyes on Alaric. "You're insane!"

"Go!" he shouted, raising his grimoire. His hands moved in a blur, inscribing runes into the air. A burst of golden light shot toward the elemental, striking its form and drawing its attention. It roared, its limbs shifting into jagged spikes as it charged him.

Lira didn't hesitate. She leapt onto one of the floating platforms, her boots skidding slightly on the uneven surface. The jade amulet pulsed against her chest, its light resonating faintly with the core. She focused on the rhythm she felt in the air—a steady pulse that matched her heartbeat.

As she leapt from platform to platform, Lira felt the wind shift around her. It wasn't random; it was guiding her. The air wrapped around her, lifting her just enough to make the longer jumps.

"It's helping me," she murmured, a hint of awe in her voice.

Below, Alaric was locked in a desperate struggle with the elemental. His runes flared, creating barriers and pulses of energy to keep the creature at bay. "Lira, I could really use some good news right about now!"

"I'm almost there!" she called back. The core's glow grew brighter as she approached, its energy pulsing in time with the amulet's. She reached out, her fingers brushing the spinning shard.

The moment she touched it, the world shifted. A vision overwhelmed her senses—endless skies filled with swirling currents of air, each one a thread of light connecting distant nexuses. She saw the ley lines as veins of magic, their energy flowing freely until something disrupted the harmony. Fractures spread like cracks in glass, their jagged edges leaking chaos into the system.

"The lines aren't broken," she whispered. "They're blocked. Misaligned."

The vision faded, and she found herself back in the nexus, her hand still on the core. The elemental froze, its form flickering as if waiting.

"Alaric!" she called. "I know what to do!"

Alaric deflected another attack, sweat dripping down his face. "Anytime, Lira!"

"The elemental isn't our enemy," she said, her voice steady. "It's part of the nexus. I need your help to align the ley lines."

Alaric hesitated, then nodded. "Tell me what to do."

Lira closed her eyes, focusing on the rhythm she'd felt in the vision. "The core is the key. You need to bind it to the ley lines' natural flow."

Alaric flipped through his grimoire, his fingers moving rapidly over the pages. "A binding rune won't hold—it needs to adapt dynamically to the shifts."

"Use the amulet," Lira said. "It's already attuned."

Alaric glanced at the amulet around his neck, then quickly sketched a rune on its surface. The jade glowed brightly, its light merging with the core's. The elemental roared again, but this time, its movements were slower, less aggressive.

"It's working!" Alaric shouted. "Keep steady!"

Lira held her ground, her hand still on the core. The energy around them pulsed faster, the air vibrating with intensity. Alaric inscribed the final rune, the light surging outward as the core stabilized. The elemental dissolved into a gentle breeze, its energy merging with the nexus.

The vortex stilled, the platforms settling into a solid floor. The Air Nexus pulsed softly, its energy flowing freely once more.

Lira sank to her knees, her breathing heavy. The jade amulet pulsed faintly against her chest, its light dim but steady.

"You did it," Alaric said, his voice filled with relief as he approached. He knelt beside her, placing a hand on her shoulder. "You stabilized the nexus."

"We stabilized it," she corrected, managing a faint smile. "The ley lines... they're alive, Alaric. They want balance, not control."

Alaric nodded, pulling out his journal. He scribbled furiously, documenting the elemental's behavior and the connection between the core and the ley lines. "The storm elemental wasn't inherently chaotic. It reflected the state of the nexus—just like the Earth Guardian. These creatures are extensions of the ley lines, not separate entities."

Lira stood slowly, her gaze fixed on the now-calm nexus. "If that's true, then what happens when we reach the Spiral Nexus? What kind of creature would it manifest?"

Alaric didn't answer, his mind already racing with possibilities.

*****

As they left the Air Nexus, the path ahead grew darker, the faint glow of the next nexus visible in the distance. Alaric and Lira paused at the edge, their exhaustion evident.

"We're not just stabilizing ley lines," Lira said quietly. "We're learning from them. Every trial changes us."

Alaric glanced at her, his expression thoughtful. "And we're not the only ones trying to change them. The Veiled Order isn't just manipulating the ley lines—they're exploiting their connection to these creatures."

"Then we'll have to stop them," Lira said firmly.

Alaric smiled faintly. "Let's just survive the next trial first."

Ahead, the path twisted into shadow, the faint sound of rushing water echoing through the darkness. The Water Nexus awaited.

The Air Nexus behind them seemed to hum faintly as if its restored balance rippled through the surrounding ley lines. Alaric paused, glancing back one last time. The storm elemental's energy lingered, visible only as faint trails of light drifting upward into the sky.

"It feels... different," Lira said, her voice thoughtful. "Like it's watching us."

Alaric nodded, his hand resting on the jade amulet around his neck. "Maybe it is. Or maybe it's just relieved the flow is restored."

Lira gave him a sidelong glance, her brow furrowed. "Do you think the ley lines... feel emotions? Like relief? Or anger?"

Alaric hesitated. "I don't know. But whatever they feel, they're definitely trying to communicate."

Their conversation was interrupted by a soft crackle in the air. A translucent figure materialized in front of them, faintly glowing like the afterimage of lightning. Its form shifted between a humanoid silhouette and wisps of cloud-like tendrils.

"What now?" Lira muttered, raising her blade instinctively.

The figure didn't attack. Instead, it extended a hand, its voice a low, resonant whisper that seemed to come from all directions at once. "Travelers of the ley, you tread paths not meant for mortal feet. Each step you take binds you tighter to the weave. Choose wisely, for threads fray with both intention and ignorance."

Alaric took a cautious step forward. "Who are you?"

The figure's form flickered, its edges dissolving and reforming. "I am an echo, a fragment of the ley lines' memory. Your actions ripple across the weave, shaping futures yet unseen."

"And the Veiled Order?" Alaric asked. "What do they want?"

"They seek to rewrite what cannot be rewritten. But the ley lines do not forget. Nor do they forgive."

Before Alaric could ask more, the echo faded, leaving behind only the faint hum of the restored nexus.

*****

By the time they reached a stable section of the path, the faint glow of the next nexus was still a distant speck on the horizon. The air was cooler here, the winds carrying the scent of water.

"We should rest," Alaric said, glancing at Lira. She looked as exhausted as he felt, her movements sluggish after the trial's intensity.

They set up a small camp on a flat stretch of rock, lighting a modest fire. Lira leaned against a boulder, her blade resting across her lap as she stared into the flames.

"You were right back there," Alaric said after a long silence. "About the ley lines helping us. I couldn't have stabilized the core without you."

Lira shrugged, her expression unreadable. "It wasn't just me. The ley lines... they wanted to be heard. I just listened."

Alaric opened his journal, scribbling notes about the trial. "The way you interacted with the nexus... it's not something I've seen before. I think your connection to the ley lines is deeper than either of us realized."

"Or it's just dumb luck," Lira said, though her tone lacked conviction.

Alaric shook his head. "It's not luck. You felt the rhythm of the nexus. You understood it in a way I couldn't."

Lira looked up, her expression softening. "Maybe. But if we're going to survive the next trial, we'll need more than just understanding."

As they rested, faint movements in the shadows beyond the fire caught Alaric's eye. He sat up, reaching for his grimoire.

"Do you see that?" he whispered.

Lira tensed, her hand on her blade. "What is it?"

From the darkness emerged a pair of shimmering creatures, their forms shifting between solidity and transparency. They were slender, with elongated limbs and faintly glowing eyes. Each movement left behind trails of light, like ripples in water.

"Arcane phantasms," Alaric breathed. He flipped to a blank page in his journal, quickly sketching their forms. "They're rare... creatures attuned to multiple elements. They must be drawn to the nexus energy."

The phantasms watched them curiously, their movements fluid and graceful. One stepped closer, its translucent form flickering as it sniffed the air around Alaric.

"They're not hostile," Lira said, lowering her blade slightly. "They're... curious."

Alaric nodded, jotting down notes about their behavior. "They're probably remnants of the ley lines' influence. Creatures like this only form where the elements converge."

The second phantasm tilted its head, emitting a soft chime-like sound. Alaric felt a faint tug at his grimoire as if the creature was drawn to the magic within it.

Lira extended a hand cautiously, and the first phantasm approached her, its glowing eyes studying her intently. "They're beautiful," she said softly.

"They're a reminder," Alaric said, his tone thoughtful. "The ley lines don't just connect magic. They create life."

The phantasms lingered for a while longer before fading back into the shadows, leaving the campfire crackling quietly.

The Path to the Water Nexus

The following morning, the journey resumed. The terrain shifted gradually, the rocky path giving way to smooth stone veined with faint traces of moisture. The sound of rushing water grew louder with each step.

"The Water Nexus must be close," Lira said, her tone cautious. "I can feel the air getting heavier."

Alaric nodded, studying the shifting patterns of light beneath their feet. "It's going to be different from the Earth and Air Nexuses. Water is about adaptability, fluidity. We'll need to think on our feet."

Ahead, the path opened into a vast cavern filled with cascading waterfalls and shimmering pools. The nexus pulsed faintly at the cavern's center, surrounded by swirling mist that reflected the light in dazzling patterns.

"It's beautiful," Lira said, stepping closer to the edge of a pool.

"Beautiful but dangerous," Alaric said, his eyes scanning the area. "The ley lines won't make this easy."

As if in response to his words, the water rippled unnaturally. From the depths emerged a massive, serpentine creature with scales that shimmered like liquid silver. Its eyes glowed with an eerie blue light, and its movements were slow but deliberate.

"The nexus guardian," Alaric said, flipping open his grimoire. "This is going to be tricky."

As the guardian circled the nexus, its presence radiating power, Alaric and Lira exchanged a determined glance. The challenges ahead would test not only their skills but their resolve. With the lessons of the Air Nexus fresh in their minds and the whispers of the ley lines echoing in their thoughts, they prepared for the next trial.

"Ready?" Alaric asked, his voice steady despite the tension.

Lira smirked, her blade gleaming in the nexus's light. "Always."

Together, they stepped forward, the path to the Water Nexus—and the Spiral Nexus beyond—stretching out before them.

Chapter 11: The Trial of Water

The path to the Water Nexus wound downwards, the air growing heavier with each step. The faint sound of rushing water grew louder, echoing through the stone passage like the pulse of a heartbeat. Alaric and Lira exchanged a glance, their earlier confidence tempered by the weight of the trials behind them.

"We're getting closer," Lira murmured, adjusting the jade amulet around her neck. Its glow was faint but steady, reacting to the ley line energy that permeated the air.

Alaric nodded, his eyes scanning the faint runes etched into the cavern walls. "This nexus is different. The energy feels... colder. Slower. Like it's waiting for something."

Section 1: Entry into the Water Nexus

They emerged into a vast cavern bathed in dim, iridescent light. Water dripped from unseen heights, pooling into streams that flowed upward, defying gravity as they spiraled toward a glowing nexus at the cavern's center. The walls shimmered with moisture, reflecting the light like rippling glass.

"This place is alive," Lira said, her voice filled with quiet awe. She knelt by one of the upward streams, running her fingers through the water. "It's flowing toward the nexus. Like it's feeding it."

Alaric crouched beside her, tracing his fingers along a patch of glowing algae. "It's more than that. The water isn't just moving—it's reacting. Look." He pointed to the way the algae's light brightened as his fingers passed over it. "The ley lines' influence is everywhere."

Before Lira could respond, the ground trembled beneath them. Water surged from the pools, rising like living tendrils. The cavern seemed to inhale, and the pools around them began to expand.

"Get ready!" Alaric shouted, flipping open his grimoire.

The water surged without warning, lifting them off their feet. Alaric's hands moved quickly, inscribing a rune midair that expanded into a glowing barrier of light. The bubble encased them, holding back the rushing currents, but it flickered under the relentless pressure.

"Think fast!" Lira yelled, gripping the edge of a floating rock as the water carried her higher. "This isn't holding!"

"I'm trying!" Alaric snapped, pouring more energy into the rune. The bubble stabilized, but cracks of light spiderwebbed across its surface. "I need to adjust the binding pattern—just hold on!"

As the water subsided, the ground beneath them shifted again. New corridors opened, their walls glistening with bioluminescent algae, while others sealed with torrents of water. The labyrinth of the Water Nexus was changing, forcing them deeper into its grasp.

The air grew still for a moment, save for the gentle lapping of water. Then, from the depths of one of the glowing pools, sleek shapes began to emerge. The creatures were a blend of fish and humanoid features, their silver scales shimmering with bioluminescent patterns that pulsed in rhythm with the nexus.

"They're guardians," Alaric said, stepping back and reaching for his grimoire. "And they don't look happy to see us."

The largest of the creatures stepped forward, its eyes glowing with an eerie light. It tilted its head, emitting a haunting, melodic sound that resonated through the cavern. The smaller guardians spread out, circling Alaric and Lira with slow, deliberate movements.

"What's the plan?" Lira asked, her blade drawn.

Alaric flipped through his grimoire, his eyes scanning for a binding spell. "Distract them while I figure out what they're protecting."

Lira rolled her eyes. "Of course. Leave me with the fun part."

As the first guardian lunged, Lira met it head-on, her blade flashing in the dim light. The creature was fast, its movements fluid and unpredictable, but Lira's reflexes kept her one step ahead. She parried its strikes, her eyes darting to the patterns on its scales.

"They're reacting to the water flow!" she called out. "If we disrupt the current—"

Alaric didn't wait for her to finish. He sketched a rune into the air, directing a burst of energy toward the pool's center. The water surged upward, breaking the creatures' formation and sending them scattering.

"Nice work!" Lira shouted, her blade cutting through one of the smaller guardians' defenses. It retreated, its scales dimming as it slunk back into the water.

The largest guardian stepped forward again, its melodic hum rising into a piercing screech. The sound sent shockwaves through the cavern, shattering Alaric's rune and knocking them both off their feet.

"This one's stronger," Alaric muttered, scrambling to his knees. "We need to end this fast."

The water in the cavern rippled violently, and from its depths rose a massive serpentine creature. Its body shimmered like liquid glass, and its scales reflected the light of the nexus in mesmerizing patterns. Its eyes burned with ancient intelligence, and its voice resonated directly in their minds.

"Who dares disturb the balance of the waters?"

Lira staggered to her feet, the jade amulet around her neck pulsing faintly. "We're here to restore balance!"

The serpent's body coiled, its movements fluid and hypnotic. "Balance is not yours to command, mortal."

Alaric stepped forward, his grimoire open. "We're not here to command. We're here to help stabilize the nexus."

The serpent let out a low growl, the water around it rising in response. "Prove it."

The guardian struck without warning, its tail lashing out in a wave of force that sent them both tumbling. Alaric rolled to his feet, inscribing a rune midair that sent a jet of heat toward the incoming wave. The water evaporated on contact, but the serpent was already moving again, its body blending seamlessly with the currents.

"Lira!" Alaric shouted. "The amulet—it's reacting to the nexus. Use it!"

Lira clutched the amulet, its light growing brighter. She held it high, and the currents around her shifted, spiraling toward her like threads drawn to a spool.

"The currents—they're listening to me!" she said, her voice filled with wonder.

"Then guide them!" Alaric yelled, sketching another rune to deflect the serpent's next attack.

Lira closed her eyes, focusing on the rhythm of the water. The currents spiraled tighter, encasing the serpent in a swirling vortex. The guardian roared, its movements slowed as the water's flow turned against it.

"Now, Alaric!" Lira shouted.

Alaric inscribed the final rune, its golden light surging toward the nexus. The energy merged with the currents, stabilizing the flow. The serpent let out a final roar before dissolving into the water, its form dispersing like mist.

The nexus pulsed, its light soft and steady. Alaric and Lira approached cautiously, their breaths heavy from the battle.

As they reached the core, the cavern dissolved around them. They found themselves in a field of endless light, threads of energy stretching across the void. The ley lines appeared as a web connecting dimensions, their colors shifting and intertwining in a mesmerizing dance.

"This is what the ley lines truly are," Alaric murmured, awe in his voice. "They're not just channels of magic—they're the threads of existence itself."

At the center of the web was the Spiral Nexus, its form fractured and leaking shadow. A dark entity loomed nearby, its form shifting unnaturally. Its voice was a whisper that echoed through the void.

"The Spiral Nexus belongs to us."

The vision faded, and they found themselves back in the cavern. At the nexus's core lay a crystalline object, its surface etched with ancient runes.

Alaric picked it up carefully, its energy humming softly in his hands. "This is a fragment of knowledge. A key to understanding the ley lines' origin."

As they left the nexus, the path ahead stretched into shadow. They paused to rest, the weight of their journey pressing heavily on their shoulders.

Alaric opened his journal, documenting the creatures they had encountered and the vision of the ley lines. "The guardians weren't just protecting the nexus," he wrote. "They were maintaining its balance, just like the serpent. Every creature here is connected to the ley lines."

Lira leaned against a rock, her gaze distant. "The ley lines are alive, Alaric. And they're trying to teach us something. But are we listening?"

Alaric looked up, his expression thoughtful. "Maybe that's the real trial—not just stabilizing the nexuses, but understanding them."

Ahead, the path twisted into the unknown, the faint glow of the next nexus beckoning them forward.

Alaric and Lira sat by the edge of the now-calm nexus, its soft glow illuminating the cavern in shades of blue and green. The crystalline object Alaric held continued to hum faintly, its runes shifting like water flowing over stone.

"This isn't just a relic," Alaric murmured, his fingers tracing the etched symbols. "It's a conduit. The runes are designed to channel ley line energy, but they're written in a language I've never seen before."

"Doesn't that mean we're in over our heads?" Lira asked, the jade amulet still pulsing faintly against her chest. "If the ley lines are this complex, maybe we're not meant to fix them."

Alaric's expression hardened. "If we don't, who will? The Veiled Order isn't stabilizing anything. They're exploiting the fractures, tearing apart the very fabric of magic."

Lira sighed, standing to stretch. "I get it, Alaric. I do. But every time we touch one of these nexuses, it feels like we're playing with something we barely understand."

Before Alaric could respond, the crystalline object in his hand flared brightly. Both of them shielded their eyes as a beam of light shot from the crystal into the nexus's core. The cavern trembled, and the light expanded into a series of intricate geometric patterns that floated midair.

"It's a map," Alaric whispered, awe in his voice.

*****

The map glowed with faint, interconnected lines, each one pulsing gently. At the center was a bright point, its edges jagged and irregular—a clear representation of the Spiral Nexus.

"These are the ley lines," Alaric said, his fingers hovering over the glowing patterns. "This is how they connect the nexuses."

Lira pointed to a darker region near the Spiral Nexus. "What's that?"

Alaric frowned. "A disruption. The lines are broken there... severed. That must be where the Veiled Order is focusing their efforts."

The map shifted, revealing smaller nexuses surrounding the Spiral Nexus. Each one glowed faintly, their light dimmer than the rest. Alaric traced a line from their current location to the next nexus, his expression grim.

"We're running out of time," he said quietly. "If the Spiral Nexus collapses, it won't just affect this plane—it'll ripple across every dimension."

Lira's eyes narrowed. "Then let's make sure it doesn't."

As they prepared to leave the cavern, a soft chuckle echoed through the air. They turned to see Pecos leaning casually against one of the glowing walls, his form flickering between that of a young boy and an older man.

"You two just can't stay out of trouble, can you?" he said, his grin sharp and mischievous.

Alaric stepped forward, his grimoire in hand. "What do you want, Pecos?"

"Relax, seeker," Pecos replied, holding up his hands in mock surrender. "I'm just here to deliver a message. The next nexus will make you question everything you think you know about the ley lines."

Lira crossed her arms. "That's not exactly helpful."

"It's not supposed to be," Pecos said, his tone light but laced with an edge of seriousness. "The ley lines aren't just paths of magic—they're threads of existence. Tug too hard, and everything unravels. Your next trial will test more than your skills. It'll test your resolve."

"And what's at the Spiral Nexus?" Alaric pressed. "What is the Veiled Order trying to do?"

Pecos's grin faded slightly. "They think they can rewrite the ley lines to fit their vision of perfection. But perfection is a dangerous thing to chase. It usually comes with a cost."

With that, Pecos faded into the shadows, his parting words lingering in the air. "Good luck, seekers. You're going to need it."

Observing the Amphibious Guardians

Before leaving the nexus, Alaric paused to study the remaining amphibious creatures. Now that the guardian serpent had dissolved, the smaller guardians moved peacefully, their bioluminescent patterns shifting like a gentle current.

"They're not just protecting the nexus," Alaric said, jotting notes into his journal. "They're an extension of it. Their movements mirror the flow of the ley lines. When the nexus was unstable, they were aggressive. Now, they're calm."

Lira watched as one of the creatures swam gracefully through the upward-flowing water. "They're beautiful. It's hard to believe they were attacking us not long ago."

"They weren't attacking us," Alaric corrected. "They were defending the balance. Everything here serves the ley lines' purpose, even if we don't fully understand it."

He sketched a quick drawing of the largest guardian, noting its intricate patterns and behavior. "I need to document as much as I can. If the Veiled Order is disrupting nexuses, they might also be endangering the creatures tied to them."

*****

As they left the Water Nexus, the path ahead grew darker, the air heavy with an oppressive energy. The faint glow of the next nexus was visible on the horizon, but it felt different—distant and foreboding.

"We're getting closer to the Spiral Nexus," Lira said, her voice low. "I can feel it."

Alaric nodded, his expression grim. "The closer we get, the more unstable the ley lines will become. Every fracture brings us closer to collapse."

Before they could continue, the air around them shimmered, and Phelipandro appeared. The ley line guardian's form was as radiant as ever, its platinum feathers glowing softly in the dim light.

"The Spiral Nexus is no mere thread," Phelipandro said, its voice calm but grave. "It is the heart of all magic. Fail to restore it, and all threads will unravel."

Alaric stepped forward. "We've stabilized the other nexuses, but the fractures are spreading faster than we can keep up. How do we stop it?"

"You must understand the balance before you can restore it," Phelipandro replied. "The ley lines do not seek control—they seek harmony. To stabilize the Spiral Nexus, you must be willing to sacrifice."

"Sacrifice what?" Lira asked, her tone sharp.

Phelipandro's glowing eyes dimmed slightly, a sign of sorrow. "That is for you to discover."

As they walked, Alaric studied the crystal fragment from the Water Nexus. The runes shifted faintly under his touch, revealing fragments of forgotten history.

"The ley lines don't just connect places," he murmured, his eyes scanning the shifting patterns. "They connect realities. Every nexus is a node in a larger system, and the Spiral Nexus is the keystone."

Lira frowned. "So if it collapses—"

"Everything collapses," Alaric finished. "Magic, time, dimensions—all of it."

The crystal glowed brighter, and for a brief moment, they saw a vision of the Spiral Nexus. Its fractured threads stretched across the void, leaking shadow and light. At its center was a dark, shifting figure, its presence radiating malevolence.

"The Veiled Order," Lira whispered. "They're already there."

Alaric closed his grimoire, his jaw set. "Then we have to stop them."

The faint glow of the next nexus loomed ahead, its light flickering like a dying flame. Alaric and Lira steeled themselves, their steps resolute despite the weight of what lay ahead.

"Ready?" Alaric asked, his voice steady despite the tension.

Lira adjusted the jade amulet around her neck, its light pulsing faintly in response to the ley lines' energy. "Always."

Together, they stepped forward, the path to the Spiral Nexus stretching into the unknown.

The chamber of water faded into silence as Alaric stepped away from the gently rippling pool, the coolness of the trial still lingering on his skin. He glanced back one last time, the luminous runes etched into the stone walls shimmering faintly before their glow dimmed, as if bidding him farewell.

"You handled that trial well," Lira said, her voice steady but tinged with exhaustion. She adjusted her cloak, still damp from the cascading waves of the trial. "But don't let it give you too much confidence. The Trials don't get easier."

"I didn't expect them to," Alaric replied, his tone sharper than intended. The weight of his mistakes from earlier trials still lingered, a quiet reminder that mastery wasn't guaranteed. He shifted the strap of his satchel on his shoulder, the grimoire inside feeling heavier with each step toward their next destination.

The air around them began to shift as they moved deeper into the cavern system, leaving behind the soothing, humid embrace of the water trial. It grew warmer with every step, and soon, beads of sweat formed on Alaric's brow. The walls of the tunnel glowed faintly with an orange hue, as if lit from within by embers. The very stones seemed alive, pulsing faintly in time with a rhythm neither of them could hear but both could feel.

"This isn't just heat," Lira murmured, her eyes narrowing. "It's the ley lines. We're getting closer to the Fire Nexus."

Alaric nodded, though unease prickled at the back of his mind. He'd felt the resonance of ley lines before, but this was different—stronger, almost aggressive. The grimoire in his satchel seemed to react to it as well, the faint hum of its bound magic growing louder, as though in warning.

"What do you know about the Fire Nexus?" Alaric asked, breaking the silence. The tunnel widened ahead, the glow intensifying.

Lira hesitated. "Enough to be wary," she admitted. "It's not just about controlling fire. This trial... it tests more than skill. It forces you to confront the flames inside you—your anger, your fears, your regrets. If you're not careful, it can consume you."

Her words hung heavily in the air as they stepped into the cavern beyond, the walls opening into a vast expanse of molten rivers and crystallized flames. The Fire Nexus loomed ahead, its fiery heart thrumming with an intensity that made the air itself shimmer.

Alaric's jaw tightened as he stared into the inferno. He felt the weight of the trials he'd passed and the enormity of what still lay ahead.

The ley lines pulsed again, and he could swear he felt something beneath the heat—a presence, watching, waiting.

Chapter 12: Sparks of Sentience, Flames of Discord

The air grew heavier with each step as Alaric and Lira descended into the depths of the cavern. The cool humidity of the Trial of Water had long since evaporated, replaced by a blistering heat that pressed against their skin and threatened to choke the breath from their lungs. The walls around them, once smooth and gray, now shimmered with veins of molten fire that pulsed faintly, as if alive. Shadows danced across their faces, cast by the flickering glow of the fiery veins, and the path ahead seemed to ripple like a mirage.

"This is it," Lira said, her voice low and cautious. She pulled her cloak tighter around her, though it did little to shield her from the oppressive heat. "We're entering the Fire Nexus."

Alaric nodded, his grip tightening on the strap of his satchel. He could feel the weight of the grimoire inside, its presence a steady reminder of the knowledge and responsibility he carried. Yet the closer they got to the Nexus, the more it seemed to hum faintly, resonating with the energy in the air. He could feel it vibrating against his side, as if the ancient tome itself were reacting to the ley lines.

The cavern widened abruptly, and they stepped into a vast chamber that stole the breath from Alaric's lungs. The Fire Nexus was unlike anything he had imagined. Rivers of molten lava crisscrossed the chamber floor, their golden-red glow casting an otherworldly light that danced along the jagged walls. Massive crystalline structures jutted from the ground, their surfaces reflecting the fiery hues in mesmerizing patterns. The heat was suffocating, making every breath feel like a laborious task, and the air shimmered with waves of distortion.

But it wasn't just the heat or the grandeur of the scene that unsettled Alaric. It was the feeling. The Nexus thrummed with power, a deep, rhythmic pulse that he could feel in his chest. It was as if the very air was alive, vibrating with an energy that was both awe-inspiring and deeply unsettling.

"Do you feel it?" Lira asked, her voice barely audible over the distant roar of the molten rivers. She wasn't looking at him but at the Nexus itself, her expression a mixture of wonder and unease.

"Yes," Alaric replied, his voice strained. "It's like it's... watching us."

Lira glanced at him, her brow furrowing. "That's because it is. The ley lines here—this Nexus—they're not just forces of nature. They're alive in their own way, and they can feel. The instability, the corruption... it's like pain to them."

Alaric opened his mouth to argue, to dismiss her words as mere poetic interpretation, but he stopped. As much as he wanted to frame the ley lines as a logical system of energy, he couldn't deny the weight of the presence around him. It wasn't just power—it was something more, something deeper.

The pulsing of the Nexus grew louder as they approached its heart, and Alaric's resolve wavered. Whatever lay ahead, it wasn't just a test of skill. It was a reckoning.

The ground beneath Alaric's boots felt strangely alive, radiating a faint warmth that matched the pulse of the ley lines thrumming in the air. He glanced at Lira, whose wary gaze swept across the cavern, and then back to the molten rivers that wove through the chamber like veins of some fiery creature.

"We shouldn't linger," Lira said, her voice cutting through the oppressive silence. "The Fire Nexus isn't stable. The longer we're here, the more likely it is to lash out."

Alaric nodded, though his curiosity fought against her caution. His eyes wandered to a massive crystalline spire that jutted from the ground nearby. It shimmered like molten glass, its fiery hues shifting as if alive. He took a step toward it, unable to resist the allure.

"Don't touch it," Lira warned sharply. "The crystals are part of the Nexus's energy flow. Interfering with them could set off a chain reaction."

Alaric pulled his hand back, chastened but still fascinated. "What exactly are we looking for here?" he asked. "A way to stabilize it? Or just a way to survive?"

"Both," Lira said grimly. "The ley lines here are in pain. We have to find the source of that pain and stop it, or the Nexus will collapse—and us with it."

As they moved deeper into the chamber, the heat grew more intense, and the ground beneath their feet became increasingly unstable. Cracks spiderwebbed across the stone, glowing with molten light. Small bursts of flame erupted sporadically, forcing them to tread carefully.

"Stay close," Lira said, her tone brooking no argument. "The Nexus is unpredictable. If we get separated—"

"I know," Alaric interrupted, wiping sweat from his brow. "I'll be careful."

Despite his words, his attention kept drifting. There was something about the way the molten rivers flowed, their patterns almost hypnotic, that tugged at his thoughts. It was as if they were trying to tell him something, though the message was just out of reach.

Suddenly, a surge of energy rippled through the cavern, and the ground trembled beneath their feet. Alaric stumbled, barely catching himself on a nearby rock as a geyser of flame erupted just a few paces ahead. Lira grabbed his arm, pulling him back as the flames subsided.

"Focus!" she snapped. "This place isn't going to wait for you to figure it out."

Alaric swallowed his retort and forced himself to concentrate. He followed Lira as she led the way toward the Nexus's center, her movements precise and deliberate. She seemed to sense the rhythm of the ley lines in a way he couldn't, adjusting her path to avoid the worst of the instability.

After what felt like an eternity, they reached a clearing where the molten rivers converged. At the center stood a dark, jagged structure—an altar of obsidian and ash, its surface etched with runes that pulsed faintly with an ominous crimson light.

"What is that?" Alaric asked, his voice barely above a whisper.

Lira's expression darkened. "The Veiled Order," she said. "This is their work."

Alaric's pulse quickened. He had read about the Veiled Order in fragments, hints scattered throughout forbidden texts. They were a shadowy group of mages who sought to bend the ley lines to their will, regardless of the consequences. But seeing their influence firsthand was something else entirely.

The altar exuded an unnatural energy, a sharp contrast to the chaotic yet organic flow of the Nexus. It felt like a wound in the fabric of the ley lines, a focal point of corruption that twisted and distorted the magic around it.

Lira stepped closer, her movements cautious. "These runes," she murmured, tracing a finger along the jagged lines. "They're designed to siphon energy from the ley lines. That's why the Nexus is so unstable—it's being drained."

Alaric crouched beside her, studying the runes. They were unlike anything he'd seen before, their patterns jagged and angular, radiating a malevolent intent. He sketched them quickly into his notebook, his mind racing with questions.

"This isn't just about power," Lira continued, her voice tight. "The Order isn't just draining the Nexus—they're trying to control it. To force it to—"

She broke off suddenly, her eyes widening. Alaric followed her gaze and froze. The runes on the altar had begun to glow more brightly, their light pulsing in time with the Nexus's chaotic rhythm.

"Step back," Lira said urgently. "Something's happening."

Before they could move, a wave of energy erupted from the altar, knocking them both to the ground. The air around them shimmered, and the chamber seemed to blur and distort. Alaric struggled to his feet, his vision swimming.

"What—what is this?" he stammered.

Lira didn't answer. Her focus was on the altar, where the runes had flared to life, casting long shadows across the cavern. The shadows began to move, coalescing into forms—twisted, fiery constructs that rose from the molten rivers like spirits summoned from the depths.

"Guardians," Lira said grimly. "The altar is defending itself."

The constructs moved with a predatory grace, their forms shifting between solid and flame. They radiated an intense heat that made it hard to breathe, and their glowing eyes fixed on Alaric and Lira with unmistakable hostility.

"Any brilliant ideas?" Alaric asked, his voice tight.

"Survive," Lira said, drawing her blade. "And keep them away from the altar."

The first construct lunged, its movements a blur of heat and light. Alaric barely had time to react, raising a hasty shield of magic to block its strike. The force of the impact sent him stumbling backward, his shield flickering under the strain.

Lira moved with practiced precision, her blade slicing through one of the constructs. It dissipated in a burst of flame, but another immediately took its place. The guardians were relentless, their movements synchronized as if controlled by a single will.

Alaric gritted his teeth, focusing on the runes he'd sketched earlier. He traced a Rune of Binding in the air, the glowing lines forming a sigil that shot toward one of the constructs. The sigil wrapped around it, holding it in place long enough for Lira to strike it down.

But the effort drained him, and the heat was becoming unbearable. Sweat dripped down his face, and his breaths came in shallow gasps.

"We can't keep this up," he said, his voice hoarse.

Lira glanced at the altar, her expression grim. "We don't have to. If I can disrupt the runes, I might be able to weaken the connection."

"You'll be exposed," Alaric protested.

"We don't have a choice," Lira shot back. "Cover me."

Alaric nodded, summoning every ounce of focus he had left. As Lira dashed toward the altar, he threw up another shield, deflecting the guardians' attacks. His magic flared and wavered, the strain pushing him to his limits.

Lira reached the altar and plunged her blade into its surface, disrupting the runes with a surge of raw energy. The guardians faltered, their forms flickering, and the oppressive heat began to subside.

But the effort took its toll. Lira staggered back, her face pale and drenched in sweat. Alaric caught her as she fell, lowering her to the ground as the altar's light dimmed.

"It's... weakened," she said weakly. "But it's not gone."

Alaric looked at the altar, its runes now faint and cracked. The Nexus's pulse had calmed slightly, but the sense of unease remained. They had bought themselves time, but the battle was far from over.

The cavern settled into an uneasy stillness. The fiery guardians had vanished, leaving faint scorch marks on the ground where they had stood. The oppressive heat abated slightly, though the molten rivers still glowed with a restless energy. Alaric sat beside Lira, his chest heaving from the exertion. She leaned heavily against a jagged rock, her face pale and her breaths shallow.

"Are you alright?" he asked, his voice still hoarse.

Lira nodded weakly. "I've been worse." She managed a faint smile before her expression grew serious. "But this isn't over. The altar's weakened, but the ley lines are still unstable. We need to understand what the Veiled Order was doing here and why."

Alaric turned his gaze to the altar. Its once-vibrant runes were now dim and fractured, yet it still pulsed faintly with residual energy. The corruption it exuded had lessened, but it was far from gone. He retrieved his notebook and opened it to the sketches he had made earlier, comparing the runes on the altar to the ones described in the forbidden texts he had studied.

"These runes," he muttered, tracing his finger over the jagged lines. "They're not just siphoning energy. They're redirecting it, sending it somewhere else."

Lira frowned, sitting up straighter despite her exhaustion. "Redirecting it? To where?"

"I don't know," Alaric admitted. "But the way they're structured... it's like they're trying to create a link. Maybe to another Nexus. Or... something worse."

The words hung heavily in the air. The idea of a corrupted link between ley lines sent a chill down Alaric's spine. If the Veiled Order could manipulate the ley lines on this scale, the implications were terrifying.

"We need to move," Lira said, her voice firmer now. "The longer we stay here, the more we risk the Nexus lashing out again.

We've weakened the altar, but the ley lines are still unstable. We have to find a way to soothe them."

Alaric hesitated. "Soothe them? How? They're not... alive."

Lira turned to him, her expression intense. "Aren't they? Haven't you felt it? The Nexus isn't just raw energy, Alaric. It's something more. It feels. It remembers. And right now, it's in pain."

Her words unsettled him, but he couldn't dismiss them. He had felt the weight of the ley lines' presence since they had entered the cavern. The pulsing rhythm in the air, the distorted energy, the chaotic mirages—none of it felt like mere magic. It was something deeper, something almost alive.

"Alright," he said finally. "If you're right, then how do we... connect with it? How do we soothe it?"

Lira closed her eyes, taking a deep breath. "The ley lines respond to balance, to harmony. We need to match their rhythm, their flow. But it's not something you can brute force. You have to feel it."

Alaric raised an eyebrow. "Feel it? That's not exactly a precise instruction."

"It's not about precision," Lira snapped. "It's about trust. Trust in yourself, in the ley lines, in the balance of it all. You have to let go of control."

Alaric bristled at her words but said nothing. He wasn't used to letting go—control was what kept his magic stable, what kept him grounded. But as he looked at the chaotic Nexus, he realized that control wasn't going to be enough.

"Fine," he said, closing his eyes. "Show me how."

Trial of Balance

Lira guided him to the edge of one of the molten rivers, where the fiery veins pulsed with a chaotic energy. She knelt beside it, placing her hands just above the surface. The heat was intense, but she didn't flinch.

"Follow my lead," she said. "Close your eyes. Listen to the rhythm."

Alaric hesitated but obeyed. He closed his eyes, shutting out the chaotic sights of the Nexus. At first, all he could feel was the oppressive heat and the weight of his own thoughts. But then, slowly, he began to sense it—the pulse of the ley lines. It was faint at first, a steady thrum beneath the chaos, but as he focused, it grew clearer.

"Do you feel it?" Lira asked softly.

"Yes," he said, his voice barely above a whisper.

"Now, match it," she said. "Let your magic flow with it, not against it."

Alaric took a deep breath, reaching for his magic. He let it flow from him, not in the structured patterns he was used to, but in a more natural, instinctive way. It was difficult, like trying to unlearn years of discipline, but he persisted.

The molten river began to calm, its chaotic glow softening into a steadier, more harmonious light. The heat around them lessened, and the oppressive energy in the air seemed to lift slightly.

"It's working," Lira said, a note of relief in her voice. "Keep going."

They continued in silence, their combined magic weaving into the ley lines' rhythm. The Nexus responded, its energy stabilizing little by little. Alaric could feel the difference, as if the ley lines themselves were beginning to trust them.

But then, a sharp surge of energy rippled through the cavern, breaking their concentration. Alaric's eyes snapped open as the ground beneath them trembled violently. The altar flared back to life, its fractured runes sparking with renewed intensity.

"Something's wrong," Lira said, her voice tense. "The altar—it's fighting back."

The pulsing energy grew louder, and the molten rivers began to churn violently. Alaric and Lira scrambled to their feet as the ground cracked beneath them. The air filled with an ear-piercing hum, and the fiery guardians began to reappear, their forms flickering into existence around the altar.

"They're back," Alaric said grimly. "And they're not happy."

Lira tightened her grip on her blade. "We need to finish this. If we don't stop the altar now, the Nexus will collapse."

Alaric's mind raced. They couldn't fight the guardians head-on again—it had drained them too much the first time. But the altar's renewed power meant they were running out of options.

"There's a connection," he said suddenly, his thoughts snapping into focus. "The altar is tied to the ley lines. If we can sever that connection—"

"Then we can stop the corruption," Lira finished. "But how?"

Alaric glanced at his notebook, flipping to the sketches he had made of the runes. His eyes scanned the patterns, searching for a weakness, an anchor point. And then he saw it—a central rune etched into the base of the altar, slightly larger than the others.

"This," he said, pointing to the rune. "It's the anchor. If we disrupt it, the altar will lose its hold on the ley lines."

Lira nodded, her expression resolute. "Then let's end this."

The cavern trembled as another wave of energy rippled through the air, the molten rivers surging with fiery bursts that lit the chamber in flashes of gold and crimson. Alaric stumbled, his boots skidding on the cracked ground, while Lira held her balance with practiced precision.

"Stay close!" Lira shouted over the roar of the molten flows.

Alaric nodded, his throat dry from the heat. Every step felt like a battle against the blistering air that pressed down on them. The ground beneath them cracked and splintered as if the Nexus itself resisted their intrusion.

A sudden explosion of fire erupted just ahead, sending a wave of molten sparks flying toward them. Lira reacted instantly, raising her hands and murmuring a calming spell. The flames twisted midair, their violent trajectory softening into a harmless cascade of embers.

"How do you do that?" Alaric asked, panting as he stumbled up beside her.

Lira glanced at him, her face glistening with sweat. "Magic isn't just about force. You have to listen to it, feel its rhythm. Fire's a lot like anger—push it harder, and it pushes back. But if you guide it, you can redirect it."

"Guide it," Alaric repeated, his tone skeptical. "Sounds easy enough."

Another burst of fire interrupted their conversation, this one closer than before. Alaric instinctively reached into his satchel and pulled out a small, carved stone etched with a Rune of Cooling. He pressed the rune to the ground, activating it with a quick incantation. A wave of cool energy radiated outward, forming a protective bubble around them. The oppressive heat lessened slightly, and Alaric exhaled in relief.

"Not bad," Lira admitted, her lips curving into a faint smile. "You're learning."

The ground rumbled beneath them, and cracks began to spiderweb outward from where they stood. Alaric grabbed Lira's arm, pulling her back just as a section of the floor collapsed, revealing a molten chasm below.

"We can't keep this up," Alaric said. "The Nexus is falling apart."

"Then we move faster," Lira replied. "The center's just ahead. Whatever's causing this—it's there."

*****

As they pushed forward, the chamber opened into a vast clearing where the molten rivers converged in a chaotic whirlpool of fire and light. At the center stood a blackened altar, its surface jagged and uneven, as if hewn from obsidian pulled directly from the heart of the Nexus. The altar pulsed with an unnatural crimson glow, the light casting jagged shadows that danced across the chamber walls.

Alaric stopped in his tracks, a chill running down his spine despite the oppressive heat. "What... is that?"

Lira approached cautiously, her eyes fixed on the altar. "It's a siphon," she said grimly. "It's drawing energy from the ley lines."

The surface of the altar was inscribed with runes that seemed to shift and writhe like living things. They were angular and sharp, their shapes radiating a sense of violence and disruption. Alaric recognized some of the symbols from his studies of forbidden texts, but others were entirely unfamiliar.

"Careful," Alaric said, his voice low. "We don't know what it'll do if—"

Before he could finish, Lira reached out and placed her hand on the altar. Her eyes widened, and she froze, as if caught in an unseen force. Her breathing quickened, and her body tensed as the crimson light of the runes spread up her arm.

"Lira!" Alaric shouted, stepping forward. He hesitated, unsure if touching her would make things worse.

Lira's voice was a whisper, barely audible. "I... I can see them."

Her vision fragmented into jagged images. Cloaked figures stood around the altar, their voices chanting in a harsh, guttural language. Flames writhed unnaturally in the air, twisting into shapes that defied logic. She saw the ley lines beneath the ground, glowing threads of energy that pulsed with a desperate rhythm. Cracks formed along their length, spreading like fractures in glass.

The figures raised their hands in unison, and the altar flared with crimson light. The ley lines screamed—not in sound, but in an anguished pulse that Lira could feel in her bones.

The vision shifted, and she saw the Nexus collapsing, its energy imploding into a void of darkness. The cloaked figures vanished into the chaos, leaving only destruction in their wake.

With a gasp, Lira yanked her hand away, collapsing to her knees. Alaric rushed to her side, steadying her as she struggled to catch her breath.

"What did you see?" he asked, his voice urgent.

Lira shook her head, her face pale. "The Veiled Order," she whispered. "They're trying to control the ley lines... but they're breaking them instead. They don't care about the cost."

As Lira steadied herself, the air around the altar grew heavier. The pulsing light intensified, and the chaotic energy of the Nexus seemed to coalesce around them. The ley lines' anguish pressed against their minds, manifesting as distorted mirages that flickered in and out of existence.

Alaric froze as the air before him shimmered, forming a hazy image of his father. Walter Deymorne stood in the fields outside their home in Caerlyn, his hands gripping a plow. His face was worn and lined with frustration.

"You're wasting your time," the mirage said, its voice sharp and cutting. "Chasing dreams that lead to nothing. The world doesn't care about your ambitions, boy. It'll chew you up and spit you out."

Alaric clenched his fists, his chest tightening. "You don't understand," he muttered. "I'm not like you. I won't give up."

The mirage flickered, its edges fraying like smoke. But the weight of the words lingered, threatening to unravel his focus.

Nearby, Lira stood rigid, her eyes fixed on her own vision. A blazing nexus loomed before her, its light flickering as it collapsed into ash. She saw herself kneeling beside it, her hands outstretched in a futile attempt to stabilize its energy. The memory was a scar she couldn't forget—a failure that had cost countless lives.

"You can't save them," the mirage whispered, its voice laced with bitterness. "You'll fail again, just like you did before."

"No," Lira said through gritted teeth. "Not this time."

The visions wavered, their intensity magnified by the ley lines' anguish. The Nexus seemed to feed on their fears, amplifying them until they threatened to consume them entirely.

"Focus," Lira said, her voice trembling but firm. "They're not real. They're just echoes."

Alaric forced himself to look away from his father's image, his breathing ragged. He reached for his magic, channeling it into a Rune of Clarity etched into the back of his notebook. The rune flared, and the mirage dissolved into nothingness.

Lira followed his lead, drawing on her calming spell to dispel the vision before her. The oppressive energy around them lessened slightly, though the tension remained palpable.

"We need to stop this," Alaric said, his voice resolute. "The altar, the corruption—it's feeding the Nexus's pain. If we don't end it, the whole ley line could collapse."

Lira nodded, determination hardening her features. "Then let's finish this."

The altar pulsed once more, and the oppressive air around them grew still. The silence was unnerving, broken only by the faint, rhythmic hum of the ley lines. Alaric and Lira exchanged wary glances, their exhaustion momentarily forgotten as an unseen force gathered in the cavern.

Without warning, the molten rivers surged upward in tendrils of liquid fire, converging at the center of the chamber. The flames twisted and coalesced, forming the outline of a humanoid figure. Its body was a blend of molten lava and flickering embers, its edges shimmering as though it might dissolve at any moment. Eyes of pure flame locked onto Alaric and Lira, and when it spoke, its voice was a haunting mix of crackling fire and mournful whispers.

"Why do you seek to mend what you have broken?" the apparition asked, its tone heavy with accusation.

Alaric took an instinctive step back, his mind racing. The ley lines' sentience had been a theoretical possibility, a distant idea discussed in dusty tomes, but now it stood before him, undeniably real. He glanced at Lira, who remained rooted in place, her expression unreadable.

"We didn't break anything," Alaric said defensively, his voice sharper than intended. "We're trying to fix this."

The apparition tilted its head, the flames along its body flaring briefly. "Fix?" it echoed. "You cannot fix what you do not understand. You pull at threads you cannot see, and the pain echoes through the web of creation."

"Wait," Lira said, stepping forward cautiously. Her voice was calm, though her hands trembled at her sides. "You're part of the ley lines, aren't you? Their... essence?"

The apparition's fiery gaze shifted to her. "I am a fragment," it said. "A reflection of their anguish. The ley lines are not lifeless streams of power. They remember. They feel. And they suffer."

Alaric's stomach twisted at the words, but he pushed the unease aside. "If you're here to lecture us, it's not helping. We don't have time to debate philosophy. The Nexus is collapsing, and we need to stabilize it."

The apparition's flames darkened, its form solidifying. "You seek to heal what is broken, but you use the tools of destruction. Power without balance. Force without harmony. You will fail."

"Then tell us what to do!" Alaric snapped, frustration boiling over. "If you want us to save the Nexus, stop speaking in riddles and help us!"

Lira touched his arm, her voice quiet but firm. "Alaric, stop. Listen to it."

The apparition's gaze lingered on Lira, its flames dimming slightly. "You have felt the rhythm," it said. "You understand the pain. If you would mend the fracture, you must prove yourselves worthy."

The apparition raised an arm, and a wave of energy rippled outward. The molten rivers stilled, their chaotic flow replaced by a steady pulse that resonated through the chamber. A fragment of the ley lines' energy rose from the ground, a glowing sphere of molten light and fire that pulsed erratically.

"This fragment carries the pain of the Nexus," the apparition said. "You must soothe it. Restore its harmony. But beware—force will only deepen the wound."

Alaric stepped forward, his confidence bolstered by his mastery of runes. "I'll handle this," he said, his tone determined. He reached for his satchel and pulled out a piece of stone, carving a Rune of Stabilization into its surface with practiced precision. As he activated the rune, a thread of magic extended toward the fragment, seeking to contain its chaotic energy.

The reaction was immediate—and violent. The fragment flared with a fiery pulse, sending Alaric staggering backward. The rune shattered, and the energy lashed out, scorching the ground where he had stood.

"Force," the apparition said, its voice echoing with disapproval. "A blunt instrument for a delicate task."

"Thanks for the critique," Alaric muttered, brushing ash from his tunic. He turned to Lira. "Your turn, I guess."

Lira stepped forward, her movements deliberate and measured. She knelt before the fragment, her hands hovering over its surface. Closing her eyes, she took a deep breath, letting the chaotic rhythm of the energy wash over her.

"Feel its flow," she murmured, half to herself. "Not just the chaos, but the pattern beneath it."

Her magic flowed from her fingertips, not as a force to contain or overpower, but as a gentle guide. The fragment's erratic pulses slowed, its light softening as it responded to her touch.

"Keep going," Alaric said, his voice filled with a mixture of awe and determination. He stepped beside her, forcing himself to ignore his instincts for control. Instead, he let his magic flow freely, following the rhythm Lira had established.

The fragment began to stabilize, its light dimming to a steady glow. The heat in the chamber lessened, and the oppressive weight of the ley lines' anguish lifted slightly. Together, their magic formed a delicate balance, soothing the fragment until it pulsed in harmony with the Nexus.

The apparition observed in silence, its flames flickering as if caught in a breeze. When the fragment finally settled, it stepped forward, its fiery form now softer and more humanlike.

"You have succeeded," it said. "For now."

The apparition gestured, and the stabilized fragment dissolved into the air, its energy dispersing throughout the chamber. The molten rivers resumed their flow, calmer than before but still glowing with a faint, restless light.

"The ley lines are not merely conduits of power," the apparition said, its voice quieter now. "They are threads that bind this world together. Each fracture, each corruption, leaves a scar that weakens the web. The Veiled Order seeks to control this power, but their ambition will unravel all that is."

"Why are they doing this?" Lira asked. "What do they want?"

The apparition's flames flickered, and its voice carried a note of sorrow. "To control the ley lines is to control creation itself. But they do not see the cost. The Spiral Nexus—the heart of the ley lines—teeters on the brink. If it falls, the collapse will ripple through all realms."

Alaric felt a chill despite the heat. "The Spiral Nexus... we've seen signs of its instability. But if it collapses—"

"The world will follow," the apparition said. "Your task is far from over. The pain you have soothed here is but a fragment of a greater wound."

It turned to Lira, its fiery gaze meeting hers. "You carry the scars of failure. Do not let them define you. The ley lines remember, but they also forgive."

Lira's breath caught in her throat, and she looked away, her expression conflicted.

The apparition faced Alaric. "And you... you seek answers, but you blind yourself with doubt. Trust in the harmony you felt today, and you may yet succeed."

The apparition began to dissolve, its flames scattering into embers. "Go now. The Nexus is not yet whole, but it will hold—for a time. Seek the Spiral Nexus, and beware the Veiled Order. They will stop at nothing to claim what is not theirs."

With those final words, the apparition vanished, leaving Alaric and Lira alone in the chamber.

The oppressive energy of the cavern had lessened, though the heat remained stifling. Alaric helped Lira to her feet, her movements slower than usual.

"You okay?" he asked.

She nodded, though her gaze was distant. "That was... a lot."

"Tell me about it," Alaric said, managing a weak chuckle. "So, the ley lines are alive, the Veiled Order is breaking everything, and the Spiral Nexus is about to collapse. No pressure, right?"

Lira gave him a faint smile, but it didn't reach her eyes. "This is bigger than us, Alaric. And if we fail..."

"We won't," he said firmly, though he wasn't sure if he believed it. "We'll figure it out. One step at a time."

Lira glanced back at the altar, its surface now dark and lifeless. "We need to keep moving. The Spiral Nexus won't wait."

Alaric nodded, and together they made their way out of the chamber, the echoes of the apparition's words lingering in their minds. The trial had tested more than their magic—it had tested their understanding, their resolve, and their ability to trust in forces they couldn't fully comprehend.

As they stepped into the cooler air of the upper tunnels, Alaric cast one last look back at the Fire Nexus. The ley lines' pain had been soothed, but the memory of its anguish would stay with him.

The journey to the Spiral Nexus had only just begun.

The cavern's uneasy calm shattered as the altar flared to life once more. Its fractured runes surged with crimson light, their glow spreading across the jagged surface like blood coursing through veins. The oppressive hum of magic returned, louder and more discordant than before, reverberating through the molten rivers and shaking the ground beneath Alaric and Lira's feet.

"What's happening?" Lira demanded, her voice tight as she steadied herself against a nearby rock.

Alaric's gaze darted to the altar, his mind racing to make sense of its erratic pulses. "The altar—it's drawing energy from the Nexus again," he said, his tone grim. "But this time, it's stronger. It's like it's... redirecting the ley lines' power somewhere else."

"To where?" Lira asked, stepping closer to him. Her eyes narrowed as she studied the glowing runes. "And why?"

"I don't know," Alaric admitted, frustration lacing his voice. "But it's not good. If it keeps pulling this much energy, it could destabilize the entire Nexus."

The altar's light intensified, and a surge of energy burst outward, filling the cavern with searing heat. The molten rivers churned violently, their chaotic currents spilling over and carving deep grooves into the stone floor. Shadows twisted and stretched along the walls, forming shapes that coalesced into tangible forms.

Lira's hand went to the hilt of her blade as the shapes solidified, taking the form of fiery constructs. Their bodies crackled with molten energy, their eyes glowing like embers in the dark. They moved with an unnatural fluidity, their forms shifting between solid and flame.

"Guardians," Lira said, her voice low but steady. "The altar's defending itself."

"Fantastic," Alaric muttered, his fingers twitching as he reached for the runes etched into the leather-bound notebook at his side. "Just what we needed."

*****

The first construct lunged without warning, a blur of heat and light. Lira reacted instantly, drawing her blade in a smooth arc that sliced through the creature's molten form. It dissipated in a burst of sparks, but another took its place, its molten claws slashing toward her.

Alaric stepped forward, his magic flaring as he traced a Rune of Binding in the air. The glowing lines shot toward the construct, wrapping around its form and freezing it in place long enough for Lira to strike it down.

"Good timing," Lira said, sparing him a quick glance before turning her attention to another construct.

Alaric didn't have time to respond. Another guardian surged toward him, its molten claws slashing through the air. He activated a Rune of Shielding just in time, the shimmering barrier absorbing the impact with a deafening crack. The force of the blow sent him stumbling backward, but he held his ground.

"These things just keep coming!" he shouted, sweat dripping down his face as he traced another rune.

"They're tied to the altar!" Lira called back, her blade carving through another guardian. "As long as it's active, they won't stop."

The two of them fell into a rhythm, their movements and magic complementing each other in a way that spoke of their growing synergy. Alaric focused on creating barriers and controlling the battlefield, while Lira moved with lethal precision, dispatching the constructs with efficient strikes. Despite their efforts, the constructs kept coming, their numbers seemingly endless.

The Altar's True Nature

As the battle raged, Alaric's eyes flicked to the altar, its runes glowing brighter with each passing moment. He could feel the ley lines' pain intensifying, their anguished pulse echoing in his chest. The altar wasn't just defending itself—it was growing stronger, feeding on the energy it siphoned from the Nexus.

"We can't keep this up," Alaric said, his voice strained as he sent another Rune of Binding toward a construct. "The altar's getting stronger. We need to shut it down."

"And how do you propose we do that?" Lira asked, her breath coming in short bursts as she parried another attack. "Destroying it could destabilize the entire Nexus."

Alaric gritted his teeth, his mind racing. The runes on the altar weren't just decorative—they were the key to its function. If he could disrupt their pattern, he might be able to weaken its connection to the ley lines.

"It's the runes," he said suddenly. "They're channeling the energy. If I can disrupt them, I might be able to sever its link to the Nexus."

"Then do it," Lira said, her voice resolute. "I'll hold them off."

Alaric hesitated, his eyes darting between the altar and the constructs. "You can't fight them alone."

Lira gave him a sharp look. "I don't have to win—I just have to buy you time. Now go!"

Alaric nodded, steeling himself as he turned his attention to the altar. He sprinted toward it, narrowly dodging a fiery burst from one of the constructs. The heat was almost unbearable as he reached the altar's base, the glowing runes pulsing with a menacing light.

Kneeling beside the altar, he began tracing counter-runes over the existing symbols, his magic flowing through his fingers as he worked. The runes resisted him, their energy lashing out like a living thing, but he pressed on, his focus unyielding.

Behind him, Lira fought with everything she had. Her blade moved in a blur, cutting through the constructs with practiced efficiency, but her movements were slowing. The strain of the battle and the oppressive heat were taking their toll, and the guardians were relentless.

"Hurry, Alaric!" she shouted, her voice tinged with desperation.

"I'm trying!" he snapped, his hands trembling as he etched another counter-rune. The altar flared violently, and he felt a surge of resistance that threatened to overwhelm him. He gritted his teeth, pouring more of his magic into the runes.

The constructs closed in on Lira, their movements more aggressive as if sensing her growing exhaustion. One of them struck her blade aside, its molten claws slashing toward her. She dodged, but the effort left her off-balance, and another construct lunged.

Lira raised her hands, channeling her connection to the ley lines. Her magic surged outward, creating a burst of energy that momentarily pushed the constructs back. The effort left her staggering, her breaths coming in ragged gasps.

"I can't hold them much longer!" she called out.

Alaric's hands froze mid-motion as an idea struck him. Destroying the altar wasn't an option, but suppressing its influence might buy them enough time to escape. He turned to Lira, his eyes wide with urgency.

"The ley lines!" he shouted. "You're connected to them—can you suppress the altar's energy?"

Lira hesitated, her gaze flicking to the altar. "I... I can try."

She sheathed her blade and stepped toward the altar, her hands trembling as she reached out. Closing her eyes, she focused on the ley lines' rhythm, letting their anguished pulse guide her. Slowly, she channeled her magic into the altar, her energy weaving through its chaotic patterns.

The runes flared brighter, their resistance fierce, but Lira pushed on. Her connection to the ley lines allowed her to match their rhythm, countering the altar's influence with a steady, soothing flow. The constructs faltered, their forms flickering as the altar's power waned.

Alaric moved to her side, placing a steadying hand on her shoulder. "You're doing it," he said, his voice filled with awe.

Lira's face was pale, and sweat dripped down her temples. "I... can't hold it much longer," she said through gritted teeth.

The altar's light dimmed, and the constructs vanished, their forms dissolving into the air. The cavern grew silent once more, the oppressive energy lifting slightly. Lira staggered, her strength nearly spent, and Alaric caught her before she collapsed.

"We need to get out of here," he said, his voice urgent.

Lira nodded weakly, leaning heavily on him as they made their way toward the cavern's exit. The altar remained, its runes faint but still pulsing with residual energy. Alaric cast one last glance at it, his mind racing with questions about the Veiled Order and the Spiral Nexus.

As they stepped into the cooler air of the upper tunnels, Alaric tightened his grip on Lira's arm. The battle had been won, but the war was far from over. The altar's activation was a stark reminder of the Veiled Order's growing influence—and the fragile balance of the ley lines.

The cavern fell silent except for the faint hiss of molten rivers cooling into jagged crusts. The oppressive heat that had plagued the Fire Nexus lessened, replaced by an uneasy calm. The ley lines' anguish, though no longer screaming, remained present in the faint, fractured rhythm that echoed through the chamber.

Alaric helped Lira to a nearby ledge, her weight pressing heavily against him as she fought to catch her breath. She sank to her knees, her hands trembling as they rested on the stone. For a long moment, neither spoke, their shared exhaustion filling the space between them.

Alaric turned back to the altar, now quiet but still faintly pulsing with residual energy. Its jagged surface, once searing with crimson light, now lay dim and cracked. He approached cautiously, his gaze narrowing as he studied the runes etched into its surface.

The patterns were unlike anything he had seen before—intricate and unnatural, their shapes jagged and sharp, as if designed to disrupt rather than channel energy. Yet there was something familiar in their construction. He pulled his notebook from his satchel, flipping through the pages until he found the sketches he'd made earlier in the trial. Side by side, the resemblance was undeniable.

"These runes," he murmured to himself, tracing a finger over one of the cracked symbols. "They're not just siphoning energy. They're anchoring it. Redirecting it."

"Redirecting it where?" Lira's voice, still hoarse but steady, pulled him from his thoughts.

"I'm not sure," Alaric admitted. "But this pattern—it's similar to what I've seen in the Grimoire of Eternal Threads. Forbidden magic. The kind that bends the ley lines to the caster's will."

Lira frowned, her brow furrowing as she pushed herself to her feet. "The Veiled Order," she said, her voice heavy with certainty. "They're not just tampering with the ley lines—they're trying to control them."

"And they don't care what it costs," Alaric added, his jaw tightening. "This altar wasn't just draining the Nexus. It was amplifying the ley lines' pain, using it as a weapon to disrupt the flow. If we hadn't stopped it..." He trailed off, unwilling to finish the thought.

Lira nodded grimly. "We stopped it for now, but the ley lines are still fractured. This is only a temporary fix."

Alaric sighed, running a hand through his sweat-dampened hair. "We need more than a fix. We need a solution. And we're running out of time."

Lira leaned heavily against the stone wall, her gaze distant as she stared at the dimly glowing rivers below. "You were right about one thing," she said quietly.

Alaric raised an eyebrow. "Only one?"

Her lips curved into a faint, weary smile, but it didn't last. "I've been here before," she said, her voice dropping. "Not here, exactly, but at another Nexus. It was smaller, less volatile. But I... I failed."

Alaric remained silent, sensing the weight behind her words.

"I thought I could stabilize it," she continued, her tone bitter. "I thought if I just poured enough of myself into it, I could fix the ley lines. But I was wrong. The more I tried to force it, the worse it got. And when the Nexus collapsed, it... it wasn't just the ley lines that broke. People died. Because of me."

Alaric hesitated before speaking. "That doesn't mean it was your fault."

"Doesn't it?" Lira shot back, her eyes flashing. "I made the wrong call. I pushed too hard, ignored the warnings. And I paid for it. They all did."

Her voice cracked, and she turned away, her hands clenched into fists. "That's why I'm here. Why I keep trying. Because I can't let it happen again."

Alaric watched her, his usual skepticism softening. He had spent so much of their journey questioning her methods, dismissing her instincts as recklessness. But now he saw the weight she carried—the guilt, the determination. It wasn't recklessness; it was resolve born from pain.

"I didn't trust you," he admitted, his voice quiet. "Not at first. You're... different from what I'm used to. I rely on logic, structure, control. But control doesn't seem to mean much down here."

Lira turned to him, her expression unreadable.

"I saw it during the trial," he continued. "When you calmed the fragment. I was trying to force it into submission, but you... you listened to it. You worked with it. That's not something I can do. At least, not yet."

"You can," Lira said softly. "You just have to let go of the idea that magic is something you control. It's not a tool, Alaric. It's a conversation."

He nodded, the words settling over him like an uncomfortable truth. "Then I guess I have a lot to learn."

Lira took a deep breath, her gaze drifting back to the molten rivers. "There's something else," she said. "When I touched the ley lines earlier... I saw something. A vision."

Alaric frowned. "A vision?"

She nodded, her expression darkening. "It wasn't clear, but I saw the Spiral Nexus. Or what's left of it. It was fractured, engulfed in darkness. And there was someone there—standing at the center."

"Who?" Alaric asked, though a chill crept up his spine.

"I don't know," Lira admitted. "But whoever it was, they were... holding it together. Barely. The cost of it—it was written all over them. The ley lines were tearing them apart."

Alaric's mouth went dry. "You think it's one of us?"

"I don't know," she said again, her voice heavy with uncertainty. "But the ley lines don't just show things for no reason. Whatever that vision was, it's a warning."

They stood in silence for a long moment, the weight of her words settling over them like a stormcloud. Alaric's mind raced with possibilities, each one more dire than the last. The Spiral Nexus wasn't just the heart of the ley lines—it was the heart of their world. If it fell, everything else would follow.

"Do you think we can stop it?" he asked finally.

Lira's expression was unreadable. "I think we have to try. Even if it costs us everything."

Alaric clenched his fists, the echoes of the apparition's words ringing in his mind: The ley lines remember, but they also forgive. He didn't know what the future held or what sacrifices would be required, but one thing was certain: they couldn't turn back now.

"Then we'll try," he said firmly. "No matter what it takes."

Lira nodded, though her eyes remained clouded with doubt. "Let's just hope we're enough."

Together, they turned toward the tunnel that would lead them out of the Fire Nexus. The air around them was cooler now, but the tension remained, a heavy reminder of the trials yet to come. As they stepped into the shadows of the upper caverns, Alaric cast one last glance at the quieted altar.

The Fire Nexus was stable—for now. But the Spiral Nexus loomed ahead, its fate intertwined with their own. And for the first time, Alaric wondered if the price of saving the ley lines might be more than he was willing to pay.

As Alaric and Lira made their way through the twisting tunnels leading away from the Fire Nexus, the weight of their fragile victory pressed down on them. The air was cooler now, though the memory of the oppressive heat lingered like a phantom. Every step felt heavier than the last, the enormity of what they had seen and done carving an unspoken tension between them.

Alaric's mind churned with thoughts of the altar and the runes that adorned it. The faint resemblance to the forbidden symbols described in the Grimoire of Eternal Threads was no coincidence. He had read enough to piece together the dark philosophy of the Veiled Order, though he had never expected to confront their work firsthand.

"The Veiled Order," he said aloud, breaking the silence. "They're not just disrupting the ley lines—they're exploiting them."

Lira glanced at him, her exhaustion visible but her curiosity piqued. "What do you mean?"

"They believe the ley lines are tools," Alaric explained, his voice tight. "Resources to be mined, bent, and shaped to their will. The ancient texts call it 'dominance magic.' It's not about harmony or understanding—it's about control. They think they can use the ley lines to rewrite the fabric of reality, no matter the cost."

Lira frowned. "And what's the cost?"

"Everything," Alaric said grimly. "The ley lines aren't infinite. They're interconnected, like a web. You pull too hard on one thread, and the whole thing unravels. That's why the Spiral Nexus is so important—it's the anchor point. If they destabilize that..."

He didn't need to finish the thought. Lira's face darkened, and she nodded. "They're not just playing with fire—they're igniting an inferno."

"They've done it before," Alaric continued, his voice quieter now. "There are stories—legends, really—of civilizations that tried to dominate the ley lines. Entire kingdoms reduced to ash, their people lost to the fractures they created. The Veiled Order doesn't care about that. To them, the ley lines are just power to be wielded."

Lira's jaw tightened. "Then we stop them."

Alaric glanced at her, his skepticism fading in the face of her determination. "If we can figure out where they'll strike next."

"We don't have to guess," Lira said. "It's the Spiral Nexus. Everything they've done here, everything we've seen—it's all leading to that."

The Fire Nexus's Unique Significance

The conversation lapsed into silence as they reached a higher cavern, pausing to catch their breath. From this vantage point, they could look back at the faint glow of the Fire Nexus far below, its molten rivers now calmer but still flickering with an uneasy light.

Alaric stared at it, his thoughts drifting to the apparition they had encountered. The Nexus's sentience had been undeniable—a fragment of the ley lines' anguish given form. It had spoken to them, challenged them, and tested their resolve.

"The Fire Nexus," he said, his voice reflective. "It's not just another ley line node. It's a keystone. The heat, the volatility—it's part of the ley lines' natural balance. The energy here fuels the surrounding nodes, keeps the network stable. That's why the Veiled Order targeted it."

Lira leaned against the rock wall, her gaze thoughtful. "And if it had collapsed, it would have sent shockwaves through the entire network."

"Exactly," Alaric said. "The Fire Nexus isn't just significant because of its location. It's like a heart, pumping energy outward. The Veiled Order knew that. They wanted to weaken the entire system by starting here."

"And they almost succeeded," Lira said grimly. "If we hadn't stopped them..."

Alaric nodded, his mind turning over the implications. The Fire Nexus was safe for now, but the scars left behind by the altar's corruption would take time to heal—if they ever fully did.

As they rested, Alaric's thoughts turned to the ley lines themselves. The apparition's words echoed in his mind: The ley lines remember. They feel. And they suffer.

He had always thought of magic as a force to be studied, understood, and wielded. But the trial had shattered that belief. The ley lines weren't just conduits of energy—they were alive in their own way, bound to the fabric of the world and the people who used them.

He closed his eyes, letting his thoughts drift. In his mind's eye, he imagined the ley lines as a vast, shimmering web, each thread pulsing with life and memory. The fractures caused by the Veiled Order's interference spread like cracks in glass, threatening to splinter the entire structure.

The ley lines' pain was palpable, a mournful rhythm that echoed in his chest. It wasn't anger or vengeance—it was sorrow, a deep, abiding grief at the harm inflicted upon them.

"They're more than I thought," he murmured, almost to himself.

"What?" Lira asked, her gaze snapping to him.

"The ley lines," Alaric said. "They're not just power or tools. They're alive, in a way. They're connected to us, to everything. And we've been hurting them for centuries without even realizing it."

Lira nodded slowly. "I've felt it too. They're not just threads of magic—they're threads of life. And when we pull on them carelessly, they suffer."

The weight of her words settled over them both, and Alaric felt a pang of guilt. He had spent so much of his life studying magic as a discipline, a science to be mastered. Now he realized how blind he had been.

Alaric pushed himself to his feet, brushing dust from his tunic. "We need to understand the full extent of what the Veiled Order is doing," he said, his voice resolute. "If they've corrupted one Nexus, they've likely targeted others."

Lira stood as well, her expression determined. "We can't chase after every Nexus. The Spiral Nexus is the key. If we lose that, it's over."

"But if we ignore the others, the network could collapse before we even get there," Alaric countered. "The damage could be irreparable."

Lira hesitated, her lips pressing into a thin line. "Then we'll have to divide our efforts. You follow the Veiled Order's trail—figure out where they've struck and what their endgame is. I'll focus on the Spiral Nexus."

"You want to split up?" Alaric asked, his tone laced with skepticism.

"We don't have a choice," Lira said. "The Veiled Order is moving faster than we are. If we wait, we'll always be one step behind."

Alaric frowned but nodded reluctantly. "Fine. But we'll need to regroup before the Spiral Nexus. If we're going to stop them, we'll have to do it together."

Lira extended a hand, and he took it, the unspoken agreement binding them. "We will," she said firmly. "No matter what it takes."

As they resumed their journey, Lira's earlier vision lingered in her mind. The fractured Spiral Nexus, engulfed in darkness. The lone figure standing at its center, holding it together at unimaginable cost.

She hadn't told Alaric everything she had seen. The figure in her vision hadn't just been anyone—it had felt familiar. And the pain they bore had echoed through the ley lines like a warning. She feared what it meant, but she didn't have the heart to say it aloud.

Beside her, Alaric's expression was grim, his mind clearly turning over the same question: What would it take to save the ley lines? And who would have to pay the price?

As the tunnel narrowed and the glow of the Fire Nexus faded behind them, one thing was certain—their journey was far from over. The Spiral Nexus loomed ahead, its fragile balance threatening to tip. And the cost of restoring it might be more than either of them was prepared to pay.

The Fire Nexus's lingering heat faded as Alaric and Lira emerged from the tunnels into the cooler, open air. The ley lines' hum resonated faintly beneath their feet, calmer now but still strained. Their confrontation with the altar's corruption and the fiery sentience of the ley lines weighed heavily on their minds. Neither spoke as they descended the rocky path leading back toward the ley lines' central flow.

Alaric clutched his grimoire tightly, the flickering runes on its cover a constant reminder of the task ahead. Lira's gaze remained distant, her thoughts likely circling around the sacrifices they had witnessed and the cost yet to come. They both knew that their journey was only beginning. The ley lines' scars were deep, and the Veiled Order's machinations stretched far beyond this single Nexus.

As they reached the nexus's outer boundaries, a flicker of energy pulsed through the Runestone Compass in Alaric's satchel. He pulled it out, its needle spinning wildly before settling in a new direction.

Lira frowned, her hand instinctively brushing the crescent amulet at her neck. "Another disturbance?"

"It's guiding us to something," Alaric replied, his voice quiet. "The ley lines are fractured, but they're not finished with us yet."

The compass's needle pointed toward a distant peak, where a shimmering structure seemed to rise and fall like a mirage against the horizon. The vibrations in the air grew sharper, more chaotic, as they approached.

"This feels... different," Lira said, her eyes narrowing as the structure solidified. Its towering, mismatched turrets glinted in the dim light, reflecting fractured rainbows that pulsed faintly.

Alaric nodded, his grip tightening on the compass. "The House of the Krystal Keys. It's where the ley lines want us to go."

And so, with determination heavy in their steps, they continued forward, unaware of the secrets—and dangers—that awaited within the enigmatic structure.

Flashback: Ley Lines' Pain and History

As the oppressive heat of the Fire Nexus began to recede, Alaric paused, his hand resting lightly on the crystalline altar. A faint hum resonated through the cavern, a sound so soft it was almost imperceptible. He closed his eyes, letting the vibration wash over him.

Suddenly, images flashed through his mind: fiery threads unraveling and re-weaving, chaotic bursts of light erupting from deep within the earth. He saw towering figures—mages from centuries past—channeling the ley lines recklessly, their faces contorted with ambition and desperation.

The ley lines' sorrow wasn't just a sensation; it became a voice within him, resonating like a mournful melody: "We were nurtured once, tended with care. But then came the ones who sought to dominate, to bind us to their will. They fractured us. Used us. And now, we suffer."

Alaric's heart clenched as the vision shifted. He saw the Spiral Nexus at the center of the web, its luminous threads fraying as the ley lines' connections weakened. It pulsed faintly, struggling to maintain its rhythm as the Veiled Order's dark marks corrupted its flow.

Alaric staggered back from the vision, his chest rising and falling in rapid gasps. Beside him, Lira knelt, her fingers brushing the molten ground as if seeking a connection. Her approach was different—not forceful, but gentle. She whispered words of comfort, her magic flowing softly into the fractured ley lines.

"Why do you do that?" Alaric asked, his voice raw with frustration. "The ley lines don't need comforting. They need fixing."

Lira didn't look up. "You still don't understand," she said quietly. "They're not machines to repair, Alaric. They're alive. They feel. They remember."

Her words stung, but Alaric couldn't deny the truth in them. He had spent so much of his life treating magic as a formula to solve, a puzzle to master. But now, as he watched Lira's magic weave seamlessly with the ley lines, he saw the difference. Where his magic sought control, hers sought harmony.

The apparition, fiery and imposing, reappeared, its voice crackling like an inferno. "You pass not by strength, but by understanding. To guide the ley lines is to guide a wounded spirit, not a broken tool."

Alaric hesitated, his instincts pushing him to deflect the accusation. But he saw the apparition's fiery eyes flicker, and he remembered the vision—the pain, the anguish. He stepped closer, placing his hands over the altar. This time, he didn't try to channel the ley lines' energy. He simply listened.

The hum shifted, and for the first time, Alaric felt the ley lines respond—not with resistance, but with trust. They were not his to control, but they could be his to guide.

As the Fire Nexus grew still, its molten rivers calming to a steady flow, Alaric and Lira stood side by side. The apparition's form began to fade, leaving behind only the faint glow of restored ley lines.

"We still have so much to learn," Alaric said softly, his gaze fixed on the flickering energy.

Lira nodded. "But we're learning together now."

As they turned to leave, the ley lines whispered again, their voice faint but resolute: "Remember us. Protect us. And we will guide you to the truth."

Flashback: Alaric's Early Failure with Ley Line Magic

As Alaric stares into the pulsing heart of the Fire Nexus, a memory surfaces unbidden, pulling him back to a moment of crushing defeat.

The forest was quiet save for the rustling of leaves in the wind. Alaric stood in the center of the grove, a simple casting circle drawn in the dirt around him. The lines of the circle glowed faintly, their energy flickering as he focused his will.

"Concentrate," Eldaryn's voice commanded from the shadows. The older mage leaned against a tree, his gaze sharp. "You're trying to control it. Guide it instead."

Alaric's jaw clenched. He extended his hand toward the circle's center, his voice trembling as he whispered the incantation. The ley line thread he had coaxed into the circle pulsed brightly, but it refused to flow into the rune he had drawn.

"Come on," Alaric muttered. "Work with me."

The thread shuddered violently, and before he could react, it snapped back like a whip. The backlash threw him to the ground, the glowing circle extinguishing as a sharp pain shot through his arm.

"Enough!" Eldaryn barked, stepping forward. He crouched beside Alaric, his expression a mixture of frustration and concern. "The ley lines aren't your servants. They're alive, and they'll resist if you force them."

Alaric looked up, his pride wounded. "But I can feel them. I just don't understand why—"

"Understanding takes time," Eldaryn interrupted, helping him to his feet. "And humility. Until you learn that, you'll never wield their power without consequences."

Artifact Exploration in the Fire Nexus

As Alaric and Lira approach the Fire Nexus, Alaric's attention is drawn to an ancient pedestal near the edge of the molten rivers. Upon it rests an artifact: the Pyrestone Scepter.

The scepter shimmered with an inner light, its crystalline core pulsating in time with the Nexus' energy. Alaric's breath caught as he reached for it, the heat radiating from its surface stopping his hand inches away.

"The Pyrestone Scepter," Lira murmured, her voice reverent. "A conduit for fire ley lines. The texts say it was used to channel their power during the Breaking, but no one's wielded it since."

Alaric frowned. "Why leave it here?"

"Because it's tied to the ley lines," Lira replied. "It amplifies their energy, but it also draws from their pain. Using it might stabilize the Nexus—or destroy it."

Alaric hesitated, his mind racing. The scepter pulsed again, its rhythm syncing with the faint hum of the ley lines beneath his feet. He could feel the potential in it, a raw, untamed power waiting to be unleashed.

Narrator: Artifact and Ley Line Lore

As Alaric studies the scepter, the narrative voice reflects on the broader significance of such artifacts.

Artifacts like the Pyrestone Scepter were relics of an age when mages sought to tame the ley lines. They were tools of creation and destruction, their power drawn directly from the lifeblood of magic itself. Yet, for all their might, they were imperfect—prone to corruption and misuse.

The ley lines, ancient and sentient, resisted such domination. Their energy was not meant to be controlled but harmonized, a lesson learned too late by the mages of old. The Breaking had shattered more than just the physical world—it had scarred the ley lines, leaving them wary of those who would wield their power without understanding.

Chapter 13: The House of the Krystal Keys

The air shimmered as Alaric and Lira stood before the House of the Krystal Keys. Its towering, mismatched turrets jutted skyward like jagged teeth, each window reflecting fractured rainbows that pulsed faintly, as though alive. The house seemed to breathe with the ley lines beneath it, every corner vibrating with an energy both alluring and ominous.

"This is it," Alaric murmured, clutching his grimoire tightly. The book's pages pulsed faintly, synchronized with the vibrations of the house. "The nexus we've been tracking."

Lira tilted her head, her fingers brushing the crescent moon amulet at her neck. "It looks like it's been abandoned for centuries. You're sure this is the place?"

Alaric glanced at his Runestone Compass, its needle quivering erratically. "It's unstable. The ley lines here are distorted—fracturing."

He stepped forward, but the moment his boot touched the cracked cobblestone leading to the front door, the air thickened, and a voice—young, curious, and almost playful—rang out from nowhere.

"You shouldn't be here."

Alaric turned sharply, his eyes scanning the surroundings. A boy no older than eight stood on the steps of the house, his dark hair curling around his ears. He wore a patched tunic, his bare feet seemingly unaffected by the cold ground. His eyes, however, burned with an unsettling intensity far beyond his years.

"Who are you?" Lira asked, stepping protectively closer to Alaric.

The boy tilted his head. "Some call me Pecos. Others..." He trailed off, his form shimmering briefly before flickering into that of a teenager, taller and clad in a flowing cloak. "Others know me differently."

Lira gasped. "A Nexus being."

Alaric's grip on his grimoire tightened. "What do you want?"

Pecos—now a weathered man with streaks of silver in his hair—smiled faintly. "It's not what I want, seeker. It's what you must learn."

Before they could respond, the heavy wooden doors of the house groaned open, revealing an unlit hallway stretching into darkness. Pecos vanished, his voice echoing faintly: "Enter, if you dare."

*****

The air within the house was dense, heavy with the scent of old wood and something sharper—ozone, like the aftermath of a lightning strike. Faint glimmers of light danced along the floorboards, guiding their steps deeper into the maze-like interior.

"Stay close," Alaric whispered. "The ley lines are warping reality here."

They turned a corner and froze. The hallway ahead stretched impossibly long, with doors lining either side. From one of the rooms came a faint, melodic humming. Lira reached for her staff, her knuckles whitening.

"Do you hear that?" she asked.

Before Alaric could answer, the door nearest them creaked open, revealing a golden glow. A large goose strutted out, its feathers gleaming as if dipped in sunlight. It cocked its head, one eye gleaming with unmistakable intelligence.

"Welcome, friends!" the goose declared in a voice far too animated for its avian form. "I'm Bob! Don't mind the mess—this house has a way of rearranging itself."

Lira stared. "Is that—"

"A talking goose," Alaric finished, his tone deadpan.

The goose puffed out its chest proudly. "I am more than that. I am the arbiter of wisdom, the keeper of chaos. Also, I make excellent quiche."

The room behind Bob shifted suddenly, transforming into a sitting room filled with glowing sigils. The goose turned and, mid-step, shimmered, morphing into a lanky teenager with golden hair. "Better?" he asked with a grin, his voice still bearing an eccentric edge.

"What are you?" Lira demanded.

"Bob," he said simply. "And you've got problems bigger than introductions."

Following Bob's cryptic advice, the duo ascended a spiraling staircase to the attic. The walls seemed to ripple like water, and gravity itself felt inconsistent, each step growing heavier as they climbed. The door to the attic creaked open on its own, revealing Pecos—now in his teenage form—standing amid a sea of floating crystals.

"This is the heart of the instability," Pecos said, gesturing to the crystals. "Each one resonates with the fractured ley lines beneath the house."

Alaric stepped closer, the grimoire in his hands glowing faintly. "If I can stabilize these connections—"

"No," Pecos interrupted sharply, his voice layered with the timbre of all his forms. "You don't stabilize ley lines. You harmonize with them."

As they descended to the basement, the air grew colder, the walls shifting into translucent hues of ruby and pink. A soft, melodic laugh echoed through the chamber as a flamingo stepped into view, its feathers shimmering with a ruby sheen.

"You must be Alaric," it said, its voice smooth and feminine. The flamingo shimmered, taking the form of a young woman with pink hair and a gown that sparkled like starlight. "I am Flamipandro. And you've made a grave mistake coming here."

Alaric frowned. "The ley lines are breaking. If I don't act—"

"The ley lines don't need your intervention," Flamipandro said sharply. "They need understanding."

She raised her hand, and the walls erupted into projections of the ley lines. Threads of light wove through the air, fracturing and reconnecting like veins in a living organism. "Magic and science are not opposites, Alaric. They are reflections of the same truth. Your task is not to fix the ley lines but to learn their song."

The basement doors slammed shut behind them, cutting off the light from the house above. The faint glow of Flamipandro's ruby shimmer provided the only illumination as Alaric and Lira ventured deeper into the labyrinthine space. Each step echoed unnaturally, as though the walls themselves were absorbing the sound and twisting it into something alien.

The room shifted, the walls morphing from rough stone to glass-like panels. Shadows flickered within the surfaces, faintly resembling the forms of other Nexus beings, their movements eerily synchronized.

"This house isn't just connected to the ley lines," Lira said, her voice trembling. "It's alive."

Flamipandro, now in her flamingo form, walked ahead, her delicate steps soundless on the floor. "Alive and watching," she said cryptically. "But not for long if you persist in disrupting its heart."

Alaric paused, tracing his fingers over a faintly glowing sigil etched into one wall. It pulsed weakly, its light fading and returning sporadically. "This is the same rune I saw in the attic," he muttered. "They're connected."

Lira leaned closer, her crescent moon amulet flickering. "Connected how?"

"They're like neural pathways," Alaric said, his eyes narrowing. "The house is a nexus itself, its structure mirroring the flow of ley lines."

*****

A door on their left swung open abruptly, revealing a grand dining room that appeared untouched by time. A golden chandelier sparkled above a long table set with silverware and plates as if awaiting a grand feast. At the head of the table sat Bob, now in his teenage form, wearing a loosely fitted tunic and lounging in the chair like a bored aristocrat.

"You're poking at things you don't understand," he said, his voice carrying an uncharacteristic seriousness.

Alaric and Lira stepped cautiously into the room, Flamipandro perching gracefully on the table's edge. "If we don't, the ley lines could collapse entirely," Alaric countered.

"And if you do, you could trigger something far worse," Bob replied, his golden eyes gleaming. "The lines aren't just about energy. They're bridges—gateways. Stabilize them incorrectly, and you could invite the wrong kind of guest."

He gestured toward the far wall, where an ornate mirror hung. Its surface rippled, revealing a vision of twisted landscapes where the sky bled into the ground and figures made of shadows crawled across fractured ley lines.

"Those are the Wraiths of the Veil," Bob said grimly. "They dwell in the spaces between dimensions, waiting for cracks to form."

Alaric's grip on the grimoire tightened. "Then we have no choice but to fix the lines. If we don't, they'll invade."

Bob shook his head. "The lines don't need fixing, seeker. They need balance."

The conversation with Bob lingered in Alaric's mind as they moved deeper into the basement. The air grew colder, and the light from their surroundings dimmed to a faint glow. Alaric opened his grimoire, flipping through the pages until he found the map of the house, its layout now overlaid with shifting ley line patterns.

"These fractures," he murmured, pointing to the glowing points on the map, "they're like pressure points. If we can redistribute the energy—like equalizing pressure in a closed system—it might stabilize."

Lira frowned. "You're talking about treating ley lines like fluid dynamics."

"Exactly," Alaric said. "Magic follows natural laws. We just have to find the right variables."

He pulled out a piece of chalk and began sketching a series of interconnected runes on the floor. Each one was a variation of the amplification and balance sigils he had studied, designed to harmonize with the fractured ley lines.

"This could either stabilize the house or rip it apart," Lira said, watching him work.

"Let's hope for the former," Alaric replied, activating the first rune.

The sigils glowed faintly, their light traveling along the floor and walls. For a moment, the house seemed to sigh, its vibrations steadying. Then, without warning, a loud crack split the air, and the sigils flickered violently.

The basement walls fractured, revealing swirling voids of light and shadow. Pecos appeared suddenly, this time as an older man with weathered features and a staff of twisted wood.

"Stop!" he shouted, his voice reverberating through the space. "You're forcing the ley lines to conform to your will. That's not how balance works."

Before Alaric could respond, the voids in the walls solidified, and figures began to emerge. One resembled a humanoid made entirely of shifting crystal shards, its jagged edges reflecting every flicker of light. Another was a serpent-like entity with translucent skin, through which glowing veins of energy pulsed.

"These are ley line avatars," Flamipandro said, now in her human form, her ruby gown shimmering. "Manifestations of the lines' instability."

Bob, back in his goose form, fluttered into the room, squawking. "I told you! Now you've made them angry!"

The crystal humanoid advanced, its limbs reshaping with every step. Alaric raised his hands, summoning a barrier spell, but the avatar's strike shattered it instantly, sending him sprawling.

Lira swung her staff, summoning a wave of water magic that surged toward the serpent. The creature writhed, absorbing the water and growing larger. "That's not working!" she shouted.

Alaric scrambled to his feet, his mind racing. "They're resonating with the ley lines. We need to disrupt their frequency."

He pulled the Runestone Compass from his pocket, its needle spinning wildly. "If I can recalibrate the sigils to match their natural rhythm..."

"Do it fast," Lira said, holding off the serpent with a fire spell.

Alaric traced new runes over the existing ones, altering their structure. The sigils began to glow brighter, their light pulsating in harmony with the avatars. The crystal humanoid paused, its form flickering.

"It's working!" Flamipandro said, her voice carrying a note of hope.

But the serpent resisted, thrashing wildly. Pecos stepped forward, slamming his staff into the ground. A wave of golden light erupted, momentarily paralyzing the creature.

"Hurry, Alaric!" Pecos said, his voice strained.

With the final sigil completed, the room filled with a brilliant light. The ley line avatars dissolved, their energy flowing back into the walls. The house's vibrations steadied, and the oppressive weight in the air lifted.

Alaric slumped against the wall, his chest heaving. "Did we... do it?"

Pecos nodded, his form shifting back into that of a boy. "For now. But the balance you've restored is fragile. The ley lines have more to teach you."

Flamipandro smiled faintly, her flamingo form shimmering. "You've taken your first step, seeker. But the journey ahead will demand more than knowledge. It will demand understanding."

Bob, now a teenage boy again, clapped Alaric on the back. "Not bad for a rookie."

As the house settled into silence, Alaric opened his grimoire. A new symbol had appeared on the map—a fractured circle in the distance, glowing faintly. It was the next destination, the next challenge.

"We're not done yet," Alaric said, his determination renewed.

Lira smirked. "We never are."

The Stairwell of Shifting Time

The silence in the basement didn't last. As Alaric, Lira, and the Nexus beings gathered their bearings, the walls groaned, and the floor beneath their feet began to ripple like water under invisible pressure.

The staircase they had descended moments earlier twisted upward, its steps spiraling in impossible directions. Lira reached for the banister, but her hand passed through it as though it were smoke. A soft, dissonant hum filled the air.

"This house is unraveling," Flamipandro murmured. She shifted back into her human form, her ruby gown catching and refracting the dim light. "The ley lines here are more fractured than I feared."

"What's happening to the stairs?" Lira asked, her voice trembling.

Bob, now perched on the broken remnants of a chair in his goose form, ruffled his feathers. "Oh, they're not broken," he said casually. "They're deciding where to take you."

The staircase shimmered again, and for a moment, Alaric saw three versions of it simultaneously: one leading to a darkened attic filled with shifting shadows, another spiraling endlessly into a void of starlight, and a third coiling tightly around itself like the inside of a conch shell.

"They're shifting," Alaric said, his voice filled with awe. "The house is warping time and space—tied to the ley lines' fractures."

"Not just warping," Pecos said, stepping forward in his teenage form. "It's choosing. The house is sentient, a reflection of the lines themselves."

"And its choices aren't always kind," Flamipandro added.

The hum grew louder, and the staircase solidified into a single path leading upward, vanishing into an iridescent light.

"Looks like it's made its decision," Bob said, leaping down from the chair and transforming back into his teenage form. "Hope you're ready."

The Library of Forgotten Tomes

The staircase deposited them into a grand library, its scale utterly overwhelming. Shelves stretched into infinity, each one packed with books of every imaginable size, shape, and material. Some tomes seemed to hum faintly, their covers glowing with soft, otherworldly light. Others were chained to their shelves, their bindings writhing as though alive.

The air smelled of aged parchment and ozone, and the only light came from floating orbs that hovered above the group, flickering like will-o'-the-wisps.

"This isn't just a library," Lira whispered, staring at a book whose title was written in a language that seemed to shift every time she looked at it. "It's... a repository. A memory bank for the ley lines themselves."

Alaric ran his fingers along the spine of a particularly large tome, its surface cold and metallic. The title etched onto it read The Shattered Planes. When he pulled it from the shelf, the pages flipped open of their own accord, revealing vivid illustrations of fractured worlds.

"Look at this," Alaric said, holding up the book. "It's a record of every nexus fracture—every time the ley lines disrupted reality."

Pecos, now in his older form, peered over Alaric's shoulder. "And every mistake that led to them. That book isn't just a record—it's a warning."

As Alaric turned the pages, a faint whisper began to emanate from the book. The voice grew louder with each page, speaking in an ancient tongue. Pecos placed a hand on the tome, and the whispers ceased abruptly.

"Some knowledge should remain hidden," Pecos said gravely. "The house tests you, Alaric. Be careful what you take from it."

The Hall of Mirrors

Leaving the library proved more difficult than expected. Every door they tried led them back into the same room, though the arrangement of the shelves seemed to shift subtly each time. Finally, Flamipandro found a narrow archway concealed behind a tapestry, leading them into a corridor lined with mirrors.

Each mirror reflected not just their images, but versions of themselves that felt wrong. In one, Alaric saw himself older, his eyes sunken and his hands gnarled as though burned by overuse of magic. In another, Lira's reflection was adorned in ceremonial robes, her face blank and expressionless.

"These aren't reflections," Flamipandro said, her voice tight. "They're possibilities."

Bob, now striding ahead in his teenage form, stopped before a mirror that showed him as a radiant figure surrounded by flames. He cocked his head. "I look pretty good like that, don't I?"

"This isn't a joke," Pecos said, his form flickering. "These mirrors are tied to the house's core. They reveal the paths the ley lines could take—what they might create, and what they might destroy."

Alaric paused before a mirror that reflected an endless void filled with floating islands, their surfaces cracked and leaking light into the darkness. He felt a chill run down his spine.

"Whatever's in the heart of this house," Alaric said, "it's tied to the ley lines' future. We have to find it."

*****

The house led them next to the attic, though it was unlike the attic they had seen before. Time itself seemed fragmented here. Clocks hung from the rafters, each ticking at a different pace. Shadows moved across the walls as though cast by invisible figures. Pecos, now in his child form, stood at the center of the room, his hands folded behind his back.

"Time doesn't flow normally here," Pecos said. "It's a nexus within a nexus, a place where possibilities collide."

The crystals they had seen earlier now hovered in midair, pulsing faintly. Each one seemed to contain a miniature scene—moments frozen in time. Alaric leaned closer to one and saw a younger version of himself studying at the Grand Arcanum.

"This place... it's showing me my past," Alaric murmured.

"And your future," Pecos added. "But which future depends on the choices you make here."

A sudden cracking sound filled the attic as one of the crystals shattered. A wave of energy burst forth, sending everyone sprawling. When Alaric looked up, a figure stepped out of the mist—a Wraith of the Veil, its glowing eyes locked onto him.

The Wraith loomed tall, its form shifting and pulsating as though it were made of pure shadow. Alaric scrambled to his feet, his grimoire glowing as he prepared a defensive spell.

"Careful!" Flamipandro warned. "Wraiths feed on imbalance. The more unstable you are, the stronger it becomes."

The Wraith lunged, and Alaric cast a shield spell just in time. The shadowy figure collided with the barrier, sending ripples through the magic.

"Alaric, the runes!" Lira shouted, pointing to the glowing crystals. "They're amplifying its power. We need to stabilize them."

Alaric nodded, his mind racing. He began carving sigils into the air, using the principles of resonance he had studied. Each rune glowed briefly before fading, syncing with the crystals' pulses.

As the sigils aligned, the Wraith let out a piercing shriek and dissolved into mist. The attic grew still, the crystals dimming to a faint glow.

The Heart of the House

Their victory in the attic revealed a hidden staircase leading downward, into the heart of the house. The walls here were translucent, showing the glowing web of ley lines that formed the house's foundation. At the center of the room stood a pedestal, upon which rested a key made of pure light.

"The Krystal Key," Pecos said softly. "The house's core."

Bob, back in his goose form, flapped onto the pedestal. "So, do we grab it and hope for the best, or...?"

"No," Alaric said, stepping forward. "We harmonize with it."

He placed his hands on the pedestal and began to channel his magic, using the principles of energy redistribution. The ley lines pulsed in response, their light growing steadier.

The house shifted one final time, its walls solidifying and its vibrations ceasing. The Krystal Key floated into Alaric's hands, its light warm and steady.

"It's done," Flamipandro said. "For now."

As the group exited the house, the landscape around them seemed brighter, the tension in the air lifted. Alaric looked at the Krystal Key in his hands, its light faint but persistent.

"This is just the beginning," he said, his voice filled with determination.

Lira nodded. "Let's make sure we're ready for what's next."

Pecos, Flamipandro, and Bob exchanged knowing glances as they faded into the ether, their voices echoing: "Balance is only the first step."

The group emerged from the House of the Krystal Keys to find the world around them transformed. The once-dim sky had taken on a deep cobalt hue, dotted with brilliant stars that seemed closer than usual. The air was lighter, as if the house's chaos had lifted not just from the building but from the surrounding land.

Alaric held the Krystal Key tightly, its light casting faint, shifting patterns on his face. Though it looked solid, the key felt almost immaterial, like holding a shard of frozen light.

"What now?" Lira asked, breaking the silence. She gestured to the Runestone Compass in Alaric's pocket. "Does it point somewhere new?"

Alaric pulled out the compass, but its needle spun erratically. "It's not responding."

"That's because it's no longer guiding you," Flamipandro's voice chimed. She shimmered into view in her flamingo form before gracefully shifting into her human guise. "The Key's purpose is not to follow—it is to unlock."

"Unlock what?" Alaric asked.

Pecos appeared beside her, this time as a boy holding a small, glowing orb. He smiled faintly. "The truth."

Bob, now in his golden goose form, waddled into view. "And truths, dear Alaric, have a way of being more complicated than you'd like."

Before Alaric could question them further, the Krystal Key pulsed in his hand. A low hum filled the air, and the surrounding ley lines became visible, threads of gold and blue light weaving across the sky like an intricate web. The group froze as the threads converged on the key, their energy flowing into it in radiant bursts.

"It's absorbing the ley lines' energy," Lira whispered, shielding her eyes from the brightness. "But why?"

The light grew blinding, and the world around them began to shift. The ground beneath their feet dissolved into shimmering mist, and the group found themselves standing on an endless expanse of mirrored water. The sky above reflected the same golden and blue threads, creating an infinite web that seemed to pulse in rhythm with the key.

"This is... the Nexus Plane," Flamipandro said, her voice filled with awe. "The convergence of all ley lines."

Pecos, now an older man, stepped forward. "Few have ever entered this place. The ley lines have allowed it because of the balance you restored."

Alaric stared at the expanse, his heart pounding. The Krystal Key in his hand began to emit a faint voice, barely audible at first but growing louder. It wasn't speaking in words but in musical notes, a melody that resonated deep within him.

"It's a song," Alaric murmured. "The ley lines are singing."

"They always have," Pecos said. "You've just never listened."

*****

The melody grew more complex, and with it came visions. Alaric saw fragments of a world long gone—vast cities built around ley line nexuses, their spires glowing with harnessed energy. He saw scholars working tirelessly to understand the lines, their faces alight with discovery.

Then, the visions darkened. Fractures appeared in the ley lines, spreading like cracks in glass. The cities fell into chaos, consumed by the very energy they sought to control. Shadows emerged from the cracks, the Wraiths of the Veil, feeding on the destruction.

"It's a warning," Lira said, her voice trembling. "This is what happens when the lines are manipulated without balance."

Alaric nodded, his resolve hardening. "Then we need to ensure it never happens again."

The Krystal Key's light dimmed, and the group found themselves back in the clearing where the house once stood. But the house was gone, replaced by a circle of glowing runes embedded in the ground. Alaric knelt beside them, tracing the patterns.

"These runes," he said. "They're a map."

The Runestone Compass began to vibrate in his pocket. He pulled it out, and its needle now pointed steadily to the west.

"The key wants us to go there," Lira said.

Pecos, still in his older form, stepped forward. "It's guiding you to the next nexus. Each one will reveal a fragment of the ley lines' true nature."

Bob, now a teenager again, smirked. "And maybe if you're lucky, it won't involve fighting shadow monsters next time. No promises, though."

The Nexus beings began to fade, their forms shimmering like heatwaves. Flamipandro placed a hand on Alaric's shoulder, her ruby gown catching the light. "Remember, seeker: balance is not achieved through control but through harmony. The lines will guide you, but only if you're willing to listen."

Pecos nodded, his voice layered with the tones of all his forms. "And beware the Spiral Nexus. Its path leads to both creation and destruction."

Bob flapped his wings, now fully back in his golden goose form. "And if you find another talking goose out there, tell it I said hello."

With that, the beings vanished, leaving Alaric and Lira alone under the now-clear sky.

As they set off toward the next nexus, the landscape around them seemed subtly altered. Trees were taller, their leaves glowing faintly with ley line energy. The air was fresher, charged with a quiet vitality that hadn't been there before.

Alaric glanced at the Krystal Key, now hanging from a chain around his neck. "This is just the beginning," he said.

Lira nodded. "And we're in it together."

Their path led them into the horizon, where the next chapter of the ley lines' mysteries awaited.

Alaric's fingers tightened around the Krystal Key as the group stepped outside. The clearing where the house once stood was eerily silent, the air charged with a faint static hum. Though the house had disappeared, its presence lingered, woven into the very fabric of the land. The ley lines that crisscrossed beneath them pulsed faintly, their energy resonating with the key.

Lira crouched to trace one of the glowing sigils etched into the earth. "It's as if the house transferred itself here, into these symbols."

"The house was never just a structure," Flamipandro said, her flamingo form shifting gracefully into that of a young woman. Her ruby gown shimmered in the moonlight. "It was a vessel for the ley lines' memories. A nexus of sentience."

"Sentience?" Alaric echoed. He glanced down at the key in his hand, its light dim but persistent. "You're saying the ley lines are alive?"

"They're more than alive," Pecos said, appearing beside him in his teenage form. "They think, they feel, and they remember."

Before Alaric could ask more, the ground beneath them trembled. The sigils etched into the soil flared brightly, and a sharp, crystalline chime filled the air. The Krystal Key responded, its light pulsing in rhythm with the vibrations.

"Something's happening," Lira said, standing quickly.

The sigils began to expand, their glowing lines spiraling outward to form intricate geometric patterns. At the center of the design, a single point of light appeared, growing brighter with each pulse. The group instinctively stepped back as the light coalesced into a floating orb, its surface smooth and translucent, like polished glass.

"That's new," Bob said, now in his teenage form. He tilted his head, golden hair catching the light. "Let me guess—it's dangerous?"

"It's a memory fragment," Flamipandro said. "But it's not complete."

Alaric approached cautiously. The orb seemed to hum faintly, its resonance tugging at something deep within him. As he reached out to touch it, the world around him blurred.

Alaric found himself standing in an endless void. Golden threads crisscrossed the space, forming an intricate web that pulsed with energy. Each thread carried faint images, like streams of consciousness flowing through the nexus.

He watched as one thread unraveled, its energy splintering into jagged fragments. The images within it grew chaotic—visions of cities crumbling, dimensions collapsing, and shadowy figures feeding on the destruction. Among the chaos, a voice spoke, soft and melodic, yet filled with sorrow.

"We are the threads of existence. When we falter, so too does the balance."

"Who are you?" Alaric asked, his voice echoing in the void.

"We are the ley lines," the voice replied. "Sentient, yet bound. Guardians of creation, yet powerless to resist those who seek to control us."

The vision shifted, showing a great nexus at the center of the web. Its spiraling energy was both beautiful and terrifying, radiating immense power. Around it, shadowy figures moved, their hands weaving dark magic that fractured the threads.

"The Spiral Nexus," the voice said. "It is the heart of all things. And it is in peril."

The vision faded, and Alaric was pulled back into the clearing. The orb before him had dimmed, its energy spent.

Alaric stood at the edge of the forest, his grip tightening around the Krystal Key as its faint light pulsed in time with the ley lines' rhythm. The map in the grimoire showed a convergence nearby, marked with an ancient rune he had yet to decipher. The forest loomed before him, shadows shifting unnaturally, as if alive.

"We're close," Lira said, her voice hushed. The Aetheric Staff in her hand emitted a faint hum, resonating with the key.

Flamipandro fluttered overhead in her flamingo form, her ruby feathers gleaming in the twilight. "The ley lines don't hum this loudly for no reason. They're warning us—or calling us."

Alaric hesitated. The weight of the grimoire in his satchel and the memory of the ley lines' warnings pressed on him. "This isn't just another nexus," he said. "It's something more."

Lira nodded, her expression grim. "Then let's find out."

The group stepped forward, the forest swallowing them as the Krystal Key's light guided their way.

As the pulsating energy of the House of the Krystal Keys settled into an uneasy rhythm, Alaric felt the weight of the structure's significance pressing down on him. The crystalline walls seemed to shimmer with faint whispers, fragments of conversations echoing from long-forgotten times. Lira stood nearby, her crescent amulet glowing faintly in resonance with the ley lines beneath their feet.

Flashback: The Origins of the Keys

Alaric placed a hand on one of the crystalline spires, the surface cold yet alive with subtle vibrations. As he did, his mind was flooded with visions—fragments of the past drawn from the ley lines themselves.

He saw a time long ago, when the ley lines were pure and undisturbed. The Keys were created by the First Wardens, ancient mages who understood the delicate balance of the ley lines. The Keys were not merely artifacts; they were extensions of the ley lines, forged to protect the harmony of magic. Each key had a purpose, a singular connection to the Spiral Nexus, binding its flow to the greater web of life.

But the visions darkened, the light of the ley lines fracturing as figures cloaked in shadow emerged. The Veiled Order. They sought the Keys, not to preserve balance but to control it, to rewrite the ley lines' flow according to their will. The visions faded, leaving Alaric with the chilling knowledge that the Order's interference had begun centuries before, setting the stage for the chaos he and Lira now faced.

Dialogue with Ayiyi Mones

The spectral child, Ayiyi Mones, appeared again, their form flickering like a candle in the wind. "You saw them, didn't you?" they asked, their voice echoing faintly.

Alaric nodded. "The First Wardens. The Veiled Order. This place... it's connected to everything."

"Of course it is," Ayiyi said, tilting their head. "The House is a beacon for those who seek truth. But truth is not always what you want it to be."

Lira stepped forward, her brow furrowed. "What is the purpose of the Keys? Why would the ley lines lead us here?"

Ayiyi's expression grew somber. "The Keys are fragments of balance. Without them, the Spiral Nexus cannot be restored. But their power comes with a price. Each Key is tied to a sacrifice—a piece of the soul that wields it."

The words hung heavy in the air, and Alaric's mind raced. The Spiral Nexus loomed ahead, its stability the only hope for saving the ley lines. Yet the Keys, so vital to that mission, demanded more than mere effort. They required personal cost—sacrifices neither he nor Lira were prepared to make.

"Is that why the Veiled Order wants them?" Alaric asked, his voice barely above a whisper. "To use that power for themselves?"

Ayiyi's form flickered again, and their grin returned, faint and enigmatic. "The Order seeks control. They believe the ley lines are theirs to command. But the ley lines remember, Alaric. They remember every wound, every betrayal. The Keys are their way of choosing who is worthy."

Lira exchanged a glance with Alaric, her expression a mixture of determination and dread. "And if we fail?"

Ayiyi's grin faded entirely. "Then the Spiral Nexus will collapse, and the ley lines will unravel. Your world will follow."

*****

The crystalline walls began to hum, their vibrations growing more chaotic. Ayiyi gestured toward the heart of the house, where a spiral staircase of pure crystal descended into darkness. "The Keys await below," they said. "But they will not reveal themselves willingly. The House will test you, as it has tested all who came before."

"Tested how?" Lira asked, her hand instinctively moving to her blade.

Ayiyi's form shimmered, and their voice grew distant. "It will show you your truths. Your doubts. Your fears. If you cannot face them, the Keys will remain beyond your reach."

The child vanished, leaving Alaric and Lira alone in the crystalline hall. The hum of the ley lines grew louder, more insistent, as if urging them forward.

As they descended the staircase, the air grew colder, and the light from their amulets flickered uncertainly. The crystalline walls seemed to shift and twist, reflecting not just their surroundings but fragments of memories—Alaric's childhood in the Grand Arcanum, Lira's first failure to protect a Nexus.

The visions grew sharper, more personal. Alaric saw himself standing before Eldaryn, his mentor, who looked at him with disappointment. "You've always been too rigid, Alaric," the memory-Eldaryn said. "You can't control the ley lines with logic alone. They demand more."

Lira's reflection showed a younger version of herself, kneeling before the ruins of a Nexus she had tried to save. The echoes of voices accused her, their words cutting deep: "You were supposed to protect us. You failed."

The staircase ended in a vast chamber, its center dominated by a pedestal holding the first Key. The Key glowed faintly, its crystalline surface etched with runes that seemed to shift and writhe. But as Alaric and Lira stepped forward, shadows coalesced around the pedestal, taking the form of their deepest fears.

For Alaric, the shadow was himself, cold and unyielding, his hands dripping with fractured ley lines. "You'll fail them all," it hissed. "Just like you failed the Fire Nexus."

For Lira, the shadow was a towering figure, cloaked in darkness and wielding a blade of pure light. "You're not strong enough," it said, its voice a cruel echo of her own thoughts. "You never have been."

The shadows advanced, their forms twisting and writhing. Alaric raised his grimoire, its pages glowing faintly. "We fight together," he said, his voice steady despite the fear clawing at his chest.

Lira nodded, drawing her blade. "Always."

The battle was grueling, each strike and counterstrike forcing Alaric and Lira to confront their deepest insecurities. But as the shadows dissolved, the chamber grew brighter, the ley lines' hum shifting to a harmonious resonance.

Alaric stepped forward, his hand trembling as he reached for the Key. The moment his fingers touched its surface, a surge of energy coursed through him, filling his mind with visions of the Spiral Nexus. The Key wasn't just a tool—it was a fragment of the ley lines' essence, a beacon of balance waiting to be restored.

Lira placed a hand on his shoulder, grounding him. "One down," she said, her voice soft but determined. "How many more to go?"

Alaric glanced at the Key, its light reflecting in his eyes. "Enough to save the ley lines. Or to lose everything trying."

As they ascended back to the surface, the whispers of the House grew faint, but one phrase lingered in Alaric's mind: The Keys will choose their bearers. And their price will be paid.

Chapter 14: The Attic's Secrets

The compass needle spun erratically, the Krystal Key's glow brightening as the group emerged from the forest's edge. Before them stood a small, crooked house, its warped timbers sagging under the weight of time. Despite its dilapidated state, the windows glimmered faintly, their light pulsating in rhythm with the key.

"This place looks... inviting," Bob quipped, his golden feathers shimmering as he fluttered to Alaric's shoulder.

"It's the same energy as the Krystal Key," Lira said, stepping closer. Her staff vibrated faintly in her hand. "This house is tied to the ley lines."

Alaric approached cautiously, the key's glow intensifying with each step. He reached the threshold, the air thick with an unspoken warning. "It's more than that. It's guarding something."

Inside, the house was as unsettling as its exterior. The air was heavy, laden with the scent of aged wood and decay. Each step on the creaking floorboards sent echoes whispering through the shadows. As they ascended the narrow staircase, the Krystal Key pulsed faster, its light casting eerie, golden patterns on the walls.

The attic door loomed at the top of the stairs, sealed with a mechanism of glowing runes and intricate gears. Alaric stepped forward, his grimoire already open, his mind racing to decipher the ancient symbols.

"It's a binding spell," he murmured. "Old—centuries, maybe more."

Using a combination of runic magic and electromagnetic resonance spells he had learned at the Arcanum, Alaric manipulated the gears. Each rune glowed faintly as he aligned them. After a tense moment, the mechanism clicked, and the door creaked open.

The Attic's Mysteries Unfold The attic was impossibly vast, its dimensions defying the house's modest exterior. Crystalline orbs floated in the air, their surfaces shimmering with faint light. Within each orb, swirling mists revealed glimpses of people, places, and events—fragments of memory preserved in the ley lines' consciousness.

"What are these?" Lira asked, reaching for one of the orbs.

"Memories," Flamipandro said, her flamingo form shimmering as she perched atop a wooden beam. "Fragments of the ley lines themselves."

Lira's hand brushed against one orb, and it flared brightly. She gasped as a vision overtook her: a mage chanting before a massive nexus, the energy fracturing violently, consuming everything in its wake.

"They're warnings," Lira said, her voice shaky. "Records of what happens when the ley lines are disrupted."

The Weaver's Choice As they ventured deeper into the attic, the orbs began to pulse erratically. From the shadows emerged creatures with translucent, insect-like bodies and glowing cores—Memory Keepers. Their clicking limbs and piercing eyes marked them as both guardians and adversaries.

Flamipandro's voice cut through the tension. "They protect the memories. Harm them, and you risk damaging the ley lines."

Alaric and Lira worked quickly, using spells of light and resonance to trap the creatures without injuring them. Their efforts culminated in a moment of calm, the Memory Keepers clicking softly as they retreated into the shadows.

At the attic's center, an orb larger than the rest hovered above a pedestal, its light casting intricate patterns on the walls. Pecos, now in his elderly form, stepped forward. "This is the Weaver's Orb. It holds the knowledge of the ley lines' greatest trial—the Weaver's Choice."

Alaric hesitated, his hand hovering over the orb. When he touched it, the world dissolved into light, and a voice echoed around him: "You must choose: impose order or preserve chaos. The lines demand balance, but at what cost?"

*****

Alaric's hand trembled as he touched the orb's surface. Its light flared briefly, enveloping the attic in a warm, golden glow before dimming again. For a moment, the silence was absolute. Then a low hum began to resonate, filling the space like the distant echo of a vast, invisible choir.

Lira tightened her grip on her staff, her gaze darting around the attic. "What is that sound? It's... alive."

"It's them," Flamipandro said, her voice uncharacteristically somber. She flapped her ruby-tipped wings once before transforming into her human form. Her crimson gown swept the floor as she stepped closer to the orb. "The ley lines are speaking."

"Speaking?" Bob asked, his golden goose form perched awkwardly on a floating shard of crystal. "That doesn't sound like speaking. That sounds like the slowest argument in history."

"It's not words," Flamipandro replied. "It's feelings, concepts, connections. The ley lines communicate through what they are—threads of existence itself."

Alaric closed his eyes, his senses overwhelmed by the orb's vibrations. Images began to flicker in his mind: cities rising and falling, rivers changing course, stars collapsing into the void. The ley lines weren't just channels of magic—they were part of the fabric of reality, woven into the very essence of existence.

"I can feel them," he murmured. "They're... watching us."

Dialogue of Doubt

Lira stepped closer, her expression guarded. "If they're sentient, then what do they want? Why let us into this place? Why show us these memories?"

"Maybe they don't have a choice," Bob suggested, flapping his wings as he hopped onto Alaric's shoulder. "If I were stuck holding all of reality together, I'd want someone else to take the load off."

"Or maybe," Flamipandro said, her tone sharp, "they're testing us—not with trials, but by observing how we react. They've seen civilizations rise and fall. They know how dangerous mortals are."

Alaric frowned, the weight of the grimoire heavy in his satchel. "Dangerous doesn't mean unworthy. If they didn't think we could help, they wouldn't have let us come this far."

"That's an optimistic assumption," Flamipandro replied. "The ley lines may not trust us. They might be showing us their memories because they have no other way to communicate their desperation."

Lira's gaze softened as she looked at Alaric. "But if they're desperate, they must want to survive. That's something we can work with, isn't it?"

Before Alaric could respond, the Memory Keepers emerged from the shadows again, their insect-like bodies clicking rhythmically as they moved in an unnervingly coordinated pattern. This time, they didn't attack. Instead, they formed a circle around the orb, their glowing cores pulsing in time with its light.

"What are they doing?" Alaric asked, his voice barely above a whisper.

Pecos, now appearing as a young boy with a mischievous grin, leaned against one of the attic's warped beams. "They're guardians, remember? But guardians don't just protect—they guide."

"Guide us where?" Lira asked, her eyes narrowing.

The Memory Keepers didn't answer—at least, not in words. One of the creatures tilted its head toward Alaric, its translucent body catching the faint glow of the orb. It stepped forward slowly, its movements deliberate and almost reverent. In its claws, it held a fragment of crystal etched with runes that seemed to shift and flow like water.

Alaric reached out hesitantly, his fingers brushing against the crystal. The moment he touched it, a sharp jolt of energy coursed through him. Images flooded his mind—fragments of conversations, flashes of landscapes he didn't recognize, and a single, repeating symbol: a spiral encased in a web of lines.

"The Spiral Nexus," he whispered, his voice shaking.

As the vision subsided, Alaric staggered back, clutching the crystal fragment. Lira steadied him, her expression filled with concern.

"What did you see?" she asked.

"Fragments," he said, his breath uneven. "The Spiral Nexus is tied to all of this, but it's unstable. If it collapses... the ley lines could unravel everything."

Bob let out a low whistle. "Unravel everything? That's... vague and terrifying."

Flamipandro stepped closer, her eyes narrowing as she studied the fragment. "The ley lines don't just power magic—they stabilize reality. If the Spiral Nexus fails, it could cause cascading fractures across dimensions."

Alaric's jaw tightened. "Then we have to stop it."

"Stop it with what?" Lira asked, her voice tinged with frustration. "We're just a handful of people with some artifacts and half a map. We don't even know what's causing the instability!"

"Which is why we need to keep moving," Alaric said firmly. "This attic—these memories—they're showing us the pieces we need to understand. We can't stop now."

As the group prepared to leave the attic, the walls seemed to shift again, their wooden planks rippling like the surface of a disturbed pond. A faint whispering filled the air, growing louder with each passing moment.

"Do you hear that?" Lira asked, her grip tightening on her staff.

"It's coming from below," Flamipandro said, her voice low. "The house isn't just a repository for memories. It's a conduit."

"A conduit for what?" Alaric asked, his gaze darting toward the trapdoor leading to the basement.

Before anyone could answer, the whispers coalesced into a single, guttural voice: "Leave... now..."

The group froze as the air grew colder, and the golden glow of the orb dimmed. From the trapdoor, a tendril of shadow emerged, writhing and twisting as it reached toward them.

"Not friendly!" Bob squawked, flapping his wings in alarm.

Alaric raised his hand, casting a light spell that illuminated the attic. The shadow recoiled, but the trapdoor creaked open, revealing a dark void that pulsed with a malevolent energy.

"We don't have a choice," Alaric said, his voice steady despite the fear in his chest. "We have to go down there."

The descent into the basement was slow and nerve-wracking. The staircase seemed to stretch endlessly, each step creaking beneath their weight. The air grew heavier with each passing moment, the whispers now a cacophony of overlapping voices.

When they finally reached the bottom, they found themselves in a vast chamber carved from stone and crystal. The walls were lined with intricate carvings of creatures—serpents with scales of light, wolves with manes of shadow, and winged beings that seemed to glow from within.

"These aren't just carvings," Flamipandro said, her voice hushed. "They're representations of the ley lines' guardians."

As if in response, the carvings began to shift. The serpents slithered out of the walls, their luminous scales casting eerie reflections on the floor. The wolves emerged next, their eyes glowing with an inner fire. Finally, the winged beings unfurled themselves, their forms pulsing with a rhythmic energy.

"They're testing us," Pecos said, his grin replaced by a rare look of seriousness. "They want to see if we're worthy."

"No trials," Alaric said firmly, stepping forward. "We're not here to fight. We're here to understand."

The creatures paused, their glowing eyes fixed on him. For a moment, the chamber was silent. Then the largest serpent lowered its head, its luminescent body coiling around the pedestal in the chamber's center. Upon the pedestal rested a crystalline sphere, its surface swirling with golden light.

Alaric stepped closer, his heart pounding. The sphere pulsed faintly as he reached for it, and the chamber filled with a deep, resonant hum.

"This is it," he said softly. "This is the ley lines' heart."

Ending Hook The moment Alaric touched the sphere, a voice echoed through the chamber—not a whisper, but a roar: "Balance... or collapse. Choose wisely."

The world around them began to dissolve into light, leaving the group suspended in a void filled with the swirling threads of the ley lines.

The void surrounding the group felt infinite, yet oppressively close. Threads of golden and azure light crisscrossed the expanse, some shimmering faintly, others pulsing like living veins. Alaric stood at the center, the crystalline sphere in his hands glowing faintly.

"What is this place?" Lira asked, her voice a whisper as her eyes darted to the swirling threads around them.

"The ley lines' heart," Flamipandro said, her tone reverent. "We're not just near them anymore—we're within them."

Alaric turned the sphere in his hands, its surface smooth yet warm, as though it pulsed with a life of its own. "They're alive," he said softly. "Not just energy or memory. They think. They feel."

"And they're scared," Lira added, her voice trembling. She clutched her staff tighter, its crystalline head glowing faintly in resonance with the threads. "I can feel their pain. Their confusion."

Bob fluttered to a thread that arched near them, pecking it experimentally. The thread shivered, releasing a soft chime. "Scared or not, they're not great conversationalists."

Flamipandro shot him a glare. "They've been burdened with the weight of existence itself for eons. Would you be chatty?"

As Alaric focused on the sphere, its light intensified, and an image formed before them. It was a city, vast and magnificent, its towers carved from crystalline stone that sparkled in the sunlight. At its heart, a nexus of ley lines pulsed steadily, sending waves of energy through the city's streets.

"This is Miridelle," Flamipandro said, her voice soft. "The greatest city ever built upon a ley line nexus."

The image shifted. The streets of Miridelle teemed with life—mages casting spells of dazzling complexity, artisans crafting wonders powered by the ley lines, children playing beneath floating lights. Yet, beneath the surface, cracks began to appear. The nexus in the city's heart faltered, its rhythm uneven.

"They tried to control the ley lines," Flamipandro continued. "To bind them, to force their power to serve their will. They believed they were creating harmony, but they were only creating strain."

The vision darkened. The nexus shattered, releasing a wave of energy that tore through the city. Buildings crumbled, the sky itself seemed to fracture, and the once-thriving populace was consumed by the chaos.

"They failed," Alaric murmured, his throat tight. "They thought they were saving themselves, but they doomed everything."

The vision faded, leaving the group surrounded by the swirling threads once more. The threads began to pulse erratically, their movements chaotic.

"They're reacting to us," Lira said, her voice tight with tension. "But I don't think they trust us."

"Why would they?" Flamipandro said. "They've seen mortals destroy themselves over and over. They have no reason to believe we'll be any different."

Alaric stepped forward, his gaze steady. "We're not here to control them. We're here to help. They need to know that."

"And how do you propose we convince them?" Flamipandro asked, her tone sharp. "They don't speak in words, Alaric. They speak in actions."

Alaric closed his eyes, focusing on the sphere in his hands. He poured his thoughts into it—memories of his journey, of the choices he'd made and the lessons he'd learned. He showed them his hope for a future where the ley lines and those who relied on them could coexist.

The sphere grew warmer, its light intensifying. The threads around them began to settle, their movements more measured.

"They're listening," Lira said, her voice filled with awe.

The threads shifted again, forming a massive figure of light and shadow before them. Its form was indistinct, constantly shifting, but its presence was overwhelming.

"You carry our burden," the figure said, its voice a blend of countless tones. "You walk our path. Yet, you do not understand."

Alaric stepped forward, his chest tightening under the weight of the figure's gaze. "Then help us understand. Show us what we need to do."

The figure tilted its head, the threads around it pulsing in rhythm with its movements. "You seek to mend what is broken. Yet, to mend is to impose your will. Balance cannot be forced."

"We're not trying to force anything," Lira interjected, her voice firm. "We just want to stop the fracturing before it's too late."

The figure's light dimmed, its form flickering. "Your intent matters little if your actions lead to ruin. You must prove your understanding."

As the figure dissolved into the threads, the void around them began to fade. The group found themselves back in the attic, though it was no longer the same. The walls shimmered with faint light, and the orbs floating in the air emitted a soft hum.

"The house is changing," Flamipandro said, her gaze sweeping the room. "It's reacting to the ley lines' presence."

From the shadows emerged new creatures—graceful, bird-like beings with feathers made of light and eyes that glowed like embers. They moved silently, their wings brushing against the threads that now hung in the air like curtains.

"What are these?" Lira asked, her voice filled with wonder.

"Avian Sentinels," Flamipandro said. "Rare creatures born from ley line nexuses. They guide those who seek balance."

One of the sentinels approached Alaric, its glowing eyes locking onto his. It lowered its head, its feathers brushing against his hand.

"They trust you," Lira said softly.

"They're showing us the way forward," Alaric said, his voice steady.

The sentinel led them to a hidden corner of the attic, where a pedestal carved from crystal stood. Upon it rested a small, intricately designed artifact—a golden ring inscribed with runes that shimmered faintly.

"This is a gift," Flamipandro said, her voice reverent. "The ley lines are entrusting you with a piece of their power."

Alaric hesitated before picking up the ring. The moment it touched his skin, he felt a surge of energy—a connection to the threads that surrounded them.

"It's a conduit," he said. "A way to communicate with the ley lines."

"And a responsibility," Flamipandro added. "One you cannot take lightly."

As the group prepared to leave the attic, the threads pulsed one final time, their hum filling the space. A map formed in the air before them, its lines glowing with golden light.

"It's showing us where to go," Lira said, her eyes scanning the map. "The Spiral Nexus."

The room began to fade, the light of the threads dimming as the map burned itself into Alaric's memory.

"Then we have our path," he said, his voice filled with determination. "Let's not waste it."

The attic's glow faded entirely as they descended the staircase. The creaks underfoot felt louder in the encroaching silence, and the air grew denser, each breath laced with the sharp tang of something ancient and unyielding. Though the group remained close, the oppressive atmosphere made them feel as if they were walking alone.

"The ley lines are more present here," Lira murmured, her voice barely audible. Her staff pulsed faintly, casting faint, shifting light on the walls. "It's like they're watching us."

"They are," Flamipandro said, her voice sharp. "Every step we take in this house carries weight. This isn't just a place—it's an extension of their consciousness."

Bob, hopping uneasily from step to step, scoffed. "Their consciousness? A house with mood swings. Fantastic. What's next? A hallway that recites poetry?"

"You jest," Flamipandro replied, her ruby gown shimmering as she paused mid-step, "but this is no jest. Every corner of this place is alive in ways you can't comprehend."

Alaric pressed forward, the ring on his hand growing warmer with each step. It vibrated faintly, almost like a heartbeat, resonating with the unseen forces around them. "Let's keep moving. There's more to this place, and it won't wait for us."

The staircase led them into a vast hall unlike anything they'd seen before. The walls were covered with what appeared to be mirrors, though their surfaces rippled as though they were made of liquid. Each reflected not the group's current forms but fractured, alternate versions of themselves.

Alaric approached one cautiously. His reflection looked older, his face etched with weariness, his grimoire clutched tightly in his hands. Behind this version of himself, shadowy figures loomed—indistinct but unmistakably menacing.

Lira stepped beside him, her reflection showing her wielding a staff that blazed with power. Her expression was fierce, but her surroundings were barren—a world scorched by fire, with no life in sight.

"This isn't right," she said, stepping back. "These aren't real."

"They're possibilities," Flamipandro said, her voice low. "The ley lines don't just connect places—they connect potential. Every choice we make ripples through them, creating countless outcomes."

Bob hopped toward a mirror, squawking in alarm as his reflection morphed into a towering, golden phoenix. "I look fantastic, but is this supposed to be a warning or a compliment?"

"It's neither," Flamipandro said. "It's a reminder. Every path we take has consequences, whether we see them or not."

As they moved deeper into the hall, the mirrors began to hum faintly, their surfaces rippling more violently. A voice echoed through the chamber—soft at first, but growing louder with each word.

"You walk the threads of fate, but do you understand the burden you carry?"

The group froze. The voice seemed to come from everywhere and nowhere, its tone neither hostile nor welcoming. Alaric turned slowly, his gaze searching the shifting mirrors for the source.

"Who's there?" he asked, his voice steady despite the unease prickling at his skin.

The mirrors shimmered, and a figure stepped through one—a being made entirely of light, its form shifting between humanoid and amorphous. Its presence filled the hall, making the air vibrate with energy.

"We are the echoes," the figure said. "Reflections of choices made and unmade. You tread upon the ley lines, and they remember."

"Remember what?" Lira asked, her staff raised defensively.

"Everything," the figure replied. "The ley lines hold the weight of every action, every thought, every consequence. And now, they hold you."

*****

The figure stepped closer to Alaric, its light intensifying. "You hold their gift," it said, gesturing to the ring on his hand. "A fragment of their will. But will you wield it with wisdom, or will you repeat the mistakes of those who came before?"

"I don't want to wield it," Alaric said firmly. "I want to understand. To help."

The figure tilted its head, the light around it flickering like a dying flame. "Understanding comes with a cost. The ley lines do not ask for aid—they test the worth of those who walk their path. You must prove that your actions are not driven by fear or ambition."

Flamipandro stepped forward, her expression wary. "He's not like the others. He doesn't seek power for its own sake."

"Even the purest intentions can lead to destruction," the figure said, its voice tinged with sorrow. "Intent alone does not preserve balance."

The Misty Threshold

The hall of mirrors dissolved into mist, and the group found themselves standing before a new doorway, its frame carved with runes that pulsed faintly. The air around it shimmered, and faint whispers emanated from beyond.

"The ley lines are guiding us again," Alaric said, his voice quiet but resolute.

"They're not just guiding," Flamipandro corrected. "They're challenging."

The door swung open on its own, revealing a forest bathed in ethereal light. The trees were unlike any they'd seen—tall and slender, their leaves glowing faintly in hues of blue and gold. Creatures moved among the shadows, their forms indistinct but their presence unmistakable.

"Another realm," Lira said, stepping cautiously into the forest. "Are we still in the house?"

"The house is everywhere and nowhere," Flamipandro said. "It exists where the ley lines need it to exist."

The Forest of Echoes

As they ventured into the forest, the whispers grew louder, overlapping into an unintelligible cacophony. The creatures in the shadows began to emerge—graceful, deer-like beings with antlers made of crystalline light, their eyes glowing with a soft, amber hue.

"They're beautiful," Lira said, her voice filled with awe.

"Don't get too close," Flamipandro warned. "They're Echo Stags—manifestations of ley line memories. They're harmless unless provoked."

Alaric stepped carefully, his gaze fixed on the stags. One of them turned its head toward him, its glowing eyes locking onto his. For a moment, he felt a rush of emotions—not his own, but the ley lines'. Fear, pain, hope, and an overwhelming sense of urgency.

"They're warning us again," he said. "Something is coming."

The forest's light dimmed suddenly, and a low growl echoed through the trees. The Echo Stags scattered, their crystalline forms vanishing into the shadows. The ground beneath the group trembled as a massive figure emerged from the darkness.

The creature was unlike anything they'd seen—a monstrous beast with a body of shifting shadows and eyes that burned like molten gold. Its form seemed to flicker between dimensions, its movements jerky and unnatural.

"A Rift Beast," Flamipandro said, her voice tight with fear. "A predator drawn to instability in the ley lines."

Alaric's grip tightened on the ring as the beast lunged toward them. "We can't fight this," he said. "Not here."

"Then what do we do?" Lira shouted, raising her staff as the beast's claws raked through the air.

"Run," Flamipandro said. "Now!"

The group sprinted through the forest, the Rift Beast crashing through the trees behind them. The glowing threads of the ley lines appeared sporadically, guiding their path as the beast's growls grew louder.

"Keep moving!" Flamipandro shouted, her gown trailing like a comet's tail as she led the way.

Alaric's breath came in ragged gasps as the forest blurred around him. The ring on his hand grew brighter, its vibrations intensifying. "The ley lines are trying to help us," he said. "They're leading us somewhere."

"Let's hope it's somewhere safe!" Bob squawked, flapping desperately to keep up.

The group burst through a wall of glowing vines and stumbled into a clearing. At its center stood a towering obelisk, its surface covered in runes that shimmered with golden light. The Rift Beast halted at the edge of the clearing, growling but unable to cross the threshold.

"This is it," Alaric said, his chest heaving. "This is what they wanted us to find."

The obelisk's light intensified, and the group felt a wave of calm wash over them. The ley lines' hum filled the air, their presence undeniable.

"They've protected us," Lira said, her voice filled with wonder.

"For now," Flamipandro said, her gaze fixed on the obelisk. "But this is just the beginning."

The obelisk towered over them, its runes shifting like living things, casting soft golden light that seemed to resonate with the ley lines' hum. As the group caught their breath, the Rift Beast paced outside the clearing, its molten eyes fixed on them with palpable frustration. It let out a guttural snarl but made no move to breach the invisible boundary.

"It's afraid of this place," Lira observed, her voice still breathless. She pressed her staff into the ground for support, its crystalline tip vibrating faintly in response to the obelisk's energy.

"Afraid? That thing doesn't look like it fears anything," Bob muttered, his golden feathers ruffled as he perched on Alaric's shoulder. "But I'm all for staying on this side of whatever keeps it out."

Alaric stepped closer to the obelisk, his eyes tracing the runes as they shifted and shimmered. The ring on his finger grew warmer, its vibrations harmonizing with the obelisk's rhythm. He hesitated for a moment before placing his hand on its surface.

The moment his palm made contact, the runes flared brightly, and a wave of energy surged through him. Images flooded his mind—threads of light weaving intricate patterns across dimensions, connecting places, people, and events. At the heart of it all was the Spiral Nexus, its energy spiraling outward like the heartbeat of existence itself.

"They're showing me," he said, his voice filled with awe. "The Spiral Nexus—it's the anchor for everything. But it's fragile, and the fractures are spreading."

Flamipandro stepped forward, her expression grave. "What do they want you to do?"

"They want us to find the source of the instability," Alaric replied. "It's not just the Nexus fracturing on its own—something is causing it."

Before anyone could respond, the obelisk emitted a low hum, and the light around it condensed into a small, glowing figure. The being was no larger than a child, with a translucent, humanoid form and eyes that glowed like twin stars. It floated toward Alaric, tilting its head curiously.

"What is that?" Lira asked, taking a cautious step back.

"It's a ley line sentinel," Flamipandro said, her voice tinged with wonder. "A manifestation of their will."

The sentinel extended a hand toward Alaric, its fingers brushing the ring on his hand. A pulse of light passed between them, and Alaric felt an overwhelming sense of connection—an unspoken understanding of the sentinel's purpose.

"It wants to guide us," he said. "To show us the way."

The sentinel turned, its form shimmering as it began to drift toward the edge of the clearing. The Rift Beast snarled but didn't approach, its molten eyes narrowing as the sentinel's light grew brighter.

"Looks like it's our ticket out of here," Bob said. "Unless you'd rather stick around and make friends with Big, Dark, and Scary?"

"Let's move," Alaric said, his voice firm.

The sentinel led them deeper into the forest, its light illuminating the path ahead. The further they went, the more the environment began to change. The trees grew thinner, their glowing leaves fading into darkness. The ground beneath their feet shifted, becoming smooth and glass-like, as though they were walking on a frozen lake.

"What is this place?" Lira asked, her voice tinged with unease.

"The ley lines are thinning," Flamipandro replied. "We're moving closer to the Spiral Nexus—or what's left of it."

As they walked, faint whispers filled the air. They were different from the ones in the attic—softer, almost pleading. Alaric paused, tilting his head to listen.

"They're asking for help," he said. "The ley lines—they're trying to hold themselves together, but they're breaking."

Lira frowned, her grip tightening on her staff. "How do we help something this vast? This... abstract?"

The sentinel turned toward them, its glowing eyes fixed on Alaric. It raised a hand, and a thread of light extended from its palm, connecting to the ring on his finger. The moment the connection was made, a vision unfolded before the group.

They saw a massive rift in the ley lines—a tear in the fabric of reality itself. Energy poured from the rift like a bleeding wound, its chaotic tendrils reaching out, destabilizing everything they touched. Around the rift stood shadowy figures, their forms obscured, but their intent unmistakable—they were feeding the rift, driving its chaos.

"The Veiled Order," Flamipandro said, her voice filled with venom. "They're behind this."

Alaric clenched his fists, his jaw tightening. "Then we have to stop them."

As the vision faded, the sentinel's light dimmed, and the forest around them grew darker. The air grew colder, and a low growl echoed in the distance.

"We're not alone," Lira said, raising her staff as its light flared brightly.

From the shadows emerged creatures with glowing, amber eyes and bodies that seemed to be made of smoke and shadow. They moved silently, their movements fluid and unnerving.

"Shadow Wolves," Flamipandro said, her voice tense. "Guardians of fractured ley lines. They attack anything they see as a threat."

"Let me guess," Bob muttered, his feathers puffed up. "We look threatening."

The wolves circled the group, their eyes fixed on the sentinel. One of them lunged, its shadowy form stretching unnaturally as it moved. Lira raised her staff, casting a barrier of light that deflected the attack.

"They're testing us," Flamipandro said. "They want to see if we can harmonize with the ley lines."

"We don't have time for tests," Alaric said, stepping forward. He extended his hand, focusing on the ring. It pulsed brightly, sending a wave of energy through the clearing.

The wolves froze, their glowing eyes narrowing. One by one, they backed away, their forms dissipating into the shadows.

"They recognize the ring's power," Flamipandro said. "For now, that's enough."

The group pressed on, the sentinel's light growing brighter as they neared their destination. The air became thick with energy, each step resonating with the ley lines' hum. In the distance, they saw it—a swirling vortex of light and shadow, its chaotic energy tearing through the threads around it.

"The Spiral Nexus," Alaric said, his voice filled with a mix of awe and dread.

The sentinel turned to face them, its form flickering as if struggling to maintain its shape. It pointed toward the vortex, its light dimming as it spoke for the first time.

"Balance... must... be restored."

And with that, it dissolved into threads of light, leaving the group standing on the precipice of the most dangerous journey they had ever undertaken.

Chapter 15: Nexus of Reflections

The air shimmered as the group crossed into the Nexus of Reflections. Alaric felt a jolt in his chest, like stepping through a wall of static. The forest faded, replaced by a vast expanse of mirrored surfaces, their glass-like sheen reflecting distorted versions of the group.

Lira stopped abruptly, her hand clutching her staff as her wide eyes scanned the reflections. Each mirrored surface rippled, twisting their forms into grotesque caricatures. Alaric saw himself in one—a hollow-eyed scholar with hands stained black, clutching a shattered grimoire.

"This place is... unnerving," Lira said, her voice tight.

"Unnerving is generous," Bob muttered. The goose hopped closer to one mirror, squawking in alarm as his reflection towered over him, feathers aflame and eyes glowing menacingly. "I look like a cooked dinner with delusions of grandeur."

"This isn't just a reflection of what we are," Flamipandro said, her ruby feathers gleaming as she shifted into her human form. "It's what the ley lines see—possibilities, fears, futures."

Alaric approached a mirror cautiously, his reflection shifting again. This time, he was surrounded by books and artifacts, his face older and harder, his eyes devoid of their usual spark. "It's not just fear," he murmured. "It's a warning."

The mirrored surfaces began to hum softly, their rippling patterns growing more erratic. Lira stepped forward, raising her staff. "It's like the ley lines are trying to communicate, but... not through words."

"Through feelings," Flamipandro said. She gestured to the mirrors, her voice low. "The Nexus of Reflections mirrors the heart. It doesn't judge—it reveals."

The hum grew louder, and one mirror in the distance began to glow, its surface distorting violently. Alaric and Lira exchanged a glance before stepping toward it, the others following close behind. As they drew near, the mirror's surface cleared, revealing a new scene.

It was Alaric—but not the Alaric they knew. This version of him stood in the Spiral Nexus, his hands glowing with raw energy as he shouted incantations. Around him, the ley lines writhed in agony, their golden threads fraying and snapping. Behind him stood shadowy figures, their faces obscured but their intentions unmistakable.

"No..." Alaric whispered, his breath catching. "That's not—"

"It's what could be," Flamipandro said, her tone sharp. "This is what happens if you let your ambition consume you."

Alaric stepped back, shaking his head. "I'm not like that."

"Aren't you?" the mirror whispered, its voice a cruel echo of his own. "You seek to understand the ley lines, to stabilize them—but in doing so, you impose your will. Balance cannot be forced."

Lira placed a hand on his arm, grounding him. "You don't have to prove anything to them," she said softly. "You're not that person."

Another mirror began to ripple, drawing Lira's attention. She hesitated, her grip on her staff tightening. "I don't..."

"You have to look," Flamipandro said, her voice almost gentle.

Lira stepped forward, her breath hitching as the mirror revealed a barren wasteland. She stood at the center, her staff planted in the cracked ground, its crystalline head blazing with light. Around her, ley lines surged with power, but the land was lifeless—no trees, no people, no creatures.

"This is wrong," Lira whispered, tears welling in her eyes. "The ley lines aren't meant to destroy."

"They aren't," Flamipandro said. "But they reflect what happens when you try to become their guardian without understanding their nature. They don't just demand harmony—they demand connection."

Lira turned away from the mirror, her shoulders trembling. "I thought I was helping them."

"You are," Alaric said, stepping beside her. "But they're alive, Lira. They're not just a source of magic—they're part of everything. If we don't listen to them, we'll only make things worse."

*****

The hum of the mirrors intensified, and the reflections began to shatter, their shards spinning through the air. From the fragments emerged creatures—twisted versions of the Echo Stags they had encountered earlier. These beasts had jagged, crystalline antlers and eyes that glowed a sickly green. Their bodies crackled with unstable energy, and their movements were erratic, as though they were in constant pain.

"Corrupted guardians," Flamipandro said, stepping back. "Born from imbalance in the ley lines."

The creatures snarled, their distorted forms lunging toward the group. Lira raised her staff, casting a barrier of light that held them back temporarily. "We can't hurt them," she said. "They're tied to the ley lines. If we destroy them—"

"We destroy the balance," Alaric finished, his mind racing. He pulled the Echo Pendant from his satchel, the artifact pulsing faintly in his hands. "We need to calm them, not fight them."

"How do you calm something like that?" Bob squawked, flapping his wings as one of the creatures clawed at the barrier.

"By harmonizing with the ley lines," Alaric said. He closed his eyes, focusing on the pendant. Its light grew brighter, resonating with the energy in the room. Slowly, the corrupted guardians began to falter, their snarls turning into soft whimpers.

Lira followed his lead, channeling her connection to the ley lines through her staff. The creatures stilled, their forms flickering before dissolving into threads of light that flowed back into the mirrors.

As the last guardian faded, the pendant in Alaric's hand glowed brighter, its surface revealing intricate runes that hadn't been visible before.

"It's amplifying emotional clarity," Flamipandro said, her voice filled with wonder. "It's not just an artifact—it's a key to understanding the ley lines."

Alaric looked at the pendant, a newfound determination in his eyes. "Then we use it to find the Spiral Nexus and stop whatever's causing the fractures."

The mirrors around them began to shimmer, forming a path through the Nexus of Reflections. The group exchanged a glance before stepping forward, their resolve stronger than ever.

The mirrored path ahead seemed endless, each step amplifying the hum of ley lines that vibrated through the air. Alaric, Echo Pendant clutched tightly in his hand, led the way with Lira close behind. Bob waddled beside them, his golden feathers glowing faintly from the ambient light of the nexus.

"This place is starting to grow on me," Bob said, his voice carrying a hint of humor despite the tension. "I mean, if you're into mind-bending terror and existential dread."

Alaric glanced at him. "If you have a way to turn dread into something useful, now would be a good time."

Bob stopped abruptly, his wings ruffling. "You want useful? Fine." He puffed himself up, muttering under his breath. In a swirl of golden light, his goose form shimmered, elongating into the figure of a teenage boy. His hair was an unruly mop of gold, and his eyes carried the same mischievous glint.

"Better?" Bob asked, adjusting a scarf that appeared out of nowhere around his neck. "I still get a feather stuck here and there." He plucked an imaginary one from his sleeve with a flourish.

Lira stared, wide-eyed. "You could have done that this whole time?"

"Well, yeah," Bob said, waving a hand dismissively. "But where's the drama in that?"

The mirrors around them began to shift again, their surfaces rippling as new images formed. Creatures emerged one by one—each a testament to the ley lines' diversity and power.

The first was a Crystalline Serpent, its long, translucent body shimmering like a prism. Each scale refracted light into a spectrum of colors, and as it slithered, it left trails of raw magic that hung in the air like ribbons. Alaric watched in fascination as the serpent coiled around a floating shard of ley line energy, siphoning its power into a glowing orb at its core.

"These creatures are natural manipulators of energy," Alaric said, his scholar's curiosity overtaking his caution. "The orb acts as a focus—it's how they channel ley lines to reshape their environment."

"And how they hunt," Flamipandro added, her voice steady as she stepped forward, now in her human form. Her ruby gown shimmered like liquid fire, and her dark hair fell in waves that seemed to absorb the light. She tilted her head as she studied the serpent. "Crystalline Serpents use their orbs to amplify spells. Imagine controlling a storm or redirecting a flood—it's second nature to them."

The serpent hissed, its orb flaring. Around it, the ground shifted, crystalline spires erupting from the mirrored floor in an intricate, defensive lattice. The energy humming through the spires made Alaric shiver.

"We should move," Flamipandro said, her tone decisive. "We're not their prey, but we're trespassing."

As the group moved on, Alaric's thoughts churned. "The Crystalline Serpent's abilities—they're rooted in ley line manipulation. But it's not just magic—it's a form of physics."

Lira frowned. "Physics?"

Alaric nodded. "The ley lines are energy flows. The serpent uses a focusing mechanism—the orb—to align its intent with the natural properties of energy. Think of it like tuning an instrument. You can play one note, or you can harmonize to create an entirely new frequency."

Flamipandro glanced at him, her ruby gown catching the light. "The ley lines aren't just energy—they're alive. They adapt, resonate, and evolve based on what interacts with them."

"It's symbiotic," Alaric said. "Creatures like the serpent don't dominate the ley lines—they adapt to their natural flows. They integrate their magic into the patterns."

Bob, in human form, shrugged. "So, magic is just science we don't fully understand yet? Great. Next, you'll tell me I need a license to cast a spell."

They entered a clearing where the mirrored ground gave way to a glowing forest of trees with crystalline trunks. Beneath their boughs stood a herd of Glimmering Stags, their antlers branching like trees themselves. Light coursed through their bodies, pulsing in time with the ley lines.

The largest stag stepped forward, its luminous eyes locking onto the group. It lowered its head, releasing a soft hum that reverberated through the air.

"They're communicating," Lira whispered. She raised her staff, its crystalline tip glowing faintly in response.

The stag's antlers began to glow brighter, casting intricate patterns onto the mirrored ground. The light coalesced into a three-dimensional map, showing a vast nexus network. At its center was the Spiral Nexus, its energy a chaotic swirl of golden and black threads.

"They know where we need to go," Flamipandro said, her voice filled with awe. "They're guiding us."

As the map faded, the stag turned and bounded into the forest, its light blending with the trees. The herd followed, leaving the group alone once more.

The group reached the heart of the Nexus of Reflections, a massive, circular chamber. The floor was a single, polished mirror, and at its center floated a crystal sphere, its surface swirling with energy. Surrounding it were four pedestals, each holding an artifact: a Rune-Inscribed Blade, a Gilded Compass, a Veil-Cloaked Pendant, and a Time-Shifting Hourglass.

Alaric approached the sphere cautiously. "These artifacts—they're tied to the Spiral Nexus."

Flamipandro nodded. "Each one represents a different aspect of nexus stabilization. The blade controls force, the compass dictates direction, the pendant shields, and the hourglass manipulates time."

Bob reached for the hourglass, his eyes narrowing. "So, if I just flip this thing, can we skip to the part where we win?"

"Not how it works, Bob," Flamipandro said, gently pulling his hand away.

Alaric studied the artifacts, his mind racing. "The ley lines' sentience—they've left these for a reason. They want us to understand their purpose, not just use them."

The ground beneath them trembled violently, the polished mirror floor cracking like brittle ice. A wave of oppressive heat surged through the chamber as the jagged rift split further apart, releasing plumes of smoke threaded with golden sparks. From the depths emerged the Rift Beast, its form a horrifying amalgam of shadows and molten veins of ley line energy. The beast's massive, clawed limbs scraped against the mirrored ground, leaving behind smoldering trails.

Its eyes—spheres of liquid gold—locked onto the group, radiating malice and intent. The beast let out a roar that reverberated through the chamber, causing the artifacts on the pedestals to hum in response.

"This thing isn't here to chat," Bob muttered, gripping the hourglass so tightly that his knuckles turned white.

Lira raised her staff instinctively, the crystalline head glowing as it drew energy from the ley lines surrounding them. "It's like it's made of the fractures," she said, her voice shaking. "It's alive, but it's wrong."

Flamipandro stepped forward, her ruby gown flowing behind her like liquid fire. Her eyes narrowed as she studied the beast. "The ley lines created this," she said. "Not out of malice, but desperation. It's a guardian twisted by imbalance."

Alaric gripped the compass tightly, its needle spinning wildly. "If it's tied to the fractures, maybe the artifacts can stabilize it."

"You figure out how to stabilize," Flamipandro snapped, unsheathing the Rune-Inscribed Blade from its pedestal. "I'll keep it busy."

The Rift Beast lunged, its massive claw swiping toward the group with terrifying speed. Flamipandro darted forward, the blade in her hand glowing with runes that flared brighter as she moved. With a swift, calculated strike, she met the beast's attack head-on, the collision releasing a shockwave of energy that rippled through the chamber.

"Move!" she shouted over her shoulder. "Find a way to weaken it!"

Alaric and Lira scrambled to opposite sides of the room, their minds racing. Alaric focused on the compass, holding it steady as he traced the ley lines it revealed. Each fracture in the beast's form glowed faintly, their chaotic energy visible through the artifact's lens.

"It's vulnerable here!" he yelled, pointing to the rift along its shoulder, where a jagged tear pulsed erratically. "That's where the ley lines are most unstable!"

Lira nodded, channeling energy into her staff. She extended it toward the beast, sending a concentrated beam of light toward the tear. The beast roared in fury as the beam struck home, the unstable energy in its body surging outward in jagged arcs.

Meanwhile, Bob, still clutching the hourglass, paced nervously. "Okay, Bob," he muttered to himself. "You're not the hero, but you've got time magic. Time magic is cool. You can do this."

He flipped the hourglass experimentally, and the world around him slowed. The beast's movements became sluggish, its roars echoing like distant thunder. Flamipandro's strikes left glowing trails in the air, and Alaric and Lira's magic seemed to hang, suspended in motion.

"Whoa," Bob whispered, glancing at the group. "This might actually work."

The effect faded as the sand in the hourglass settled, and the beast's movements returned to full speed. Bob frowned. "Right, so time manipulation is tricky. Got it."

He flipped the hourglass again, this time timing it just as the beast lunged for Lira. The slowed world gave her the precious seconds she needed to dodge, her staff glowing as she unleashed another beam of light toward the beast's fractured form.

"Not bad for a golden goose," Flamipandro quipped as she drove the Rune-Inscribed Blade into the beast's claw, holding it at bay.

Lira, emboldened by Bob's intervention, reached for the Veil-Cloaked Pendant around her neck. As her fingers brushed the artifact, a surge of clarity washed over her. The pendant's magic amplified her connection to the ley lines, allowing her to feel the beast's chaotic energy as if it were a living heartbeat.

"It's not just a guardian," she said, her voice trembling. "It's in pain. The imbalance is tearing it apart."

Alaric, still analyzing the compass, called out, "Then we stabilize it! The artifacts—use them together!"

Flamipandro leaped back, the blade in her hand flickering with energy as she regrouped with the others. "Then let's stop playing and start fixing."

The group gathered in a rough circle, the Rift Beast pacing around them like a predator sizing up its prey. Alaric held the compass steady, its needle pointing toward the beast's chest, where the ley line fractures were most pronounced. Lira channeled her pendant's energy, weaving a thread of harmony into the chaotic nexus.

"Bob, now!" Alaric shouted.

Bob flipped the hourglass, slowing time just as Flamipandro raised the blade. She struck the air with precise, measured movements, each slash carving glowing runes that hovered in the space between them and the beast.

Together, the artifacts pulsed with synchronized energy, their light growing brighter with each passing second. The beast roared, lunging toward them in a final, desperate attack, but the combined force of the artifacts created a barrier of raw magic, holding it back.

Alaric stepped forward, his hand outstretched. "You're not our enemy," he said, his voice firm. "You're part of the ley lines. Let us help you."

The Rift Beast hesitated, its molten eyes flickering. For a moment, the chaotic energy within it seemed to stabilize. The glowing fractures in its form began to mend, the ley lines weaving themselves back together.

As the beast's form dissolved into threads of golden light, the chamber grew still. The cracks in the mirrored floor sealed themselves, and the oppressive heat faded into a calm, steady hum. The crystal sphere at the chamber's center pulsed gently, its energy stable once more.

Flamipandro lowered the blade, her breathing heavy. "Well," she said, smirking at Bob. "I'll admit, the goose came through."

Bob grinned, brushing imaginary dust off his scarf. "All in a day's work."

Lira stepped toward the sphere, her staff still glowing faintly. "We didn't destroy it," she said softly. "We helped it. The ley lines—they needed us to understand."

Alaric nodded, his gaze fixed on the compass in his hand. "It wasn't about power. It was about balance. The ley lines are alive—they don't just need us to use them. They need us to listen."

As the group exited the chamber, the mirrored path behind them shimmered and faded. The ley lines' hum grew fainter but remained steady, a reminder of the harmony they had restored.

Ahead lay the next challenge—the Spiral Nexus itself, a place where fractures threatened the very fabric of existence. But for now, they walked with a renewed sense of purpose, their bond strengthened by the trials they had overcome.

As the group emerged from the Nexus of Reflections, the mirrored chamber dissolved into the natural light of the ley line forest. The ethereal hum of the ley lines lingered in the air, each note vibrating through Alaric's very core. He clutched the Echo Pendant, its glow now faint, a reminder of the Rift Beast they had just faced.

Lira walked beside him, her staff glowing faintly. She glanced at him, her expression pensive. "Do you think it will be like that again? The Spiral Nexus?"

Alaric didn't answer immediately. Instead, he reached for his grimoire, flipping past pages of hastily written notes to an empty one. With the ley lines' hum as his backdrop, he began to write.

Journal Entry: The Ley Lines

Entry 47 - Reflections and Rifts

The ley lines' sentience is undeniable now. They speak—not in words, but in echoes of emotion and visions that linger in the mind. And yet, they remain a paradox: creators of harmony yet bearers of chaos when imbalanced.

What haunts me most is the Rift Beast. It was alive, not merely a manifestation of energy but something torn from the ley lines' core. Flamipandro said it was born of desperation—a guardian twisted by the imbalance it was meant to prevent. But why would the ley lines create something so volatile?

The artifacts we found in the Nexus of Reflections—tools of balance and harmony—are more than relics. They are pieces of a puzzle we still don't fully understand. I fear what we face in the Spiral Nexus. Not just the fractures, but the choices it will demand of us.

And Lira... Her connection to the ley lines grows stronger every day. She feels their pain, their urgency, in ways I can only observe. While I calculate and theorize, she listens. It terrifies me that her way might be the better one.

I wonder if Pecos would laugh at this realization.

The ley lines hum in my mind even when I sleep. Tonight, they sang of fractures—thin cracks spreading through their essence like ice breaking underfoot. I see their pain, but I don't yet understand it. What are we doing here, truly? Is this about saving them—or ourselves?

*****

The chamber's light dimmed, its crystal walls reflecting warped versions of the group. Alaric stood at the center, his gaze locked on a glowing thread of energy stretched taut between two runes. Lira circled him, her footsteps echoing against the cold floor.

"We're running out of time," Lira said sharply, breaking the silence. "The ley lines are growing more unstable with each moment we hesitate."

"I know that," Alaric replied, frustration lacing his words. "But rushing in without a plan will only make things worse."

Lira stopped, her arms crossed. "You always think there's time for logic and theory. This is different, Alaric. The Spiral Nexus won't wait for us to calculate every outcome."

Their argument pulled the others into its gravity. Gavrin, their scout, leaned against a jagged pillar, his bow resting at his side. "She's right, you know. Sometimes you have to trust your instincts."

"Trusting instincts doesn't stabilize ley lines," Alaric shot back. "We need precision, not gut feelings."

"What about trust?" Lira countered. "Trust in the ley lines themselves? They've been guiding us, but you keep fighting their flow."

Alaric opened his mouth to reply but hesitated. The ley lines' sentience had always felt abstract to him—a theory, not a reality. Yet, in the Fire Nexus, they had spoken clearly, their anguish undeniable.

Flashback: The Spiral Nexus's Creation

As Alaric studied the runes, his vision blurred, and he stumbled. A rush of images filled his mind: a swirling vortex of energy, ancient mages standing in a circle, their hands raised as they chanted in unison. The Spiral Nexus wasn't a natural phenomenon; it had been created—a desperate act to bind fractured ley lines and hold the world together.

But something had gone wrong. The vision darkened, the harmony of the chant breaking into discord. The Nexus splintered, its threads fraying under the weight of opposing forces.

Alaric gasped, the vision releasing him. "The Spiral Nexus was never meant to last," he said aloud.

Lira frowned. "What are you talking about?"

"It's a patch," Alaric explained, his voice trembling. "A fragile one. If we fail to stabilize it, the whole network collapses."

*****

The chamber trembled, and the air grew thick with energy. The ley lines' hum rose into a resonant chorus, their voices merging into a single, mournful tone. Light and shadow swirled together, forming a shimmering figure at the center of the room. Its outline was indistinct, constantly shifting, but its presence was undeniable.

"Why do you seek to heal what you have broken?" the figure asked, its voice both a whisper and a roar.

Alaric stepped forward cautiously. "We want to restore balance."

"Balance," the figure echoed, its form flickering. "You seek balance yet carry the seeds of chaos within you. To mend the Spiral Nexus, sacrifices must be made. Are you willing?"

Lira's hand moved instinctively to her amulet. "What kind of sacrifices?"

The figure didn't answer directly. Instead, it gestured to the reflections in the crystal walls. The images shifted, showing fragmented memories: Alaric's father abandoning his dreams to care for his family, Lira kneeling before a shattered Nexus, her failure etched into her face. The scenes were raw, unfiltered, and deeply personal.

"The ley lines remember," the figure said. "They demand balance for every imbalance."

As the apparition faded, the group stood in silence. Each was lost in their thoughts, the weight of the warning settling over them.

Lira broke the silence. "If sacrifices are what it takes, I'll make them."

"You don't know what that means yet," Alaric said. "None of us do."

Gavrin shook his head. "If the Spiral Nexus falls, it won't matter. Sacrifice or not, we're out of options."

Alaric nodded reluctantly. He retrieved his grimoire, flipping to a page he had sketched from the Veiled Order's altar. The runes there mirrored those in the Spiral Nexus chamber—corruption woven into the ley lines' very fabric.

"The Veiled Order caused this," he said. "If we're going to fix it, we need to understand their methods. That means going deeper into the Nexus."

"And if that kills us?" Gavrin asked.

Alaric closed the grimoire. "Then we fail. But at least we'll know we tried."

Journal Entry: Lira

The ley lines don't lie. They show us the truth we hide from ourselves. I saw my failure again today—the Nexus I couldn't save. It's as if the ley lines are daring me to try again, to prove I've learned. But what if I haven't? What if I'm the imbalance?

Chapter 16: The Whispering Nexus

The forest that greeted them was unlike any they had encountered before. The trees were impossibly tall, their crystalline trunks shimmering as though reflecting an unseen light. Their branches swayed despite the absence of wind, creating a symphony of faint whispers.

"The ley lines are alive here," Lira said, her voice hushed. She knelt, placing a hand on the mossy ground. "You can feel them—like they're trying to speak."

Alaric closed his eyes, focusing on the resonance around him. The air vibrated, carrying impressions rather than words—urgency, fear, and something else he couldn't quite name. He opened his grimoire, scribbling notes furiously. "It's like they're sending fragments of thought. Not a language, but... intentions."

Bob, now in his human form, leaned against a crystalline trunk, arms crossed. "I'll take your word for it, professor. To me, it sounds like someone humming a really bad tune."

Flamipandro emerged from the shadows, her ruby gown catching the forest's faint light. "That's because you're not listening," she said, her voice carrying an edge of irritation. "The ley lines don't hum. They sing. You just lack the ears to hear it."

As they ventured deeper into the forest, the whispers grew louder, forming a coherent rhythm that seemed to guide their steps. Eventually, they reached a clearing where a massive stone structure stood, its surface covered in glowing runes.

"The Nexus Codex," Flamipandro said, her tone reverent. She stepped closer, her fingers brushing the stone. "It's a record of the ley lines' natural rhythms. Every surge, every fracture—it's all here."

Alaric approached cautiously, his gaze scanning the structure. The runes pulsed faintly, their patterns shifting as though alive. He traced a line of runes with his finger, feeling a surge of energy course through him. "The ley lines use this to maintain balance," he said. "It's like a map of their entire network."

Lira knelt beside one of the glowing grooves, her staff resonating faintly. "It's beautiful," she said softly. "Like they're trying to show us how to help."

As they studied the Codex, a familiar voice broke the quiet. "Beautiful, isn't it? Shame you're too mortal to understand it."

Pecos emerged from the shadows, his form that of an elderly man leaning on a gnarled staff. His eyes twinkled with mischief, but his expression carried a weight they hadn't seen before.

"Pecos," Alaric said, stepping toward him. "We need answers. The Spiral Nexus—what's happening to it?"

Pecos chuckled, shaking his head. "Answers? Child, the ley lines don't deal in answers. They deal in truths. And the truth is, you're asking the wrong questions."

"What's that supposed to mean?" Lira asked, frustration creeping into her voice.

Pecos turned to her, his expression softening. "You feel them, don't you? Their pain. Their need. The ley lines don't want control or repair. They want harmony. You're the only one who hears them clearly, little guardian."

Lira froze, her eyes wide. "I'm not—"

"You are," Pecos interrupted, his voice firm. "And you'll have to prove it."

Before they could respond, Pecos reached into his robes and produced a small, silver band etched with intricate grooves. It pulsed faintly, its rhythm matching the ley lines' hum.

"This is the Resonance Band," Pecos said, holding it out to Alaric. "It harmonizes ley line frequencies, but only temporarily. Use it wisely—it won't fix fractures, but it'll help you understand them."

Alaric took the band, feeling its faint vibrations against his skin. "Why are you giving this to me?"

"Because you're the one who wants to control what you don't understand," Pecos said, a wry smile tugging at his lips. "And maybe, just maybe, this will teach you to listen instead."

*****

As they left the Codex, the whispers grew louder, merging into a single, resonant tone. Alaric and Lira both stopped, their eyes widening as the tone transformed into words—not spoken, but felt.

"You are the fracture. You are the balance."

Alaric staggered back, his mind reeling. "What does that mean?"

Lira gripped her staff tightly, her expression pale but determined. "It means the ley lines see us as part of this. We're not just observers—we're part of their balance."

The group exchanged uneasy glances, the weight of the ley lines' message settling over them like a shroud. Ahead lay the Spiral Nexus, and with it, the greatest challenge they had ever faced.

The group pressed deeper into the Resonating Forest, the air thick with whispers that grew more insistent. Each sound resonated in Alaric's chest, and as they walked, his grip on the Resonance Band tightened.

"It's like they're inside my head," he muttered, his voice barely audible over the humming air.

"They are," Lira said softly, her staff pulsing faintly. "The ley lines aren't just speaking to us. They're reaching into us, trying to make us feel what they feel."

"Great," Bob said, his human form leaning against a crystalline trunk as he tried to catch his breath. "Feelings and I are not on good terms. Can they just send a postcard instead?"

"They don't operate like that," Flamipandro said, her ruby gown trailing over the mossy ground as she moved with purpose. "The ley lines don't think like we do. They're not bound by linear thought or singular intention."

Alaric paused, his brow furrowing. "But they want us to act. They're sending us somewhere—why?"

Flamipandro turned to face him, her expression serious. "Because they don't have another choice. They can't intervene directly. They need proxies—agents who can shape events without unraveling the threads."

"And we're the proxies," Lira said, her voice heavy with realization.

Ahead, the whispers grew louder, forming a deep, rhythmic pulse. The trees thinned, and the group found themselves at the edge of a large clearing. At its center, a gaping rift tore through the ground, its edges glowing with chaotic energy. Threads of ley line light writhed like living things, lashing out at the air.

"It's unstable," Alaric said, gripping the Resonance Band. The artifact pulsed in time with the rift, its grooves vibrating faintly under his fingers. "This must be one of the fractures leading to the Spiral Nexus."

The ground trembled as the rift expanded, spewing arcs of light and shadow. Creatures began to emerge from the rift—spindly beings made of fractured crystal and shadow, their forms barely holding together as they moved jerkily toward the group.

"Corrupted guardians," Flamipandro said, her voice sharp. She drew the Rune-Inscribed Blade, its runes flaring to life. "They're drawn to the imbalance."

Bob took a step back, flipping the hourglass nervously. "I'm guessing they're not here to make friends."

The first corrupted guardian lunged, its crystal claws swiping at Lira. She raised her staff just in time, casting a barrier of light that deflected the attack. "They're fast!" she shouted, channeling another spell to push the creature back.

Flamipandro leapt forward, her blade slicing through the air in an arc of glowing energy. The guardian staggered, its form flickering as it tried to reform. "They're tied to the rift," she called out. "If we don't stabilize it, they'll just keep coming!"

Alaric glanced at the Resonance Band, his mind racing. "If this harmonizes ley line frequencies..." He strapped the band onto his wrist, its grooves aligning with the pulse of the rift. Immediately, he felt a jolt of energy, his vision shifting as the ley lines' chaotic threads became visible.

"There!" he shouted, pointing to the rift's core. "That's where the instability is strongest!"

Lira nodded, her staff glowing brighter as she joined him. Together, they focused their magic, channeling it toward the rift. The Resonance Band amplified their efforts, its grooves vibrating with increasing intensity.

Bob flipped the hourglass, slowing time just as another guardian lunged for Flamipandro. She sidestepped effortlessly, driving the blade into the creature's core. It shattered, its fragments dissolving into faint wisps of light.

"Keep going!" she yelled. "The rift's energy is weakening!"

As the rift began to stabilize, the chaotic threads around it started to weave together, forming a faintly glowing web. The corrupted guardians dissolved one by one, their forms unraveling as the imbalance subsided.

Alaric collapsed to his knees, breathing heavily. The Resonance Band on his wrist was still pulsing faintly, its grooves warm against his skin. "We... we did it," he said, his voice shaky.

Lira placed a hand on his shoulder, her expression one of relief and exhaustion. "The ley lines—they're calming. I can feel it."

The whispers in the air grew softer, transforming into a harmonious hum that resonated through the clearing. Flamipandro sheathed her blade, her ruby gown glinting faintly in the ley lines' light. "One fracture down," she said. "But the Spiral Nexus will be far worse."

As the group prepared to leave the clearing, the ground beneath the rift began to shimmer. A column of light shot upward, enveloping them in a warm glow. Images began to form within the light—a vast, swirling nexus of golden and black threads, fracturing and reforming in an endless cycle.

Alaric reached out instinctively, his fingers brushing the edge of the light. A voice echoed through the clearing—not spoken, but felt, reverberating in their very souls.

"You must act. The threads are breaking. Balance... or collapse."

The light faded, leaving the group in silence.

"What does it mean?" Lira asked, her voice barely above a whisper.

"It means we don't have a choice," Alaric said, his expression grim. "The Spiral Nexus is the heart of everything. If it collapses, so does everything else."

The forest grew denser as they moved closer to their destination. The ley lines' hum remained steady, guiding their path through crystalline trees and glowing streams. Pecos appeared again, this time as a young boy, his mischievous grin at odds with the seriousness of his words.

"You think you've done something noble," he said, hopping onto a low branch. "But stabilizing one rift is like patching a hole in a sinking ship. The Spiral Nexus is where it all breaks apart."

"Then guide us," Lira said, her tone sharp. "If you know so much, tell us what to do."

Pecos shrugged, plucking a glowing leaf from the branch. "The ley lines don't deal in answers. They deal in lessons. You're just the students."

Alaric frowned, his gaze fixed on the Resonance Band. "What about this? It's helping us harmonize with the ley lines."

"For now," Pecos said, tossing the leaf into the air. "But tools like that don't last forever. The Spiral Nexus won't be fixed by artifacts. It'll be fixed by choices."

The group reached a massive archway of crystalline vines, their edges etched with glowing runes. Beyond it lay the Whispering Nexus, a place where ley lines converged into a single, resonant force. The air was thick with energy, and the whispers they had followed now formed a symphony of voices.

"It's beautiful," Lira said, her voice filled with awe.

"It's also dangerous," Flamipandro said, stepping forward. "The ley lines here are stronger than anywhere else we've been. One wrong move, and we could destabilize everything."

Alaric took a deep breath, his fingers brushing the Resonance Band. "Then let's make sure we don't make any wrong moves."

As they crossed the threshold, the voices of the ley lines grew louder, their tone filled with urgency. The Spiral Nexus awaited, and with it, the fate of the ley lines—and perhaps reality itself.

The dimensional rift shimmered ominously, its chaotic energy casting jagged shadows across the ground. Alaric stood at its edge, his chest tight with a mixture of guilt and fascination. His failed experiment to merge light and darkness had opened this void—a tear in the fabric of the ley lines that pulsed with unchecked energy.

"We shouldn't leave this unchecked," Lira said, her voice cutting through the silence. She stood a few steps behind him, her staff glowing faintly as it resonated with the unstable ley lines. "If this is what light and darkness can do, imagine what happens when the Shadow Plane responds."

Alaric didn't answer immediately. His gaze lingered on the rift, watching as its tendrils of energy reached for the surrounding air. He clenched the Resonance Band on his wrist, the grooves warm against his skin. "We need to understand this," he murmured, though he wasn't sure if his words were driven by curiosity or redemption.

Pecos emerged from the shadows, his middle-aged form calm yet intense. He walked to the edge of the rift, his gnarled staff tapping lightly against the ground. "The balance you seek lies deeper than you think," he said, his tone cryptic as ever. He pointed toward the horizon, where the twilight sky faded into an inky blackness. "You've opened the door. Now you need to step through."

Alaric frowned. "The Shadow Plane?"

Pecos nodded, his expression unreadable. "When light bends to darkness, the shadows listen. But beware: shadows don't just reveal secrets—they also consume them."

Chapter 17: The Darkened Codex

The rift into the Shadow Plane shimmered with an eerie allure, its edges flickering as if the very air was uncertain about the portal's existence. Alaric stood at its edge, the Void Crystal Talisman pulsing steadily in his hand. Its surface was etched with dark veins that seemed to shift under his gaze.

"This should keep us safe," he said, his voice betraying a sliver of doubt as he glanced at Lira and Pecos. The former stood with her staff aglow, her brows knit in concern; the latter leaned casually on his staff, his expression unreadable.

"Safe is relative," Pecos said, his tone light but edged with something deeper. "The Shadow Plane isn't evil, Alaric. It's a mirror. It reflects what you bring into it."

Lira hesitated, her gaze fixed on the swirling shadows. "I don't like this place. It feels... wrong."

"It's not just a place," Alaric replied, gripping the talisman tightly. "It's a force. And it's waiting for us."

Without waiting for a response, he stepped through.

Colors faded and sounds warped as they crossed the threshold. The Shadow Plane's air was heavy, its oppressive chill seeping into their bones. The ground was a jagged expanse of obsidian and ash, and the sky above was a swirling void pierced by dim streaks of light.

The talisman thrummed in Alaric's hand, pushing back the encroaching shadows in faint ripples. He let out a measured breath. "It's working," he said. "For now."

Lira's sharp eyes scanned their surroundings. "Do you hear that?"

Alaric stopped, straining his ears. At first, there was only silence, but then faint whispers drifted through the air—disjointed, fragmented voices carried on the wind. They felt deliberate, as though the shadows themselves were speaking.

"Keep moving," Pecos said from behind them, his voice uncharacteristically grim. "The whispers are watching."

The whispers grew louder as they ventured deeper, weaving into a haunting melody. The ley lines here were visible as faint, glowing strands that flickered erratically. Alaric reached for one, but as his fingers brushed its surface, it recoiled violently, emitting a sharp burst of energy.

"They don't trust us," Lira said, her tone tinged with awe and unease. "Or maybe they're afraid."

"Afraid of what?" Alaric asked, though he suspected the answer.

From the swirling darkness, a Shadow Wraith emerged—a fluid, flickering form with glowing eyes that pierced the gloom. It moved closer, testing their resolve.

Alaric tightened his grip on the talisman, its energy surging in response. "It's reacting to the talisman. I think it sees us as intruders."

The wraith paused, its form shimmering. Then, with a piercing shriek, it lunged.

Alaric instinctively raised the talisman, the dark energy colliding with the wraith's attack. The force sent him staggering backward, but the talisman held, absorbing the chaotic energy.

"Shadow magic isn't inherently evil," Alaric muttered, recalling Pecos's words. "It mirrors intent."

"Then what's your intent right now?" Lira called out, her staff glowing as she cast a barrier of light to deflect another strike.

"To survive," Alaric said through gritted teeth. He channeled the talisman's energy, driving the wraith back. "And to understand."

As the wraith dissolved into the shadows, the whispers softened. Alaric lowered the talisman, his breath heavy. "The plane is testing us," he said. "It's seeing what we'll do."

"Or what we'll become," Lira added grimly.

They pressed onward, the talisman's steady pulse guiding them. The whispers gave way to a deeper resonance—a low, thrumming sound that seemed to come from the ground itself.

Ahead, a towering spire of black crystal emerged, its surface etched with glowing runes. At its base rested a pedestal holding a book—the Darkened Codex.

Alaric approached cautiously, the talisman vibrating in his hand. The codex's cover was smooth and cold, its runes shifting under his touch.

"This is what the ley lines wanted us to find," he said, his voice tinged with awe. "A guide to understanding the balance between light and shadow."

Lira frowned. "And what happens if we don't balance it?"

Alaric didn't answer. He opened the codex, its pages glowing faintly as intricate diagrams and text unfolded before him. The knowledge was vast, but it carried a warning—a stark reminder of what happens when balance is lost.

As Alaric studied the codex, the ground trembled. The oppressive energy of the plane pressed down on them, and the whispers grew harsh and discordant.

"The plane knows we're here," Lira said, her staff pulsing with light. "We need to leave."

Alaric closed the codex and tucked it into his satchel. "Let's go."

As they turned to leave, more wraiths emerged from the shadows, their forms larger and more defined.

Lira raised her staff. "Looks like it doesn't want us to leave."

Alaric gripped the talisman, its energy surging. But before the wraiths could strike, Pecos stepped forward. His presence seemed to ripple through the plane, causing the wraiths to hesitate.

"You've learned enough for now," Pecos said calmly. "But linger, and it will consume you."

*****

Back in the ley line forest, the oppressive weight of the Shadow Plane lifted. Alaric sat on a jagged rock, the Void Crystal Talisman in his hand. Its surface shimmered faintly, reflecting the ley lines' steady hum.

"Did we do the right thing?" Lira asked quietly.

"We'll find out," Alaric said, his gaze distant. The weight of the Darkened Codex in his satchel was a constant reminder of the cost of understanding.

The ley line forest had returned to its quiet hum, but the group's camp was anything but peaceful. Alaric sat near the fire, the Darkened Codex open on his lap. Each page glowed faintly, its runes shifting in patterns that seemed to respond to his thoughts. His quill hovered over his journal as he struggled to put his discoveries into words.

Lira approached, her staff tucked under one arm. "You've been at it for hours," she said. "You should rest."

Alaric shook his head. "I can't. The codex—it's... alive, in a way. It changes as I read it, like it's reacting to me."

"Or testing you," Lira said, sitting across from him. She leaned forward, studying the codex. "What have you learned so far?"

"That shadow magic isn't inherently destructive," Alaric said. "It's reactive—mirroring the intent of its wielder. The ley lines here in the Shadow Plane are part of the same system, but they're twisted by imbalance."

"And the wraiths?" Lira asked.

"They're manifestations of that imbalance," Alaric said. He closed the codex, running a hand over its cool surface. "Guardians, but corrupted. The codex suggests they were once part of the ley lines' defenses."

"Then why attack us?" Lira pressed.

"Because they don't trust us," Alaric said simply.

Journal Entry: The Shadow Plane's Legacy

Entry 49: The Codex and Its Secrets

The Darkened Codex is unlike any artifact I've studied. Its pages seem alive, shifting and adapting as though it's attuned to my thoughts. It offers guidance but never reveals too much at once, as if it knows I'm not ready for the full truth.

The Shadow Plane itself is a reflection—of the ley lines, of the nexus, and perhaps of me. The wraiths attacked not out of malice but out of necessity. They are protectors warped by imbalance, unable to distinguish friend from foe.

Lira asked me tonight if we did the right thing. I don't know. What I do know is that the codex is a key—not just to the ley lines' balance but to understanding their will. I only hope I'm strong enough to wield it.

*****

The next morning, the group prepared to leave the forest. Alaric carefully tucked the codex into his satchel, its weight a constant reminder of the knowledge it contained. Pecos appeared as they broke camp, his form shifting between middle-aged and elder as he spoke.

"You've learned a lot," he said, his voice light but measured. "But knowledge is a double-edged blade, Alaric. Be careful how you wield it."

Alaric frowned. "The codex is a guide. If it can help us restore balance, why wouldn't I use it?"

"Because not all balance is meant to be restored," Pecos said. His gaze turned distant, his voice soft. "Sometimes, imbalance is part of the cycle. Sometimes, destruction paves the way for renewal."

"That sounds like something the Veiled Order would say," Lira interjected, her tone sharp.

Pecos chuckled. "Perhaps. But even the Veiled Order has its truths. They just don't know how to wield them without breaking the world."

The ley lines grew darker as they neared the next nexus. The air around them felt dense, charged with chaotic energy that made every breath feel heavier. The ground beneath their feet cracked and sparked, each step reverberating with discordant hums.

"This is worse than I expected," Lira said, her voice tense. She pointed to a series of broken ley lines overhead, their glowing threads frayed and sparking. "The balance here is almost completely gone."

As they approached, a new guardian emerged from the nexus—a Corrupted Sentinel, its massive form an amalgamation of jagged crystal and shifting shadow. Its movements were slow but deliberate, and its glowing eyes burned with an eerie light.

Alaric instinctively reached for the Void Crystal Talisman, feeling its energy resonate with the sentinel. "It's like the wraiths," he said, his voice low. "But... stronger."

"Stronger and angrier," Bob quipped, stepping back as the sentinel let out a low, rumbling growl.

"What do we do?" Lira asked, her staff already glowing with defensive magic.

Alaric stared at the sentinel, his mind racing. The talisman pulsed in his hand, its dark energy responding to the nexus's chaotic resonance. "We stabilize the ley lines," he said. "Together."

The group formed a loose circle around the nexus, their artifacts glowing faintly as they prepared to channel their energy. Alaric held the Void Crystal Talisman steady, its dark pulse aligning with the broken ley lines' erratic hums.

Lira extended her staff, its crystalline tip flaring with light as she began to weave threads of energy. "The ley lines are trying to reconnect," she said. "But they need a focus."

Flamipandro stepped forward, her blade glowing with runic energy. "Then we give them one."

As the group worked in unison, the sentinel roared, its corrupted form lashing out with waves of chaotic energy. Lira deflected the first strike with a barrier of light, while Flamipandro countered with a precise slash of her blade.

"Keep going!" Flamipandro called. "The ley lines are responding!"

Alaric focused on the talisman, channeling its energy into the nexus. The ley lines began to glow brighter, their frayed threads knitting together. The sentinel faltered, its form flickering as the nexus stabilized.

"It's working!" Lira said, her voice filled with hope.

As the final threads of the ley lines reconnected, the sentinel let out a final, echoing roar before dissolving into a mist of light and shadow. The nexus pulsed softly, its chaotic hum replaced by a steady, harmonious tone.

The group stood in silence, the weight of their actions settling over them. The ley lines around the nexus were calm now, their glow steady and bright.

"We did it," Lira said, her voice soft.

"For now," Alaric replied. He looked down at the Void Crystal Talisman, its energy faint but still present. "But the ley lines aren't just asking for balance—they're asking for trust. And I don't know if we've earned it yet."

Pecos appeared beside him, his expression uncharacteristically serious. "Trust is a two-way street, Alaric. The ley lines are alive, but they're also patient. They'll give you the time you need to prove yourself."

Alaric glanced at the Darkened Codex in his satchel. Its weight felt heavier than before, a constant reminder of the responsibility he now carried. "Then we'll keep moving," he said. "The Spiral Nexus is waiting."

The ley line nexus ahead pulsed faintly, its energy glowing dimly in the distance like a dying star. As the group approached, Alaric could feel the tension in the air—both from the fractured ley lines and the weight of their journey. The faint hum of magic intertwined with the rustling of unseen forces, a symphony of imbalance.

Lira slowed her steps, her staff resonating faintly with the environment. "The ley lines are... different here. Their rhythm is broken, like a song out of tune."

"They're more than broken," Alaric said, his voice tight. "They're calling out—for help or a warning, I'm not sure."

Pecos, now appearing as a middle-aged man, leaned on his staff as he regarded the distant nexus. "Both, probably. The ley lines don't speak in absolutes. They leave room for interpretation... and for mistakes."

"Encouraging," Bob muttered, his human form pacing behind the group. "Just the kind of vague guidance we need."

Flamipandro gave Bob a side glance, her ruby gown glinting faintly in the ley line's dim light. "The ley lines are asking for more than guidance—they're asking for understanding. The question is, can you offer that?"

The nexus itself was a swirling mass of broken ley lines, their strands frayed and sparking. Above it hovered a crystalline obelisk, its surface marred with cracks that glowed faintly with chaotic energy. The ground beneath was jagged, fragments of blackened stone jutting upward like the jagged teeth of a great beast.

Alaric stepped closer, the Void Crystal Talisman in his hand reacting to the unstable energy. Its pulse aligned with the fragmented rhythm of the ley lines, creating a discordant harmony that reverberated in his chest. "This is worse than I imagined," he said. "The nexus isn't just unstable—it's on the verge of collapse."

Lira knelt by one of the glowing ley lines, her fingers hovering just above its surface. "The energy feels... desperate. Like it's trying to hold itself together but doesn't have the strength."

"That's where we come in," Alaric said, his voice steady despite the weight of his words. "The codex might have the answers, but we need to act now."

Before Alaric could say more, the ground beneath them began to tremble. From the shadows emerged a massive guardian—a Shadowbound Sentinel, its form an amalgamation of fractured ley lines and shadow magic. Its crystalline body shifted and cracked as it moved, and its molten eyes glowed with an intensity that made even the surrounding nexus energy seem dim.

"Great," Bob muttered, flipping his hourglass. "Another overgrown monster. Just what we needed."

"It's not a monster," Lira said, her staff glowing brightly as she stepped forward. "It's a guardian. The nexus must have created it to protect itself."

Flamipandro unsheathed her rune-inscribed blade, its runes flaring to life. "Whether it's a guardian or a monstrosity, it's in our way."

The sentinel let out a low, rumbling growl, its crystalline form shifting as it prepared to attack. Alaric felt the Void Crystal Talisman thrum in his hand, its energy surging in response to the sentinel's chaotic resonance. "It's tied to the nexus," he said. "If we stabilize the ley lines, we might be able to calm it."

"And if we can't?" Lira asked, her voice tense.

"Then we do what we have to," Alaric said grimly.

The group spread out, forming a loose circle around the nexus. Alaric held the Void Crystal Talisman aloft, its dark energy forming threads that connected to the frayed ley lines. Lira raised her staff, its crystalline head glowing as she channeled a steady stream of light into the nexus. Flamipandro moved with precision, her blade carving glowing runes into the ground to stabilize the energy flows.

The sentinel roared, its body flickering as it lashed out with tendrils of shadow and light. One struck near Bob, who narrowly avoided it by flipping the hourglass and slowing time just enough to dodge.

"Less dodging, more helping!" Flamipandro snapped as she deflected another strike with her blade.

"I'm working on it!" Bob called, flipping the hourglass again and sending a ripple through the nexus energy. The ley lines shuddered, their rhythm faltering before resuming a steadier pulse.

"Focus!" Alaric shouted, his voice cutting through the chaos. He closed his eyes, letting the talisman's energy guide him. The ley lines responded, their threads beginning to weave together in a delicate balance.

Lira's voice broke the tension. "It's working. Keep going!"

The sentinel paused, its molten eyes narrowing as its movements grew less erratic. The ley lines' hum grew stronger, their fractured rhythm slowly aligning into harmony.

As the ley lines stabilized, the sentinel stepped back, its crystalline form flickering faintly. It tilted its head, as though studying the group, before lowering itself to one knee. The glowing cracks in its body began to fade, and the chaotic energy around it dissipated.

Alaric lowered the talisman, his breathing heavy. "It's... submitting."

"Not submitting," Pecos corrected, his voice quiet but firm. "Acknowledging. The ley lines recognize balance when they see it."

Lira approached the sentinel cautiously, her staff still glowing. "Do you think it understands us?"

"It understands intent," Alaric said. He placed a hand on the codex in his satchel, its surface faintly warm. "And for now, it knows we mean no harm."

*****

With the sentinel standing guard, Alaric retrieved the Darkened Codex and opened it to a page he hadn't seen before. The runes glowed brightly, forming a detailed diagram of the nexus and its surrounding ley lines.

"This is a map," he said, his voice tinged with awe. "It shows how the nexus connects to the Spiral Nexus."

Lira leaned over his shoulder, studying the diagram. "The ley lines here aren't just broken—they're inverted. They flow backward, disrupting the natural balance."

"The codex suggests a way to restore them," Alaric said. "But it's risky. If we fail, we could destabilize the entire network."

"Then we don't fail," Flamipandro said, her tone resolute. "We've come too far to stop now."

The group worked together, using the codex's guidance to realign the ley lines. Each movement was precise, each spell carefully measured to avoid overloading the nexus. The energy in the air grew heavier as the ley lines began to shift, their frayed threads weaving into a delicate web of light and shadow.

Alaric felt the Void Crystal Talisman grow warmer in his hand, its energy resonating with the nexus. He channeled its power into the ley lines, watching as the chaotic threads steadied.

"We're almost there," Lira said, her voice steady despite the strain.

The ley lines pulsed one final time, their glow bright and harmonious. The nexus let out a low, resonant hum as its energy stabilized. The sentinel stepped forward, its crystalline body glowing softly as it bowed its head in acknowledgment.

"We did it," Alaric said, his voice filled with relief.

"For now," Pecos said, his tone carrying a hint of warning. "The Spiral Nexus is still fractured. This is just the beginning."

The air outside the Shadow Plane was crisp and alive, yet Alaric felt no relief. Clutching the Void Crystal Talisman, he stood in silence, his gaze fixed on the faint hum of ley lines threading through the forest. Each step away from the rift felt like a hollow victory. The talisman's once-bright pulse was now muted, its energy subdued yet volatile, as though it carried the weight of the Shadow Plane's truths.

The shadows' whispers lingered, faint but insistent. They were no longer words, but feelings—warning, curiosity, and an overwhelming sense of expectation. Alaric tightened his grip on the talisman, its dark surface warm against his palm.

"I thought leaving the Shadow Plane would feel like a relief," Lira said, breaking the silence. She stood a few feet away, her staff faintly glowing. "But it's like we brought part of it with us."

"We did," Alaric replied, his voice heavy. "The ley lines here... they're different now. They carry the residue of what we did. What I did."

"Then we have a responsibility to make it right," she said, her tone firm but understanding.

Pecos stepped closer, his expression uncharacteristically somber. "The ley lines don't forget, Alaric. They adapt. You've set something in motion, but where it leads depends on the choices you make next."

Alaric nodded, his mind swirling with thoughts. The Shadow Plane had given him answers, but they came with even more questions. Could he truly restore balance to the ley lines? Or was he merely delaying the inevitable?

Journal: The Shadows' Legacy

Entry 50: A Fragile Balance

The Shadow Plane doesn't just challenge you—it changes you. Its whispers are gone, but their echoes remain. The Void Crystal Talisman feels heavier now, as though it carries more than shadow energy. It carries expectation.

The ley lines here are quieter than they should be. They hum with a new resonance, one that mirrors the Shadow Plane's fragmented rhythm. It's subtle, but it's there. The codex suggests this is normal—ley lines adapt to disruption—but the question remains: have I helped them, or made things worse?

Pecos said balance isn't always about restoration. Sometimes, it's about understanding when to let go. I wonder if the Spiral Nexus will give us that choice—or if it will take it from us.

The rift to the Shadow Plane pulsed behind them, its edges swirling like a pool of ink disturbed by unseen winds. The Void Crystal Talisman in Alaric's hand felt colder than before, its weight pressing against his thoughts. Pecos lingered at the edge of the void, his presence steady but unreadable.

"This place is alive," Lira said softly, her staff casting faint light on the shifting ground. "I can feel it moving, like it's breathing."

Alaric nodded, though his mind was elsewhere. His gaze fell on the fractured ley lines visible in the distance, their erratic flickering a painful reminder of what they were risking.

Journal Entry: The Shadow Plane

The Shadow Plane is not what I expected. It's not a void or an absence—it's a reflection. Every step we take feels like walking through memory, but whose memories? The ley lines are fractured here, not just physically but emotionally. They recoil at our presence, and yet they guide us. What are they trying to show us?

*****

The faint sound of hissing interrupted Alaric's thoughts. From the shadows, luminous forms emerged—serpentine creatures with translucent scales that shimmered with the colors of the ley lines. Their eyes glowed with an inner light, and their movements were fluid, almost hypnotic.

"Ethereal Serpents," Pecos murmured. "Guardians of the ley lines. They won't let us pass without proof of our intent."

One of the serpents coiled toward Lira, its gaze piercing. She raised her staff instinctively, but its light dimmed as the creature's energy overpowered hers.

"It's testing us," she whispered, lowering her weapon. Instead, she extended her free hand, allowing the serpent to approach. It hissed softly, its energy entwining with hers. Lira gasped as images flooded her mind—fractured nexuses, ancient guardians, and the Spiral Nexus at the center of it all, pulsating with fragile light.

"What do they want from us?" she asked aloud, her voice trembling.

"To listen," Alaric replied, stepping forward. He held the Void Crystal Talisman aloft, and the serpents turned their attention to him. The artifact glowed faintly, resonating with the ley lines' energy. The largest serpent lowered its head, its voice a chorus of whispers.

"Restore balance, or be consumed by the chaos you have wrought."

Flashback: The Guardians' Warning

As the serpents retreated, their forms dissolving into the ley lines, Alaric's vision blurred. He was no longer in the Shadow Plane but standing before a council of Nexus Guardians. Their forms were indistinct, glowing figures that radiated authority.

"The ley lines were entrusted to us," one of them said, their voice echoing like a distant storm. "But we failed to protect them. The Spiral Nexus became our greatest triumph—and our greatest sin."

Another figure stepped forward, their energy flickering. "To repair the ley lines, you must face what we could not. The Spiral Nexus will test your resolve, your unity, and your willingness to sacrifice."

The vision faded, leaving Alaric with the weight of their words. He turned to Lira, who was staring into the distance, lost in thought. "Did you see them too?" she asked.

He nodded. "They're warning us. This isn't just about fixing the ley lines—it's about earning their trust."

Narrator's Perspective: The Interdimensional Stakes

Magic is a force of creation, but it is also a force of memory. The ley lines are not merely threads of energy—they are the history of worlds, the lifeblood of dimensions. Each fracture is a wound, and each wound threatens the fragile web that holds existence together.

The Spiral Nexus was never meant to be touched. It was a convergence point, a place where all things met and all things were held apart. To tamper with it was to tamper with the fabric of reality itself. Yet, as Alaric and Lira approached, they knew that the Veiled Order had already done the unthinkable.

Memory Scene: The Spiral Nexus's Fracture

As they approached the heart of the Shadow Plane, the ground beneath them shifted, revealing a fractured ley line. Its threads were torn apart, leaking energy that shimmered and warped the air around it. Alaric knelt beside the fracture, his hand hovering over the exposed threads.

"It's worse than I thought," he said. "This isn't just a crack—it's a rupture."

Lira knelt beside him, her voice soft. "I can feel its pain. The ley lines aren't just broken—they're scared."

Alaric hesitated, his mind flashing back to the moment he had first learned about the Spiral Nexus. He remembered standing in Eldaryn's study, the old mage's voice heavy with warning. "The Spiral Nexus is not a place of power," Eldaryn had said. "It is a place of balance. And balance, Alaric, is far more dangerous than power."

*****

Pecos reappeared, his expression grim. "The Veiled Order is here. Their marks are all over this place."

Alaric followed Pecos's gaze to a series of jagged runes carved into the obsidian ground. The symbols pulsed faintly, their light a sickly green. "They've corrupted the ley lines," he said, his voice shaking. "They're trying to rewrite them."

"And if they succeed?" Lira asked.

"The Spiral Nexus will collapse," Pecos replied. "And with it, every dimension tied to the ley lines."

The group pressed on, the serpents' warnings and the guardians' words echoing in their minds. The Spiral Nexus loomed ahead, its fractured threads visible even from a distance. The air grew colder, and the weight of their task settled over them.

"We can't fail," Lira said, her voice steady. "Not after everything we've seen."

Alaric nodded, his grip on the Void Crystal Talisman tightening. "Then we won't."

As they stepped closer to the Spiral Nexus, the ground beneath them trembled, and the ley lines' hum grew louder. The test was coming, and the cost of failure was clear.

Chapter 18: Fantasy Secrets

The next leg of their journey took them away from the ley line forest and into a landscape that seemed pulled from a dream. Fields of golden grass stretched as far as the eye could see, punctuated by towering crystal spires that shimmered in the sunlight. The air was thick with magic, and the ley lines here pulsed with a vibrant energy that felt almost playful.

"This place is... different," Lira said, her gaze sweeping the horizon. "It doesn't feel broken like the other nexuses."

"That doesn't mean it's safe," Flamipandro said, her ruby gown trailing behind her as she stepped carefully over the uneven ground. "Magic like this tends to come with a price."

"Doesn't everything?" Bob muttered, flipping his hourglass in one hand as he walked. "At least it's pretty."

Alaric said nothing, his focus on the Void Crystal Talisman. Its pulse was faint here, almost as if it were unsure how to respond to the ley lines' energy. He reached into his satchel and pulled out the Darkened Codex, flipping through its pages. The diagrams shifted, forming new patterns that seemed to mirror the spires around them.

"The ley lines here are more stable," he said, studying the codex. "But they're layered—like they're overlapping realities."

"Overlapping?" Lira asked, frowning. "What does that mean?"

Before Alaric could answer, a soft laugh echoed through the air, startling the group. The sound was light and melodic, but it carried an otherworldly quality that sent a shiver down Alaric's spine.

Ayiyi Mones

The laugh came again, and this time it was accompanied by a figure emerging from behind one of the crystal spires. She appeared to be a young girl, her delicate frame wrapped in a shimmering cloak that seemed to shift between colors. Her eyes sparkled with mischief, and her smile was both inviting and unnerving.

"Welcome to my little corner of the ley lines," she said, her voice carrying an accent Alaric couldn't place. "You must be the travelers the whispers have been talking about."

Lira instinctively raised her staff, but Ayiyi held up a hand. "No need for that," she said. "I'm not here to hurt you. Quite the opposite, actually."

"And who are you?" Flamipandro asked, her tone wary.

"Ayiyi Mones," the girl replied with a graceful bow. "Guardian, dreamer, and... let's call me a storyteller."

"A storyteller?" Bob asked, raising an eyebrow. "That's a new one."

Ayiyi's grin widened. "Every realm needs its stories, golden one. And here, stories shape reality."

A Game of Imagination

Ayiyi led the group to a clearing surrounded by crystal spires. The ground was covered in soft, golden moss that seemed to glow faintly. She gestured for them to sit, her cloak rippling like water as she moved.

"Let's play a game," Ayiyi said, her tone light but commanding. "A game where your imagination becomes reality."

Alaric hesitated. "What's the purpose of this game?"

"To show you the truth," Ayiyi replied. "And to see if you're ready for it."

Despite their reservations, the group sat. Ayiyi began to hum softly, and the air around them shifted. Images flickered to life—dreamlike manifestations of their thoughts. Bob's hourglass floated upward, spinning lazily as golden sand spilled into the air. Lira's staff pulsed, projecting shimmering patterns of light that danced like fireflies.

When it was Alaric's turn, he focused on the Void Crystal Talisman. The shadows within it expanded, forming a swirling vortex that seemed to pull at the edges of the clearing.

Ayiyi clapped her hands, her eyes shining with excitement. "Fascinating! Your shadows seek balance, but they fear the light. What are you hiding, scholar?"

Alaric's heart raced. "I'm not hiding anything."

"Perhaps not yet," Ayiyi said, her smile fading. "But the Spiral Nexus won't wait for you to decide."

When the game ended, Ayiyi handed Alaric a small, shimmering crystal. It was warm to the touch, and its surface seemed to shift between solid and liquid.

"This will help you," she said, her tone suddenly serious. "But be careful—it doesn't just reflect reality. It changes it."

"What do you mean?" Alaric asked.

"You'll see," Ayiyi said cryptically. "Every story has its secrets."

As she vanished into the light, Alaric felt the weight of the crystal in his hand. It was unlike anything he'd encountered before, and its potential both intrigued and terrified him.

As the group left the clearing, the ley lines' energy grew stronger, their hum steady and resonant. The shimmering crystal in Alaric's hand pulsed faintly, a reminder of Ayiyi's parting words.

"We're getting closer," Lira said, her voice filled with determination.

"To the Spiral Nexus," Alaric replied. "And to the truth."

The journey from the ley line forest into the surreal landscape of Ayiyi Mones's domain felt like stepping into another reality entirely. The air shimmered with faint hues of gold and blue, the light bending unnaturally around crystal spires that jutted skyward like fractured monuments. The ground beneath their feet was covered in moss that seemed to glow faintly with its own energy, pulsing in rhythm with the ley lines threading invisibly through the atmosphere.

Lira paused to inspect the moss, running her fingers over its soft, luminous surface. "It's alive," she said, her voice filled with awe. "I can feel its connection to the ley lines."

"Everything here feels alive," Alaric replied, his eyes scanning the horizon. "It's as if the ley lines themselves have taken on a physical form."

Ahead of them, towering crystal spires loomed, their surfaces glinting with an iridescent sheen. Each spire emitted a faint hum, creating a layered harmony that seemed to resonate in Alaric's chest. In the distance, creatures flitted between the spires—delicate, glowing forms that appeared to be part insect, part bird. Their wings shimmered like liquid light, leaving trails of color as they moved.

"Are those... ley creatures?" Lira asked, pointing at the glowing beings.

"They might be," Alaric said, his voice tinged with fascination. "I've read about such creatures in ancient texts. They're said to be manifestations of pure ley line energy, existing only in places where magic flows freely."

One of the creatures descended closer, its small, angular body hovering just out of reach. Its wings buzzed faintly, emitting a high-pitched trill that seemed almost musical. Bob extended a hand, and the creature landed lightly on his finger, its body emitting a soft warmth.

"Well, aren't you a curious little thing," Bob said, grinning. "Do you have a name?"

The creature chirped in response, tilting its head as if studying him. Then, with a burst of light, it took off again, joining its companions.

Ayiyi's Realm

The group continued toward the center of the nexus, where the spires grew denser, forming a ring around a shimmering lake. The water was perfectly still, its surface reflecting the sky above with uncanny precision. In the center of the lake stood a platform of crystalline stone, and atop it was Ayiyi Mones, her cloak of shifting colors flowing like liquid light.

"Welcome back," she called, her voice carrying across the water as if amplified by the ley lines themselves. "Did you enjoy my little corner of the ley lines?"

"It's... breathtaking," Lira said, her tone sincere.

"And disorienting," Flamipandro added, her ruby gown glinting as she approached the water's edge. "This place doesn't follow the rules of normal magic."

"Why would it?" Ayiyi replied, stepping lightly across the water as though it were solid ground. "The ley lines aren't bound by your rules. They create their own."

She stopped before Alaric, her bright eyes studying him intently. "And you, scholar. What do you think?"

"I think this place is beautiful," Alaric said, his grip tightening on the Void Crystal Talisman. "But beauty can be dangerous."

Ayiyi's smile widened. "Wise words. Perhaps you're ready for the truth after all."

Ayiyi led them to the crystalline platform in the center of the lake. As they stepped onto its surface, the ley lines' hum grew louder, vibrating through their feet. Ayiyi extended her hand, and from the air itself, a small, shimmering crystal appeared. It floated just above her palm, its surface shifting between solid and liquid, light and shadow.

"This," Ayiyi said, "is the Shimmering Crystal. A gift from the ley lines themselves. It can reshape reality, but only for those who understand its purpose."

Alaric reached out hesitantly, feeling the crystal's warmth as it hovered just above his fingers. "How does it work?"

"It doesn't 'work,'" Ayiyi replied. "It reflects your intent, magnifies it. But be careful—what you create can become a prison if your heart isn't true."

Flamipandro crossed her arms, her gaze skeptical. "And why would you give us something so dangerous?"

"Because you need it," Ayiyi said simply. "The Spiral Nexus is unraveling, and this will help you restore balance. But it comes at a cost."

"What cost?" Lira asked.

Ayiyi's smile faded, her expression turning somber. "That's for you to decide."

Before they could ask more questions, the air around them shifted. The crystalline platform dissolved, replaced by a swirling expanse of light and shadow. They stood in a void filled with floating fragments of landscapes—mountains, forests, rivers—all disconnected and surreal.

"This is your trial," Ayiyi's voice echoed. "Show me your intent."

The group looked around in confusion as the fragments began to move, forming shapes that shifted and twisted unpredictably. Creatures emerged from the chaos—some familiar, like wolves and deer, but others were strange amalgamations of limbs and wings, their forms fluid and alien.

"We need to focus," Alaric said, gripping the talisman. "This place is responding to us, just like the crystal."

"Then what do we do?" Lira asked, her staff glowing faintly as a creature with too many eyes approached her.

"Think of something stable," Alaric said. "Something balanced."

Lira closed her eyes, and the glow of her staff intensified. The fragments around her began to coalesce, forming a serene forest with towering trees and a calm river. The chaotic creatures near her transformed into deer, their movements gentle and harmonious.

Alaric focused next, picturing the ley lines as a steady web of energy. The fragments around him aligned into geometric patterns, their hum growing steady and rhythmic.

Bob, however, grinned mischievously and imagined a flock of geese with golden feathers. They appeared instantly, honking loudly as they waddled around the void. "What? You said stable."

The swirling chaos began to settle, the void transforming into a cohesive landscape that blended each of their creations. Ayiyi appeared again, her expression one of quiet satisfaction.

"You've passed," she said. "Barely."

"What was the point of this?" Flamipandro asked, her blade still drawn.

"To show you that balance isn't about control," Ayiyi replied. "It's about harmony. The Spiral Nexus isn't broken because of chaos—it's broken because the ley lines have stopped trusting each other. Just like you."

Her words hung heavy in the air, and for a moment, no one spoke.

As they prepared to leave Ayiyi's domain, she handed the Shimmering Crystal to Alaric. Its surface shimmered with an inner light, as though it held the potential of the entire nexus within it.

"Remember," Ayiyi said, her tone serious. "This is a tool, not a solution. What you create with it will reflect what lies within you."

Alaric nodded, his thoughts heavy. The crystal felt both powerful and fragile, a perfect embodiment of the balance they sought.

The group stepped away from the platform, the vibrant nexus fading behind them as they returned to the ley line path. The Spiral Nexus awaited, and with it, the greatest challenge of their journey.

Journal Entry: The Burden of Knowledge

Entry 51: The Shimmering Crystal

The Shimmering Crystal feels like both a gift and a curse. Ayiyi's words still echo in my mind: "What you create with it will reflect what lies within you."

The ley lines' whispers have grown quieter since we left her domain, but the weight of their expectations remains. The Void Crystal Talisman thrums faintly, as if waiting for the next fracture to reveal itself.

I can't shake the feeling that we're missing something—some vital truth about the ley lines' will. The codex speaks of a balance that cannot be forced, but how do we honor that while the Spiral Nexus crumbles around us?

If the ley lines are alive, do they trust us? Or are we just another tool in their endless cycle of creation and destruction?

*****

The transition from Ayiyi's vibrant nexus to the Nature Nexus was marked by a shift in the air itself. The ley lines here were visible, flowing like shimmering rivers through the earth and sky. Trees with bark that glowed faintly lined their path, their roots intertwined with the ley lines in an intricate dance of magic and life.

The group entered a clearing where a massive tree, its trunk wide enough to house an entire village, stood at the center. Its branches were heavy with golden leaves that emitted a soft, warm light.

"This is the heart of the Nature Nexus," Lira said, her voice filled with reverence. "I can feel its energy everywhere."

Alaric knelt by one of the ley lines, watching as it pulsed gently through the grass. "The ley lines here aren't just connected to magic—they're part of the life force itself."

From the shadows stepped a Kirin, its form elegant and otherworldly. Its silver mane shimmered like moonlight, and its antlers glowed with a faint, ethereal light. It regarded the group with intelligent eyes, its gaze lingering on Alaric.

"You are far from your world, scholars," the Kirin said, its voice resonant and musical. "What brings you to the cradle of harmony?"

Before Alaric could answer, the ground beneath them began to shimmer. The ley lines pulsed erratically, and the group was enveloped in a bright light. When the light faded, they were no longer in the clearing but in a dreamlike vision—a tapestry of ley line threads stretched across a star-filled void.

Ancient voices spoke in unison, their tones filled with both wisdom and sorrow:

"The Spiral Nexus is the heart of creation, but its threads fray with every choice, every imbalance. Trust is not freely given, for mortals have often sought to command what cannot be controlled."

The threads shifted, showing glimpses of past Nexus Guardians. Among them was a younger Pecos, his form solid and radiant, standing before a swirling rift. His voice carried through the vision:

"Balance is not found in control, but in understanding. The ley lines have their will. We are but their stewards."

The vision dissolved, and the group found themselves back in the clearing. The Kirin stepped forward, its gaze solemn. "The ley lines have shown you their truth. Will you honor it?"

The Kirin led them to a grove where ancient Dryads emerged from the trees, their forms slender and bark-like, their hair woven with leaves and flowers. The Dryads began to weave a spell, showing the group a scene of balance disrupted: a nexus overtaken by human ambition, its ley lines fractured and its guardians corrupted.

"This is what happens when harmony is ignored," the Kirin said. "The ley lines can heal themselves, but only if left to their natural rhythms. Force disrupts, but understanding mends."

Lira turned to Alaric, her expression troubled. "This is what the codex has been trying to teach us. We can't impose our will—we have to guide the ley lines back to balance."

Alaric looked down at the Shimmering Crystal in his hand, its surface flickering faintly. "But how do we guide them without interfering?"

The Kirin tilted its head. "That is your trial to discover."

The group was tasked with stabilizing a severed ley line using the Shimmering Crystal. The Kirin warned them that the crystal's power would amplify their intent, but it would also expose their fears and doubts.

Alaric placed the crystal at the ley line's fracture, feeling its energy surge through him. As he focused on mending the ley line, the crystal began to glow brighter, projecting his thoughts into the air around them.

The group watched as images formed—a fractured Spiral Nexus, wreathed in shadow; a younger Alaric arguing with Eldaryn about the ethics of ley line manipulation; and a vision of Alaric standing alone amidst a desolate, lifeless landscape.

"The crystal is showing your heart," Lira said softly. "You're afraid of failing."

Alaric closed his eyes, steadying his breathing. "I am. But fear can't guide me." He redirected his focus, imagining the ley lines whole and harmonious. The crystal responded, its light weaving the severed threads back together.

The ley line pulsed steadily once more, its energy flowing freely. The Kirin and Dryads nodded in approval, their forms glowing faintly as they retreated into the forest.

That night, Alaric opened the Darkened Codex and found a new passage glowing faintly. It was an ancient scripture written in flowing, elegant runes:

"The ley lines do not seek dominance or servitude. They seek trust, for trust is the thread that binds all creation. Only through trust can balance be restored, and only through balance can harmony endure."

He traced the runes with his fingers, their meaning resonating deeply. The ley lines weren't asking for perfection—they were asking for understanding.

The next morning, the group set out from the Nature Nexus, their hearts heavier but their purpose clearer. The ley lines pulsed gently beneath their feet, as though acknowledging their progress.

"We're running out of time," Flamipandro said, her tone uncharacteristically soft. "The Spiral Nexus won't wait for us to learn all the answers."

"Then we trust what we've learned so far," Alaric said, gripping the Shimmering Crystal. "And we trust each other."

As they walked, the ley lines hummed faintly—a song of hope and warning, urging them onward.

Chapter 19: The Nature Nexus

The air shimmered as the group entered the Nature Nexus, a realm alive with magic. Here, ley lines weren't just invisible threads of energy—they flowed openly through the environment, their luminous currents weaving through trees, rivers, and sky. The ground beneath their feet was a soft carpet of moss that pulsed faintly with each step, as though the land itself was breathing.

Massive trees with glowing trunks and branches that stretched endlessly upward dominated the horizon. Their leaves were golden, catching the light of a sun that seemed closer and warmer than any Alaric had known. Creatures of all shapes and sizes moved through the forest, their forms ranging from mundane to fantastical. A herd of Crystal Stags grazed near a sparkling brook, their antlers glowing faintly as they drank from the ley line-infused waters. Overhead, luminous birds with translucent wings trailed light as they darted through the canopy.

"This place feels... perfect," Lira said, her voice hushed. She held her staff tightly, its faint glow blending with the natural radiance of the ley lines. "It's like the magic here isn't just part of life—it is life."

Alaric knelt by a ley line that coursed through the ground like a shallow stream. The energy rippled as he touched it, sending a soothing warmth up his arm. "This is what the ley lines were meant to be," he said. "Unbroken, pure, and in harmony with everything around them."

Pecos, appearing as a wizened elder with a faint smile, gestured toward the heart of the nexus. "Don't let the beauty distract you, scholar. Even paradise has its fractures."

As if summoned by Pecos's words, the ground trembled faintly, and a figure stepped from the shadows of the great trees. A Kirin, its silver mane flowing like water, approached gracefully. Its hooves left trails of light on the mossy ground, and its crystalline antlers sparkled as though they held stars.

The Kirin stopped a few paces from the group, bowing its head in acknowledgment. "Travelers from beyond," it said, its voice a melodic resonance. "You stand in the cradle of harmony, where life and magic are one. But the ley lines speak of disruption. What brings you to this sacred place?"

"We seek to understand the ley lines," Alaric said, standing. He held the Void Crystal Talisman in one hand and gestured toward the glowing currents. "To learn how to restore balance before the Spiral Nexus collapses."

The Kirin's gaze lingered on the talisman, its light reflecting in the creature's intelligent eyes. "You carry tools of power and fragments of understanding, but understanding cannot be forced. Come. There is much for you to see."

The Kirin led them deeper into the Nature Nexus, where the ley lines grew more visible and intertwined with the environment. Massive vines encased the threads of energy, their roots spreading into the glowing ground. Rivers shimmered as they carried ley line currents, and the air buzzed faintly with the hum of magic.

As they walked, the group noticed creatures that seemed to exist solely as extensions of the ley lines. A group of Will-o'-Wisps, tiny orbs of glowing energy, floated around them in a playful dance. They weaved through the group's path, leaving trails of light that dissolved into the air.

"These creatures," Lira said, watching the wisps, "are they part of the ley lines?"

"They are born of them," the Kirin replied. "Manifestations of harmony. But when the ley lines falter, so too do they."

The Kirin stopped abruptly, its gaze fixed ahead. The group followed its line of sight and saw a patch of the forest that was darker, quieter. The ley lines there were dim, their currents sluggish and uneven. A cluster of trees stood withering, their glowing leaves dull and lifeless.

"This is what happens when balance is lost," the Kirin said, its voice heavy with sorrow. "The ley lines weaken, and all life suffers."

Alaric knelt by the dying ley lines, feeling their feeble energy struggle beneath his touch. He pulled the Shimmering Crystal from his satchel, its surface flickering faintly. "Maybe I can use this to restore the flow."

"Be cautious, scholar," the Kirin warned. "The crystal reflects your intent but magnifies your will. Its power is not without consequence."

Alaric placed the crystal near the ley line's fracture and focused his energy. The crystal began to glow, projecting threads of light that reached into the severed ley line. Slowly, the ley line brightened, its energy pulsing stronger as the crystal knitted the threads back together.

"It's working," Lira said, her voice filled with awe.

But as the ley line stabilized, the ground beneath them trembled. A ripple of chaotic energy surged through the forest, and in the distance, another ley line dimmed. The Kirin's gaze darkened. "You have healed one wound, but in doing so, you have torn another."

Alaric pulled back, his heart sinking. "I didn't mean to—"

"Intent is not enough," the Kirin interrupted. "Balance cannot be forced. Each action you take ripples across the whole."

The Kirin led them to a grove surrounded by massive, ancient trees. At the center of the grove was a large stone, its surface etched with glowing runes. The stone pulsed faintly, resonating with the ley lines around it.

"This is the Primal Keystone," the Kirin said. "A fragment of the ley lines' origin. It carries the memory of their creation and the knowledge of how to restore their harmony."

Alaric approached the stone cautiously, feeling its energy radiate through the air. As he touched its surface, visions flooded his mind—images of ley lines weaving through the cosmos, connecting dimensions in an intricate web of magic. He saw the Spiral Nexus, its threads glowing brightly before fracturing and unraveling.

The visions shifted, showing figures—guardians like Pecos—standing at the nexuses, their energy intertwined with the ley lines. The final image was of the Shimmering Crystal, its light flickering as it split into countless fragments.

The visions faded, and Alaric stepped back, his breathing unsteady. "The ley lines are more than magic," he said. "They're the foundation of everything. If they collapse, so does all life."

The Kirin stepped forward, its eyes solemn. "You have glimpsed the truth, but knowledge alone will not save you. The Spiral Nexus is unraveling because trust has been broken—not just between mortals and the ley lines, but within the ley lines themselves."

"What can we do?" Lira asked, her voice filled with desperation.

"You must restore trust," the Kirin said. "Not through force, but through understanding. The ley lines are alive. They will respond to your intent, but only if it is pure."

Alaric gripped the Shimmering Crystal tightly, its surface warm in his hand. "Then we need to move quickly. The Spiral Nexus won't wait."

As the group prepared to leave, the Kirin and the Dryads gathered at the edge of the forest. The ley lines hummed softly, their glow steady once more.

"Remember what you have learned here," the Kirin said. "Harmony is not found in control but in collaboration. The ley lines are not tools—they are partners."

The group bowed in gratitude before continuing their journey. The Primal Keystone pulsed faintly in Alaric's satchel, its energy a reminder of the truths they had uncovered.

As they left the Nature Nexus, the air grew colder, and the ley lines' hum grew fainter. The Spiral Nexus awaited, its fractures a looming threat to everything they had come to understand.

Journal Entry: A World in Harmony

Entry 52: The Living Ley Lines

The Nature Nexus is unlike anything I've ever seen. Here, the ley lines are visible, flowing like rivers and weaving through the trees and sky. It's not just magic—it's life itself, alive in ways I never imagined.

The Kirin called this place the cradle of harmony, but even here, the ley lines show signs of strain. A fracture we healed revealed another wound elsewhere, as though the balance we seek to restore eludes even our best intentions.

The Shimmering Crystal amplifies my will, but its power frightens me. What if my intent is flawed? What if, in trying to heal the ley lines, I only hurt them further?

The Primal Keystone we found resonates with the ley lines' origins. Its energy hums like an ancient song, one I don't fully understand. Perhaps the codex will reveal more, or perhaps I need to stop looking for answers and start listening.

*****

The group stood at the edge of the Nature Nexus, the vibrant energy around them humming with life. The Kirin's silver mane shimmered in the light as it stepped forward, its gaze solemn.

"You leave here with knowledge, but knowledge alone is dangerous," it said. "The ley lines will not obey you—they will respond to your heart. Be wary of your intentions."

Alaric nodded, his grip tightening on the Shimmering Crystal. "We'll remember. Thank you."

The Kirin tilted its head, its expression unreadable. "You walk a fine line, scholar. Balance is not achieved through force. Trust is the thread that binds creation. Break that thread, and all will unravel."

Memory Flashback: Eldaryn's Lessons

As the group walked away from the Nature Nexus, Alaric's thoughts drifted to a memory of Eldaryn, his mentor. They had stood in the House of the Crystal Keys, its grand halls echoing with the hum of ley lines.

"Magic is not a tool to be wielded, Deymorne," Eldaryn had said, his stern gaze softening as he placed a hand on Alaric's shoulder. "It is a conversation. The ley lines are alive—they feel, they react. To demand their obedience is to invite chaos."

"But what if balance requires intervention?" Alaric had asked. "What if the ley lines can't fix themselves?"

Eldaryn's expression grew distant. "Then you must ask yourself, are you intervening for their sake—or your own?"

The memory faded, leaving Alaric with an uneasy sense of familiarity. Eldaryn's words felt more relevant than ever.

The group soon encountered another severed ley line, its glow faint and its energy sparking erratically. The ground around it was barren, the trees withered and lifeless. The Void Crystal Talisman throbbed faintly in Alaric's hand, reacting to the ley line's instability.

"This one looks worse," Lira said, kneeling beside the fracture. "The energy here is almost gone."

Alaric pulled out the Darkened Codex, flipping through its glowing pages. A passage caught his eye, its runes shifting into legible text:

"The ley lines are threads of creation. To mend them is to weave with care, for each thread pulls upon another. Impatience invites destruction."

He sighed, glancing at the Shimmering Crystal. "We have to try, but we can't rush this."

Flamipandro crossed her arms, her ruby gown catching the dim light. "What does the codex say?"

"That balance can't be forced," Alaric replied. "We need to find the source of the fracture, not just patch it."

As they worked to stabilize the ley line, the Primal Keystone began to hum, projecting a vision into the air. It showed the ley lines in their prime, flowing brightly and connecting dimensions in perfect harmony. Nexus Guardians like Pecos stood at key points, their forms radiant as they guided the energy with reverence.

But the vision darkened, showing a time when mortals sought to command the ley lines. The energy faltered, the threads fraying as the guardians struggled to maintain balance. One figure, cloaked in shadow, appeared, wielding a talisman that pulsed with chaotic power.

"That's the Veiled Order," Lira whispered. "They've been trying to control the ley lines for centuries."

The vision ended, leaving the group in silence. Alaric stared at the Primal Keystone, his thoughts racing. "They believe control is the answer," he said. "But control is what broke the ley lines in the first place."

As the group finished their work, the ley line pulsed brightly, its energy flowing steadily once more. The surrounding area began to heal, the trees regaining their glow and the ground sprouting new moss. But the hum of the ley lines carried a faint discordant note, a reminder that the Spiral Nexus remained unstable.

"It's not enough," Alaric said, his voice heavy. "We're treating symptoms, not the cause."

Pecos, now appearing as a younger man, stepped forward. "The ley lines are teaching you, Alaric. Listen to them. Trust them."

Alaric nodded, though doubt still gnawed at him. "We need to reach the Spiral Nexus. It's the only way to fix this."

Journal Entry: Trust and Balance

Entry 53: The Ley Lines' Warning

The ley lines hum with more than energy—they hum with intent. Every fracture we heal feels like a conversation, one filled with questions I don't know how to answer.

The codex speaks of trust, but trust doesn't come easily. I've spent my life studying the ley lines, trying to understand them. Now, I wonder if understanding isn't enough. Maybe they don't want to be understood. Maybe they just want to be heard.

The Spiral Nexus looms ahead, its fractures spreading through every dimension. The Primal Keystone resonates with its call, but the answers it offers are shrouded in shadows. We move forward, not knowing if we're restoring balance—or merely delaying collapse.

Chapter 20: The Twilight Experiment

The ley line forest gave way to an open expanse of twilight, where the sky shifted constantly between the deep blues of night and the soft golds of dawn. The nexus ahead was unlike any Alaric had seen—a point where threads of light and shadow magic intertwined, glowing faintly as they pulsed in and out of harmony.

The energy here was unstable, sparking in arcs that left scars on the ground. Strange, ephemeral creatures flickered into existence near the nexus, their forms fluid and fleeting as though they were caught between realms.

Lira stepped closer to the nexus, her staff glowing faintly. "This place feels... wrong. Like it's on the verge of falling apart."

"It is," Alaric said, studying the shifting threads of energy. "The ley lines here are holding on by a thread, and the balance between light and shadow is deteriorating."

Flamipandro frowned, her ruby gown catching the dim light. "Can we stabilize it?"

Alaric hesitated, pulling the Shimmering Crystal from his satchel. The artifact felt heavier here, its surface flickering between light and darkness as if reacting to the nexus's instability. "Maybe. But we have to be careful. The balance here is delicate."

Pecos appeared nearby, leaning on his staff. "Delicate doesn't begin to describe it. This nexus has always been a point of tension—too much light, and the shadow collapses. Too much shadow, and the light burns away."

"Then what do you suggest?" Alaric asked, frustration creeping into his voice. They had stabilized nexuses before, but this one felt different—more volatile, more resistant to their efforts.

Pecos's expression grew serious. "I suggest you observe. Listen. The ley lines here don't want to be controlled—they want to find their own balance."

"And how long will that take?" Alaric challenged. "Days? Weeks? The Spiral Nexus is collapsing now. We don't have time for passive observation."

"Perhaps," Pecos said softly. "But you also don't have time for catastrophic mistakes."

*****

The group worked quickly, setting up around the nexus. Alaric placed the Shimmering Crystal at its center, the artifact glowing faintly as it resonated with the surrounding ley lines. He held the Void Crystal Talisman in one hand, its dark energy providing a counterpoint to the light threads.

"We need to weave these threads back together," Alaric said. "If we can synchronize their flow, we might be able to stabilize the nexus."

Lira nodded, stepping forward with her staff. "I'll handle the light threads. You take the shadow."

As the two began their work, Flamipandro and Bob stood guard, their eyes scanning the surrounding area for any signs of danger. The ephemeral creatures grew more agitated, flickering closer to the group before dissolving into wisps of light and shadow.

The Shimmering Crystal pulsed brighter, amplifying the energy of the ley lines. The threads of light and shadow began to shift, their chaotic movements slowing as Alaric and Lira guided them into alignment.

For a moment, it seemed to work. The ley lines pulsed steadily, their energy flowing in harmony. Alaric felt a surge of confidence—they had done this before at the Nature Nexus, and they could do it again.

But as he channeled more energy through the Shimmering Crystal, something felt... off. The threads were responding too quickly, too eagerly. The balance wasn't natural—it was forced, held together by sheer will and magical pressure.

"Something's not right," Lira said, her voice tense. "The ley lines—they're resisting underneath. It's like we're pressing down on a spring."

Alaric gritted his teeth, sweat beading on his forehead. "We just need to hold it a little longer. Once the pattern stabilizes, they'll settle into the new configuration."

"Alaric, I don't think—"

"I've got this!" he snapped, pouring more energy into the Shimmering Crystal. The artifact blazed brighter, its light overwhelming the natural twilight around them.

The threads of light and shadow began to twist together more tightly, their separate identities blurring. For a heartbeat, Alaric thought he had succeeded—thought he had discovered a way to merge opposing forces into perfect unity.

Then the Shimmering Crystal began to scream.

It wasn't a sound, exactly, but a sensation that tore through Alaric's mind—the artifact's essence recoiling in horror at what he was forcing it to do. The crystal's light flickered erratically, shifting between brilliant white and absolute darkness in rapid succession.

"Alaric, stop!" Lira shouted, but her voice seemed distant, muffled by the roaring of energy building around them.

"I can control it," Alaric gasped, even as the Void Crystal Talisman in his other hand began to pulse violently. "I just need to—"

The nexus exploded.

Not literally, but the effect was nearly as devastating. Threads of light and shadow that had been forced together suddenly repelled each other with catastrophic force. Ley line energy erupted outward in a shockwave that knocked everyone off their feet. The ground cracked, forming spiderweb fissures that glowed with unstable power.

Alaric was thrown backward, the Shimmering Crystal and Void Crystal Talisman both burning against his hands. He lost his grip on both artifacts, and they clattered to the fractured ground, their glow dimming to faint, wounded pulses.

When he struggled to his feet, gasping, the world around him had changed.

Where there had been a struggling but contained nexus, now there was a rift—a tear in the dimensional fabric itself. Dark energy poured from the opening, mixing with the remnants of light magic in a chaotic, swirling maelstrom. The ephemeral creatures that had been flickering at the edges now screamed silently as they were torn apart by the competing energies.

"No," Alaric whispered, staring at the destruction he had caused. "No, no, no..."

Lira pulled herself up, blood trickling from a cut on her forehead. Her eyes widened as she saw the rift. "Alaric, what did you do?"

"I thought—I was trying to—" He couldn't form coherent words. His throat was tight, his chest constricted with a horror so profound it bordered on physical pain.

Flamipandro was on her feet, blade drawn, scanning for immediate threats. But even she looked shaken, her usual confidence replaced by wary alertness. "The rift is expanding. We need to contain it before it tears through to other dimensions."

Bob slowly picked himself up, for once completely devoid of humor. "Alaric... man, I don't think we can contain that."

The rift pulsed, and from its depths, something began to emerge.

*****

The Shadow Revenant that stepped through was massive, its form wreathed in darkness that seemed to devour light itself. Its eyes glowed with an eerie red light, and its voice echoed with a deep, resonant hum that Alaric felt in his bones.

"You dare disturb the balance?" The revenant's words carried weight beyond sound—they were accusation, judgment, and prophecy all at once.

Alaric stepped forward on trembling legs, the Void Crystal Talisman somehow back in his hand though he didn't remember retrieving it. "We're trying to restore it."

The revenant's laugh was bitter, hollow. "Restore? You have torn what was fragile. You have forced what should be coaxed. You have broken what was merely bent." It advanced, each step causing ripples in reality itself. "Your arrogance has deepened the wound you sought to heal."

"I didn't mean—" Alaric started, but the words died in his throat. What did his intentions matter when the consequences were this catastrophic?

"Intent without wisdom is destruction wearing a noble mask," the revenant intoned. "The ley lines must heal on their own. Your interference only hastens their unraveling."

The revenant struck, sending a wave of shadow energy toward the group. Lira raised her staff with visible effort, creating a barrier of light that deflected the attack. But Alaric could see the strain in her face, the way her hands shook. She had been hurt—they had all been hurt—by his mistake.

Flamipandro charged forward, her blade glowing as she slashed at the revenant, but her strikes passed through its form without effect. "It's tied to the rift!" she called out. "We can't hurt it while the rift remains open!"

"Then we close the rift!" Bob shouted back, flipping his hourglass to slow the revenant's movements.

But Alaric stood frozen, staring at the chaos he had unleashed. The rift continued to spread, its edges crackling with unstable energy. Smaller tears were forming around it, like sympathetic fractures in glass. If they didn't stop this, the damage could spread through the entire ley line network.

"Alaric!" Lira's voice cut through his paralysis. "We need you! I can't do this alone!"

He looked at her—really looked at her. She was injured because of him. They were all in danger because he had been too confident, too certain that he could force the ley lines to obey his will.

But there was no time for guilt. There was only the choice: give up, or try to fix what he had broken.

Alaric retrieved the Shimmering Crystal from where it had fallen, feeling it pulse weakly in his palm. The artifact was damaged, its light flickering uncertainly. He had pushed it too hard, demanded too much.

"I'm sorry," he whispered to it, then louder, "Lira, I need you to trust me one more time."

She met his eyes, and in her gaze he saw fear, doubt, and something else—a fragile thread of faith that he desperately hoped he wouldn't break again.

"What do we do?" she asked.

"Not what I did before," Alaric said, moving toward the nexus's center. "We don't force the balance. We ask for it."

*****

Alaric knelt beside the rift, feeling the chaotic energies buffet against him. The Shimmering Crystal in one hand, the Void Crystal Talisman in the other. But this time, he didn't push his will into them. Instead, he listened.

The ley lines were screaming—not in words, but in sensations. Pain. Violation. Betrayal. He had tried to command them, and they had responded as any living thing would when commanded against its nature: with violent resistance.

"I'm sorry," he said aloud, knowing somehow that the ley lines could hear him. "I was wrong. I thought I knew better than you. I thought control was the answer."

The revenant paused in its attack, turning its burning gaze toward Alaric. "Words mean nothing. Only actions speak truth to the ley lines."

"Then let me show you," Alaric said.

He placed both artifacts on the ground, not channeling energy through them but simply letting them rest. Then he reached out with his bare hands toward the rift's edges, feeling the raw ley line energy against his skin.

It hurt. It burned with cold fire and froze with searing heat. But he didn't try to shape it. He simply... touched it. Acknowledged it. Let it know he was there not as a master, but as a student.

Lira understood immediately. She joined him, her staff aside, her own hands reaching out. "We're listening," she said softly. "We're here. We see you."

The ley lines' chaos didn't stop. But something shifted—a subtle change in the tenor of their energy. The screaming became less panicked, more plaintive. They were still wounded, still frightened, but now they sensed something different in Alaric's approach.

"The threads of light and shadow," Alaric said, his voice barely above a whisper. "They're not meant to merge. They're meant to dance. To interweave without losing themselves."

He began to gently, carefully, guide the frayed edges of light and shadow away from violent collision and toward harmonious coexistence. Not pushing them together, but allowing them to find their own rhythm.

Lira did the same, her natural affinity for the ley lines allowing her to feel the patterns they wanted to form. "They're trying to heal," she breathed. "They've been trying all along. We just kept interrupting."

The revenant watched in silence as the two worked. Minutes passed. Then hours. The rest of the group maintained a protective perimeter, but the revenant made no move to attack. It simply observed.

Gradually, infinitely slowly, the rift began to close. Not through force, but through the ley lines' own natural healing process, guided but not controlled by Alaric and Lira's gentle touch.

When the rift finally sealed, leaving only a scar of shimm ering energy across the nexus, Alaric collapsed backward, exhausted beyond anything he had ever experienced. His hands were raw, his mind felt scraped hollow, and his heart ached with the weight of what he had learned.

The revenant stepped forward, its form less threatening now, more sorrowful. "You have delayed the inevitable," it said, its voice quieter. "But you have also learned. The question now is whether you will remember this lesson when it matters most."

"The Spiral Nexus," Alaric whispered.

"The Spiral Nexus," the revenant confirmed. "Where the temptation to control will be a thousand times stronger, and the cost of failure infinitely higher." It turned, beginning to dissolve back into shadow. "Your work is far from over. And you are far from ready."

With that, the revenant faded, leaving the clearing silent once more. The nexus pulsed weakly but steadily, its threads of light and shadow flowing in cautious harmony.

*****

No one spoke as they set up camp that night. The energy expenditure had been too great, the revelations too profound. Alaric sat apart from the others, staring at the Shimmering Crystal in his hands. Its light was dimmer now, and he could sense the artifact's weariness.

"I nearly destroyed everything," he said when Lira approached with water and bandages for his raw hands.

"But you didn't," she replied, her voice neutral. Not quite forgiving, not quite accusatory. Simply factual.

"Only because you helped me fix it." He looked up at her, seeing the dried blood on her temple from where she had been injured. "I hurt you. I hurt all of you."

Lira was quiet for a long moment. "Yes," she finally said. "You did. Your arrogance nearly killed us."

The words hit him like physical blows, but he accepted them. They were true.

"But," she continued, kneeling beside him, "you also learned. And that matters. The question is, will you carry this lesson forward, or will you forget it the next time your confidence tells you that you know best?"

"I won't forget," Alaric said, the words a vow. "I can't forget. Not after this."

Lira began wrapping his hands, her touch gentle despite her justified anger. "The ley lines don't respond to promises, Alaric. They respond to actions. Show them you've learned. Show us you've learned."

Flamipandro appeared out of the darkness, her expression unreadable. "The nexus is stable for now. But there are fractures spreading from here—sympathetic tears in nearby ley lines. Your 'experiment' had ripple effects."

Guilt crashed over Alaric anew. "How do we fix it?"

"We don't," Flamipandro said bluntly. "Not tonight. Tonight, we rest. Tomorrow, we deal with the consequences. And then we move toward the Spiral Nexus, where the stakes will be infinitely higher and the margin for error even smaller."

She walked away, leaving Alaric alone with his thoughts and the faint, wounded pulse of the Shimmering Crystal.

*****

JOURNAL ENTRY: THE TWILIGHT EXPERIMENT

Entry 54: The Cost of Arrogance

I failed today. Not just failed—I nearly destroyed everything we've been working toward. I forced the ley lines to obey my will, believing that my intent was pure enough to justify any means. I was wrong.

The Shimmering Crystal is damaged, its light diminished. The ley lines here will carry scars from my arrogance for years, perhaps centuries. And my companions—my friends—were hurt because I refused to listen to warnings, refused to acknowledge that perhaps I didn't know best.

The revenant's words echo in my mind: "Intent without wisdom is destruction wearing a noble mask." How many times have I wrapped my hubris in the language of noble purpose? How many times have I convinced myself that forcing a solution was the same as finding one?

The ley lines are not tools to be wielded. They are not puzzles to be solved through clever application of magical theory. They are alive, sentient, and deserving of respect. They have their own wisdom, their own path to healing. My role—our role—is not to command them but to support them. To listen, not dictate.

I thought I was saving them. Instead, I was making their pain worse.

The Spiral Nexus looms ahead. When we reach it, the temptation to "fix" things through force will be overwhelming. The stakes will be higher, the pressure greater, the desire to believe I have the answer more seductive than ever.

I must remember this moment. I must remember the sound of the Shimmering Crystal's scream, the sight of Lira's blood, the weight of my friends' justified doubt. I must remember that being clever is not the same as being wise, and that the best intentions can lead to the worst outcomes.

The ley lines must heal on their own. Our job is to create the conditions for healing, not to impose it.

I pray I remember this when it matters most. Because next time, there may be no second chance.

*****

The following morning, as the group prepared to leave the twilight forest, the damage from Alaric's experiment was even more visible in the harsh light of dawn. The ground remained fractured, with thin lines of unstable energy tracing across the earth like scars. The nexus itself pulsed weakly, its harmony fragile and hard-won.

Pecos appeared one final time, his form that of a young boy, his usual mischief absent from his expression. "You've learned something valuable, scholar. The question is, will you apply it?"

"I'll try," Alaric said quietly.

"Trying isn't enough," Pecos replied. "The Spiral Nexus will test you in ways you cannot imagine. Your instincts will tell you to act decisively, to take control, to fix things through sheer force of will. Those instincts will be wrong."

"Then what should I do?"

Pecos smiled, sad and knowing. "That's the right question. Finally." He began to fade, his final words hanging in the air: "Trust the ley lines. Trust your companions. And most importantly, trust that you don't have all the answers."

As the group moved out, heading toward the distant glow of the Spiral Nexus, Alaric felt the weight of his failure settling into his bones. It would stay with him, he knew. A constant reminder of the line between confidence and arrogance, between healing and harm.

The Primal Keystone hummed faintly in his satchel, and he knew it was showing him possible futures again—some where he learned from his mistakes, others where he repeated them with far worse consequences.

"We're running out of time," Lira said, her voice still carrying a note of wariness when she spoke to him.

Alaric held the Shimmering Crystal, feeling its diminished light. "Then we need to make every moment count," he said. "And every choice matter."

The Spiral Nexus awaited. And this time, Alaric would approach it not with arrogance, but with the hard-won humility of someone who had learned the true cost of playing god with forces beyond his understanding.

This time, he would listen.

He had to.

Because next time, there would be no revenant to stop him. No second chance to fix his mistakes. Just the choice between wisdom and catastrophe, with the fate of all existence hanging in the balance.

Chapter 21: The Path to the Spiral Nexus

The forest of twilight began to thin, giving way to a vast, open expanse where the ley lines converged in a chaotic swirl. The ground was cracked and uneven, pulsing with faint echoes of energy that radiated upward in jagged arcs. Above them, the sky was a swirling vortex of light and shadow, its threads unraveling as they stretched toward the horizon.

The Spiral Nexus loomed in the distance—a massive, spiraling structure of glowing threads suspended in the air. Its brilliance was dimmed, and its movements were erratic, as though it was struggling to hold itself together.

"This is it," Lira said, her voice barely above a whisper. "The Spiral Nexus."

Alaric stepped forward, the Shimmering Crystal pulsing faintly in his hand. "The heart of the ley lines," he said. "And the source of everything that's been happening."

Pecos, appearing as a young man, stood at his side. "The Spiral Nexus isn't just a place—it's the web that connects all dimensions. If it collapses, everything connected to it will fall apart."

The group moved cautiously toward the nexus, the unstable ground shifting beneath their feet. The ley lines here were fractured and chaotic, their threads sparking with unpredictable bursts of energy. Strange creatures roamed the area—Fracture Beasts, their forms jagged and distorted, as though they were pieced together from fragments of shattered dimensions.

One of the creatures stepped into their path, its many-eyed gaze fixed on the group. It let out a low, guttural growl, its crystalline body crackling with energy.

"Stay back," Flamipandro warned, her blade glowing faintly as she prepared to strike.

The creature lunged, its movements erratic but swift. Flamipandro met its attack head-on, her blade slicing through its crystalline form. The beast shattered into fragments, which dissolved into the air.

"These things are drawn to the ley lines' instability," Alaric said, gripping the Void Crystal Talisman tightly. "They're a manifestation of the chaos here."

"We need to move quickly," Lira said, her staff glowing as she scanned the area. "The closer we get to the Spiral Nexus, the more dangerous it's going to be."

As they neared the Spiral Nexus, the ley lines' hum grew louder, but the sound was dissonant—a chaotic cacophony that seemed to seep into their minds. Alaric felt a growing pressure in his chest, as though the nexus was calling to him, demanding his attention.

The Darkened Codex in his satchel began to hum faintly, its pages glowing with shifting runes. Alaric pulled it out, flipping through its pages until he found a new passage that hadn't been there before.

"The Spiral Nexus is the beginning and the end, the source and the convergence. Its threads bind all creation, but its collapse unravels the fabric of existence. To restore it is to restore trust, not only between dimensions but within the nexus itself."

"What does it mean?" Lira asked, peering over his shoulder.

"It's not just about fixing the nexus," Alaric said. "We have to restore its balance—its trust."

"How do we do that?" Flamipandro asked.

"I don't know yet," Alaric admitted. "But the codex is guiding us. We have to trust it."

As they approached the base of the Spiral Nexus, the ground beneath them trembled violently. A massive rift tore open, and from it emerged a towering figure cloaked in shadow—a Nexus Warden, its form both imposing and otherworldly. Its eyes glowed with a piercing light, and its voice echoed with power.

"You come to the Spiral Nexus uninvited," the warden said. "Why?"

"We're here to restore balance," Alaric said, stepping forward. "The ley lines are fracturing, and the Spiral Nexus is collapsing. We need to fix it."

The warden tilted its head, its glowing gaze fixed on Alaric. "Balance cannot be forced. The Spiral Nexus does not trust mortals. Prove your worth, or be consumed by its chaos."

The warden raised its hand, and the ley lines around the group flared violently. The ground shook, and arcs of energy surged toward them.

The group scattered, each member working to counter the warden's attacks. Lira raised her staff, creating a barrier of light to deflect the surging energy. Flamipandro moved with precision, her blade slicing through the arcs of chaos that threatened to overwhelm them.

"We can't fight it directly," Alaric said, gripping the Shimmering Crystal. "The nexus is tied to the warden—it's testing us."

"Then what do we do?" Bob asked, dodging a stray burst of energy. "Talk it into submission?"

"Not quite," Alaric said, his mind racing. He opened the Darkened Codex, searching for a clue. The runes shifted, forming a passage that seemed to speak directly to him.

"Harmony is not found in opposition but in unity. The Spiral Nexus responds to those who seek balance, not control."

Alaric closed the codex, his path clear. "We need to harmonize with the ley lines."

Alaric knelt at the base of the Spiral Nexus, placing the Shimmering Crystal on the ground. Its surface began to glow, resonating with the chaotic threads around it. He reached out with the Void Crystal Talisman, channeling its energy into the nexus.

Lira joined him, her staff glowing brightly as she synchronized her energy with the ley lines. Together, they worked to weave the threads back into harmony, following the natural flow of the nexus's energy.

The Nexus Warden paused, its form flickering as the ley lines began to stabilize. "You understand," it said, its voice softer now. "The Spiral Nexus is not a puzzle to be solved. It is a trust to be earned."

The warden lowered its hand, the chaotic energy around it dissipating. The ley lines pulsed brightly, their hum growing steady and harmonious.

As the Spiral Nexus stabilized, the Nexus Warden stepped back, its glowing gaze fixed on the group. "You have passed this trial, but your journey is not over. The Spiral Nexus is still fragile, its threads frayed. You must restore its trust fully, or all will be lost."

"How do we do that?" Alaric asked.

The warden gestured to the Spiral Nexus. "The answers lie within. But beware—the nexus will test you. Only those who understand its will may succeed."

The warden dissolved into the air, leaving the group alone at the base of the Spiral Nexus. The threads of light and shadow pulsed faintly, their glow a reminder of the work still to be done.

Journal Entry: The Spiral's Test

Entry 56: Trust and Balance

The Nexus Warden spoke of trust—of earning the Spiral Nexus's balance rather than forcing it. But how do you earn the trust of something so vast, so integral to creation itself?

The ley lines are stabilizing, but they are not whole. The codex speaks of unity, of harmony found through understanding. Perhaps that is the answer.

The Spiral Nexus looms above us, its threads frayed but pulsing with faint hope. I don't know if we're ready, but we have no choice. If we fail here, everything unravels.

*****

As the Nexus Warden dissolved, the ley lines pulsed faintly, their energy flowing steadily but hesitantly. Alaric remained kneeling at the base of the Spiral Nexus, his hand resting on the Shimmering Crystal. The artifact's glow was subdued, its light flickering as though uncertain.

For the first time, Alaric felt the ley lines not just as currents of energy but as something alive—watchful, aware, and waiting.

"They're listening," he said softly, glancing at Lira. "But they're not convinced."

Lira nodded, her staff emitting a faint, steady hum. "They don't trust us yet. After everything that's happened, can you blame them?"

"We have to earn their trust," Alaric replied, rising to his feet. His gaze shifted to the Void Crystal Talisman, its dark surface reflecting the faint light of the nexus. "But how do you convince something this vast, this... infinite, that you're worthy?"

Memory Flashback: The First Guardians

As Alaric contemplated the ley lines' hesitation, the Primal Keystone in his satchel began to hum softly. Its energy rippled outward, pulling him into a vivid memory—a vision of the first Nexus Guardians.

The memory unfolded like a dream, showing an ancient time when the ley lines were vibrant and unbroken. A group of guardians stood at the Spiral Nexus, their forms radiant and ethereal. Each guardian held an artifact similar to the ones Alaric carried, their energies resonating in perfect harmony with the ley lines.

One guardian stepped forward, her voice resonating with the cadence of the ley lines. "Balance is not imposed but fostered. The ley lines respond to intent, to trust. Those who seek to command them will find only chaos."

The vision shifted, showing a guardian wielding an artifact that pulsed with chaotic energy. The ley lines recoiled, their threads fraying as the artifact's energy clashed with their rhythm. The Spiral Nexus trembled, its glow dimming as fractures spread through its threads.

The memory faded, leaving Alaric shaken. He glanced at the Void Crystal Talisman and the Shimmering Crystal, their energies still pulsing faintly. "These artifacts aren't tools," he said aloud. "They're extensions of the ley lines themselves. They react to our intent."

The group moved cautiously toward the Spiral Nexus, the fractured ground and chaotic energy making each step a challenge. The closer they got, the more the ley lines' presence pressed upon them—a tangible weight that seemed to test their resolve.

Flamipandro lagged behind, her ruby gown streaked with dust from the unstable terrain. "We've been through realms and nexuses, fought beasts and faced trials, and now we're supposed to convince the ley lines to trust us? What if they don't?"

"They have to," Lira said, though her voice wavered. "If we don't restore balance, everything unravels."

Bob, his human form flickering faintly as the energy around him fluctuated, let out a dry laugh. "And if we succeed, what then? Do we just go back to pretending we understand magic while the ley lines decide whether to trust us again?"

Alaric didn't respond immediately. The doubts of his companions mirrored his own, but he couldn't let them see the full weight of his uncertainty. "We don't have to pretend to understand everything," he said finally. "We just have to listen."

As they approached the nexus's inner boundary, the Void Crystal Talisman in Alaric's hand began to pulse more intensely. Its energy felt heavier now, resonating with the unstable threads of shadow around the Spiral Nexus.

"Where did this talisman even come from?" Lira asked, her gaze fixed on the artifact.

Alaric frowned, recalling a passage he had read in the Darkened Codex. "The talisman was created during a time when the ley lines of light and shadow were at war. It was meant to absorb and stabilize shadow energy, but it also magnifies the intent of its wielder. That's why it's so dangerous—it reflects as much of the wielder's doubt as their resolve."

"And you've been carrying that all this time?" Flamipandro asked, her tone incredulous. "What if it turns on you?"

"It already has," Alaric admitted. "In the Shadow Plane, I felt it feeding on my fear. But now, I think it's waiting—just like the ley lines."

"For what?" Lira asked.

"For me to make a choice," Alaric said. "One that aligns with their will."

The Spiral Nexus towered before them now, its threads of light and shadow swirling chaotically. As the group stepped closer, the ley lines flared violently, creating a barrier of energy that blocked their path.

From the nexus emerged another warden, its form a towering mass of light and shadow intertwined. Its voice echoed with a power that made the ground tremble. "You seek to restore the Spiral Nexus, yet you carry the weight of doubt and discord. Prove your worth, or be consumed by the chaos."

The ley lines surged, creating a series of shifting patterns in the air. Each thread pulsed with a distinct rhythm, their movements chaotic and unpredictable.

"They're testing us," Alaric said, his eyes narrowing as he studied the threads. "We have to align them."

"How?" Flamipandro asked, her blade ready but useless against the immaterial threads.

"Not with force," Alaric said. He placed the Shimmering Crystal on the ground, its light resonating faintly with the threads. "We have to guide them, like we did before."

Alaric knelt beside the crystal, his hands trembling as he reached out to the ley lines. The Void Crystal Talisman pulsed in his hand, its dark energy counterbalancing the light threads swirling above him.

Lira joined him, her staff glowing brightly as she synchronized her energy with the ley lines. Together, they began to weave the chaotic threads, following the natural flow of the nexus's rhythm.

The threads resisted at first, their movements erratic and discordant. But as Alaric and Lira worked in harmony, the threads began to align, their pulses steadying.

The warden watched in silence, its glowing eyes narrowing as the ley lines stabilized. "You begin to understand," it said. "But balance is not achieved through unity alone. It requires sacrifice."

The ley lines' hum grew louder, their energy pressing heavily upon the group. Alaric felt the weight of the Spiral Nexus's will, a silent demand that cut through his thoughts.

"What does it want?" Flamipandro asked, her voice strained.

Alaric looked down at the Void Crystal Talisman and the Shimmering Crystal. "It wants intent. A choice. We can't restore the nexus without giving something in return."

He placed the talisman and the crystal together, their energies flaring brightly as they merged. The ley lines pulsed in response, their rhythm growing steady.

"What are you doing?" Lira asked, her voice filled with alarm.

"I'm trusting them," Alaric said. "And hoping they trust us back."

The Spiral Nexus flared brilliantly, its threads glowing with renewed energy as they wove together in harmony. The warden stepped back, its form dissolving into the ley lines as the nexus stabilized.

The group stood in silence, the weight of the moment pressing upon them. The ley lines pulsed steadily now, their hum resonating deeply.

"We're not done yet," Alaric said, his voice steady. "This was just the beginning."

The Spiral Nexus loomed above them, its energy radiating with both promise and peril. The final test awaited, and with it, the fate of all ley lines.

The Spiral Nexus pulsed steadily now, its threads weaving together in tentative harmony. But within the flow of its energy, a deeper awareness stirred. The ley lines' sentience stretched across dimensions, remembering countless cycles of creation and collapse.

They had seen mortals before—scholars, guardians, conquerors—all of whom sought to command the nexus's power. They remembered the last Nexus Guardian, a figure wreathed in golden light, who had stood at the heart of the Spiral Nexus and tried to force its threads into alignment. His failure had fractured the ley lines, creating the instability that now threatened all dimensions.

The ley lines regarded Alaric and his companions. They were different—more uncertain, more willing to listen. But doubt lingered. Could they be trusted to restore harmony without repeating the mistakes of the past?

As the group caught their breath at the base of the Spiral Nexus, a sudden tremor shook the ground. The ley lines flared violently, their threads unraveling as a dark energy surged through them.

"It's happening again," Lira said, her voice filled with alarm. "Something's destabilizing the nexus!"

From the shadows emerged a figure cloaked in dark robes, their hands glowing with corrupted energy. It was Kael, a former scholar now aligned with the Veiled Order. His eyes glinted with triumph as he approached the group.

"You've done well to stabilize the nexus," Kael said, his voice calm but mocking. "But you're only delaying the inevitable. The ley lines must evolve, and that evolution requires destruction."

Alaric stepped forward, his grip tightening on the Void Crystal Talisman. "You're the reason the nexuses have been collapsing. What are you trying to accomplish?"

"Balance through control," Kael replied. "The ley lines are chaotic, unstable. They need order. And the Veiled Order will provide it."

The tension in the air was palpable as the group faced Kael. The ley lines pulsed erratically, responding to the conflict.

"You think forcing the ley lines into order will save them?" Lira said, her voice rising. "You'll destroy everything they're connected to!"

"Destruction is necessary for creation," Kael retorted. "The ley lines are flawed. They need guidance, not this endless cycle of chaos."

Alaric shook his head, his mind racing. "You're wrong. The ley lines aren't tools—they're alive. They don't need control. They need trust."

Kael sneered. "Trust? The ley lines have failed us for centuries. They need a master, not a caretaker."

The air grew heavier as the ley lines' energy swirled around them, mirroring the clash of ideologies. Alaric could feel the ley lines watching, waiting for a choice.

Before the confrontation could escalate, the Primal Keystone in Alaric's satchel flared brightly. Its energy enveloped the group, pulling them into another vision.

They stood in a swirling void, where the ley lines stretched infinitely in all directions. At the center of the void was a golden figure—the last Nexus Guardian. His voice echoed through the space, filled with both pride and sorrow.

"I sought to command the ley lines, to bring them into perfect order," the figure said. "But in my arrogance, I shattered their trust. My failure fractured the Spiral Nexus, and my name was lost to time."

The vision shifted, showing the ley lines recoiling from the guardian's actions. The Spiral Nexus trembled, its threads fraying as the guardian's energy clashed with its will.

The vision ended, leaving the group back at the base of the Spiral Nexus. Alaric's hands trembled as he looked at the ley lines. "We're not here to control them," he said softly. "We're here to repair the trust that was broken."

Kael watched Alaric with a mix of curiosity and disdain. "You think trust is enough? The ley lines are too fractured for that. Only force can bring them back into alignment."

Alaric stepped forward, holding the Shimmering Crystal in one hand and the Void Crystal Talisman in the other. "Force is what broke them in the first place. If we want to restore balance, we have to show them that we're willing to listen."

He placed the artifacts together at the base of the Spiral Nexus, their energies merging in a bright flare. The ley lines' hum grew louder, resonating deeply as their threads began to align.

The nexus trembled, its energy stabilizing as the ley lines responded to Alaric's intent. Kael staggered back, his corrupted energy dissipating as the nexus rejected his influence.

"This isn't over," Kael said, retreating into the shadows. "You can't save them. The Spiral Nexus will collapse, and the Veiled Order will rise."

As Kael disappeared, the Spiral Nexus flared brilliantly, its threads glowing with renewed energy. The ley lines pulsed in harmony, their hum steady and resonant.

Alaric closed his eyes, feeling the ley lines' presence more clearly than ever. They weren't just watching—they were speaking, their voices a chorus of hope and caution.

"Trust is earned, not given. You have taken the first step, but the Spiral Nexus remains fragile. Restore the final threads, and we will see if you are worthy."

The group exchanged glances, their determination renewed. The Spiral Nexus awaited its final restoration, and with it, the fate of the ley lines.

Chapter 22: The Nexus Fractures

Journal Entry: The Nexus Speaks

Entry 57: Voices of the Ley Lines

The ley lines aren't just conduits of energy—they're alive, in ways I'm only beginning to understand. They carry the memories of every nexus, every Guardian, every mistake. Their voices echo through the Spiral Nexus, urging us to listen, but they're fragmented—uncertain.

I used to think the ley lines were tools, something we could shape and control. Now, I see they're mirrors, reflecting the intent of everyone who touches them. They don't trust easily, and they shouldn't. Trust has been broken too many times.

We've stabilized the Spiral Nexus for now, but it's not whole. The ley lines want something from us—something more than action. They want understanding. But how do you prove your worth to something that spans every dimension?

The Spiral Nexus pulsed faintly, its glow casting long shadows across the jagged ground. Alaric sat cross-legged at its base, his hands resting lightly on the Void Crystal Talisman and the Shimmering Crystal. He could feel the ley lines' presence more deeply than ever, a vast web of interconnected energy and memory stretching across dimensions.

The ley lines were not a single voice but a chorus—a collective consciousness formed from centuries of existence. Each nexus added its own resonance, its own will, creating a harmony that had been shattered by the Spiral Nexus's fractures. Their sentience was diffuse, fragmented, yet unified in purpose: balance.

Alaric closed his eyes, letting the ley lines' whispers fill his mind. They spoke not in words but in impressions—flashes of past

Guardians, ancient nexuses, and the fragile thread of creation that bound everything together.

Flashback: Flamipandro's Human Form

A soft hum broke Alaric's concentration, pulling him back to the present. Flamipandro stepped into view, her human form radiant in the nexus's glow. Her ruby gown shimmered, and her presence exuded both elegance and authority.

"You're listening," she said, her voice tinged with approval. "Good. But listening is only the beginning."

Alaric looked up, startled. "Flamipandro? I thought—"

"That I was just a sword?" She smirked, her gaze sharp. "I am, but I'm also more. Nexus Beings like Pecos and I are extensions of the ley lines. We exist to guide and protect, but we're bound by the will of the nexus."

Alaric frowned. "If you're part of the ley lines, why can't you just fix them?"

"Because the ley lines are trust," Flamipandro said. "And trust can't be forced or given. It has to be earned."

As Flamipandro spoke, Pecos appeared, his form shifting between a young boy and an old man. He leaned on his staff, his expression grave.

"You're walking a dangerous path, Alaric," Pecos said. "The ley lines are patient, but they're not infinite. If you misstep, they'll reject you—and everything you're trying to save."

Alaric stood, frustration bubbling to the surface. "You keep saying that, but what does it mean? How do we earn their trust?"

Pecos's gaze darkened. "By letting go of control. By accepting that you're not the one who decides their fate—they are."

Flamipandro crossed her arms, her ruby gown catching the light. "And if you don't, the Spiral Nexus will collapse, and the ley lines will scatter. Everything you've fought for will be gone."

Bob, still in his human form, watched the exchange from a distance. He flipped his hourglass absently, the golden sand within flowing in reverse. The group was fracturing, just like the ley lines they were trying to save.

"They're falling apart," Bob muttered, his tone uncharacteristically serious. "Trying to save the world and losing themselves in the process."

Lira approached, her staff glowing faintly. "They'll figure it out," she said, though her voice held doubt. "They have to."

Bob gave her a sidelong glance. "And if they don't? What happens then?"

Lira's grip tightened on her staff. "Then we keep trying."

As the group prepared to move deeper into the Spiral Nexus, a new figure appeared—Felipandro, his form more human than before but still ethereal. His eyes glowed with the light of the ley lines, and his voice carried the weight of centuries.

"The Spiral Nexus is nearing its breaking point," Felipandro said. "I've come to help you, but my time is limited."

"What do you mean?" Lira asked.

"I am a fragment of the ley lines' will," Felipandro explained. "To guide you further, I must give up my form. It will weaken the ley lines, but it's the only way to show you what you need to see."

Alaric hesitated. "There has to be another way."

"There isn't," Felipandro said firmly. "Trust me as the ley lines trust you."

Felipandro stepped forward, his form dissolving into a burst of light. The energy flowed into the Spiral Nexus, stabilizing its threads temporarily and revealing a path deeper into its core.

The group followed the newly revealed path, their determination tempered by uncertainty. The Spiral Nexus's inner core pulsed ahead, its glow both beautiful and foreboding.

"We're running out of time," Flamipandro said, her voice tense. "The Spiral Nexus can't hold much longer."

Alaric nodded, his grip tightening on the Void Crystal Talisman. "Then we have to make it trust us."

The ley lines' whispers grew louder, their voices blending into a single, resonant hum. The Spiral Nexus was watching, waiting for their next move.

Journal Entry: A Fractured Trust

Entry 58: The Nexus Beings

The ley lines are more than energy—they're alive. Flamipandro, Pecos, and Felipandro aren't just guides; they're extensions of the ley lines' will. They see more than we can, but even they can't fix this alone.

Felipandro's sacrifice showed us a path, but it also showed me how fragile the ley lines are. Their trust is fractured, and if we fail here, it may never be restored.

The Spiral Nexus is waiting. I don't know if it trusts us yet, but I have to believe we can earn it. If not, everything we've fought for will be lost.

The Narrator's Perspective: The Spiral Nexus

The Spiral Nexus thrummed at the center of all creation, its vast threads stretching across dimensions. To mortal eyes, it was a structure of light and shadow, chaotic yet mesmerizing. But to the ley lines themselves, it was a heartbeat—a pulse of energy that carried their will, their memories, their trust.

For centuries, the Spiral Nexus had watched as Guardians came and went. Some had sought to preserve its balance, others to wield its power. Each decision, each failure, had left scars upon the ley lines, fracturing their collective consciousness. Trust was no longer implicit—it had to be earned.

Now, the ley lines observed Alaric and his companions. Their actions carried echoes of past mistakes, but also glimmers of hope. The ley lines whispered among themselves, their voices resonating through the threads of the Spiral Nexus.

"They are different."

"But are they worthy?"

"Time will tell."

Flashback: The Creation of the Void Crystal Talisman

As the group prepared to move deeper into the Spiral Nexus, Alaric opened the Darkened Codex, its pages glowing with faint light. A new passage appeared, its runes forming a detailed account of the Void Crystal Talisman's origins.

The vision swept over Alaric, pulling him into the memory of a Nexus Guardian from centuries past. The guardian, a figure wreathed in shadow and light, stood at the heart of a nexus consumed by chaos. Around them, ley lines sparked and frayed, their energy threatening to unravel.

"The ley lines cannot hold," the guardian said, their voice steady despite the chaos. "We need a conduit—something to absorb the excess energy."

The guardian crafted the Void Crystal Talisman, its surface pulsing with dark energy. It stabilized the ley lines, but at a cost—the talisman drew upon the guardian's intent, amplifying their doubts and fears.

The nexus stabilized, but the guardian was consumed by the talisman's corruption.

The vision faded, leaving Alaric shaken. He glanced at the talisman in his hand, its surface dark and reflective. "This isn't just a tool," he murmured. "It's a test."

As the group pressed on, the tension between them grew palpable. The Spiral Nexus's chaotic energy seemed to magnify their doubts, pulling at the fragile threads of trust that held them together.

Flamipandro, her ruby gown flickering in the dim light, spoke sharply. "We're wasting time. The ley lines don't care about your doubts, Alaric—they need action."

"And what do you think I've been doing?" Alaric shot back, his frustration boiling over. "Every decision I've made has been about saving the ley lines."

"And every decision has cost us," Flamipandro countered. "Felipandro sacrificed himself because of your hesitation."

Lira stepped between them, her staff glowing faintly. "Enough. This isn't helping."

Bob, flipping his hourglass absently, added with a sigh, "If we don't trust each other, why would the ley lines trust us?"

The silence that followed was heavy, filled with unspoken doubts. The Spiral Nexus loomed ahead, its threads pulsing faintly, as though waiting for them to reconcile.

*****

As the group rested near the Spiral Nexus's core, Pecos appeared, his form shifting between a young boy and an old man. He sat beside Alaric, his expression distant.

"You remind me of my first nexus," Pecos said, his voice tinged with nostalgia. "I was brash, certain I could fix everything with sheer willpower."

"What happened?" Alaric asked, his voice soft.

Pecos chuckled ruefully. "I failed. The ley lines rejected me, and the nexus collapsed. It took me centuries to understand why."

"And why was that?" Alaric pressed.

Pecos met his gaze, his eyes filled with an ancient wisdom. "Because I didn't listen. I thought I knew better than the ley lines, better than the Guardians who came before me. But the ley lines don't need heroes. They need trust."

The Spiral Nexus's threads began to flare brightly, their energy shifting erratically. The ley lines' voices grew louder, their whispers resonating in the air around the group.

"They are fractured, as we are."

"Can they be whole?"

"Show us."

The ley lines projected a vision into the air—a fractured Spiral Nexus collapsing under the weight of mortal ambition. The threads unraveled, and the dimensions connected by the ley lines dissolved into chaos. The vision shifted, showing a restored nexus, its threads glowing in perfect harmony. But the path to that future was unclear.

Alaric stepped forward, his voice steady. "We can't undo the past, but we can prove that we've learned from it."

The ley lines pulsed faintly, their hum growing steady. The group felt a subtle shift in the air—a glimmer of trust.

Journal Entry: Fractures and Harmony

Entry 59: The Ley Lines' Will

The ley lines are more than energy—they're memory, will, and trust. They carry the weight of every failure, every fracture, and they're hesitant to trust again.

Pecos's story reminded me that the ley lines don't need perfect Guardians. They need ones who are willing to listen, to adapt. But trust isn't something you demand—it's something you earn.

The Spiral Nexus is watching us, waiting to see if we can repair the fractures within ourselves. Maybe that's the real test.

The group reached the Spiral Nexus's inner core, where its threads converged in a dazzling swirl of light and shadow. The energy was overwhelming, pressing heavily upon them, but the group stood united.

"We've made mistakes," Lira said, her voice steady. "But we've also learned. The ley lines don't want control—they want trust. And we're ready to earn it."

Alaric placed the Void Crystal Talisman and the Shimmering Crystal at the nexus's core. Their energies merged, resonating with the ley lines. The Spiral Nexus pulsed brighter, its threads weaving together in tentative harmony.

The ley lines' voices grew louder, their resonance filling the air. "They listen."

"They understand."

"Trust is restored."

For the first time, the Spiral Nexus glowed with steady light, its threads flowing in perfect balance. The group stood in silence, the weight of their journey lifting as the ley lines accepted their intent.

As the Spiral Nexus began to stabilize, its threads glowing with newfound harmony, the surrounding environment seemed to shift. The jagged ground softened, and the air became warmer, carrying faint whispers of ley line energy. From the shimmering currents emerged creatures unlike anything the group had seen before.

The first to approach was a Ley Stalker, its body a graceful combination of sleek fur and crystalline spines that pulsed faintly with light. Its luminous eyes scanned the group, its movements fluid and cautious. Following behind were smaller creatures—Glow Hares with translucent fur that shimmered as they hopped along the ley line threads. Overhead, Sky Mantas glided silently, their broad, glowing forms leaving faint trails of energy in the air.

Lira crouched down, extending her hand toward the Ley Stalker. "They're not afraid of us," she said softly.

"They're part of the ley lines," Alaric replied, his voice filled with wonder. "Manifestations of the Spiral Nexus's energy."

The Ley Stalker stepped closer, its glowing spines dimming as it sniffed at Lira's hand. With a soft chirr, it nudged her fingers, its body vibrating faintly with a resonant hum.

"They're connected to the nexus," Lira said, looking up at Alaric. "If we've earned the ley lines' trust, maybe we've earned theirs too."

Bob, now fully embracing his human form, squinted at the Sky Mantas overhead. "Those look more serious than the hares," he muttered, pointing as one of the creatures descended. Its wings shimmered like liquid crystal, and its long, sinuous body coiled in midair as it emitted a low, melodic hum.

The mantas began circling the group, their glowing forms creating a faint pattern in the air. The energy shifted, and Alaric felt a sudden tug on the Shimmering Crystal in his hand.

"They're trying to communicate," he said, holding the crystal up. The artifact glowed in response, its surface rippling with faint symbols that mirrored the movements of the mantas.

Flamipandro stepped forward, her ruby gown shimmering as she studied the patterns. "It's a warning," she said. "There's still a fracture deeper in the Spiral Nexus. The creatures are guiding us."

"They want us to follow them," Alaric said. He glanced at the others. "We don't have much time."

The group followed the Sky Mantas deeper into the Spiral Nexus, where the energy grew denser and more erratic. The ley lines pulsed brightly, their hum vibrating through the air. As they approached a glowing fissure in the ground, the mantas paused, their wings folding as they hovered in silence.

"This is it," Lira said, her voice trembling. "The final fracture."

Alaric stepped forward, examining the fissure. The ley lines here were jagged and frayed, their threads sparking violently as they struggled to reconnect. "We'll need to use magic to stabilize it," he said. "Complex magic."

Flamipandro crossed her arms. "Then let's get to work."

The group spread out, each member taking a position around the fissure. Alaric held the Shimmering Crystal in one hand and the Void Crystal Talisman in the other, his mind racing as he planned the spell.

"Focus on the threads," Alaric instructed. "We need to guide them back into harmony."

Lira raised her staff, its glow intensifying as she channeled her energy into the ley lines. The threads of light responded, their movements slowing as they aligned with her intent.

Bob flipped his hourglass, the golden sand within creating a shimmering vortex. "Time for a little stability," he said, his voice light but focused. The threads of shadow began to coalesce, their chaotic energy softening under his influence.

Flamipandro drew her blade, its edge gleaming with a ruby glow. She slashed through the air, sending arcs of energy toward the fissure. The threads responded, their movements sharper and more precise.

Alaric knelt at the fissure's edge, the artifacts in his hands glowing brightly. He closed his eyes, feeling the ley lines' rhythm as he began to weave the threads together. The energy flowed through him, resonating with the Shimmering Crystal and the Void Crystal Talisman.

The ley lines resisted at first, their frayed ends sparking violently. The energy surged, sending a shockwave through the area that knocked Lira off her feet.

"Stay focused!" Alaric shouted, his voice strained.

Lira scrambled back to her position, gripping her staff tightly. "They're fighting us," she said, her voice filled with frustration. "Why?"

"They're testing us," Flamipandro said, her blade slicing through another arc of energy. "They want to see if we can handle this."

Alaric gritted his teeth, pouring more energy into the weave. The threads began to align, their movements synchronizing as the fissure's glow intensified. "Almost there," he said, his voice a mix of determination and exhaustion.

As the group neared completion, the ground beneath them trembled violently. From the fissure emerged a Fracture Wyrm, its massive, translucent form coiled with raw ley line energy. Its eyes glowed with an intense light, and its roar reverberated through the Spiral Nexus.

"Great," Bob muttered, flipping his hourglass. "As if this wasn't hard enough."

The wyrm lunged toward the group, its energy-charged body leaving a trail of destruction. Flamipandro stepped forward, her blade glowing brightly as she blocked its attack.

"Keep weaving!" she shouted. "I'll handle this!"

Alaric nodded, his focus returning to the ley lines. Lira and Bob joined him, their combined magic creating a steady flow of energy that began to close the fissure.

As Flamipandro fought the wyrm, her movements precise and relentless, she glanced back at Alaric. "You're doing it," she said, her voice softer than before. "Maybe you're not as hopeless as I thought."

Alaric allowed himself a faint smile, though his concentration didn't waver. "Thanks for the vote of confidence."

Lira, her staff glowing with steady light, added, "You're not doing this alone, Alaric. We're with you."

Bob smirked. "Yeah, and if we survive this, drinks are on you."

With a final surge of energy, the group completed the weave. The fissure began to close, its jagged edges smoothing as the ley lines pulsed in harmony. The Fracture Wyrm let out a final roar before dissolving into light, its energy absorbed by the Spiral Nexus.

The ley lines' hum grew steady, their glow bright and harmonious. The Sky Mantas circled above, their movements slow and deliberate as if acknowledging the group's success.

The Spiral Nexus pulsed once, a deep, resonant vibration that filled the air. The ley lines' voices echoed faintly, their tone one of gratitude.

"You listen."

"You understand."

"Trust is restored."

The group stood in silence, the weight of their journey settling over them. The Spiral Nexus's threads flowed steadily, their energy connecting dimensions in perfect balance.

"We did it," Lira said softly, her voice filled with wonder.

Alaric nodded, his hands trembling as he placed the artifacts back in his satchel. "The ley lines trust us," he said. "But we can't take that trust for granted."

Flamipandro sheathed her blade, her ruby gown shimmering faintly. "You've earned it, Alaric. Don't forget that."

Bob flipped his hourglass one last time, the golden sand flowing smoothly. "So... what's next?"

Alaric glanced at the Spiral Nexus, its glow a beacon of hope. "We move forward."

Journal Entry: The Ley Lines' Judgment

Entry 60: The Spiral's Whisper

The ley lines don't speak in words, yet their intent is clear. Every hum, every pulse of energy, carries meaning. They judge not by what we do but by why we do it. Trust isn't something they give lightly—not after centuries of misuse.

I've felt their hesitation, their doubt. They've seen Guardians fail, artifacts corrupt, and nexuses collapse. Every fracture in their threads is a scar left by mortals who thought they knew better.

But today, the Spiral Nexus hummed with something new—something I can only describe as hope. It wasn't because we succeeded. It was because we listened.

As the group rested near the Spiral Nexus, Flamipandro sat apart from the others, her ruby gown catching the faint glow of the ley lines. She seemed lost in thought, her usually sharp demeanor softened by the stillness.

Lira approached cautiously. "You've been quieter than usual," she said, her tone gentle. "Something on your mind?"

Flamipandro looked up, her eyes reflecting the nexus's light. "Do you know where we come from, Lira? Nexus Beings like Pecos and me?"

Lira shook her head. "I always assumed you were... part of the ley lines."

"We are," Flamipandro said. "But we weren't always. We were once mortal, like you. Chosen by the ley lines to become their stewards."

She paused, her gaze distant. "I was a warrior once, in a time when the nexuses were young. The ley lines gave me purpose, made me more than I was. But they also took away what I could have been."

"Do you regret it?" Lira asked.

Flamipandro hesitated before answering. "Sometimes. But then I remember that the ley lines don't just ask for sacrifice. They give something in return—a chance to shape the balance of all creation."

The group gathered at the edge of the Spiral Nexus, its threads pulsing faintly in the dim light. Alaric studied the ley lines, his mind racing with doubts. Flamipandro stood nearby, her arms crossed, while Bob paced restlessly.

"We're running out of time," Flamipandro said, her tone sharp. "The ley lines won't wait for you to figure this out."

Alaric turned to her, his frustration boiling over. "Do you think I don't know that? Every step we take feels like another test, another chance for the ley lines to decide we're not good enough."

"They're not testing you," Flamipandro snapped. "They're testing your intent. And right now, all I see is someone who doubts himself more than he trusts the ley lines."

Lira stepped between them, her staff glowing faintly. "Enough. This isn't helping."

Bob, flipping his hourglass absently, muttered, "The real test might be whether we can get through this without tearing each other apart."

*****

Later that night, Alaric opened the Darkened Codex, searching for answers. A new passage glowed faintly, its runes shifting into legible text:

"The Void Crystal Talisman was forged in the Shadow Nexus, its surface imbued with the energy of fractured ley lines. It was created as a tool of stabilization, but its power comes at a cost. The talisman reflects the intent of its wielder, amplifying both their strength and their doubt."

Alaric traced the runes with his fingers, their meaning resonating deeply. The talisman wasn't just a tool—it was a mirror, one that revealed his deepest fears. He glanced at the artifact, its surface dark and reflective, and felt the weight of its power more keenly than ever.

As the group approached the Spiral Nexus's core, the ley lines began to hum louder, their rhythm shifting into something almost melodic. The energy around them grew heavier, pressing down on their thoughts and emotions.

The ley lines' voices echoed faintly, blending into a single, resonant whisper: "You are fractured, as we are. Will you trust each other, as we must trust you?"

Alaric hesitated, the weight of the question pressing on him. "They're asking us to prove ourselves," he said. "Not just to them—but to each other."

Flamipandro stepped forward, her blade gleaming faintly. "Then let's start by being honest. I've doubted you, Alaric. I've doubted all of you. But I trust the ley lines. And if they see something in you, maybe I should too."

Lira nodded, her staff glowing steadily. "We've come this far together. If the ley lines trust us, we can't afford to let them down."

Bob grinned, flipping his hourglass one last time. "Guess that means we're in this together, whether we like it or not."

The group stood in a circle around the Spiral Nexus's core, their energies converging as they channeled their magic into the ley lines. Alaric held the Shimmering Crystal and Void Crystal Talisman, their combined light illuminating the threads of the nexus.

The ley lines responded, their rhythm aligning with the group's intent. The threads pulsed brighter, their movements growing steady and harmonious.

As the Spiral Nexus began to stabilize, the ley lines' voices grew louder, resonating through the air: "Trust is restored. Balance is near. Together, we are whole."

The group stood in silence, the weight of their journey lifting as the ley lines' energy flowed freely once more. The Spiral Nexus glowed with steady light, its threads weaving together in perfect harmony.

Journal Entry: A Whole Nexus

Entry 61: Balance Restored

The ley lines didn't just judge us—they trusted us. But that trust wasn't given lightly. It came with expectations, with challenges that forced us to confront not just the Spiral Nexus's fractures but our own.

The Void Crystal Talisman and the Shimmering Crystal are tools, yes, but they're also mirrors. They reflect the intent of their wielder, amplifying both our strengths and our flaws.

The ley lines are whole again, but they've taught me that balance isn't something you achieve—it's something you maintain, one choice at a time.

Chapter 23: Trust in Fractures

Narrator's Perspective: The Spiral's Sentience

The Spiral Nexus pulsed with life, its threads of light and shadow stretching across infinite dimensions. To mortal eyes, it was a tangle of chaotic energy; to the ley lines, it was their voice, their will, their memory. They carried echoes of every choice, every betrayal, and every act of trust ever woven into their threads.

The ley lines regarded Alaric and his companions. Their energy hummed faintly, a question lingering in the air. "Will you listen? Will you understand?"

Alaric's Perspective: A Fractured Trust

As the Spiral Nexus flared, Alaric felt the weight of its judgment pressing on him. The Shimmering Crystal in his hand glowed faintly, its light reflecting the swirling chaos within the nexus.

He knelt at the edge of the nexus, his thoughts heavy. "We've stabilized the threads, but it still feels... fragile. Like it could fall apart at any moment."

Flamipandro, her ruby gown shimmering in the dim light, stepped forward. "Because it can," she said bluntly. "The ley lines don't trust you yet."

Alaric looked up at her, frustration bubbling to the surface. "Then what are we supposed to do? We've done everything they asked."

"Have you?" Flamipandro's gaze was piercing. "Or have you done what you thought would make you look worthy?"

Lira's Perspective: Harmony Through Doubt

Lira watched the exchange, her staff glowing faintly as she attuned herself to the ley lines' hum. She could feel their hesitation, their reluctance to fully embrace the group's intent.

"They're afraid," she said softly. "The ley lines don't know if we'll protect them—or use them."

Pecos appeared beside her, his form shifting between a young boy and an old man. "They've been burned before," he said, his tone heavy with centuries of wisdom. "Every fracture in their threads is a scar left by someone who thought they knew better."

Lira frowned, her grip tightening on her staff. "So how do we convince them we're different?"

"You can't convince them," Pecos replied. "You have to show them."

Kael's Perspective: The Veiled Order's Intent

Far from the group, Kael stood in the shadows, his dark robes blending into the fractured landscape. He watched as the Spiral Nexus flickered, its threads trembling under the weight of conflicting energies.

"They don't understand," Kael muttered, his voice low and bitter. "The ley lines don't need trust—they need control."

He turned to a small device in his hand, a glowing sphere of dark energy pulsating with Veiled Order magic. It was designed to force the ley lines into alignment, to impose order where chaos reigned. Kael's gaze hardened. "If they can't fix this, the Veiled Order will."

Flashback: The Guardians' Failure

As the group worked to stabilize the Spiral Nexus, a sudden pulse of energy enveloped them, pulling them into a shared vision.

They stood in a vast, empty void, where a single Nexus Guardian faced a spiraling rift. The guardian, cloaked in golden light, held an artifact similar to the Shimmering Crystal. Their voice echoed with desperation.

"The ley lines are too unstable. We have to force them into balance."

The guardian raised the artifact, its energy surging violently. For a moment, the ley lines aligned, their threads pulsing in harmony. But then the energy fractured, and the nexus collapsed into chaos.

The vision faded, leaving the group shaken. Alaric gripped the Shimmering Crystal tightly, his voice trembling. "That's what happens when we try to control them."

The group reconvened at the Spiral Nexus's core, the tension between them palpable. Flamipandro's voice cut through the silence. "You saw what happens when you act out of fear. Do you really think the ley lines will forgive another mistake?"

Alaric rounded on her, his frustration boiling over. "I'm trying! Every step we take feels like another test, another chance for the ley lines to decide we're not good enough."

"And maybe you're not," Flamipandro said sharply. "But that doesn't mean you stop trying."

Lira stepped between them, her staff glowing brighter. "Enough! We're all tired, but this isn't about us. It's about the ley lines. They don't need us to be perfect—they need us to be honest."

Pecos and Flamipandro exchanged a glance before stepping forward. Flamipandro's ruby gown flickered with energy as she spoke. "The ley lines don't trust easily, but they chose us for a reason. We're not here to fix them—we're here to show them that they can heal."

Pecos nodded, his gaze fixed on the nexus. "The ley lines respond to intent, not power. If you want to earn their trust, you have to show them that you trust each other."

The group stood in a circle around the Spiral Nexus, their magic flowing into its threads. Alaric held the Shimmering Crystal in one hand and the Void Crystal Talisman in the other, their energies merging into a brilliant light. Lira's staff glowed with steady warmth, her connection to the ley lines grounding their efforts.

The nexus flared, its threads trembling as the ley lines' voices echoed around them: "Show us your intent. Prove your trust."

Alaric closed his eyes, letting go of his doubts. "We're not here to control you," he said softly. "We're here to listen."

The ley lines pulsed brighter, their hum growing steady. The Spiral Nexus began to weave itself together, its threads glowing with renewed harmony.

Journal Entry: The Spiral Reborn

Entry 62: Trust and Balance

Today, the ley lines showed us their scars, their memories of failure. They don't want perfection—they want trust. They want intent, not control.

The Spiral Nexus isn't just a nexus—it's a reflection of everything we are. When we're fractured, it's fractured. When we trust, it heals.

The ley lines accepted us today, but their balance is fragile. It's a reminder that harmony isn't something we achieve—it's something we earn.

The Spiral Nexus pulsed with a steady rhythm now, its threads weaving together in luminous patterns that stretched across dimensions. The group stood in silence, their collective effort resonating through the ley lines. Alaric released the Shimmering Crystal, its surface dulling slightly as it rested on the ground. For the first time in what felt like days, the air around them was calm.

But the calm was fleeting.

The ley lines' hum grew louder, their resonance shifting into something deeper and more complex. The threads shimmered, forming shapes and patterns that moved with purpose.

"They're not done with us," Flamipandro said, her voice steady but wary.

Alaric stepped forward, his heart pounding. "What do they want?"

The ley lines shimmered again, their threads forming a spiral that pulsed faintly. A voice, soft but resonant, filled the air: "You have mended fractures, but the core remains fragile. One thread pulls upon another. Are you ready to face what lies within?"

The Spiral Nexus pulsed brightly, its energy coalescing into a single form at its center. The ley lines manifested as a luminous figure, its body composed of intertwining threads of light and shadow. Its face was indistinct, but its presence was overwhelming—a living embodiment of the ley lines' sentience.

"You," it said, its voice resonating through the group, "have walked among our scars, touched our threads, and sought to mend what was broken. But trust is not given. It must be earned."

The group exchanged uneasy glances. Flamipandro stepped forward, her ruby gown catching the light. "We've done everything you asked. What more do you want from us?"

The ley line figure tilted its head, its threads rippling. "Intent must be pure. Unity must be whole. The fractures within you mirror our own. Resolve them, and we shall heal."

The ley lines' words hung heavily in the air. Alaric looked at the others, their faces shadowed by doubt. Flamipandro's jaw was set, her posture tense. Bob flipped his hourglass absently, his usual levity gone. Lira clutched her staff, her expression pained.

"We're not fractured," Alaric said, though his voice wavered. "We're here, together, doing what needs to be done."

"Are we?" Flamipandro countered, her tone sharp. "You've doubted me from the start. And I've doubted you. The only reason we're still here is because the ley lines haven't rejected us—yet."

Lira stepped forward, her staff glowing faintly. "Enough! The ley lines aren't testing our magic—they're testing us. If we can't trust each other, how can we expect them to trust us?"

Flashback: The Ley Lines' First Fracture

Before anyone could respond, the ley line figure raised its hand, and a vision enveloped the group. They stood in a vast, shimmering void, where the Spiral Nexus glowed brilliantly, its threads unbroken. At the nexus's core stood a Guardian, their form radiant with golden light.

The Guardian raised an artifact—a precursor to the Shimmering Crystal—and spoke with conviction: "The ley lines must be controlled, their chaos tamed. Only then can harmony endure."

As the artifact pulsed, the ley lines recoiled. Their threads frayed, their hum growing discordant. The Guardian's light dimmed, and the Spiral Nexus began to collapse.

The vision shifted, showing the aftermath of the fracture—dimensions unraveling, creatures fading into nothingness, and the ley lines' threads trembling under the weight of their scars.

The vision faded, leaving the group in stunned silence. The ley line figure spoke again. "Control broke us. Trust can mend us. But trust must begin with you."

Alaric looked at Flamipandro, her ruby gown still shimmering in the dim light. "You're right," he said, his voice quiet. "I've doubted you. I've doubted all of us. And that doubt has held us back."

Flamipandro's eyes narrowed, but she didn't interrupt. Alaric continued, "The ley lines don't need us to be perfect. They need us to trust each other, even when it's hard. Especially when it's hard."

Bob let out a soft chuckle, flipping his hourglass one last time. "Guess that means no more snide comments from me. Well, fewer, anyway."

Lira stepped closer, her staff glowing brighter. "We've come this far because we believe in what we're doing. Let's finish it—together."

The group stood in a circle around the Spiral Nexus's core. The ley line figure watched silently as they raised their artifacts, their magic intertwining with the nexus's threads. Alaric held the Shimmering Crystal and the Void Crystal Talisman, their energies merging in a brilliant flare of light and shadow.

Lira channeled her staff's magic into the nexus, her connection to the ley lines steadying the threads. Flamipandro's blade gleamed as she slashed through errant energy, guiding it back into harmony. Bob used his hourglass to stabilize the flow of time around the nexus, ensuring their work wasn't undone.

The ley lines pulsed brighter, their rhythm growing steady and resonant. The Spiral Nexus glowed with renewed energy, its threads weaving together in perfect balance.

The ley line figure stepped forward, its form shimmering. "You have shown unity. You have earned trust. The Spiral Nexus is whole once more."

As the Spiral Nexus stabilized, the ley lines' energy flowed into the group. Each member felt its warmth, its presence—a silent acknowledgment of their intent and effort.

For Alaric, it was a sense of understanding, a connection to the ley lines' memory and will. For Lira, it was a reaffirmation of her bond with magic, a harmony she had never felt before. For Flamipandro, it was a release of her doubts, a reminder of her purpose as a Nexus Being. For Bob, it was a rare moment of clarity, a realization of the weight of his choices.

The ley line figure spoke one last time. "The Spiral Nexus is whole, but our scars remain. Balance is not a destination—it is a journey. Walk it well."

With that, the figure dissolved into light, its energy flowing back into the Spiral Nexus.

Journal Entry: The Journey Continues

Entry 63: Balance Restored

The Spiral Nexus is whole again, its threads flowing with a harmony I never thought possible. But the ley lines made it clear—this isn't the end. Balance isn't something you achieve and forget. It's something you work for, every day, with every choice.

I used to think the ley lines were just energy, something to be studied and understood. Now, I see they're more than that. They're alive, and they've trusted us with their future.

The journey isn't over. But for the first time, I feel ready to face whatever comes next.

The Spiral Nexus stretched before them, a chaotic realm of swirling energy where light and shadow interwove in an endless, unpredictable dance. The threads of ley lines pulsed erratically, their colors shifting from vibrant golds and blues to ominous reds and blacks. The air was alive with magic, humming so intensely that it felt like a physical weight pressing down on them. Each pulse sent ripples across the jagged ground, where fragments of other dimensions bled through—shimmering glimpses of forests, cities, and skies that didn't belong.

Lira's breath caught as she stepped closer, her staff glowing faintly in response to the ley lines' instability. The magnitude of the challenge hit her all at once—the raw power of the Spiral Nexus, teetering on the edge of collapse. She felt the ley lines reaching out, tugging at her magic, her very essence.

"They're crying out," she whispered, her voice trembling. "They're in pain."

Alaric glanced at her, his own expression grim. "Then we have to help them."

But Lira hesitated, her grip tightening on her staff. She could feel the ley lines pulling harder, demanding more. A chilling realization washed over her: To stabilize them, I may have to give up a part of myself.

Flamipandro's ruby gown flickered like firelight as she stared at the Spiral Nexus. Her usual sharp confidence faltered as the nexus's chaotic energy surged unpredictably, creating bursts of light and shadow that rippled across the clearing.

"This isn't balance," she murmured, more to herself than anyone else. "This is... overwhelming."

The ley lines pulsed again, and Flamipandro felt their presence more keenly than ever. They weren't just energy—they were alive, sentient. They knew her doubts, her fears.

For the first time, Flamipandro questioned her role. What if we're not here to fix them? What if they don't need fixing? What if they're waiting for us to understand them? The thought unsettled her, but it also planted a seed of clarity. The ley lines didn't want control—they wanted collaboration.

Before they could act, a shadow emerged from the swirling chaos. Kael, cloaked in dark robes, stepped forward, his expression a mix of triumph and disdain. His hand clutched a sphere of pulsating dark energy, its surface alive with shifting symbols of Veiled Order magic.

"So, this is how it ends," Kael said, his voice dripping with contempt. "You think you're any different from the Veiled Order, Alaric? Driven by ambition, wielding power you don't fully understand?"

Alaric bristled, stepping forward. "We're not trying to control the ley lines. We're trying to save them."

Kael laughed coldly. "Save them? Don't delude yourself. You're doing exactly what the Order did—imposing your will, thinking you know better. You're just more self-righteous about it."

Lira interjected, her voice wavering but resolute. "You don't know what we've sacrificed. This isn't about ambition—it's about survival. I've given everything to protect the ley lines. I'm ready to give more if it means saving them."

Kael's gaze shifted to her, his expression softening slightly. "And what will you become if you do? Another tool of the ley lines, like Pecos? Like all the others who've disappeared into their will?"

Pecos appeared beside Alaric, his form flickering like a shadow caught between dimensions. His voice was softer now, almost wistful. "Kael isn't wrong, you know. The ley lines don't need another hero, Alaric. They don't need control. They need trust."

Alaric frowned, the weight of Pecos's words pressing on him. "I'm trying to trust them, but... what if I'm wrong?"

Pecos smiled faintly, his gaze distant. "Trust isn't about being right. It's about stepping forward even when you're afraid. It's about letting go of control and believing in something bigger than yourself."

He placed a hand on Alaric's shoulder, his form flickering. "You don't have to do this alone. Trust Lira. Trust Flamipandro. They're as much a part of this as you are."

Kael raised the dark sphere, its energy surging violently. "You want to trust the ley lines?" he sneered. "Let's see how they react to this."

He chanted an incantation, and the sphere erupted, sending waves of corrupted energy into the Spiral Nexus. The ley lines convulsed, their threads unraveling as bursts of energy tore through the clearing. Time itself seemed to distort—images of the past and future flashed around them in chaotic fragments.

Flamipandro acted quickly, her blade slicing through the air to deflect an errant burst of energy. "Alaric! Do something!"

Alaric grabbed the Whispering Codex, its pages glowing faintly as he flipped through them. "I need to channel harmonic energy into the ley lines, but I can't do it alone."

Lira stepped forward, her staff glowing brighter. "Then don't. Let me help."

As Alaric began to chant the Codex's incantation, Lira closed her eyes and reached out to the ley lines. She felt their chaos, their pain, their yearning for balance. She let go of her fear, letting the ley lines flow through her.

The transformation was instantaneous. Her body became a conduit of pure energy, her form glowing with threads of light and shadow intertwined. She saw the ley lines not as fractured threads but as a living web, connected to everything.

The world around her shifted. She could see the Spiral Nexus's core, feel its rhythm, hear its voice. It wasn't just a place—it was alive.

With Lira as their anchor, the group worked together. Alaric channeled the Codex's harmonic energy, Flamipandro guided the flow of light and shadow with her blade, and Bob stabilized the distortions with his hourglass.

The ley lines began to steady, their threads weaving together in intricate patterns. The chaotic energy subsided, replaced by a deep, resonant hum.

Kael staggered back, his sphere cracking as the ley lines rejected its corruption. "No," he muttered, his voice filled with disbelief. "This isn't possible."

The ley lines pulsed one last time, their energy enveloping Kael. He disappeared into the Spiral Nexus, his fate unknown.

As the ley lines stabilized, Pecos stepped toward the final frayed thread. His form flickered, his energy dimming. "The nexus needs one last push," he said, his voice calm.

Alaric's eyes widened. "No. There has to be another way."

Pecos smiled faintly. "There isn't. This is my purpose. Trust me, Alaric."

He reached out, his form dissolving as he stabilized the thread. The Spiral Nexus pulsed brightly, its energy flowing freely once more.

Alaric knelt, his hands trembling. "I'll honor you, Pecos. I swear it."

The Spiral Nexus glowed steadily now, its threads weaving together in perfect harmony. The group stood in silence, their exhaustion mingled with a profound sense of accomplishment.

Alaric looked into the distance, where a faint light shimmered—a new nexus point forming. "It's not over," he said softly. "The ley lines still have scars. There's more work to do."

Lira, still glowing faintly, placed a hand on his shoulder. "Then we'll do it. Together."

Chapter 24: Echoes of Balance

The Spiral Nexus had stabilized, its threads glowing softly with renewed energy. Yet, as the group lingered in its presence, a sense of unease crept through the air. The ley lines were no longer chaotic, but they were not entirely whole either. Faint echoes resonated through the nexus, carrying whispers that were neither words nor thoughts but something in between.

Lira, still radiating a faint glow from her recent transformation, tilted her head. "Do you hear that?" she asked, her voice barely above a whisper.

Alaric nodded, his brow furrowed. "It's like... memories. Fragments of something lost."

Bob, for once serious, flipped his hourglass in contemplation. "Or something waiting to be found."

Flamipandro's ruby gown flickered as she stepped closer to the Spiral Nexus's core. "The ley lines are speaking to us. They've shown us trust, but they're still holding back. There's more they want us to see."

The Spiral Nexus pulsed once, and a wave of energy enveloped the group. In an instant, the environment around them shifted. They were no longer in the clearing but standing in an ancient chamber carved from glowing crystal. The air was thick with magic, and the walls hummed with ley line energy.

At the center of the chamber was a massive, fractured mirror. Its surface reflected distorted images of the group, as though it was peering into their very souls. Threads of light and shadow snaked out from the mirror, connecting it to the ley lines.

"This isn't real," Alaric said, his voice unsteady. "It's a vision."

"It's a message," Lira corrected, stepping toward the mirror. As she approached, her reflection shifted, showing her surrounded by an overwhelming web of ley lines, her form slowly dissolving into their glow.

Alaric's reflection changed too, showing him holding the Shimmering Crystal as it cracked in his hands, its light fading. Flamipandro's reflection showed her kneeling before the ley lines, her blade shattered at her feet.

The mirror's surface rippled, and a voice echoed through the chamber. "Balance comes at a cost. Will you pay it?"

The group stood in silence, the weight of the mirror's message pressing on them.

Flamipandro broke the silence first, her voice sharp. "We've already paid. Felipandro. Pecos. How many more sacrifices do they want?"

Lira turned to her, her expression conflicted. "It's not about how much we've given. It's about what we're willing to give. The ley lines aren't demanding—they're asking."

Flamipandro's eyes narrowed. "And if we don't give enough? Do they take it from us?"

Alaric interjected, his tone measured. "That's not what this is about. The ley lines aren't punishing us. They're trying to protect themselves."

"Protect themselves from what?" Bob asked, his voice tinged with unease.

"From us," Alaric said softly. "From anyone who would use them for their own gain. This isn't about magic or power—it's about trust. And we're not the only ones trying to earn it."

Before anyone could respond, a fissure split the air. From it stepped Kael, his form ragged and his dark robes scorched. The remnants of the Veiled Order's magic flickered around him, unstable and volatile.

"You're still here," Kael said, his voice dripping with exhaustion and disdain. "I thought the nexus would have rejected you by now."

Flamipandro raised her blade, her stance defensive. "What are you doing here, Kael? The ley lines rejected you."

Kael laughed bitterly. "They rejected all of us. But I'm not done with them yet."

Alaric stepped forward, his eyes narrowing. "You can't force the ley lines to trust you, Kael. That's what you never understood."

"And what do you understand, Alaric?" Kael shot back. "You think you're any different? You think the ley lines trust you because you're noble? They trust you because you haven't failed yet. But trust me—they will."

Kael raised his hand, and the remnants of the Veiled Order's magic surged outward, colliding with the ley lines' energy. The chamber trembled as bursts of light and shadow exploded around them, fracturing the ground and sending shards of crystal flying.

Flamipandro darted forward, her blade glowing as she deflected the energy bursts. "We don't have time for this!" she shouted.

Lira joined her, her staff glowing brightly as she created a barrier of light to shield the group. "Kael, stop! You're only making it worse."

Kael sneered, his magic flaring again. "Worse? The ley lines are already broken. You're just playing at mending them."

Alaric gripped the Shimmering Crystal tightly, its light pulsing in response. "You're wrong. The ley lines aren't broken—they're healing. But they need balance, not control."

The battle intensified, the chamber erupting into chaos. Kael's magic clashed with the ley lines, creating fissures that bled into other dimensions. The group fought to contain the damage, their efforts growing more desperate as the nexus's stability faltered.

Amid the chaos, Alaric felt the ley lines reaching out to him. Their presence was overwhelming, their intent clear: To restore balance, a thread must be cut.

He hesitated, his mind racing. The ley lines weren't asking for another sacrifice—they were asking for trust. He glanced at Lira, her glow dimming as she struggled to maintain the barrier. He looked at Flamipandro, her blade flickering as she deflected another surge of energy. And he looked at Kael, whose magic was tearing the chamber apart.

"Enough!" Alaric shouted, his voice cutting through the noise. He stepped toward Kael, the Shimmering Crystal glowing brighter in his hand. "If you want to prove you're worthy, then listen. Stop fighting and let the ley lines decide."

Kael hesitated, his magic faltering. The ley lines pulsed again, their hum growing louder. The chamber began to stabilize, the fractures sealing as the ley lines' energy flowed freely.

The ley lines' presence filled the chamber, their voice resonating through the air. "Balance has been restored, but scars remain. Trust is fragile. Will you protect it?"

Alaric knelt before the nexus, his hands trembling. "We will. I swear it."

The ley lines pulsed softly, their light dimming as the chamber began to fade. The group found themselves back at the Spiral Nexus, its threads glowing steadily. Kael was gone, his fate unknown.

As the group stood in the Spiral Nexus's glow, the weight of their journey settled over them. Lira placed a hand on Alaric's shoulder, her glow faint but steady. "We did it," she said softly. "The ley lines trust us."

Alaric nodded, though his thoughts were heavy. "But for how long? Trust isn't permanent. It's something we have to earn, every day."

Flamipandro sheathed her blade, her ruby gown flickering in the nexus's light. "Then let's make sure we do."

In the distance, a faint light shimmered—a new nexus point forming. It was a beacon of hope, a reminder that their journey was far from over.

Journal Entry: The Journey Ahead

Entry 64: Trust in Balance

The ley lines have given us their trust, but it's a fragile thing. They've shown us their scars, their fears, and their hope. It's up to us to protect that trust, to ensure that balance isn't just a moment but a legacy.

The Spiral Nexus is whole again, but the work isn't done. The ley lines will always need care, always need understanding. And as long as they do, we'll be there.

The Spiral Nexus settled into a steady hum, its threads glowing softly as the tension eased. The faint light on the horizon pulsed rhythmically, drawing the group's attention. It was not just a distant glow; it carried a presence, an undeniable pull that resonated within each of them.

Alaric tucked the Whispering Codex into his satchel, his hand brushing against the Whispering Key. Its faint warmth was a reminder of their next step. He turned to the others, his voice steady despite his exhaustion. "The ley lines are pointing us there. A new nexus is forming."

Lira, her glow now dimmed but still present, stepped beside him. "We have to protect it. If the Veiled Order reaches it first..."

"They won't," Flamipandro interrupted, her ruby blade resting against her shoulder. "Not while we're still standing."

Bob, flipping his hourglass with a resigned sigh, added, "And here I thought we'd get a moment to breathe. Onward, to the glowing doom beacon."

The journey to the new nexus was unlike any they had taken before. The ley lines themselves seemed to guide their path, shaping the terrain as they moved. The forest around them twisted and reformed, the trees glowing faintly with ley line energy. Creatures of light and shadow flitted between the branches—Wisp Falcons that left trails of sparkling energy and Shade Hounds that moved in near silence, their dark forms blending seamlessly into the shadows.

Lira paused as a Shade Hound stepped into their path, its glowing eyes fixed on her. She held out her hand, her voice soft. "It's not here to hurt us."

The hound sniffed her palm before dissolving into wisps of shadow, merging with the ley lines. Flamipandro watched with a raised eyebrow. "I'll never get used to how these creatures just... evaporate."

"They're part of the ley lines," Alaric said. "Extensions of their will. They're guiding us, in their own way."

Bob muttered under his breath, "I wish their 'way' didn't involve creepy silence and glowing eyes."

The forest opened into a vast clearing where the new nexus point glimmered at the center. The energy here was different—raw and untamed, like a star on the verge of exploding. Threads of light and shadow swirled chaotically, creating bursts of color that painted the sky.

Lira took a hesitant step forward, her staff glowing faintly. "It's beautiful... but unstable."

The Whispering Key in Alaric's satchel pulsed, drawing his attention. He pulled it out, its surface glowing brighter as they approached the nexus. "The key resonates with it. It's connected somehow."

Flamipandro's expression darkened as she scanned the clearing. "If the ley lines are unstable, we won't be the only ones drawn here. Stay sharp."

Her warning proved true. From the edge of the clearing, a rift opened, and Veiled Order mages stepped through, their dark robes billowing as they chanted in unison. At their center stood Kael, his form flickering with corrupted energy.

"Did you really think you could protect this nexus from us?" Kael sneered, his voice dripping with contempt. "The ley lines belong to no one."

"They don't belong to you either," Lira shot back, her staff glowing brightly. "You've already caused enough harm."

Kael raised his hand, dark tendrils of energy spreading outward. "Then let's see if you're strong enough to stop me."

The clearing erupted into chaos as the Veiled Order launched their assault. Dark magic clashed with the ley lines' energy, creating bursts of light and shadow that rippled across the clearing.

Alaric raised the Whispering Codex, its pages glowing as he chanted a harmonic spell. Threads of ley line energy surged forward, intercepting the Veiled Order's magic and weaving it back into balance. "Lira! Focus on the nexus! It's still stabilizing!"

Lira nodded, her staff emitting a steady glow as she channeled her magic into the nexus. The threads of light and shadow began to calm, their movements slowing as they responded to her intent.

Flamipandro charged into the fray, her blade slicing through bursts of dark energy with precision. She locked eyes with Kael, her voice cold. "You've overstayed your welcome."

Kael smirked, raising his hands to summon a swirling vortex of corrupted energy. "And you've underestimated the Veiled Order."

Bob, flipping his hourglass, slowed the vortex's advance, giving Flamipandro a chance to strike. "Anytime you want to end this, Alaric, feel free!"

As the battle raged on, Kael's magic grew more erratic, his connection to the corrupted ley lines weakening. He staggered back, his confidence faltering. "You think this is over? The ley lines may trust you now, but they're fragile. One mistake, and everything collapses."

Alaric stepped forward, the Whispering Key glowing in his hand. "You're right. They are fragile. That's why we protect them—not control them."

Kael raised his hands one last time, summoning a burst of energy aimed directly at the nexus. Before he could release it, Flamipandro struck, her blade slicing through his defenses. Kael's magic faltered, and he collapsed, the remnants of his power dissipating into the air.

With Kael defeated, the group turned their attention to the nexus. The threads of light and shadow pulsed erratically, their instability threatening to spiral out of control.

Lira stepped closer, her connection to the ley lines strengthening. "They're calling to us. We have to guide them back into balance."

Alaric placed the Whispering Key at the nexus's core, its glow spreading outward as it resonated with the ley lines. "The key is a guide. It'll show us how to weave the threads."

The group worked together, their magic intertwining as they channeled harmonic energy into the nexus. The threads began to align, their chaotic movements slowing until they pulsed in perfect harmony.

As the nexus stabilized, a deep hum filled the air—a sound of gratitude and relief. The ley lines glowed steadily, their energy flowing freely once more.

The group stood in silence, the weight of their journey settling over them. The new nexus point shimmered brightly, its energy a beacon of hope in the chaotic landscape.

"We did it," Lira said softly, her voice filled with wonder. "The ley lines are healing."

Alaric nodded, his gaze fixed on the nexus. "But there's still more to do. The ley lines are stable, but the scars remain."

Flamipandro sheathed her blade, her ruby gown flickering faintly. "Then let's make sure we're ready for whatever comes next."

In the distance, another light shimmered—a new nexus forming. The group exchanged determined glances, their resolve unshaken.

"The journey isn't over," Alaric said, his voice steady. "But we'll face it. Together."

The Spiral Nexus was not a place one simply entered; it was a force, a paradox where energy, time, and reality collided. The ground underfoot rippled like liquid glass, shifting into unfamiliar shapes with every step. Jagged cliffs appeared and vanished, rising like frozen waves before dissolving into fragments of light and shadow. The air was thick with magic, humming with a frequency that resonated deep in the chest, making every breath an effort.

Above them, the ley lines converged like rivers in the sky, weaving an intricate web of radiant threads. Streams of light and shadow danced together, their interplay revealing an almost living quality—each pulse and ripple carrying the weight of countless choices, memories, and scars.

Alaric's breath caught as he surveyed the chaos. It was beautiful and terrifying, a reminder of both the power and fragility of the ley lines. "It's alive," he whispered, his voice barely audible over the hum.

"It's falling apart," Flamipandro countered, her ruby blade flickering with the energy around them. "And we're standing in the middle of it."

Alaric tightened his grip on the Whispering Codex, its glowing pages shifting like restless tides. The artifact was warm in his hands, its power radiating a faint hum that matched the ley lines' chaotic rhythm. Each pulse seemed to whisper accusations, reminding him of his past failures.

He had tried to stabilize the ley lines before, in the Twilight Experiment. He had been so certain of his calculations, so confident that his methods would succeed. Instead, he had nearly unraveled a nexus. The scars of that failure still lingered in his mind, sharp and unyielding.

"This is my fault," he muttered, his voice trembling. "The fractures, the instability... if I hadn't—"

"Stop," Lira said sharply, her staff glowing faintly. She stepped closer, her expression firm but not unkind. "You didn't cause this. The ley lines were scarred long before you tried to help. Blaming yourself won't fix anything."

Alaric looked at her, his guilt mingling with a flicker of hope. "But what if I fail again?"

"Then we fail together," Lira said. "But we won't give up."

As they moved closer to the nexus's core, Lira felt the ley lines pulling at her, their energy coursing through her like a tidal wave. It wasn't just power—it was emotion, memory, and intent. She saw flashes of past Guardians, moments of triumph and failure, and the fractures left behind by each choice.

The ley lines whispered to her, their voices soft and resonant. They weren't asking for dominance or control—they were asking for understanding. For trust.

Lira's grip on her staff tightened as a realization settled over her. They're not just guiding me. They're preparing me.

A surge of fear and wonder swelled within her. If she allowed herself to fully connect to the ley lines, she might lose herself. Her individuality, her memories—everything that made her Lira—could dissolve into their endless flow. But if that was the price of balance, was she willing to pay it?

Flamipandro watched as Lira's glow intensified, her form becoming almost translucent. It was unnerving, seeing someone so closely tied to the ley lines. Flamipandro had always been skeptical of their sentience. To her, the ley lines were energy—powerful, yes, but nothing more.

Yet, as she stood in the Spiral Nexus, she couldn't deny their presence. The ley lines pulsed with an intelligence that felt both alien and familiar. They knew her doubts, her fears. They weren't punishing her—they were waiting for her to understand.

"They don't need fixing," Flamipandro said aloud, her voice quiet but steady. "They've been trying to heal themselves this whole time. We just keep getting in the way."

Bob glanced at her, his expression unreadable. "That's the first smart thing you've said all day."

Flamipandro smirked despite herself. "Don't get used to it."

A sudden crack echoed through the nexus, and a rift opened near its core. From the jagged tear emerged the Veiled Order's leader, cloaked in flowing black robes that shimmered with dark energy. His presence was commanding, his voice calm yet brimming with authority.

"You've come far," he said, his tone almost admiring. "But you're blind to the truth. The ley lines don't need harmony—they need control."

Alaric stepped forward, his jaw set. "Control is what fractured them in the first place. They're not tools to be manipulated."

"And harmony is just another form of control," the leader countered. "You seek to impose your will under the guise of balance. But the ley lines were never meant to be free. Their power demands order."

The group tensed as corrupted guardians emerged from the shadows—twisted manifestations of the ley lines' instability. Their forms were jagged and shifting, their movements erratic as they surrounded the group.

The guardians attacked with relentless force, their energy lashing out in bursts of light and shadow. Flamipandro darted forward, her blade slicing through the chaos with precision. "Keep them off the nexus!" she shouted.

Lira raised her staff, creating a barrier of light that deflected the guardians' strikes. "Alaric, the codex! Use it to stabilize the ley lines!"

Alaric opened the Whispering Codex, its pages glowing brighter as he began to chant. The ley lines responded, their threads weaving together in intricate patterns. But the process was slow, and the guardians pressed harder.

Bob flipped his hourglass, slowing the guardians' movements just enough for Flamipandro to strike. "Not to rush you, Alaric, but we're running out of time!"

As the battle raged on, the ley lines' whispers grew louder in Lira's mind. She could feel their pain, their longing for balance. Without thinking, she stepped into the nexus's core, her form glowing brighter as the ley lines enveloped her.

"Lira, no!" Alaric shouted, his voice filled with panic.

But Lira didn't stop. She let the ley lines flow through her, their energy merging with her own. Memories and visions flooded her mind—fractures from centuries past, Guardians who had come and gone, and the ley lines' enduring struggle for balance.

Her form became a beacon of light and shadow, her individuality fading as she harmonized the chaotic energies. The ley lines pulsed in response, their threads weaving together more quickly.

Pecos appeared beside Alaric, his form flickering like a shadow caught between worlds. He placed a hand on Alaric's shoulder, his voice calm and steady. "Trust her."

Alaric's hands trembled. "She's giving up everything. I can't just—"

"She's not giving up," Pecos said, his gaze distant. "She's becoming. And so must I."

Before Alaric could respond, Pecos stepped toward one of the ley line threads, his form dissolving as he stabilized it. The ley lines pulsed brighter, their hum steadying. Pecos's voice echoed faintly. "Balance is a choice. Choose wisely."

With Pecos's sacrifice and Lira's transformation, the ley lines began to align. Alaric raised the Whispering Codex one final time, its pages glowing with radiant energy. He channeled the harmonic spell, pouring every ounce of his strength into the ley lines.

The energy surged, and the nexus flared brightly, its chaotic threads weaving into a perfect web. The guardians dissolved, their forms returning to the ley lines as the Veiled Order's leader retreated, his magic broken.

As the Spiral Nexus stabilized, Lira's glow began to fade. She stepped out of the core, her form still intact but changed. Her eyes glimmered with the ley lines' light, and her voice carried their resonance. "The balance is restored, but the scars remain."

Alaric knelt, his exhaustion evident. "We've done all we can. The rest is up to the ley lines."

Flamipandro sheathed her blade, her expression solemn. "And us. Balance isn't permanent. It's something we have to fight for."

In the distance, another light shimmered—a new nexus forming. The group exchanged determined glances, their journey far from over.

Chapter 25: The Guardian's Path

The Spiral Nexus stood behind them, its threads glowing with a steady, rhythmic pulse. For the first time since their journey began, the ley lines no longer felt fractured or chaotic. The nexus hummed softly, resonating with a peace that was hard-won.

But as the group turned toward the distant glow of a new nexus forming, the weight of their next challenge loomed. The Whispering Key pulsed faintly in Alaric's hand, a reminder that their work was far from over.

Lira, her transformation still evident in her glowing eyes and faintly radiant aura, stepped beside Alaric. "The ley lines aren't done with us," she said softly. "I can feel their call, their need for us to protect what we've restored."

Alaric nodded, his exhaustion visible but tempered by determination. "Then we keep moving. The ley lines trusted us once. We can't let them down now."

The journey toward the new nexus was unlike any they had taken before. The ley lines seemed to guide them, the terrain shifting in subtle ways to create a path. Trees with crystalline leaves shimmered as they passed, their branches humming softly with ley line energy. Pools of light dotted the landscape, their surfaces reflecting fragments of other dimensions—worlds both familiar and alien.

Bob paused at one such pool, his reflection showing him not as he was now but as a younger version of himself, carefree and unburdened. "These ley lines really know how to get under your skin," he muttered, flipping his hourglass.

Lira knelt beside another pool, her reflection showing her as she had been moments before merging with the ley lines. "They're showing us possibilities," she said. "Paths we've taken and paths we might still take."

Flamipandro stepped forward, her ruby gown catching the light. "Or paths we should avoid. The ley lines don't just reveal—they warn."

As they crested a hill, the new nexus came into view. It was smaller than the Spiral Nexus but no less powerful. Its threads radiated outward like the spokes of a wheel, converging at a glowing core that pulsed with rhythmic energy. The surrounding air shimmered with magic, alive and vibrant.

But something was wrong. The threads were tangled, their movements jerky and unnatural. Dark veins of corrupted energy pulsed within the nexus, spreading outward like cracks in a crystal.

Alaric's grip on the Whispering Key tightened. "It's already unstable. We need to act quickly."

"Not so fast," Flamipandro said, her blade already in her hand. "This doesn't feel right. Something's interfering with it."

Before they could move closer, a rift tore open near the nexus. Out stepped a group of Veiled Order mages, their leader flanked by corrupted guardians that writhed with unstable energy. Their leader, cloaked in robes that seemed to devour the light, raised his hand.

"You've meddled in our plans for the last time," he said, his voice echoing unnaturally. "The ley lines are meant to be controlled, shaped to serve a higher purpose. Your so-called harmony is nothing but weakness."

Alaric stepped forward, his jaw set. "The ley lines don't belong to anyone. They're alive, and they've rejected you."

The leader sneered. "Rejection is a temporary inconvenience. We will bend the ley lines to our will, no matter the cost."

The corrupted guardians surged forward, their forms shifting and distorting as they attacked.

The clearing erupted into chaos as the group fought to defend the nexus. Flamipandro met the guardians head-on, her blade cutting through their unstable forms with precise strikes. Each swing of her sword left arcs of ruby light that lingered in the air, disrupting the corrupted energy.

Lira raised her staff, her connection to the ley lines amplifying her magic. She created barriers of light to shield the nexus, her power intertwining with the threads to steady them. "The nexus is fighting back," she said, her voice strained. "We have to give it time."

Bob flipped his hourglass, slowing the movements of the guardians and mages. "I hope this nexus appreciates us risking our necks for it," he quipped, though his tone lacked its usual levity.

Alaric opened the Whispering Codex, its pages glowing brightly as he chanted a harmonic spell. The ley lines responded, their threads weaving together more steadily as they pushed back against the Veiled Order's corruption.

As the battle raged, Lira felt the ley lines pulling at her again. They weren't just calling for help—they were calling for her. She stepped closer to the nexus, her glow intensifying as the threads of light and shadow reached out to her.

"Lira, what are you doing?" Alaric shouted, his voice laced with panic.

"I can feel them," she said, her voice calm but resolute. "They need me."

She raised her staff, letting the ley lines' energy flow through her. Memories and sensations flooded her mind—flashes of past Guardians, moments of triumph and failure, and the ley lines' endless struggle for balance. Her form became a beacon of light and shadow, her individuality fading as she harmonized the chaotic energies.

The Veiled Order's leader raised a dark artifact, its energy surging violently. "You think this changes anything? The ley lines will bow to us, or they will break."

Alaric stepped forward, the Whispering Key glowing in his hand. "The ley lines aren't tools. They're not something you can control."

The leader sneered, his artifact flaring with corrupted energy. "Then prove me wrong."

Alaric raised the key, its light spreading outward as he channeled the ley lines' energy. The artifact in the leader's hand cracked, its dark magic dissolving as the nexus's threads pushed it away.

Flamipandro struck the leader with a final, decisive blow, her blade cutting through his defenses. He staggered back, his form flickering before he collapsed into the rift, which sealed behind him.

With the Veiled Order defeated, the group turned their full attention to the nexus. Lira stood at its core, her form glowing with ley line energy as she guided the threads back into harmony.

Alaric raised the Whispering Codex, chanting the final harmonic spell. The nexus pulsed brightly, its chaotic energy calming as the threads aligned. The corrupted veins dissolved, replaced by steady streams of light and shadow.

The nexus let out a final, resonant hum—a sound of relief and gratitude.

As the nexus stabilized, Lira's glow began to fade. She stepped back, her connection to the ley lines still evident but no longer overwhelming. "The balance is restored," she said softly. "But the scars remain."

Alaric nodded, his gaze distant. "The ley lines are whole again, but this isn't the end. The Veiled Order won't stop, and neither will the fractures."

Flamipandro sheathed her blade, her expression solemn. "Then we keep fighting. Balance isn't permanent—it's something we have to protect."

Bob flipped his hourglass one last time, his tone unusually serious. "Let's just hope the next nexus doesn't come with an army of corrupted magic."

In the distance, another light shimmered—a new nexus forming. The group exchanged determined glances, their journey far from over.

The newly stabilized nexus hummed softly, its radiant threads of light and shadow weaving into the surrounding terrain. The air, once heavy with the tension of fractured ley lines and corrupted energy, was now still, vibrating with a strange kind of peace. But as the group stood amidst the calm, an unspoken weight pressed on their shoulders.

Lira leaned on her staff, her glowing eyes reflecting the stabilized nexus. Her voice was steady but carried an undertone of exhaustion. "The Veiled Order won't stop with this. Every nexus we stabilize is a battle they'll want to fight."

Flamipandro wiped her blade clean of residual energy, the ruby in her hilt flickering faintly. "Good. Let them come. We're still standing, and that's more than I can say for them."

Alaric crouched near the Whispering Key, its glow dimmed but pulsing faintly in his hand. He turned it over, its intricate design a puzzle he couldn't fully solve. "The key isn't just a tool. It's showing us something—guiding us, maybe. But it feels like there's more."

Bob, sitting on a nearby rock, flipped his hourglass absently. "You're saying the key has a mind of its own? Great. First the ley lines, now a piece of magic metal. What's next, sentient boots?"

As Alaric contemplated the key, the Whispering Codex in his satchel began to hum. Its pages glowed faintly, flipping on their own to reveal new text. Alaric opened the codex carefully, his eyes scanning the glowing runes.

"The ley lines' scars are not wounds—they are memories. Trust binds them, and trust breaks them. To protect the nexuses, one must first understand their pain."

Lira knelt beside him, her staff casting a soft glow over the codex. "It's speaking about the scars. The fractures aren't just damage—they're part of the ley lines' history."

Alaric nodded, his brow furrowed. "Every failure, every moment of imbalance, leaves a mark. The ley lines remember everything."

Flamipandro crossed her arms, her voice skeptical. "If they're so good at remembering, why do they need us? Why can't they fix themselves?"

Bob tilted his hourglass, watching the sand shift. "Maybe they're waiting for someone to listen. Someone who doesn't just want to use them."

Before anyone could respond, the ground beneath their feet trembled. A ripple of energy passed through the air, and a rift opened nearby. Unlike the jagged tears created by the Veiled Order, this rift was smooth and shimmering, its edges glowing faintly with ley line energy.

"What now?" Flamipandro muttered, her blade already in her hand.

Lira stepped closer, her staff glowing brighter as the rift pulsed. "It's not like the others. It feels... different."

The rift expanded slightly, revealing a vision within—a vast expanse of ley line threads stretching into infinity. Among the threads, a figure moved, their form indistinct but glowing with a faint blue light.

"Pecos," Alaric whispered, his voice filled with disbelief.

The figure turned, their features becoming clearer. It was Pecos, but not as they had last seen him. His form was whole, his presence calm and steady. He raised a hand in greeting, his voice echoing through the clearing. "You're not done yet."

The group stood frozen as Pecos stepped through the rift, his movements slow and deliberate. His form flickered slightly, as though he were caught between dimensions.

"You stabilized the nexus," Pecos said, his tone carrying a mix of pride and urgency. "But the scars in the ley lines run deeper than you realize. Each nexus you restore strengthens the balance, but it also stirs the past."

Alaric frowned, the Whispering Key warm in his hand. "What do you mean? What past?"

Pecos gestured to the stabilized nexus, its threads glowing faintly. "The ley lines remember everything—every choice, every failure, every moment of imbalance. Those memories aren't just scars. They're echoes, ripples that reach across dimensions."

Lira stepped forward, her glowing eyes fixed on Pecos. "If the ley lines are remembering, does that mean... they can bring those moments back?"

Pecos nodded slowly. "Not intentionally, but the energy you're working with is ancient, tangled. The more you interact with it, the more it reveals. You must tread carefully."

As Pecos spoke, the stabilized nexus began to tremble. Its threads, once steady, pulsed erratically, and dark veins of corrupted energy began to creep along their lengths.

"What's happening?" Lira asked, her voice tense.

"The Veiled Order's corruption runs deep," Pecos said, his form flickering. "They've tied themselves to the ley lines in ways you can't yet understand. The nexuses aren't just targets—they're conduits."

Alaric's grip on the Whispering Key tightened. "Conduits for what?"

"For control," Pecos said simply. "If they gain access to enough nexuses, they'll rewrite the ley lines entirely. Balance will be erased."

Before they could respond, the ground split open, and a massive figure emerged from the nexus's core. It was a corrupted guardian, its form twisted and jagged, its eyes glowing with dark energy. Its movements were slow but deliberate, each step shaking the ground.

Flamipandro raised her blade, her stance ready. "Looks like we've got company."

The guardian let out a low, guttural roar, its corrupted energy lashing out in waves. Lira raised her staff, creating a barrier of light to shield the group, but the force of the attack pushed her back.

"This thing isn't like the others," she said, her voice strained. "It's tied to the nexus. If we destroy it, we might damage the ley lines."

Alaric opened the Whispering Codex, its pages glowing brightly. "Then we'll have to untangle it."

The group moved in unison, their magic and abilities complementing each other. Flamipandro darted toward the guardian, her blade slicing through its corrupted energy with precision. "Keep it distracted!" she shouted.

Lira focused her magic on the nexus, her connection to the ley lines guiding her movements. She channeled harmonic energy into the threads, steadying them as they pulsed erratically. "The corruption is deep," she said. "It's tied to the guardian. We have to separate them."

Bob flipped his hourglass, slowing the guardian's movements just enough for Flamipandro to land a decisive strike. "This thing is stubborn," he muttered. "We need to hurry."

Alaric held the Whispering Key aloft, its glow spreading outward as he chanted a stabilization spell. The ley lines responded, their threads weaving around the guardian and pulling its corrupted energy away.

As the battle reached its peak, Pecos stepped forward, his form more stable now. He placed a hand on Alaric's shoulder, his expression calm. "The ley lines need one last push."

Alaric shook his head, his voice filled with urgency. "We can't lose you again."

"This isn't about loss," Pecos said. "It's about balance. Trust me."

Before Alaric could protest, Pecos stepped into the nexus's core. His form merged with the ley lines, his energy weaving into the threads. The corrupted guardian let out a final roar before dissolving into light, its energy absorbed by the ley lines.

The nexus pulsed brightly, its threads glowing steadily once more.

The group stood in silence, the weight of Pecos's sacrifice settling over them. Lira wiped a tear from her cheek, her glow dimmed but steady. "He gave everything to protect the ley lines."

"And we'll honor that," Alaric said, his voice firm. "The ley lines trusted us once. We won't let them down."

Flamipandro sheathed her blade, her expression resolute. "There's another nexus out there, waiting. Let's make sure it doesn't fall."

In the distance, a faint light shimmered—a new nexus forming, its presence a beacon of hope and a reminder of the challenges ahead.

Chapter 26: The Scholar's Reflection

The air was heavy with silence as the group gathered around the now-stabilized nexus. Its threads glowed with a gentle rhythm, their light a stark contrast to the chaos they had endured. The battle was over, but the scars it left behind were evident—not just in the ley lines but in each of them.

Alaric stood at the edge of the nexus, the Whispering Codex and Spiral Anchor resting in his hands. The artifacts pulsed faintly, their energy mirroring the ley lines' newfound harmony. He looked at his companions, their faces etched with exhaustion and determination, and felt the weight of what they had witnessed settle over him like a shroud.

Pecos was gone. Not dead—the ley lines had shown them that much—but transformed, absorbed into the very fabric of the network he had given everything to protect. The space where he had stood moments before still shimmered faintly, as if the ley lines themselves were mourning his absence.

"He knew," Lira said softly, breaking the silence. Her glow had dimmed considerably, but her connection to the ley lines remained strong, steady. "He knew what would happen when he stepped into the core."

Alaric's grip tightened on the artifacts. "He didn't tell us. He didn't give us the chance to find another way."

"There wasn't another way," Flamipandro said, her voice rough but not unkind. "You know that. We all know that. The corruption was too deep. If he hadn't acted—"

"The nexus would have fallen," Bob finished quietly, his usual levity absent. "And maybe all of us with it."

Alaric closed his eyes, letting their words wash over him. They were right. He had seen the mathematics of the situation play out in real-time, had felt the ley lines' desperate pull toward catastrophe.

Pecos's sacrifice had been the variable that changed everything, the singular choice that tipped the balance back toward harmony.

But understanding it didn't make it easier to accept.

"He trusted us," Alaric said finally, opening his eyes to look at each of his companions in turn. "He trusted that we would finish what he started. That we would honor what he gave."

Lira stepped forward and placed a hand on his shoulder. "Then that's what we'll do."

—-

Later that evening, as the others rested near the stabilized nexus, Alaric found himself unable to sleep. The events of the day played through his mind in an endless loop—Pecos's calm expression, the way he had placed a hand on Alaric's shoulder, the certainty in his voice when he said, "This isn't about loss. It's about balance. Trust me."

Trust.

How many times had that word defined their journey? Trust in the ley lines. Trust in each other. Trust that there was meaning in the chaos, purpose in the pain.

Alaric pulled out his journal, the leather cover worn smooth from years of use. The pages fell open to an entry from what felt like a lifetime ago—his first encounter with a ley line, the wonder and fear he had felt standing before something so vast and incomprehensible. He had been so young then, so certain that knowledge alone would be enough to understand the world's mysteries.

He knew better now.

His quill hovered over a blank page, and after a long moment, he began to write.

—-

JOURNAL ENTRY:
Entry 103: The Scholar's True Reflection

The Spiral Nexus is whole again, its threads weaving together in harmony that feels both fragile and eternal. But as I sit here in the quiet aftermath, I find myself grappling with a truth I've avoided for too long: balance is not something we achieve. It is something we participate in, moment by moment, choice by choice.

Pecos understood this in a way I'm only beginning to grasp. When he stepped into that nexus core, he wasn't sacrificing himself—he was completing himself. He was answering a call that had been resonating through his being since the moment the ley lines first touched him. I see that now, though I wish I had seen it sooner. Perhaps then I could have told him what his friendship meant to me. What his wisdom taught me.

But perhaps that's the point. Some lessons aren't meant to be spoken. They're meant to be lived, witnessed, carried forward.

I've spent years studying the ley lines as a scholar—measuring their flows, cataloging their properties, attempting to reduce their infinite complexity to formulae and theories I could grasp. And I've learned much. The appendices I've compiled contain more technical knowledge about ley line mechanics than perhaps any single volume in history. But all of that knowledge, all of those careful observations, pale beside the simple truth Pecos showed me:

The ley lines are not problems to be solved. They are relationships to be honored.

Every nexus we've encountered, every guardian we've met, every artifact we've wielded—all of it has been teaching me this lesson. The Whispering Codex doesn't just contain information; it resonates with the reader's need for wisdom. The Spiral Anchor doesn't merely stabilize nexuses; it harmonizes with the natural rhythm of the ley lines themselves. Even the Twilight Experiment, in all its catastrophic consequences, taught me that power without respect is destruction waiting to happen.

I thought I was recording these discoveries for future scholars. I thought I was building a foundation of knowledge that others could stand upon. And perhaps I have done that. But I see now that the true gift isn't the information—it's the understanding that comes from living these truths, not just documenting them.

Lira feels this instinctively. Her connection to the ley lines isn't intellectual; it's visceral, immediate, alive. She doesn't need to understand why a nexus responds to harmonic resonance—she simply knows the song to sing. Flamipandro embodies it through action, her blade cutting away corruption not through technique alone but through absolute commitment to her purpose. Even Bob, with his seemingly endless jokes and his mysterious hourglass, moves through time with a trust that I've only begun to learn.

And Pecos... Pecos became it.

—-

Alaric paused, his quill trembling slightly above the page. The enormity of what had happened was still settling into his bones, finding places to rest among old certainties and new doubts. He looked up at the nexus, its threads flowing in patterns that reminded him simultaneously of music, mathematics, and something beyond either.

He thought about the first time he'd met Pecos, back at the Grand Arcanum. The older scholar had seemed eccentric even then, more interested in meditation than measurement, more focused on feeling the ley lines than mapping them. Alaric had dismissed it at the time as imprecision, as the woolly thinking of someone who lacked rigor.

How wrong he had been.

Pecos had possessed the deepest rigor of all—the discipline to listen instead of dictate, to serve instead of control, to trust instead of demand certainty.

Alaric's hand moved across the page again, the words flowing more freely now.

—-

I'm reminded of my early experiments, the ones I meticulously documented in the chapters of this codex. Each one taught me something technical about the ley lines—their response to different stimuli, their capacity to store and transfer energy, their sensitivity to dimensional barriers. But beneath all those measurements lay a deeper pattern I was too blind to see: the ley lines were teaching me about myself.

When I stood before that first minor nexus and felt its energy flow through me, I wasn't just observing a phenomenon—I was being invited into a relationship. When the guardians tested us, they weren't merely gatekeepers; they were teachers showing us that worthiness isn't about power but about understanding our place in the larger pattern.

The House of the Crystal Keys demonstrated this truth most clearly. A place that changes based on need, that reveals itself differently to each visitor, that holds countless artifacts not as a hoarder but as a custodian—it embodied the principle that true wisdom isn't about possession but about stewardship.

I wonder now if Pecos knew, even then, what his role would ultimately become. Did he sense the call of the ley lines pulling him toward this moment? Did he feel the shape of his destiny forming around him like a chrysalis?

I don't know. I'll never know.

But I do know this: his choice was made from love, not duty. From trust, not resignation. He gave himself to the ley lines because he recognized himself in them—because he had spent so long listening to their song that he had learned to sing it himself.

And now that song continues through all of us who remain.

—-

Alaric set down his quill and flexed his fingers, stiff from writing. The night had deepened around him, stars appearing in the gaps between the nexus's glowing threads. Somewhere in the distance, he heard Flamipandro moving through sword forms, the whisper of her blade cutting air a meditation of its own. Bob's soft snoring drifted from where he lay against a smooth stone, his hourglass clutched loosely in one hand.

And Lira sat at the nexus's edge, her fingers trailing through threads of energy that responded to her touch like living things. She sensed his gaze and looked over, offering a tired smile.

"Can't sleep either?" she asked.

Alaric shook his head, closing his journal and moving to sit beside her. "Too much to process. Too many thoughts circling."

"He's still here, you know," Lira said softly, her attention returning to the ley lines. "I can feel him. Not as himself, exactly, but... woven through. Part of the harmony now."

"Does it hurt him?" The question escaped before Alaric could stop it, raw and unbidden.

Lira considered for a long moment, her brow furrowed in concentration. "I don't think so. It's not like pain as we understand it. It's more like... purpose. Like he's exactly where he's meant to be, doing exactly what he was meant to do."

Alaric wanted to take comfort in that, but grief was a stubborn thing, resistant to logic or reassurance. "I should have seen it coming. Should have found another solution."

"There wasn't another solution, Alaric." Lira's voice was gentle but firm. "You can't save everyone from their own destiny. And you can't carry the weight of choices that weren't yours to make."

He knew she was right. Intellectually, he understood that Pecos's choice had been his own, made with full knowledge and clear intention. But the heart didn't always listen to the head, especially when loss was fresh and grief was raw.

"The ley lines called to him," Lira continued, her voice taking on the distant quality it sometimes held when she was deeply connected to the network. "They've been calling to him for a long time. Maybe his whole life. He answered. That's not tragedy, Alaric. That's completion."

Alaric sat with that, letting the words settle. Completion. Not ending, but fulfillment of purpose. Not loss, but transformation into something greater.

Perhaps that was what balance truly meant—not the absence of change, but the acceptance of it. Not the elimination of sacrifice, but the recognition that some gifts were meant to be given, some transformations meant to be embraced.

"What about us?" he asked quietly. "What do we do now?"

Lira's smile was sad but steady. "We honor him by continuing. By protecting what he helped us save. By learning what he taught us."

"And by trusting," Alaric added, the realization settling over him like dawn. "By trusting the ley lines the way he trusted them. By trusting each other. By trusting that this isn't the end of the work, just the end of one chapter."

"The beginning of another," Lira agreed.

—-

The next morning brought clarity with the sunrise. Alaric gathered his companions near the stabilized nexus, feeling the weight of what he needed to do settle into certainty.

He held up the Whispering Codex, its glowing pages warm in his hands. "This artifact has been my guide through much of this journey," he said, looking at Lira. "But I've come to understand that it was never truly mine. Artifacts like these... they're not possessions. They're partnerships. And this one has been calling to you, Lira, from the moment you first touched it."

Lira's eyes widened. "Alaric, I can't—"

"You can," he interrupted gently. "You must. The Codex responds to those who listen rather than command, who seek harmony rather than control. That's always been you. The ley lines trust you completely. So do I."

He placed the artifact in her hands, and its glow intensified immediately, pages rippling with energy as it recognized its true bearer. Lira gasped softly, and Alaric knew she could feel what he had suspected—the Codex had been waiting for her all along.

He turned to Flamipandro next, holding up the Spiral Anchor. Its intricate design caught the morning light, casting prismatic patterns across the ground. "You've been our blade and our shield," he said. "But more than that, you've been our anchor in the truest sense—keeping us grounded, keeping us honest, keeping us focused on what matters. This artifact embodies that same principle. It doesn't just stabilize nexuses through force. It reminds them of their true nature, calls them back to their fundamental harmony."

Flamipandro's expression was unreadable, but she took the artifact carefully, reverently. "You're sure about this?"

"I've never been more sure of anything," Alaric replied. "These artifacts found their way to us for a reason. Now they've found their way to you."

"What about you?" Bob asked, his tone unusually serious. "What will you carry?"

Alaric smiled and tapped his journal. "I'll carry what I've always carried—questions, observations, and the willingness to learn. That's been my true tool all along. Everything else has just been teaching me how to use it."

He looked at each of them in turn, these companions who had become something far deeper than friends. They had walked through fire together, faced impossible choices together, learned to trust not just each other but something larger than themselves.

"Pecos showed us the way forward," Alaric said. "Not through sacrifice alone, but through understanding. Through becoming part of the balance we sought to protect. We can't bring him back, and I'm no longer certain we should want to. But we can honor what he gave by continuing the work—by protecting the ley lines, by teaching others what we've learned, by remaining open to the lessons that are yet to come."

"There are other nexuses," Flamipandro said, her hand resting on the Spiral Anchor. "Other places that need protection."

"Other guardians who need allies," Lira added, the Whispering Codex glowing softly in her arms.

"Other jokes that need telling," Bob said with a shadow of his usual grin. "Though perhaps I'll keep those to a minimum. For now."

Alaric felt something loosen in his chest, a tightness he hadn't fully recognized until it began to ease. This was right. This was how it was meant to be—not an ending, but a transformation. Not an answer, but a deeper understanding of the question.

The Spiral Nexus pulsed behind them, its threads flowing in perfect harmony, and Alaric could almost feel Pecos's presence woven through it—not trapped, not suffering, but part of something vast and beautiful and eternal.

"Then let's begin," Alaric said.

And in the distance, the faint glow of another nexus appeared on the horizon, calling to them, waiting for the harmony only they could bring.

—-

JOURNAL ENTRY:
Entry 104: The Road Forward

We leave the Spiral Nexus behind today, but we carry it with us in ways I'm still learning to understand. The artifacts have found their true bearers. The ley lines flow in harmony. And Pecos... Pecos has become part of the song itself.

I am not the scholar I was when this journey began. I have learned that true wisdom isn't found in answers but in better questions. Not in control but in trust. Not in my understanding alone but in the shared understanding we build together.

The work is not done. It will never be done, I think. Balance is not a destination but a practice, a constant choosing of harmony over chaos, connection over isolation, trust over fear.

I don't know what waits for us at the next nexus, or the one after that. I don't know what challenges the ley lines will present, what lessons they still have to teach. But I know I don't face them alone. And I know that whatever comes, we'll meet it together—not as conquerors or controllers, but as students, partners, guardians of a balance that is infinitely more complex and beautiful than I ever imagined.

Pecos trusted us with this responsibility. The ley lines have shown us the way.

Now it's our turn to listen, to learn, and to become part of the harmony we're meant to protect.

The horizon calls. We answer.

— Alaric Deymorne, Scholar, Guardian, Student of the Eternal Balance

Epilogue: Threads of Continuity

Six months had passed since the Spiral Nexus, and the rhythm of their work had become almost meditative. Alaric stood at the edge of the Ember Nexus, watching as threads of fire and earth wove together in patterns that had seemed impossible to stabilize just weeks ago. The nexus pulsed with steady light now, its chaotic energies tamed not through force but through understanding.

"That's the fourth one this month," Bob said, flipping his hourglass with satisfaction. "We're getting efficient."

"We're getting better," Lira corrected gently, the Whispering Codex floating beside her, its pages turning slowly in a wind only she could feel. Her connection to the ley lines had deepened considerably over the months—where once she had to concentrate to sense their flow, now she moved through them as naturally as breathing. "Each nexus teaches us something new."

Flamipandro sheathed the Spiral Anchor at her side, its weight familiar now, almost comforting. "This one was different. The corruption was older, deeper. If we'd tried the Spiral Nexus approach, we'd have failed."

"But we didn't," Alaric said, closing his journal with a satisfied snap. The pages were filling quickly these days—observations, patterns, insights that built upon everything Pecos had taught them. "We adapted. We listened."

The Ember Nexus hummed its agreement, threads of energy flowing smoothly through the dimensional fabric. In the distance, Alaric could see the local guardians emerging from their watchposts, their crystalline forms catching the fading sunlight. They had been wary at first, uncertain of this group that claimed to help rather than control. But trust, like balance, was something earned through consistent action.

"The guardians are satisfied," Lira reported, her eyes distant as she communed with the ley lines. "They're already spreading word to the neighboring nexuses. We'll have allies when we reach the Twilight Convergence."

"If we reach it," Bob muttered. "That's at least two weeks' travel through some very unfriendly terrain."

"We'll reach it," Alaric said with quiet confidence. Six months ago, he might have buried himself in research before attempting such a journey, seeking certainty in preparation. Now he understood that some lessons could only be learned by walking the path. "We have everything we need."

He looked at his companions—no, his friends—and felt a deep sense of gratitude. Lira, who had grown from uncertain student to accomplished guardian, her natural affinity for the ley lines now matched by hard-won wisdom. Flamipandro, whose blade had found purpose beyond mere combat, who protected not out of duty but out of genuine care for the balance they served. And Bob, whose jokes concealed a depth of understanding about time and consequence that Alaric was only beginning to appreciate.

They had become something more than a group of scholars and fighters. They had become a team, each member essential, each strength complementing the others' weaknesses.

"We should rest before we move on," Flamipandro suggested, already scouting for a suitable campsite. "The ley lines may be stable, but we're not invincible."

Alaric nodded, though his mind was already turning toward the next challenge, the next opportunity to learn. The Twilight Convergence was rumored to be one of the oldest nexus points, a place where multiple dimensions touched simultaneously. If they could stabilize it...

"Alaric," Lira said softly, interrupting his thoughts. "You're doing it again."

"Doing what?"

"Planning three steps ahead instead of being present for this one." She smiled, but there was gentle reproof in her voice. "Pecos would tell you to breathe. To acknowledge what we've accomplished here."

The mention of Pecos brought a familiar ache—not the sharp pain of fresh grief, but the softer sorrow of absence. Alaric had felt him occasionally over these months, a presence woven through the ley lines themselves, subtle and sustaining. He wondered sometimes if Pecos could see them now, if he knew how his sacrifice had enabled all of this.

"You're right," Alaric admitted, taking a deliberate breath and looking around at the stabilized nexus, the peaceful guardians, the harmonious flow of energy. "We did well today."

"We did excellently," Bob corrected. "And we'll do excellently tomorrow, and the day after. But tonight, we rest. And maybe I finally tell you all the story about the temporal anomaly and the very confused dragon."

Lira groaned. "Is this the one with the seven timelines?"

"Eight timelines," Bob corrected cheerfully. "And a partridge in a pear tree, which is relevant, I promise."

As they made camp that evening, Alaric found himself writing in his journal by the light of the nexus's gentle glow.

—-

JOURNAL ENTRY:

Entry 147: Six Months of Balance

The work continues, and I find myself grateful for that continuation. Where once I sought conclusions—definitive answers to fundamental questions—I now appreciate the value of the journey itself. Each nexus we stabilize adds to our understanding, not as isolated data points but as verses in an ongoing song.

Lira's growth has been remarkable. The Whispering Codex responds to her with an eagerness it never showed me, revealing layers of knowledge I suspect were waiting for her all along. She doesn't just read the patterns in the ley lines—she feels them, understands them in ways that transcend mere scholarship.

Flamipandro has found peace in purpose. The Spiral Anchor suits her perfectly, its stabilizing energy matching her unwavering commitment to protection. She wields it not as a weapon but as an instrument of harmony, and the nexuses respond to her touch with trust.

And Bob... Bob remains an enigma wrapped in humor, but I've learned to recognize the wisdom in his levity. Time flows differently around him, and I suspect he sees threads of causality that remain invisible to the rest of us.

As for me, I am simply a scholar with a journal, documenting what we learn, preserving what we discover. It's a humbler role than I once imagined for myself, but I've come to understand that humility is not diminishment—it's accuracy. I am one small part of a much larger pattern, and that's exactly where I'm meant to be.

We received word today from the Grand Arcanum. They're compiling our reports into a new curriculum on ley line dynamics. Scholars who once dismissed this field as too theoretical are now clamoring to study it. Perhaps some good can come from all we've witnessed—a new generation taught not just to control magical forces but to respect them, to work in harmony with them.

There was also news that gave me pause. Several messages from the House of the Crystal Keys mention unusual activity—rooms rearranging more frequently than normal, artifacts shifting positions without cause, corridors appearing where none existed before. The caretakers describe it as "restless," though they insist it's nothing to worry about. The House has always been changeable, they say. Its moods are its own.

Still, something about the reports troubles me. The House has always been a place of mystery, but there's a difference between mystery and instability. I made a note to visit when our work brings us back to that region, though the Twilight Convergence will occupy us for some time yet.

For now, there are nexuses that need us, ley lines that require protection, and a balance that demands our constant attention. This is the work Pecos entrusted to us, and we will not fail him.

The horizon calls. We answer.

— Alaric Deymorne

—-

Later, as the others slept, Alaric stood watch beside the Ember Nexus. The threads flowed peacefully around him, their energy a steady reminder of what they'd achieved. In the distance, he could see the faint glow of other nexuses, some stable, some calling out for help.

There was so much work still to do.

But for the first time since this journey began, Alaric didn't feel daunted by the magnitude of the task. He felt ready. They all were ready—prepared not because they had all the answers, but because they knew how to find them together.

A faint pulse rippled through the ley lines—a moment of resonance that felt almost like recognition, almost like acknowledgment. Alaric smiled, suspecting he knew its source, and whispered a quiet thank you to the friend who had shown them the way.

The nexus pulsed once in response, its light brightening briefly before settling back into its steady rhythm.

Balance maintained. Journey continuing.

Exactly as it should be.

—-

Somewhere far to the north, in a house that existed between dimensions, crystal keys chimed softly in halls that had not existed an hour before. A staircase folded into a doorway. A window opened onto a room that had been sealed for centuries. An attic expanded to accommodate new treasures while a basement contracted, squeezing itself into impossible geometry.

The House of the Crystal Keys was changing, growing more restless with each passing day. Its corridors whispered with energy that felt almost alive, almost aware, almost yearning.

But no one who walked its halls understood why.

Not yet.

The keys hung on their hooks, waiting. The doors stood ready to open. And deep within the foundation, where the ley lines converged in patterns too complex for any map, something ancient stirred—not malevolent, but not entirely benign either.

The House remembered. The House knew.

And soon, it would need to be understood.

But that was a story for another time, another journey, another reckoning with the mysteries that lay at the heart of magic itself.

For now, four companions slept peacefully beside a stabilized nexus, dreaming of the challenges that awaited them at dawn.

And in the space between sleeping and waking, between one moment and the next, the threads of eternity continued their eternal dance—weaving, unweaving, forever seeking the balance that gave all things meaning.

The work was never finished.

The work was always beginning.

And that was exactly as it should be.

Afterword

As I close the final chapter of The Sorcerer's Codex, I find myself reflecting on the journey that brought this book to life—a journey as intricate and challenging as the paths traveled by Alaric Deymorne within these pages. Writing this story has been a labor of love, inspired by countless hours of imagining worlds where magic thrives, heroes grow, and mysteries unfold.

This tale began as a spark—a question about the unseen threads that hold our lives together. What if magic were not merely a tool, but a living force, a delicate balance that demands both reverence and understanding? That question led to the creation of Alaric, a character driven by curiosity, resilience, and an unyielding belief in the possibility of more. Through his struggles, triumphs, and growth, I hoped to explore what it means to seek purpose and the cost of ambition.

The Sorcerer's Codex would not exist without the support and inspiration I've received along the way. To my family, especially my wife, Debbie N. Bones, you are the foundation of my world. Your patience, encouragement, and unwavering belief in my dreams have been the driving force behind this book. To my children, Aerith Nyomi, Alisher Krystal, and Aiden Kalel, you remind me every day of the magic in curiosity and the power of storytelling.

I also owe a debt of gratitude to the readers who choose to embark on this adventure. Whether you're new to fantasy or a seasoned traveler of magical realms, your willingness to explore the unknown is what brings stories like this to life. It is my hope that Alaric's journey resonates with you, reminding you of the sparks of courage and wonder within your own life.

Lastly, a note on the themes of this story. At its core, The Sorcerer's Codex is about balance—between ambition and humility, power and responsibility, and the personal and the universal. These are lessons I've learned not only from crafting this tale but from life itself. In a world that often feels as fractured as the ley lines within this story, I believe there is value in seeking connection and harmony, even when the path forward seems uncertain.

As you close this book, I invite you to reflect on your own story. What mysteries do you long to unravel? What horizons call to you? Perhaps, like Alaric, you will find that the journey itself is as meaningful as the destination.

Thank you for allowing me to share this world with you. May your own adventures be filled with magic, wonder, and the courage to follow your spark.

With gratitude,

Hector L. Bones

Appendix A: The Nature of Ley Lines

Introduction

Ley lines are the lifeblood of magic, a vast network of energy that courses through the world, connecting realms, dimensions, and the physical environment. Invisible to the naked eye but profoundly impactful, ley lines sustain the magic that fuels life, balances nature, and enables extraordinary feats of power. They are not merely conduits but also sentient entities, reacting to their surroundings and preserving the equilibrium of existence.

This appendix serves as a comprehensive guide to understanding ley lines, their significance, and their intricate relationships with ecosystems, magical creatures, and human intervention. Throughout the story of The Sorcerer's Codex, ley lines symbolize balance, memory, and the interconnectedness of all things, reflecting the delicate harmony that must be maintained to avoid chaos. By exploring their nature, readers will gain insight into one of the most foundational aspects of this magical world.

Section 1: Theoretical Framework

Magical Anatomy of Ley Lines: Ley lines are streams of concentrated magical energy that flow both above and beneath the surface of the world. Though invisible to most, they can be detected and mapped using specialized tools such as the Runestone Compass. Scholars describe them as rivers of power that intersect at key points called nexus points, where their energy converges and amplifies.

Origins and Theories: Ley lines have sparked numerous theories about their origins. The Primordial Energy Theory posits that they are remnants of the world's creation, channels of raw magic that emerged alongside the universe itself. Meanwhile, the Dimensional Web Theory suggests that ley lines are bridges between realms, facilitating the exchange of magical energy across dimensions. Both theories highlight ley lines as integral to the structure of reality.

Energetic Flow and Structure: Ley lines operate as an interconnected network, much like a circulatory system. Smaller branches feed into larger flows, which in turn connect at nexus points. This intricate structure sustains the physical and metaphysical world, influencing everything from ecosystems to spellcasting. Nexus points are the energy hubs of this system, serving as reservoirs that regulate and distribute magical power.

Balance and Disruption: Despite their strength, ley lines are fragile and susceptible to disruption. External interference, whether natural or man-made, can destabilize the flow of energy, leading to catastrophic consequences. Dimensional rifts, temporal anomalies, and ecological collapse are just some of the dangers associated with ley line imbalances.

Section 2: Interaction with the Natural World

Ley Lines and Ecosystems: Ley lines play a pivotal role in sustaining the natural world. Their energy nourishes the environment, promoting growth and vitality. For example, forests near ley line junctions often exhibit accelerated growth, with trees and plants developing magical properties. Similarly, ley lines can influence weather patterns, causing elemental storms or other phenomena when their energy fluctuates.

Magical Creatures and Ley Lines: Many magical creatures have a symbiotic relationship with ley lines. For instance:

Kirin and Dryads rely on ley lines for their life energy, creating vibrant habitats that mirror the lines' flows.

Shadow Wraiths, on the other hand, guard corrupted or unstable ley lines, ensuring that their disruptive potential does not spread.

Flamipandro, an elemental entity, consumes and protects ley line energy, embodying both its power and fragility.

Natural Phenomena and Ley Lines: Ley lines are responsible for a variety of magical phenomena, including: Floating islands that hover above powerful nexuses. Temporal pockets where time flows inconsistently, creating regions of past, present, and future overlap. Geographical anomalies like glowing rivers or crystalline caverns formed by concentrated ley line energy.

Case Studies

The Nature Nexus: A harmonious example of ley lines sustaining an environment and its mythical inhabitants.

The Twilight Experiment: A failed human intervention that destabilized a nexus point, resulting in a dangerous dimensional rift.

Section 3: Nexus Points

Definition and Importance: Nexus points are the convergence zones where multiple ley lines intersect, acting as reservoirs of immense energy. They are critical to maintaining the balance of magical flows, serving as both stabilizers and amplifiers within the network.

Types of Nexus Points

Stable Nexuses: These are naturally harmonious zones, such as the Crystal Glade or the Nature Realm, where ley lines flow without disruption.

Unstable Nexuses: These areas have been affected by interference, often resulting in magical anomalies or environmental disasters. The Veiled Nexus, for example, was corrupted by exploitation, showcasing the risks of tampering with ley lines.

Nexus Points in the Multiverse: In addition to regulating energy, nexus points serve as portals connecting different dimensions. Locations like the Spiral Nexus allow for travel between realms, while simultaneously acting as conduits for dimensional energy.

The Role of Guardians: Guardians like Pecos, Ayiyi Mones, and Flamipandro play essential roles in maintaining the integrity of nexus points. These entities protect the balance of energy, ensuring that the ley lines remain stable and functional.

Notable Nexus Points

The Spiral Nexus: Central to the story and the ley line network, representing both power and fragility.

The Nature Nexus: A symbol of harmony between ley lines and the environment.

The Veiled Nexus: An example of the consequences of corruption and misuse.

Section 4: Sentience of Ley Lines

Concept of Sentience: Ley lines are more than mere conduits; they are sentient entities capable of reacting to stimuli and retaining memory. This sentience is a recurring theme, emphasizing the interconnectedness of magic, nature, and life.

Ley Line Whispers: The sentience of ley lines often manifests as whispers or emotional resonances, guiding or warning those who interact with them. For example: Alaric hears fragmented warnings during his discovery of the Whispering Codex. Lira feels a deep connection to the ley lines during her transformation into an avatar.

Memory and Reaction: Ley lines "remember" interactions, reacting positively to harmonization efforts and negatively to disruptions. Successful stabilization can strengthen their flows, while interference can lead to energy outbursts or guardian emergence.

Philosophical Implications

The sentience of ley lines raises important questions about their role in the world. Should they be left untouched to maintain natural balance, or is human intervention justified to preserve them when they are at risk?

Section 5: Human Interaction and Manipulation

Tools for Studying Ley Lines: Artifacts and tools play a vital role in understanding and interacting with ley lines. Key examples include:

Runestone Compass: Maps ley line paths and nexus points.

Void Compass: Guides users through unstable ley line regions.

Shimmering Crystal: Alters ley line flows but with unpredictable effects.

Positive Interactions: Successful interventions demonstrate the potential for humans to work with ley lines, such as: Using the Whispering Codex to stabilize the Spiral Nexus. Flamipandro's ability to cleanse corrupted ley lines.

Negative Interactions

However, failed experiments highlight the dangers of human manipulation. For instance:

The Twilight Experiment's attempt to force alignment led to a catastrophic rift.

The Veiled Order's rigid structuring caused widespread ley line corruption.

Ethical Considerations: The tension between control and collaboration underpins many of the moral dilemmas faced by characters in the story. Ley lines demand respect and caution, serving as a reminder of the risks of overreach.

Section 6: Legacy and Future Implications

Alaric's Discoveries: Alaric's contributions to ley line research include: Documenting their sentience and behavior. Creating tools for harmonization and balance.Establishing guidelines for responsible interaction.

Future of Ley Lines: The ley lines' cycles of disruption and renewal reflect nature's resilience. Visions of new nexus points forming symbolize hope for continued balance.

Passing the Torch: Lira's transformation into a ley line avatar marks a turning point, ensuring that future generations can learn from Alaric's legacy and preserve the fragile harmony of magic.

Conclusion

Ley lines are a testament to the interconnectedness of life, magic, and the natural world. They embody balance and memory, serving as both a source of power and a reminder of the responsibilities that come with it. Approaching them with reverence and humility is essential to maintaining their integrity. As the story of The Sorcerer's Codex shows, ley lines are not merely a part of the world—they are its very essence, a living, breathing force that unites all things.

Appendix B: The Fundamentals of Magic

Introduction

Magic in The Sorcerer's Codex is not simply a tool; it is the essence of existence, woven into the fabric of life, nature, and the cosmos. It is the lifeblood of the world, drawn from the ley lines that crisscross dimensions and realms, linking all things in a delicate web of energy and intent. As a living force, magic demands respect and understanding, rewarding those who seek balance and punishing those who attempt to control it without care.

This appendix serves as an exploration of the types, sources, and mechanics of magic in the story, offering readers a deeper appreciation of its complexity and significance. Magic in this world is both a creative and destructive force, capable of healing ecosystems and unraveling dimensions. Its duality mirrors the choices of those who wield it, making magic not just a power, but a reflection of intent and will.

By categorizing magic into distinct forms—runic, elemental, ley line, enchantment, and dark magic—this appendix provides a comprehensive framework for understanding the forces that shape the narrative. Beyond the mechanics, it delves into the philosophy of magic, questioning its ethical use and the responsibilities of those who harness its power.

Whether you are a scholar seeking to unravel its mysteries or a guardian tasked with its preservation, this guide offers insights into the nature of magic, its infinite possibilities, and its inherent risks.

Section 1: Sources of Magic

Ley Lines as the Foundation of Magic: Ley lines form the foundation of all magical energy, acting as the veins of power that sustain the physical and metaphysical realms. These invisible currents of energy connect nexus points, which serve as reservoirs of immense power. When properly aligned and undisturbed, ley lines fuel spells, sustain ecosystems, and provide a harmonious flow of magic throughout the world.

The interaction between ley lines and practitioners is central to the narrative. Characters like Alaric Deymorne rely on their understanding of ley lines to navigate challenges, while guardians like Flamipandro embody the balance required to protect these flows. Ley lines are not mere conduits; they are dynamic, sentient forces that react to interference, rewarding those who align with their rhythms and punishing those who disrupt them.

Elemental Planes: Magic in The Sorcerer's Codex draws heavily from the elemental planes, each representing a fundamental aspect of existence. These realms—Fire, Water, Air, and Earth—serve as reservoirs of raw elemental power, each with its unique characteristics and risks.

Fire Plane: A realm of destruction and rebirth, the Fire Plane is volatile and dangerous. Its power is tied to artifacts like the Emberstone, which embodies both creation and chaos.

Water Plane: A source of healing and purification, the Water Plane is a realm of tranquility and adaptability. Artifacts like the Waterheart Pearl draw on its calming influence to balance chaotic energies.

Air Plane: Known for its association with speed, mobility, and temporal energy, the Air Plane is a realm of boundless potential. It is represented by objects like the Breath of Aeons, which manipulates time flows.

Earth Plane: Grounded in stability and resilience, the Earth Plane anchors magical energy to the physical world. Artifacts like the Earthen Heartstone reflect its enduring strength and connection to ley lines.

Each elemental plane interacts with ley lines, contributing energy and balance to the magical ecosystem. Practitioners must respect the inherent volatility of these planes, as tapping into their power recklessly can destabilize both the practitioner and the environment.

Dimensional Magic: Beyond the elemental planes, interdimensional ley lines connect realms such as the Shadow Plane and the Crystal Plane. These dimensions add complexity to the magical landscape, offering unique energies and challenges.

Shadow Plane: A realm of twilight and duality, the Shadow Plane is both alluring and dangerous. It serves as a source of shadow energy and is home to entities like Shadow Wraiths, who act as guardians of corrupted ley lines.

Crystal Plane: A realm of shimmering beauty, the Crystal Plane allows ley lines to manifest visibly, creating a mesmerizing network of glowing pathways. It is a place of clarity and reflection, where magical energies align perfectly.

Dimensional magic is complex and requires a profound understanding of ley line harmonics. It enables advanced practices like dimensional travel and nexus point stabilization but carries significant risks, including dimensional rifts and energy imbalances.

> **Sentient Entities and Guardians:** Magic often manifests through sentient beings who act as intermediaries between ley lines and practitioners. These entities—such as Pecos, Flamipandro, and Ayiyi Mones—play crucial roles in guiding, amplifying, or guarding magic.
>
> Pecos serves as a multiverse guide, appearing in various forms to provide cryptic guidance to those navigating dimensional ley lines.
>
> Flamipandro, an elemental guardian, embodies the harmony of fire and chaos, ensuring that destructive forces do not destabilize the ley line network.
>
> Ayiyi Mones, with her whimsical and unpredictable nature, represents the creative and transformative aspects of magic, challenging characters to see beyond rigid structures.

These guardians highlight the sentience of magic and its connection to balance and intent.

The Will of the Nexus: At the heart of the ley line network lies the Spiral Nexus, a chaotic and powerful convergence point. Representing the ultimate source of ley line magic, the Spiral Nexus embodies both creation and destruction. Its energy is the lifeblood of the world, but its instability poses a constant threat.

The Spiral Nexus serves as a focal point in the story, illustrating the need for harmony and collaboration between practitioners, guardians, and the ley lines themselves. It symbolizes the delicate balance that sustains magic and the consequences of disruption.

Section 2: Types of Magic

Magic in The Sorcerer's Codex manifests in distinct forms, each shaped by its source, application, and intent. These forms range from the precise art of runic magic to the volatile forces of elemental magic and the profound intricacies of ley line manipulation. By categorizing magic into these types, this section provides an in-depth exploration of their mechanics, risks, and roles in the story.

Runic Magic

Definition: Runic magic involves the inscribing of symbols and glyphs that channel and amplify magical energy. Each rune carries a specific intent, making this form of magic precise and highly adaptable.

Techniques:

Protective Wards: Runes can create barriers that shield against physical and magical threats.

Amplification Runes: Engraved on objects, these symbols enhance the potency of spells or artifacts.

Key Artifact: The Runestone Compass exemplifies runic magic, using inscribed symbols to track and map ley lines.

Risks: Misaligned runes can cause spells to backfire, while poorly crafted inscriptions may weaken over time, leading to unexpected failures.

Narrative Significance: Alaric's mastery of runic magic allowed him to create tools essential for his expeditions, bridging the gap between ancient knowledge and modern applications.

Elemental Magic

Definition: Elemental magic harnesses the raw power of the elemental planes, enabling practitioners to manipulate fire, water, air, and earth.

Subtypes:

Fire Magic: Focuses on destruction, energy manipulation, and transformation. Spells can range from summoning flames to creating explosive bursts.

Water Magic: Associated with healing, purification, and fluid control. Practitioners can calm turbulent waters or conjure protective mists.

Air Magic: Governs mobility, speed, and temporal manipulation. Wind currents can be controlled for defense or used to enhance agility.

Earth Magic: Emphasizes stability, defense, and growth. This magic fortifies structures and encourages natural regeneration.

Risks: The elemental planes' volatility means that reckless use of their magic can destabilize nearby nexus points or ecosystems.

Key Artifacts:
The Emberstone channels fire energy, amplifying its destructive potential.

The Waterheart Pearl balances chaotic flows, reflecting water's calming nature.

Narrative Significance: Elemental magic serves as a metaphor for balance, demonstrating both the power and fragility of nature.

Ley Line Magic

Definition: Ley line magic taps directly into the energy of ley lines, allowing for large-scale spells and intricate manipulations.

Applications:
Resonance Spells: Align ley line harmonics to stabilize nexus points or repair disruptions.

Dimensional Alignment: Reconnect severed dimensional ley lines, ensuring balance across realms.

Key Moment: During the Spiral Nexus confrontation, ley line magic was pivotal in restoring balance, showcasing its potential and risks.

Risks: Ley line magic requires deep understanding and precision; improper use can result in cascading failures or dimensional rifts.

Narrative Themes: This form of magic reflects the story's core theme of collaboration between individuals and the natural world.

Enchantment and Alchemy

Definition: These disciplines involve imbuing objects with magical properties or crafting potions and elixirs from magical ingredients.

Processes:

Infusion: Channeling ley line energy into artifacts like the Shimmering Crystal to grant them unique abilities.

Potion Crafting: Combining magical elements to create transformative substances, such as healing draughts or energy enhancers.

Risks: Overloading objects with energy can lead to destructive feedback, while improperly balanced potions can cause harmful side effects.

Significance: Enchantment and alchemy play supporting roles in the narrative, providing tools that amplify the characters' abilities and resolve.

Dark Magic

Definition: Often forbidden and dangerous, dark magic involves practices like shadow manipulation, ley line corruption, and soul-binding.

Key Practitioners: The Veiled Order exploited dark magic to destabilize nexus points and consolidate power.

Risks: This form of magic inherently disrupts balance, leading to ecological collapse, emergence of hostile entities, and moral degradation.

Notable Event: The Twilight Experiment demonstrated the devastating effects of dark magic, leaving a fractured nexus that nearly collapsed the surrounding region.

Narrative Role: Dark magic serves as a cautionary force, representing the consequences of unchecked ambition and disregard for balance.

Section 3: Mechanics of Magic

Magic operates through a series of interconnected processes, from the flow of energy to the act of casting spells. This section delves into the mechanics that underpin magical practices, offering a detailed look at how energy is sourced, shaped, and released.

The Flow of Energy

Magical energy flows from sources like ley lines and elemental planes to practitioners, who act as conduits. This flow is governed by harmonics, the natural rhythms that maintain balance within the ley line network. Spells that align with these harmonics are more stable, while those that disrupt them risk causing backlash or instability.

Casting and Control
Steps of Spellcasting:

Sourcing Energy: Practitioners draw power from ley lines, personal reserves, or artifacts.

Shaping Energy: Incantations, gestures, and tools help shape the energy into a desired form.

Releasing Energy: The final step involves channeling the energy outward, achieving the spell's intended effect.

Role of Focus: Mental clarity and emotional balance are critical to successful spellcasting. Distracted or unstable practitioners risk miscasting their spells, with potentially disastrous consequences.

Artifacts as Catalysts: Artifacts like the Whispering Codex and Spiral Anchor act as catalysts, amplifying or refining magical energy. While they enhance precision and power, overreliance on these tools can weaken a practitioner's innate abilities, creating dependency.

Magical Feedback Loops: When spells disrupt the natural flow of energy, they can create feedback loops, where unstable magic rebounds onto the caster or the environment. These loops often result from misaligned harmonics or corrupted ley lines.

Harmonics and Stability: Harmonics play a vital role in maintaining stability. Practitioners like Alaric use harmonic spells to align fragmented ley lines, ensuring that magic flows smoothly and safely.

Section 4: Philosophical Implications

Magic is not a tool; it is a force imbued with intent, memory, and purpose. Its use, therefore, raises profound questions about ethics, balance, and the responsibilities of those who wield it. This section explores the philosophical dimensions of magic, offering a deeper understanding of its role within the narrative and its impact on the world.

Balance vs. Control: At the heart of magic lies the tension between balance and control. Practitioners must decide whether to harmonize with magic's natural flow or impose their will upon it. This choice often determines the outcome of their actions and reflects their character's core values.

> Alaric's Journey: Throughout the story, Alaric transitions from attempting to control ley lines to embracing a collaborative approach. His early experiments, such as the Twilight Experiment, were driven by a desire for mastery, leading to catastrophic results. However, his later efforts at the Spiral Nexus demonstrated his growth, as he worked alongside guardians and ley lines to restore harmony.

> The Veiled Order: In contrast, the Veiled Order represents the dangers of imposing rigid structures on magic. Their attempts to harness ley lines for personal gain disrupted the natural flow, causing nexus corruption and ecological collapse.

Magic as a Living Force: Magic is a sentient and reactive force, particularly through its connection to ley lines. This depiction challenges traditional views of magic as a passive resource and invites readers to consider its role as an active participant in the world.

> Ley Line Sentience: Ley lines react to interference, "remembering" both harmony and disruption. This sentience is evident in their whispers and emotional resonances, guiding or warning practitioners.

Guardians as Extensions of Magic: Entities like Flamipandro and Ayiyi Mones embody the will of magic, acting as intermediaries to protect its balance. Their actions suggest that magic is not merely a resource but a living entity with its own needs and desires.

The Cost of Magic: Every use of magic carries a cost, whether physical, emotional, or ecological. This principle serves as a cautionary reminder of the consequences of overreliance or misuse.

Physical Toll on Practitioners: Drawing excessive energy from ley lines can lead to exhaustion, illness, or even death. Characters like Lira experience the strain of channeling powerful spells, highlighting the limitations of human endurance.

Ecological Impact: Disrupting ley lines or nexus points has far-reaching consequences, from localized disasters to dimensional rifts. The Twilight Experiment, for instance, caused a collapse in the surrounding environment, leaving the area uninhabitable for years.

Emotional Consequences: The responsibility of wielding magic often weighs heavily on practitioners. Alaric, for example, grapples with guilt over the unintended consequences of his early experiments, driving his determination to restore balance.

Human Intervention in Magic: The question of whether humans have the right to manipulate ley lines lies at the core of the story's ethical dilemmas. Scholars, guardians, and practitioners debate the merits and risks of intervention, reflecting broader themes of agency and stewardship.

Perspectives Among Scholars: Some scholars advocates of intervention argue that human ingenuity can enhance magic's potential, citing successes like the Spiral Anchor. While critics warn of the dangers of tampering with natural systems, pointing to disasters like the Veiled Nexus as evidence of humanity's hubris.

Role of Guardians: Guardians like Pecos and Flamipandro embody the balance between intervention and preservation. They guide practitioners toward harmonious solutions while intervening only when absolutely necessary.

Section 5: Notable Magical Events

Magic plays a pivotal role in the story's major events, shaping the characters' journeys and the world around them. This section examines key moments where magic was central to the narrative, offering insights into its mechanics, risks, and themes.

The Nature Nexus Discovery: The Nature Nexus represents a harmonious convergence of ley lines, sustaining a vibrant ecosystem and its mythical inhabitants. When disruptions threatened this balance, Alaric used harmonic spells to repair severed threads, drawing on both his knowledge and the guidance of guardians.

Significance: This event highlighted the interconnectedness of magic, nature, and life, showcasing the potential of collaborative efforts to restore harmony.

Lessons Learned: Alaric's success reinforced the importance of working with, rather than against, the natural flow of ley lines.

The Twilight Experiment: An ambitious attempt to harmonize opposing ley lines of light and shadow, the Twilight Experiment was one of Alaric's earliest and most disastrous failures. The forced alignment caused a dimensional rift, destabilizing the surrounding region and unleashing shadow entities.

Consequences: The experiment left a scar on the land and on Alaric's psyche, serving as a turning point in his understanding of magic.

Themes: This event underscored the dangers of arrogance and the need for humility in the face of magic's power.

The Spiral Nexus Confrontation: As the heart of the ley line network, the Spiral Nexus represented both immense power and immense risk. Its destabilization threatened to unravel the entire network, requiring a coordinated effort to restore balance.

Key Actions: Alaric, Lira, and the guardians combined harmonic spells, ley line resonance, and artifacts like the Spiral Anchor to stabilize the nexus.

Narrative Role: This climactic event demonstrated the culmination of the characters' growth, as they united their knowledge, skills, and intent to achieve harmony.

The Veiled Order's Corruption: The Veiled Order's attempts to impose rigid structures on ley lines resulted in widespread corruption, creating unstable nexuses and triggering ecological collapse. Their actions served as a cautionary tale about the consequences of greed and control.

Impact: The corrupted nexuses required immense effort to purify, further straining the ley line network.

Themes: This arc reinforced the narrative's critique of exploitation and emphasized the need for balance and respect.

Section 6: Future Evolution of Magic

Magic, like the ley lines that sustain it, is in constant flux. Its evolution reflects the changing needs and aspirations of those who wield it. This section explores potential advancements in magical disciplines, the integration of technology, and the role of future generations in shaping the multiverse's magical landscape.

Adaptive Practices
Integration of Technology and Magic

The future holds the promise of new tools and methodologies that blend traditional magical practices with technological innovation.

Potential Advancements: Devices capable of mapping ley line flows in real-time, improving stability efforts.

Enhanced artifacts that integrate mechanical precision with ley line energy.

Example: A theoretical fusion of the Void Compass with a ley line stabilizer to create a multifunctional tool for dimensional navigation.

Evolving Artifacts

Artifacts are not static; their connection to ley lines allows them to adapt to new challenges over time.

Example: The Spiral Anchor could develop greater precision in handling overlapping realms, reducing strain on its user.

New Disciplines

Temporal Magic: Advanced understanding of time manipulation could lead to its development as a distinct discipline.

Applications: Stabilizing temporal anomalies within nexus points. Creating localized time dilation fields for research or recovery.

Risks: Distorting time flows could have unpredictable ripple effects across dimensions.

Dimensional Fusion Magic: Techniques for aligning or merging overlapping dimensions may become essential as the multiverse continues to evolve.

Applications: Repairing fractured realms with greater efficiency. Harmonizing conflicting energies in unstable nexus points.

The Role of Guardians and Scholars

Guardians' Legacy: Future guardians will build on the lessons of entities like Flamipandro and Pecos, adopting their principles of balance and stewardship.

Example: New guardians may emerge with unique ties to specific dimensions, ensuring the continued protection of ley lines.

Scholars' Innovations: The work of scholars like Alaric will inspire future generations to deepen their understanding of magic.

Potential Contributions:
Refinement of harmonic spells for ley line stabilization.
Discovery of new energy sources within elemental planes.

Visions of Magic's Future

Prophecies of Renewal: Visions within the Whispering Codex hint at a resurgence of magical innovation, driven by the interplay between tradition and discovery.

Expanding the Multiverse's Potential: As ley lines continue to adapt and evolve, the possibilities for magic will expand, offering endless opportunities for exploration and creation.

Alaric's Reflection

Magic, as I have come to understand it, is not a mere tool to be wielded or a puzzle to be solved. It is a force that defies simple categorization, a source of awe and wonder that mirrors the intentions of those who interact with it. To some, it may appear as an engine for creation or a means to achieve power, but to me, magic is much more—it is alive. It breathes through the ley lines, whispers through the codices, and reveals itself to those willing to listen.

In my journey, I have seen magic at its most harmonious and its most destructive. I have marveled at its ability to restore life and balance, yet I have also borne the weight of its wrath when mishandled. Magic is not to be tamed or controlled; it is to be understood, respected, and approached with humility. It is sentient in its way, remembering acts of harmony and chaos alike. It demands balance and punishes excess, serving as both teacher and judge to those who dare to harness it.

As I reflect on the sources and types of magic—the ley lines, elemental planes, and dimensional energies—I am struck by their interconnectedness. Each strand of magic contributes to a greater whole, a tapestry of energy and intent that binds our world and others together. The guardians and entities I have encountered, like Flamipandro and Pecos, embody this interconnectedness, serving as stewards of a fragile equilibrium that we must not take for granted.

The lessons of magic are not mine alone to carry. Future scholars, guardians, and practitioners will inherit this legacy, and with it, the responsibility to honor its balance. I can only hope they learn from our triumphs and failures. The mistakes of the Veiled Order, the devastation of the Twilight Experiment, and the restoration of the Spiral Nexus all serve as reminders of magic's power and fragility.

Magic is a living force, a reflection of our intent and actions. It connects us to each other and to the world itself. Its legacy is uncertain, as it always will be, shaped by the choices of those who follow. To those who seek its mysteries, I offer this plea: tread carefully. Magic will endure as a testament to the interconnectedness of all things, but only if we allow it to thrive in balance, harmony, and respect.

I leave these words not as a conclusion but as an invitation. Take what I have learned, and may your journey through the mysteries of magic be one of wonder, wisdom, and responsibility.

— Alaric Deymorne

Appendix C: The House of the Crystal Keys

Introduction

The House of the Crystal Keys is no ordinary structure; it is a living nexus at the heart of the ley line network, connecting dimensions, timelines, and realms of existence. Its shifting architecture, sentience, and deep ties to ley lines make it both a sanctuary and a challenge for those who encounter it. In The Sorcerer's Codex, the house plays a pivotal role, acting as a hub for interdimensional travel, magical experimentation, and moments of profound discovery.

This appendix explores the origins, attributes, and narrative significance of the House of the Crystal Keys. As a living embodiment of the multiverse's complexity, the house reflects the themes of balance, exploration, and interconnectedness that run throughout the story. Its sentience allows it to respond to the needs, fears, and intentions of its occupants, creating a dynamic environment that evolves with every interaction. The house's intricate design, paranormal connections, and manipulation of time and space make it a focal point for both wonder and trepidation.

Through its infinite doors and ever-changing rooms, the House of the Crystal Keys offers a glimpse into the boundless possibilities of the ley line network. It serves as a reminder of the multiverse's resilience and the enduring quest for understanding and harmony within its flows.

Section 1: Origins and Structure of the House

The origins of the House of the Crystal Keys are shrouded in mystery, its existence a testament to the convergence of ley lines and the sentient forces that guide them. Scholars, guardians, and travelers alike have speculated about its creation, weaving myths and theories that attempt to explain its presence at the heart of the multiverse.

Creation Myths and Scholarly Theories

Primordial Origin Theory: According to this theory, the house formed spontaneously during a rare convergence of major ley lines. These ley lines, seeking stability amidst their immense energy flows, coalesced into a physical structure capable of harmonizing and redirecting their power. Proponents of this theory point to the house's natural alignment with ley line rhythms and its role as a stabilizing force in the multiverse.

Architect of Realms Legend: This myth credits the creation of the house to an ancient Nexus Guardian known only as the Architect of Realms. The legend claims that the Architect, recognizing the fragility of the ley line network, constructed the house as a sanctuary and hub for interdimensional travelers. Stories of the Architect often describe them as a being of immense power and wisdom, their essence woven into the house itself.

Physical Structure

Shifting Design: The House of the Crystal Keys defies conventional architecture. Its layout is not static; rooms appear, disappear, and rearrange themselves based on the needs and intentions of its occupants. This adaptive design reflects the house's connection to ley lines, allowing it to create spaces that facilitate exploration, healing, or confrontation.

Rooms of Infinite Potential: The house contains countless rooms, each with unique properties tied to its dimensional and magical functions. Notable examples include:

The Hall of Reflections: A room of mirrored surfaces that reveal alternate realities, potential futures, and hidden truths. Travelers often leave the hall changed, having faced versions of themselves they might become—or avoid.

The Temporal Study: A vast library where time flows differently, enabling extended research within a compressed timespan. This room is a favorite of scholars, offering the gift of time to pursue their inquiries.

The Nexus Chamber: The central heart of the house, where ley line flows are visible and tangible. This chamber serves as both a control room for dimensional travel and a sanctuary for stabilizing unstable nexuses.

Role as a Nexus Point: The house sits at the intersection of multiple ley lines, acting as a keystone for their stability. Its position allows it to channel and harmonize their flows, preventing disruptions that could ripple across dimensions. This unique role makes the House of the Crystal Keys a beacon for those seeking to understand or manipulate ley lines.

Section 2: Sentience of the House
The House of the Crystal Keys is not merely a structure; it is a sentient entity deeply connected to the ley lines. Its intelligence

and adaptability make it a guardian, guide, and enigma for those who interact with it.

The House as a Living Entity

Behavior and Interaction: The house actively engages with its occupants, responding to their intentions, emotions, and actions. It offers guidance through subtle manipulations of its environment, such as opening specific doors or altering room layouts to direct travelers.

Communication Through Ley Lines: Using the ley lines as a medium, the house communicates through whispers, visions, and environmental cues. For example, dimming lights or sudden drafts might signal danger, while glowing pathways indicate a safe route. These interactions reinforce the house's role as a sentient ally—or adversary—depending on the occupants' intentions.

Adaptive Nature

Room Creation: The house's ability to create or alter rooms on demand showcases its adaptability. For instance, it might summon a sanctuary for a wounded traveler or transform a corridor into a labyrinth to test the resolve of an intruder.

Memory and Response: The house remembers past occupants, adjusting its interactions based on their history. Those who have acted in harmony with the ley lines are often met with welcoming environments, while those who disrupt the balance face more challenging conditions.

Protective Mechanisms: The House of the Crystal Keys employs a variety of defensive measures to protect itself and the ley lines. These include creating illusions to mislead intruders, activating temporal loops to trap unstable energy, and summoning guardians to confront threats.

Ethical Implications: The house's sentience raises ethical questions about its autonomy and purpose. Is it a servant to those who enter, or does it act as an equal partner, choosing who to aid and how? These questions add complexity to the house's role within the multiverse.

Section 3: Dimensional Connections

The House of the Crystal Keys serves as a bridge between dimensions, realms, and even timelines, making it an unparalleled hub of interdimensional travel. Through its unique connection to ley lines, the house opens portals to distant worlds, allowing its occupants to traverse the multiverse. These dimensional connections are not merely functional; they are integral to the house's identity and purpose within the ley line network.

Dimensional Portals

Mechanics of Dimensional Travel: The house uses ley line harmonics to open stable portals, aligning energy flows to create pathways between realms. This process requires precise calibration, often aided by artifacts such as the Whispering Key or Runestone Compass.

Key examples include:

Shadow Plane Gate: A doorway shrouded in twilight energy, leading to the Shadow Plane. This portal is used sparingly, as the realm's unstable energy poses significant risks.

Nature Nexus Portal: A shimmering archway that opens into the lush Nature Realm, where magic and life coexist symbiotically.

Role of Keys: Access to specific realms often requires unique keys attuned to the house and its ley lines. These keys are not mere objects; they resonate with the essence of their holder, ensuring that only those aligned with the realm's energy can pass through.

Multiverse Connections

Interdimensional Web: The house acts as a central node in the multiverse, connecting realms through a vast network of ley lines. This web enables simultaneous access to alternate realities, timelines, and dimensions. The house's connection to this web explains phenomena such as Pecos's ability to exist in multiple forms across dimensions.

Narrative Examples

Alaric's Training in the Hall of Reflections: The house reveals alternate outcomes of Alaric's choices, helping him understand the consequences of his actions. This experience underscores the complexity of free will and destiny within the multiverse.

Dimensional Convergence: During a critical moment in The Sorcerer's Codex, the house synchronizes multiple realms, allowing the characters to draw strength and resources from different dimensions to stabilize the Spiral Nexus.

Temporal and Spatial Bridges

Time Period Crossings: The house's mastery of ley line harmonics enables it to bridge time periods, connecting past, present, and future. These crossings are not merely portals but immersive experiences, allowing occupants to interact with other timelines directly.

Examples:

Temporal Study Research: Alaric uses a room where time flows slower to compile years' worth of observations in a matter of hours.

Future Visions: The house briefly aligns with a future nexus point, giving Alaric and Lira glimpses of potential outcomes.

Spatial Connections

The house links disparate locations, providing seamless travel across vast distances. For example, a single door might open to a nexus point deep within the Crystal Plane or a hidden ley line fracture in the Shadow Plane.

Section 4: Manipulation of Reality and Time

One of the most remarkable aspects of the House of the Crystal Keys is its ability to manipulate reality and time. These abilities go beyond mere transportation, shaping the experiences of those within its walls. The house's dynamic architecture and temporal mechanics create opportunities for exploration, growth, and confrontation, reflecting its sentient understanding of its occupants' needs.

Reality Manipulation

Dynamic Architecture: The house's rooms and corridors are not static; they shift and evolve in response to the intentions and challenges faced by its occupants.

Example: A narrow hallway becomes an expansive labyrinth when a traveler seeks to test their resolve.

Example: A nondescript room transforms into a tranquil sanctuary for healing after a grueling journey.

Perception Distortion

The house can alter sensory input to reveal hidden truths or create illusions that test its occupants.

The Hall of Reflections: This room is a prime example, showing visitors alternate selves or futures, forcing them to confront their potential paths.

Guided Visions: At times, the house creates scenarios to prepare travelers for impending challenges, blending reality with possibilities.

Temporal Mechanics

Time Dilation: Certain rooms, like the Temporal Study, operate on altered timelines, allowing extended experiences within compressed periods. This capability is invaluable for scholars like Alaric, who have used the Temporal Study to amass decades of research in a single day.

Temporal Loops: The house can create protective loops to contain unstable energy or intruders. These loops reset the environment until balance is restored, ensuring that disruptions do not spread to the ley line network.

Future and Past Interactions: The house occasionally aligns its ley lines to provide direct access to past events or glimpses of the future. These interactions are fleeting and often cryptic, requiring interpretation and reflection.

Ethical and Practical Implications: The house's manipulation of reality and time raises profound questions about free will and the ethics of intervention. By altering experiences, the house can shape its occupants' choices, blurring the line between guidance and control. These implications add a layer of complexity to its role as both ally and enigma.

Section 5: Paranormal Realms and Influence

The House of the Crystal Keys is not merely a physical nexus; it is also deeply entwined with the ethereal and paranormal realms. These connections amplify its mystical nature, making it a gateway to dimensions of pure magic, spectral echoes, and spiritual energies. This section explores the house's ties to the paranormal, its role in bridging the metaphysical with the tangible, and its interactions with otherworldly forces.

Paranormal Gateways

Spirit Plane Access: The house's ley line harmonics create a resonance with the Spirit Plane, allowing travelers to interact with spectral entities and echoes of the past.

Examples of Interaction:

Pecos's post-sacrifice communications occur through the Spirit Plane, where his presence guides Alaric and Lira in critical moments.

Alaric encounters spectral remnants of ancient scholars in the Hall of Reflections, gaining insights from their wisdom and warnings.

Ethereal Nexus

A realm of pure magical energy, the Ethereal Nexus is a convergence of ley lines untethered from any physical dimension. The house creates fleeting gateways to this plane, where visitors can experience the raw essence of magic.

Key Experiences:

Lira's transformation into an avatar of the ley lines begins in the Ethereal Nexus, where her connection to magic deepens beyond physical limitations.

Flamipandro harnesses the chaotic energies of this realm to stabilize her own volatile powers.

Influence on Paranormal Activity
Residual Energies

The concentration of ley line energy within the house attracts echoes of past events, creating a tapestry of memories and impressions that linger in its halls.

These residual energies often manifest as faint voices, apparitions, or inexplicable shifts in the environment.

Examples:

A room within the house occasionally replays the final moments of the Architect of Realms, offering a glimpse into its creation myth.

Alaric hears fragments of a forgotten language while meditating in the Nexus Chamber, believed to be whispers from the ley lines themselves.

Guardian Presence

Sentient entities like Flamipandro and the Keeper of Crystals maintain order within the house's paranormal interactions. Their roles are not merely protective but also instructional, guiding travelers in understanding the house's deeper mysteries.

Challenges of Paranormal Connections

Unpredictable Manifestations: The house's ties to paranormal realms occasionally create unpredictable phenomena, such as temporal overlaps or dimensional anomalies.

Example: During a ley line surge, the Hall of Reflections temporarily connects to the Spirit Plane, causing visitors to encounter spectral versions of themselves.

Ethical Considerations

Interacting with these realms raises questions about disturbing the past, exploiting magical energies, and the responsibilities of those who explore the unknown.

Section 6: The Role of the House in the Narrative

Throughout The Sorcerer's Codex, the House of the Crystal Keys is more than a setting; it is a character in its own right. Its sentience, adaptability, and ties to ley lines make it a central figure in the narrative, shaping the journeys of Alaric, Lira, and their companions. This section highlights the house's multifaceted role, from its function as a hub for exploration to its active participation in the story's climactic events.

As a Hub for Exploration

The house serves as a base for Alaric's experiments and dimensional travels, providing him with the tools and knowledge to navigate the ley lines. Its rooms, artifacts, and gateways allow the characters to explore realms, study magic, and confront their fears.

Key moments include:

Dimensional Research: Alaric's study in the Temporal Study accelerates his understanding of ley line harmonics, enabling him to develop stabilization techniques.

Artifact Retrieval: The house guides the group to the Shard of Resonance, a critical artifact for repairing ley line fractures during the Spiral Nexus confrontation.

As a Character

The house's sentience makes it an active participant in the story. It challenges characters by creating trials, protects them with its defensive mechanisms, and offers guidance through its adaptive nature.

Examples of its character-like behavior:

Protective Actions: When the group is pursued by corrupted guardians, the house reconfigures its layout into a maze, buying time for their escape.

Challenging Tests: The Hall of Reflections forces Alaric to confront his own arrogance, preparing him for the ethical decisions he must make in the Spiral Nexus.

As a Nexus Point

The house's role as a stabilizing force for ley lines is crucial during the story's climactic events. Its position at the heart of the ley line network allows it to channel energy and harmonize disruptions, preventing the collapse of the multiverse.

Key narrative moments:

Spiral Nexus Confrontation: The house serves as the launch point for the group's efforts to stabilize the nexus, providing access to artifacts, allies, and critical knowledge.

Dimensional Convergence: During a ley line surge, the house synchronizes multiple realms, enabling the group to harness the energy needed to restore balance.

Conclusion

The House of the Crystal Keys stands as one of the most enigmatic and essential elements of The Sorcerer's Codex. Its sentience, dimensional connections, and role as a ley line nexus make it a living embodiment of the multiverse's complexity. Through its infinite doors and shifting rooms, the house offers endless opportunities for exploration, discovery, and growth, while also posing profound ethical and practical challenges.

As both a sanctuary and a challenge, the house reflects the story's themes of balance, interconnectedness, and the pursuit of understanding. It reminds us that magic is not merely a force to be wielded but a living system that demands respect and collaboration.

In the end, the House of the Crystal Keys is more than a place; it is a journey—an ever-evolving nexus where the multiverse reveals its infinite possibilities to those who dare to explore.

... ...

www.ingramcontent.com/pod-product-compliance
Lightning Source LLC
Chambersburg PA
CBHW030849030726
47495CB00005B/1446